The Uncovered Legacy

Anne Tweddle and Isobel Elliott are born four centuries apart, Isobel in the time of the Border Reivers, yet their lives are irrevocably entwined.

by
B. A. Silcock

A CIP catalogue record for this title is available from the British Library.

ISBN   9798867787691

WILSON & WALTER
BOOK PUBLISHING

Sycamore Gap

there is no answer to why
as the last of my standing people
I had to go, I had to die
for centuries I have guarded this gap
poised and balanced, rooted in purpose
loved and adored by all

I hear your outpouring of grief
as I lie here atop the wall
as my seedlings still hang close
I speak to my companion, Hawthorn,
'I had no choice but to fall your way
yet together our friendship will hold'

but my roots hold fast
my stump remains, I will regrow
for your generations yet to come
and once more I shall watch over
the landscape, our home and see you,
by now, ancestors, come and go

but only a small part of me has gone
in this senseless human act
although my heart is torn
and my sadness knows no depths
and our collective souls are ripped
yet, I will not leave you

I wrote this poem in honour of The Sycamore, on Hadrian's Wall, illegally felled.
23rd September 2023

Dedication

For my children
Rebecca and Benjamin
And my grandchildren
Isabelle, Jocelyn
Austin and Aaron

When the leaves have fallen from the trees and
snow has obliterated all trace of me from the earth
then look for me in the heavens where you will see my soul
soaring still among the stars
watching over you all.

Author's Note

This book is a work of fiction, loosely based on places and families living in the time of the Border Wars of the 16th Century. But it is also a story where historical fact and legend have a part to play.

Spellings of names and places change over generations. So, to be consistent and for clarity I have used the current modern versions where I could.

Some of the conflict may seem confusing. In those turbulent times it was not uncommon for men to change sides for brief periods when borders could be crossed to suit common interests. At other times, their grievances against the enemy were so great that alliances could be temporarily broken as they rode together to settle old debts, and take revenge for past feuds, whose history had often long been forgotten. Debts would be settled, new ones set in play, spoils divided, and men returned.

It is not for us to judge our ancestors born in these lawless times. These families survived the best way they could, and we should be grateful for the heritage they have left us.

We were not there, we cannot know.

PART 1
The Calling

Prologue

The song of the woods filtered into Anne's thoughts. Memories awoke. Nettles guarded the path against unwanted feet and shadows of shimmering new green leaves blended into the landscape. She smiled to herself as she brushed her hands across the fragrant bluebells and watched them dance in the warm breeze.

Then a gentle voice made her look skywards. Clouds parted and something spoke to her.

'Anne Tweddle we are your ancestors. Hear us. It is spring 1560, the season for raiding, stealing, kidnapping and bloodletting. The Scottish and English borders are in turmoil. We are the people who live in these borderlands and pay a heavy price for our birth right, caught between powerful families.'

Anne stood still, staring at the now cloudless sky, confused by what she had just heard. Then a hawk flew in front of her, so close she could feel the touch of its wing on her face. She sensed it was a messenger and had come to help her to look at her life, to free herself from unnecessary baggage and to connect with her ancestors.

In that moment, she knew she had been sent a gift. Something momentous was about to happen. The sky darkened and a light sprinkle of rain fell on her face.

Chapter 1

Middle Moor Tower. Scottish Borders
Mid-16th Century.

The kitchen, in the middle of a large stone tower, was full of men shouting and arguing. Various cooking pots, metal pans, clay bowls, wooden spoons, plates, and jugs littered the floor. The scene was chaotic with children crying and clinging to women's skirts and dogs barking and yelping as they were kicked out of the way. A hunched old woman was standing by the fire vigorously stirring a pot, as if she was trying to bury something in it. A fair-haired girl in a long green linen dress, elaborately embroidered with flower designs, stood over a man who was laid, with a bleeding leg, on a table. Her Celtic knot necklace dangled over his mud engrained face. Then a tall elegant middle-aged woman entered the room with a basket full of green herbs and shouted.

'Isobel, have you finished cleaning up Turnbull's leg? I've more comfrey for the poultice if you need it.'

'It's clean, Mam, but I can't stop the blood flowing.' She continued binding narrow strips of cloth round a slanted open wound.

A stout middle-aged man, with a mass of unruly red hair and long greying beard, burst into the room and started to shout,

'Wardens coming… James, get the guns out from under the top floor bed…Bring them all lad. I curse the day we ever took young Turnbull in …should have finished him off properly.

The young girl spoke. 'It's a bad wound, Father. By the look of it, a sword. Slashed clear to the bone.'

'Should have finished him off.' Her father's sentiment was met with a curse and scream from the man on the table.

'Lucky to get away alive. They jumped us in Willington gap.'

'Did you get the money? Where is it? What happened to the cattle?'

'No…they were upon us when we got to the ford. We were betrayed. The cattle bolted. That snivelling wretch Nick Robson changed sides. I saw the smirking little sod. I was lucky to escape with my life.' Turnbull struggled to sit up but quickly fell back weeping, clutching his gashed leg.

'And now they've followed you here. Out of my way lad,' said the older man as he pushed past a flustered young boy standing in front of a threadbare tapestry, which hid a narrow stone stairway, and continued shouting instructions.

'Fergus, go help your brother get the guns and all the ammunition…Bring the bows as well.'

James turned. 'How many guns?'

'All of them. We'll need the lot by the sound of all the gunfire. Must be forty or more of them by the look of the dust rising from Toppling Gate Wood. They'll be well-armed.'

'The bastards,' he muttered under his breath.

'Be quick, carry as many as you can. They're under the bed, lads. Under the bed…go on get going…Go. Go.'

A young man ran towards James. 'Forty you say. By God that's a lot of fighters, James. Are you afraid?'

'Nah. But you should be, little brother.' He smacked his back and laughed.

'Isobel, clean that blood off the table. Make haste girl,' said the middle-aged woman who was rushing about gathering bloodied bandages and torn clothing and throwing them onto a well stoked open fire.

The older man continued to issue instructions. 'Weapons, lads. Weapons. Get Turnbull off that dammed table. Come on, Tom. Robb, get to the grain store. Seth, get up to the parapet. Ned, check outer doors are secure. Will, get the horses out of the stables…the bastards aren't having my horses. Be quick. Be quick. We'll meet the bastards in the west courtyard.'

Then came the voice of a disheveled looking man holding open a heavy door, who looked at the young girl. 'Be quick, girl. Get him out of here. Wardens coming…We'll all hang for this.'

The injured man, groaning, rolled off the table and landed with a heavy thud on the floor.

'He's dead, he's dead,' she screeched.

'Leave him, girl. Leave him. 'Get out of here. By God, they'll be upon us any minute.'

Chapter 2

Wydon Farm. Northern England.
2018

Anne became absorbed by the scene developing in front of her and tried hard to focus on the people in the kitchen. But the tall, fair-haired girl, who she now believed to be called Isobel, having just heard the middle-aged woman speak to her, had turned and gazed up to the ceiling with a puzzled expression on her face, as if she was being observed. Then the sights and sounds faded, and Anne returned to the present and the sound of the tractor and trailer rattling up the field track.

She had woken with a start and shivered in the cool of the late afternoon. She pulled up the collar on her full-length, green, cord coat with its rainbow braided belt, put on her hand knitted, woollen gloves and gently wrapped her long greying plait into her blue scarf. She wiggled her toes and readjusted her cold feet, quite stiff in their multi-coloured leather Doc Martins. A faint whiff of wood smoke tickled her nostrils and the vibration of distant machinery, leading another load of hay from the newly baled field, made her sit up and think about what had just happened. She had sat under this gnarled old oak tree many times and fallen asleep and dreamed. These visions had a recurring theme of something that took place a long time ago. They were now becoming more vivid, and the people and their voices were clearer and easier to understand.

*

Anne sensed a light breeze as something soft wafted across her face. She looked up and there, towering above her, stood a large black and white Crane. How odd she thought we don't usually have cranes in England, this one must have been on migration and blown off course. Her grandmother had a favourite hat in those colours, so she decided to call it Grandmother Crane. But, before she could speak, the bird lifted its wings and gently flew away into the low-lying clouds. Entranced by this graceful creature as it disappeared, her thoughts turned to what the Crane could represent. Something about balance; being alone but working with others?

Anne looked skywards and spoke. 'Why am I spending so much time connecting with this girl, Isobel?' But no one answered. She sighed and sat hugging her knees, quietly humming to herself. After a while she noticed a gap appearing in the eastern sky and a dark shape approached. Grandmother Crane returned and, with open wings, made a soft landing at her feet. A moment or two of silence followed, then the bird leant forward and spoke.

'Are you aware of the wisdom you carry?'

Anne beamed with delight. She could understand the words. She'd always been able to communicate with animals. Their thoughts were often inside her head. It had started early in her childhood, roaming through the fields with only the dog and her horse, Molly, for company. With nowhere to go and long days to herself, she would sit under trees or on top of old wooden gates, lie in hedge gaps or doze on the riverbank and absorb the natural world. Observing animal behaviour had become normal and, over the years, she had come to understand how they communicated with each other and, gradually, developed the ability to read their minds. Eventually the practice had been reciprocated and had led to a career in animal welfare. Now this bird was communicating. Grandmother Crane lifted her head and hopped from one leg to the other.

'You have the ability to enable souls to journey to their inner world, at a point of transition.'

Anne frowned, uncertain of what she meant.

'Transition? you mean dying?'

The bird paused for a moment, then became restless and walked round in a circle, flattening daises with her feet.

'You hold secret knowledge, and, with practice, you can open the door. Be patient. Trust yourself. You have a remarkable gift.'

'Gift. What gift?'

Road kills came into her mind. Each time she found a dead rabbit, pheasant, or crow, which had met some hideous death as a result of human misdeeds, she would talk to its soul and release it to take its rightful place in the other world. Long ago, one cold winters night, she'd sat in the stable with Molly when her foal had died of pneumonia and, together, they'd eased the colt's passage into the spirit world. Anne paused, nodded, and acknowledged, yes, she did have a gift.

'There is someone trying to connect with you.'

'Me! WHY?'

'Try to understand yourself better. All will become clear. Be patient and we will reveal all to you.'

Anne stared at this tall bird with its dancing wings and was filled with a mixture of awe and excitement. She held out her hand to touch the magical creature.

'We?'

Grandmother Crane straightened her body and peered into Anne's green eyes.

'I understand it confuses you. You must learn to acknowledge your abilities and not deny the wisdom you bear.'

Anne put her outstretched arms into the air and shouted, 'Why?'

'The girl Isobel has chosen you to help her. She waits for you.'

'Is this thing I have to develop something to do with the other world?' Anne asked.

Grandmother Crane bounced up and down, padding her feet on the grass.

'It could be.'

B. A. Silcock

Tilting her head to one side, Anne felt she needed to find answers. 'What was this conversation all about? Am I learning to journey to other worlds, observe different events, times, and places because that's what I seem to be doing?'

The bird turned her head to look at Anne and said, *'All that.'* Then she stretched her long neck, opened her grey wings, ruffled her curved tail feather, looked skywards, lifted her feet off the ground and, with the grace of a gazelle, flew upwards into the evening sky and soon disappeared into the cumulus above.

This left Anne with an array of puzzling thoughts. Appreciating this magical experience was easy but understanding the message was harder. What was this unknown force driving her? It was as if she was sitting on the top edge of a vast chasm between mountains, knowing she could fly but unsure of in which direction. Anne looked up at the darkening sky and shivered. She stood up, wrapped the blue scarf around her neck and set off back to the farmhouse with a renewed sense of purpose. She had a mission. Now was the time in her life to find it.

Returning home, she found a pile of letters on the hall table. Her brother Jack came out of the sitting room, picked them up, lifted his eyebrows and grinned.

'Anne, this one is for you. It's handwritten, nice writing too. Do I recognise that posh handwriting and he cocked his head and winked.'

She took the letter from him, glanced at the words and her heart began to flutter. Her face flushed, as a warm tingling feeling spread through her body. She looked at her brother's inquisitive face, cleared her throat and quickly stuffed the letter safely into her pocket.

'Thanks, I will read it later.' She wasn't ready to open up to him about its contents. It was all still too raw, and she didn't want her brother to launch into solution mode. At the moment it was her secret.

Jack frowned and returned to the sitting room. Anne took off her Doc Martins, hung up the old coat and calmly went upstairs. She flopped onto the bed, took the letter out of her pocket, letting her fingers gently caress the address and first-class stamp. She sighed. Memories of their last meeting flooded back. Months ago, they had sat together on the cobblestones at the bottom of the Washburn Pack Horse bridge. They talked and talked about their futures. But Michael had been unable, or unwilling, she wasn't sure which, to answer her questions and put her fears to rest. They had sat in silence for a long time. Then he stood up, his face wet with tears, bent down and cupped her head in his hands and gently kissed her on the brow.

'Please trust me. Don't leave me. I love you.' Michael had bowed his head and, hands in pockets, had slowly walked across the bridge. She had wanted to run after him to tell him she was sorry. She would forgive him for anything. Instead, she had turned her head and taken one last look at the man she loved walking away, out of her life.

Anne's sweaty hands quivered. The envelope, now crumpled and damp, was difficult to peel open. She pulled out the piece of cream coloured paper and began to read...

The Uncovered Legacy

Dearest Anne,

I am so sad that you left me, but I understand why. I am lost without you. My life is empty. There are parts of my life that, over the last few months, I have been unable to share with you. I feel trapped by circumstances, not of my making. If you love me, and I know you do, please do not walk away. I couldn't bear it. You are my world. I have waited all my life for you. Don't leave me now. Wait. I understand how you must feel; betrayed and lied to. But there is a big difference between being lied to and not being told the "whole truth". I am not in a position at this time to be open with you. Others are involved and I must protect them. Please believe me. It is important you trust me. I will explain later when I am free to do so. I will come to you soon and all will be explained. Please believe me when I say how much I love you and miss you.

All my love, Michael xxx

Anne read it over and over, trying hard to understand. After a while the letter fell from her hands onto the floor. She sat very still, tears welling up in her eyes, unable to take it all in.

None of it made any sense, none of it. She yawned. It had been an extraordinary day. The dream had taken her back to a time, hundreds of years ago, when she had witnessed men and women shouting and panicking and a girl called Isobel, who she thought she knew. Grandmother Crane had appeared and the conversation between them had been unsettling. Now, Michael's letter… She bent down, picked it up, and held it close to her heart. She looked around her old room; moving back to the farm had given her breathing space. Exhausted, she laid back on the bed and quickly fell asleep.

Chapter 3

S everal months ago, Anne Tweddle had returned to her family home, Wydon Farm, to live with her brother Jack and father Alan. One morning in early January they had received a letter to say she was coming home and would be staying for the foreseeable future. No explanation had been given and on her arrival none had been forthcoming.

Wydon dated back to 1291. At various times it had been a hamlet, a farm and later a large, fortified manor house, enclosed on three sides by a barmkin wall. Different occupants would have altered its layout. There was archaeological evidence of steep ditches, a moat and two courtyards. In its heyday the entrance would have been through a stout oak door held in place by a heavy drawbar, on the north side of the west wall.

A spacious, well-appointed hall would have led to an attached wing that housed the kitchen, and the three floors connected by a narrow staircase. There were garderobes on the second and third floor, a chapel on the third and a poorly lit basement, which housed the dungeon.

All floors would have been strewn with dried moor grasses and aromatic herbs and spaces separated by tapestry curtains and wall hangings. Narrow windows on the upper floors, possibly only small slits, their window seats decorated with cushions. It was a house, strategically situated close to the South Tyne River and Irthing Gap, built of dressed stone, pillaged from Hadrian's Wall.

Over the centuries the Tweddles had owned the property and its accompanying lands and settlements, then lost them for various reasons to do with debt, betrayal, intrigue, and war. Several generations ago, Anne's family had regained ownership and expanded the land holding to include Belister Haff Farm, across the Tyne. Thick, matted ivy covered the south frontage of the house, obscuring windows and darkening rooms. A rectangular half-acre garden was predominantly laid to grass. The large Sycamore tree on the east side of the garden which dated back to 1640, shaded the farmhouse even more. Over time, it had pushed against the stone garden wall creating a space behind itself just large enough for children to make a den, and lovers to hide from prying eyes.

Most of the old farm buildings had been modernised but not the tool shed, which had always been Anne's favourite place to meet up with her grandfather for his '10 o'clock tea breaks'. Fields surrounded the cattle sheds, milking parlour, stables and barns. It was an isolated farm with only one narrow access track leading to Haltwezell and a footpath to Fetherstone village.

Anne was a tall, slim, mother and grandmother with long fair hair, greying now, which she wore tied in a single neat plait that hung down to her knees. A kind, generous woman, yet lonely, strangely intriguing but troubled by her visions of an unseen force pulling her into the past, she felt she did not 'fit into the world' of people. But animals were a different matter. Over the years she had become a proficient shape shifter and spent many hours journeying with them, listening and learning. It was exhausting work and could take her several days to fully return to the present, much to the annoyance of those around her. These wanderings could often leave her unsure of who or where she was.

*

One afternoon when out walking the dog, Anne found herself sitting under the old oak, thinking about her life and trying to understand its purpose. As the day wore on the temperature dropped the wind had begun to blow chaos across the fields bringing devastation and fear to the emerging insects alighting on the bright green vegetation. The constant buzz of the bees had faded, as they were blown off course, leaving behind the pungent smell of the flowering ramsons. She sat observing the dwindling sunlight against the darkening sky and longed for clarity of mind. Anne closed her eyes and allowed the coming darkness to envelope her and cast away the shattered shadowy memories of Michael… her husband.

After a while the soft noise of rain and the tickling sensation of a snail, gently progressing onto the palm of her hand, made her look down and smile.

'Hello little one. This is no place for you to be.' She tenderly stroked its shell, lifted it onto a small patch of rotting undergrowth and watched as it crawled slowly away to safety. Anne thought about the squashy body of the gastropod that carried its protective shell home around with it. An animal completely focused on its survival… focus…focus…a useful lesson for Anne to think about.

She stood up, put her hand in a front pocket and felt a bag of Fisherman's Friends lingering in the lining. They were Michael's favourite throat sweets. She had bought them at Newcastle railway station on her way back to Wydon, when an old woman's overpowering perfume hit the back of her throat, giving her an irritating cough.

It was six o'clock on a grey overcast Wednesday morning. The platform had emptied apart from a middle-aged man with his tongue wedged down the throat of a much younger woman, his arms caressing her back. She had been short, smartly dressed and stood with both arms clinging to his body. Eventually, he had released his grip, let go and walked away but not before turning back with a smile and blowing a long seductive kiss. Anne had watched as he had climbed the stairs over the bridge and made his way down to the other platform where a beaming middle-aged woman and two tired looking little girls, still in their pyjamas, were smiling and shouting as they ran towards him, the children screaming, 'Daddy...Daddy...Daddy.'

Anne wiped her eyes and thought of Michael's behaviour. Had he betrayed her? Were all men the same? Something was nudging her hand. She looked down, patted the dog, and smiled. 'Yes, Nip. I know he's gone. It's over. Come on, Nip, let's go home.' The dog barked, wagged his tail and together they walked back to the farm under the guidance of the moon, who tried to whisper her mystical secrets along the way.

B. A. Silcock

Jack leaned on the stackyard gate and watched the distant shape of Anne as she hurried home. He was a restless man, struggling with his own sense of place in the world, a farmer, landowner, and highly respected for his knowledge and wisdom. A man with a powerful presence, he didn't mind being listened to; always related a story in great detail and in chronological order, from 'thread to needle,' and woe betide anyone who interrupted him. As the years had passed, Jack had mellowed, becoming kinder and more generous with his time and he loved having Anne back home.

In the past he had had little time for his "airy fairy" sister and thought she was "light in the head." There was a history of "lightheaded" women in the family. Aunty Janet was peculiar, and her daughter had ended up in a mental asylum in Carlisle. There were rumours of a great grandmother who was taken away and locked up. Uncle Jasper, who made yearly visits on his 1930's Norton motor bike, was odd and had two equally odd sisters, who knew they were not "right in the head" and promised to remain single and not pass anything on. There was something strange that ran through the female line of his family and he hoped against all hope it had passed Anne by. But it was more than likely that these relatives had suffered from some sort of depression and been at the mercy of the ignorance of the time.

'Hello, Sister dear. Decided to come home then?' Anne returned his broad smile, put her arm through his and together they walked across the yard to the farmhouse kitchen.

'It's good to have you back home but, you know, Anne, you have changed. Sadder perhaps?'

'I know Jack. I feel different,' she said fiddling with the ring on her finger.

'What is it you do up there, sitting for hours and hours?'

She shook her head. 'You wouldn't understand.

'I might.'

'Well … I have these visions and it's as if I am somebody else in another time, in another place.' She shrugged her shoulders and rolled her eyes skywards.

'Yes. I know you have been having these, whatever they are … all your life. I find it frightening when I look at you.'

Anne raised her eyebrows, 'Frightening! Why?'

'It's as if you are here with me but your mind is elsewhere.'

'Yes, that's how it feels.' She smiled at him, and they grinned at each other.

'It's strange and can be disturbing. I don't know whether it's a gift or a curse.'

'Do you see things?'

'Yes, I see everything. It is as if I am there…you know, actually there.'

They paused to peer over the Pasture gate, lost in their own thoughts.

After several minutes Jack broke the silence. 'Anne, you have always been a healer, do you remember setting the lamb with a broken leg? You made creams for sore hands and hair preparations for removing hay lice, put a splint on the snipe I found after the dog had caught it and snapped its leg in two. You grew things in the garden for brewing and made paste from the leaves of comfrey for bruises. The 'townies' would venture up here and ask for remedies. You were always busy helping people.'

'Yes, I had forgotten all that but there is always more to do. I wonder if that part of me is lost. I seem to be living in two worlds more and more. I don't understand what this connection is to this girl, Isobel, but she seeps into my thoughts so often.'

'Yes, you have told me about this girl, Isobel, before. Could she be trying to tell you something?' But Anne's attention was suddenly drawn away.

'Oh, Jack look! It's a barn owl silently flying over our heads. It is so beautiful, isn't it? You know Jack, I wonder why I am seeing this owl now?'

'Dunno. It's looking for a tasty vole… nothing more.'

'No Jack. Owls fly at the shimmering time of moonlight and, if we are sensitive to their teachings, we can connect to the otherworld and the inner soul of nature.' Anne stood transfixed as the owl quartered the pasture. 'It is exciting, isn't it?' she said jumping up and down laughing, like an excited child.

'Here, wipe your eyes.' Jack gave her a clean hankie. 'Come on let's go and have a bedtime cup of tea and one of them fruit scones left over from yesterday.'

Chapter 4

O ne evening, several days later, Jack was out playing pool and their father Alan was laid up in bed nursing his aching back. Anne smiled at the thought of her father, who had some understanding of her visions. In his youth he had seen many inexplicable things but when spoken about them, he'd been ridiculed and quickly learned not to. He was a man with a strong sense of his inner self, faithful, honest, loyal and had never betrayed anyone in his life. A clever man, who had been devastated when he was taken out of grammar school at the age of fourteen to work on the farm, his hopes, and dreams of becoming an engineer crushed. He had learned to bury himself in work and had become a sad, unhappy man, unable to reach his potential. But Anne loved him dearly and enjoyed spending time with him and exploring other worldly happenings. She took a casserole out of the oven, cut up a fresh loaf of bread, made a cup of tea, went upstairs, and knocked on his bedroom door.

'Dad, are you awake?'

'Yes, just coming round. Come in, come in.'

'I've got your supper here.'

'Come in, come in, Annie.'

'How is your back?'

'Not bad. I'm not much use on the farm anymore, can't do the heavy lifting and Jack has to do all the work now. Don't go far now a days, I just potter about and keep an eye on things.'

'I'm sure he doesn't mind. Now let's look after you shall we.'

Anne put the tray of food down, fluffed up his pillows, then followed his gaze to the other end of the room. He was looking intently in the direction of the television, and, after a few seconds, he said, in a matter-of-fact voice.

'Is that a swan sitting in my armchair next to the TV?' They looked at each other and smiled.

'Yes, it's a white swan, a Bewick, I think? Anne looked lovingly at him, and a huge smile appeared on his face. They could see the same thing.

'We understand each other, Dad, don't we? We know things, can see things that others can't.'

He leaned back on his bed, straightened the covers, and nodded his head. 'Yes, Annie, if only we had spent more time together when you were young. I sometimes wonder if playing by the book, always doing the right thing, was to my detriment.' Tears rolled down his face. Anne chose to ignore this outburst. What was done was done.

'Dad, do you remember the meaning of Swan energy? Why has it appeared now and what has it come to say?'

Alan folded his arms across his chest and sighed. 'There is a field over the back called the Swaynes. I spent a lot of time there in my youth and these birds were often around me. I felt drawn to them and would sit for a short time watching. I didn't understand what they wanted to tell me.' Anne came over to the bed and sat down and held his hand.

'The swan is a bird of the threshold; they represent the part of us that can travel into the other world. They fly over many lands and through many worlds, collecting knowledge as they go.'

'I didn't have the time as a boy to spend much time there. But now, listening to you, I am wondering if it's here, in my chair, telling me it's time to go.'

'Go, Dad, what do you mean, go?' Her heart began to race, alarmed at what he could be thinking. He began to mumble, and she had difficulty following him.

'Go, time I left here. You know, go,' he said staring at her and shuffling further down the bed. Anne laughed and squeezed his hand.

'No dad, I think it's come for me.'

He raised his eyebrows. 'For you?

'Yes, I am having more visitations from all sorts of different creatures at the moment.'

'Why?'

'Not sure yet. But it's something I've got to do. It's like a life's purpose. Sometimes they come to me in dreams, but they all have a similar message. It's something about wisdom, being true to myself and acknowledging who I am.'

'So why come into my room?'

'Perhaps it thought you may be able to help me.'

'I have always been a bit afraid of these things, Annie. You know I never followed anything through or made any attempt to find out more. Too busy and all that. I regret it now. I could have done with some magic when I was young.' He pulled himself back up the bed and sighed. An unfamiliar noise came from across the room. They paused, looked at the chair and saw the swan had gone.

'Come now and eat your supper, then rest. Do you need any more painkillers, your back rubbed?'

'No thanks, Annie, I am alright for now but perhaps later?' Anne bent over and gave him a loving kiss on his forehead.

'Thank you, Annie, my dear. It does me good to look at you, so different from the rest of us,' he said, his face a beaming smile.

'Oh, get away with you, Dad. Here eat your supper before it gets cold.'

She propped him up on his pillow and switched the TV over to what she considered a suitable channel and quietly went back to the kitchen.

Chapter 5

Nip the dog and the two cats were asleep on the kitchen rag mat. Anne slumped easily into her mother's old rocking chair, pulled grandmother's woolen shawl around her shoulders, and watched the fire in the hearth die down. She closed her eyes, enjoyed the comfort of knowing the day's work had ended and quickly fell asleep. She was awakened by sweltering heat burning her face. She glanced at the clock which read ten past two and realised it was the middle of the night. Anne sat forward in her chair, rubbed her eyes, dropped the shawl onto the floor and gazed into the fire wondering why it was burning so fiercely because no coal had been put on for several hours. The flames were growing, getting bigger, roaring up the chimney, hissing, crackling, demanding her attention, long tall flames swishing and swirling, making different shapes as if devouring something. There was a noise coming from the fire of galloping horses and people shouting. Nip and the two cats at her feet didn't seem to notice anything had changed and slept on.

Anne became mesmerised as she stared into the images the flames were creating and, after a few moments, she felt herself being drawn into the scene in front of her.

Buildings were on fire. Several hundred men, women and children were shouting, loose horses and livestock were panicking, everything was fleeing. It was a scene of fear and chaos. Some of these people were familiar as she had seen them recently when sitting meditating under the old oak. Others not so. Her attention was drawn to a good-looking man, probably in his mid-twenties, who sat on his horse like he was born in the saddle. He wore a quilted jacket with metal, bone, or perhaps horn fastenings, stout leather boots on his legs and a steel bonnet on his head which allowed his trapped long dark hair to stay fixed in place. It looked like he wore woolen trousers held up by an elaborately decorated belt around his waist with a sharp looking dagger hanging perilously from its edge. He carried a basket-hilted backsword as did some of his companions, while others carried lances. On the outskirts of the settlement, she could just make out the girl she knew to be Isobel. Anne looked more closely at the black, unshod, sure footed, shaggy ponies and knew them to be "hobblers". How did she know that? It was such a familiar scene. Then she remembered that the "hobblers" belonged to the Border Reivers, Raiders of the 16th century. Was she accessing the Border Wars?

*

Then the scene changed, and Anne observed a conversation between Isobel and another girl.

'We have to find the book, Margaret.' It was Isobel talking to a younger girl; perhaps 16 years old.

'Look behind that cupboard,' said Margaret. 'It's not in this Kist.'

'Where could she have left it? It must be hidden. Would she risk carrying it around with her when she heard the reivers coming?'

'I think Katie Nixon must have hidden it.'

'She didn't leave it anywhere,' replied a throaty male voice.

Isobel and Margaret spun round to see a short, grubby, young man waving, the book they sought. Isobel screamed, 'RIDLEY!' Then, stumbling backwards into a rocking chair, she let out a torrent of verbal abuse.

'So, you have it, you grotesque youth, not big enough to be called a man. A sneak thief, that's what you are.' A smile of pride beamed across his face. 'Always managing to wriggle your way out of dangerous situations, changing sides as often as night and day. You are a notorious outlaw. What are you doing here? I know the men wouldn't have let you join them on this raid into the Nixon settlements. Better turn and run back to the Debatable lands where you can easily hide, betray confidences for money and elevate your worth as a spy.'

'Well, I am here now.' He left the doorway and stepped closer to the girls.

'Why are you here?' she shouted.

'Following you, my dear Isobel, you know what I want.'

'You, Robert Ridley, have been following me since we were children, chasing me through fields and woods. I despise everything about you!' Isobel was red in the face and looked as if she could explode with rage.

'You have bewitched me, Isobel. I can't stop thinking about you.'

'I have not.'

'Yes, you have. Do you remember when we were young, and I came to you and your mother Elinor with an open leg wound?'

'Yes, I remember. You were a filthy boy just as you are now.'

'You poured some foul-smelling liquid into my wound and chanted some incoherent nonsense.'

'They were powerful healing words. Your leg got better, didn't it?'

'Not before you had cast a spell on me.' He lifted both eyebrows and grinned. 'Isobel, we are bound together. You bewitched me that day and now I can't rid you from my mind.' He moved closer to her as he spoke. Isobel took a step backwards and put her hand onto the kitchen wall for support lest her legs would give way. She stood with hands on hips, took a deep breath and quickly changed the conversation, and glared at him straight in the eyes.

'Where did you get that book from?'

'Wouldn't you like to know.' He tossed his head to one side, lifted one eyebrow as he curled his lip with a sneer that did not want to be ignored.

'How did you come by Katie Nixon's book? She always kept it in her healing bag and would not have let the likes of you have it. How did you get it?'

Ridley kept grinning as he held the leather-bound brown book high in the air.

'I caught her running away through the wood. She was trying to steal my horse. We had a bit of a tangle. She cut my face, so I slit her throat. No number of witches potions could save her.' He let out a hoarse laugh so loud a small clay pot fell off the table and shattered on the stone floor. Isobel's hands flew to her mouth, she seemed to realise the danger she and Margaret were in. Ridley paused, frowned, and asked, 'What's so important about this book anyway?'

'If you didn't think it was important, why did you steal it?'

'I took everything she was carrying. I emptied her pockets. Little trinkets can fetch a good price,' he said, winking at her. 'What's so important about it, why do you want it, it's just a tatty book, not worth much?' He twisted his filthy, matted, stained beard with two equally dirty fingers.

'It's a herbalist's book and full of important information about herbs and plants. At least we hope it is. Next time you are injured, break a leg, or get stomach rot, you might be glad of what's in there. Please give it to me!' He was quiet for a moment, looked thoughtful then said, 'I trade you for it.'

Isobel looked flabbergasted. 'Trade? I have nothing to trade.'

'Yes, you do.' A sickening smile returned to his face.

'Give me a kiss, come on Isobel, you're always smiling at me. I know you want to.'

'You evil bastard, get away from me, I would rather kiss a warty toad. I despise you, every bit of your snot riddled dirty beard, your bent nose.' She stopped. Ridley was laughing.

'Well, aren't we making a protest?'

'I hate you and am sick of you spying on me.' She stamped her foot several times on the floor.

'What me, spying?' His eyes were wide open, aghast at the suggestion. He moved forward to lean against the wall where he had a better view of both girls.

'I see the way you look at me, Isobel, when no one's looking.'

'It's a look of disgust. I shall tell my brother, William, and then you will be sorry.'

'Oh, I don't think so. He's too busy. Just kidnapped one of them Nixon girls.' Robert Ridley looked as if he was enjoying the thought. 'Run off with her he has. All the prisoners are being marched back down the valley so you two are all on your own with me.' His menacing smirk grew wider.

Candles were still lit in the room. There appeared to be a bare amount of wooden furniture, some of it broken. Belongings were strewn about the floor. Someone had already ransacked this house. The two girls looked at each other, nodded and then, with a sudden movement, lunged towards Robert Ridley, who was taken by surprise and within seconds all three of them landed on the floor, Ridley on his back and the two girls on top of him, pounding away with their fists on his chest. He returned blow for blow, trying hard to hit them but failing because his left hand was trapped under one of the girls' legs. There was a lot of kicking, hitting, swearing, and spitting, that would have alerted anyone close by. Isobel put her free hand down into the top of her boot, pulled out a dirk from its scabbard and proceeded to stab him in the leg. Ridley screamed, threw the girls off him and grabbed his bleeding leg.

He staggered to his feet clutching his wounded leg. 'You witch, you witch. I will kill you for this.'

The Uncovered Legacy

'Look, Margaret, look. It's the book. He's dropped it. Look it's over there.' But, as they both dived forward, Isobel tripped over some abandoned clothes, fell head long and screamed.'

'Margaret, help me, my dress is caught on a nail.' Margaret rushed to her side and both girls tore at the dress to free it. Then there was a terrifying shriek. Ridley had staggered back to them, lifted a broken chair leg and in one fell swoop had brought it down on Margaret's head.

'You witch. You witch. You'll pay for this.' Again, and again he brought the chair leg down on her head and shoulders. The girl quickly stopped screaming. But Robert Ridley seemed to be beyond reason and continued his frenzied attack on her. Again and again, he raised the broken chair leg and battered her head, until the leg became stuck in her neck, entangled in her matted hair. He stopped. Her dress was ripped, her back covered in open wounds. Splinters of the chair leg had become more embedded with every blow. Her breathing slowed and yet she somehow managed to crawl towards the light of the open door, where she curled up into a ball and lay in a pool of her own seeping blood.

'You won't forget that lesson now will you.' He kicked the lifeless body with his foot and made his way to the door. The room fell silent.

'Margaret, Margaret where are you. Let's go. We must get out of here. I have the book.' Isobel turned, her eyes focused on a heap in the doorway and moved towards it. Ridley stopped his abuse of the body on the floor, turned and stared in disbelief at Isobel who stood before him.

'You are still alive. You evil witch. I've killed Margaret, the wrong sister, damn and blast you girl.' He beat his fists against the wall shrieking, so many fearful words pouring out of his mouth that Isobel backed herself against the cupboard, hands scrabbling round for something to protect herself with. Then, finding some courage, clutching a piece of wood, she screamed.

'You will pay for this when my father finds out. He'll come for you. He'll kill you, kill you. Do you hear me, you revolting boy, you disgust me, I hate you, do you hear me? I hate you, hate you.'

'It's not my fault Isobel, you drove me to it, you bewitched me. You got the better of me this time, but I'll have you.' He bent down, picked up a chair and threw it at her, then fled through the open door clutching his bleeding thigh, mounted his horse as best he could and galloped away as if the devil himself was behind him. The back of the chair had shattered against the wall. Some sections had flown onto her head, causing Isobel to momentarily clasp her chest to steady her breathing. She was hysterical, crying and screaming,

'Help. Help. Please, I need help, please. Margaret... I need help. Somebody, please, help.' She collapsed onto Margaret's body and tried to drag it through the open doorway when she heard a familiar voice behind her.

Chapter 6

John stared at her. 'What the hell were you doing in there? I saw Robert Ridley stagger out. We fell into each other in the yard. He was sweating and dragging his bloodied leg.'

Isobel was sobbing, 'John, John, oh thank goodness you are here… he killed Margaret! He killed Margaret! She's dead! She's dead!' Isobel looked up at him. John looked anxious and there was an urgency in his voice.

'Come on, Isobel, we must leave. The Nixon's will be on their way back now. We must go. 'He took her arm and pulled her outside.

'I'm not leaving without her.' She freed herself from his grip, ran inside and fell on top of her dead sister.

'She is dead Isobel. We must leave, NOW!' His voice was urgent. Isobel continued to fight him with flailing arms and flying feet.

'Stop. I want to take my sister.'

'You little fool you are putting both our lives in danger.' He picked her up, carried her outside, slung her over the front of his horse, mounted behind and together they trotted off, winding their way through the burning settlement. After a few minutes he caught up with another Reiver. As John pulled his horse to a halt Isobel slithered to the ground. John dismounted and lifted her onto the saddle, to ride behind him.

'Are we being followed? Have we got all the stragglers, covered our tracks, as I instructed?

'That's one of the Elliott lasses, isn't it, John? No one is behind us yet. We only lost three men, Jamie Bell, young Todd, and old Neil.'

'How many prisoners did we take?'

'Twenty or more men, a few women and children. Some ran off when they heard us coming. Tom Ogle got his wife back from that murdering bastard Willy Bruse. We need to get back to Wydon, reinforce our defenses, divide the spoils.' He steadied the unsettled horse.

'Come on, John, let's go, the Nixon's will be on the Hot Trod. They'll find us soon.'

'Not if you hide them in Herds Glen, Edgar. Now be off, get there as fast as you can.'

Looking at Isobel seated behind John, he raised his eyebrows and smiled. 'You not coming with us, John?'

'I'm taking Isobel Elliott home. She is injured. I will explain what happened later.'

'Better get your story right or there will be trouble.' He lowered his gaze and curled his lip as if jealous of John's new possession.

'Don't worry, I'll lay the blame fair and square where it belongs: on Robert Ridley. He attacked Isobel and her sister Margaret.'

'I expect old man Elliott will be in hot pursuit?'

'As long as he isn't after us.'

'And the lass's sister?'

'She's dead. I got there too late.' John shook his head and then whacked the rump of Edgar's horse so hard it leapt forward, and they were soon out of sight. John seemed angry now and turned around to Isobel.'

'What the hell were you two doing in there? I saw you both trailing behind some of the Armstrong men this morning and wondered what you were about.'

'We heard about the Nixon raid and hoped we would get a chance to steal Katie Nixon's herb remedy book.'

'You stupid girls!'

'Don't you dare speak to me like that, John Tweddle. We knew the Reivers were going to the Nixon's and we wanted to get Katie Nixon's book and learn its secrets. Our mother needs them. Margaret thought we could steal it in the chaos, but Riley got there first. You know he killed her, and he took the book then thought he could barter it for me.' She said weeping and hitting his back with her fists, but it didn't seem to have any effect and they rode off. A few miles further on John halted.

'You're telling me you went with the raid to get a stupid book. Isobel, I saw Robert Ridley eyeing you up. Show me this book.'

Drawing the herbal remedy book from the pocket in the dress, she placed it in his hand. 'I saw him too, in the distance, but thought we would be safe, with so many of you about.'

'I am surprised you put yourself in so much danger for this,' he said leafing through the pages, 'but that's what you seem to have a habit of doing.'

Isobel had a sudden outburst, 'I hate Robert Ridley! I hate him!'

'Will Tomson told me the evil, little, creepy bastard had been bragging, round the camp, he was going to have you and what he was going to do with you. He hung back when we were on our way home to Wydon. None of us could find him. That's why I turned back. Because I couldn't see you or Margaret either.'

'I am glad you did.'

'You were lucky it was me that found you and not one of the Nixon's.'

'Lucky you call it, lucky!' She beat his back again with her fists. 'Margaret's dead, John. She is dead. Beaten to death by that cowardly bastard.'

'That's raiding, Isobel, and you know that,' John said, passing the book back to her. 'You should not have been here.' She looked enraged as if John Tweddle wasn't going to tell her what she could and couldn't do.

'Let me go. Let me go, back to my sister.'

'You little fool I can't protect you if you go back.'

'Protect me! Is that what you call this?'

Isobel struggled free, fell to the ground, and began to run back the way they had come. 'I'm going back for her!'

'No Isobel you are not! I care too much for you, my little firebrand, to see you die as well. You forget how well I know you; we have been friends since childhood, we've spent years together hunting, poaching, roaming the border hills, spying on our neighbours, collecting valuable information to help our families plan the next raid and I am not going to lose you now. Isobel, COME BACK HERE!' He swung his horse round and set off at a gallop after her muttering under his breath, 'You belong to me Isobel Elliott. Me!... Isobel, Isobel, stop. You can't go back. Margaret's gone; she is dead.' But his words were lost to the wind. As he brought his horse parallel to the running girl he leant over, put his arm round her waist and lifted her kicking and screaming back onto his horse.

'Isobel, I am taking you home!'

Chapter 7

As they turned a sharp corner into Spittle Wood, a tawny owl flew, out of the trees, straight towards them. Its outstretched wing clipped the ear of John's horse, causing the animal to jump sideways, rear up and toss its head from side to side, covering Isobel in copious amounts of white froth. John lost his balance and his hold on Isobel weakened. She slid onto the mossy carpet of the woodland floor. John steadied the horse and returned to a very disheveled Isobel, who was laughing. He dismounted, bent over, lifted her up, folded her into his arms and kissed her hard on the mouth. He loosened his grip, 'Are you alright?'

'No, I am not alright! Look where we are in this dark wood. It's dusk, the owls are calling and flying. Isn't that what spooked your horse?'

John smiled and rolled his eyes upwards, deep in thought, 'Yes, it was a tawny owl, lovely bird. I have owl feathers on my lance.'

'Why?'

'It's a sign of strength and wisdom.'

Isobel sighed and looked down at her ragged appearance. Her dress was ripped, and her hair untied and straggling down her back. The horse's wet snot had stuck hair to her face, some of which was embedded in the cuts and scratches on her head and neck. Her legs were covered in mud and tears began to flow as she saw one of her leather boots had torn. Isobel's beautiful little hands now resembled dismembered bits of bread stumps covered in a dark pink combination of mud and blood. She screwed up her nose and sneezed. Perhaps it was the smell of her own body, mixed with the sweat of the horse and froth from its mouth and neck that was so overpowering. She looked back along the track, 'I'm going back for my sister.' She ran down the path.

John, exasperated with this wayward creature, raised his voice.

'Come here, its late, we need shelter, and you need help.' He ran after the stumbling girl, who had not gone far and was easily caught. She wriggled in his arms but seemed to put little effort into it. John looked down at her and smiled.

'It's hard not to kiss that beautiful little face looking up at me, always so pretty and now wet with tears.' Isobel seemed lost for words.

'Yes, I want you to kiss me, kiss me all the time John, but not now, while Margaret is lying in a crumpled heap in that kitchen.' John's arms tightened around her.

'Let me go, please, John. She was my sister, and I can't just leave her like that, all alone and in a mess. I want to take her home, wash her, look after her, you know, do things properly.' John stood firm. He pushed her to arm's length.

'No! We are too many miles away now and you need help, and we must hurry. We have wasted too much time already.' He lifted his hand and slapped her hard across the face. She slumped against him. He struggled to stop her falling and dissolving into the ground. Carrying her back to his horse he lifted her in front of him, climbed on behind her and set off. It looked cold and the trees seemed to be whispering to each other as if bemused by what they had witnessed. As Isobel came round, rubbing her face, she raised her head,

'I can smell woodsmoke coming from the far end of the wood.'

'It's drifting from above the trees. Its old Meg's place.'

'The witch?'

'Yes, the witch. She will give us shelter for the night, I'm sure.'

'The moon is hiding, making it difficult to see where we are going. The track is well overgrown with brambles, ivy, and all manner of dead branches. I am wondering if someone has laid these obstacles across the path on purpose, as a disguise?'

'I can see a small light. It's a long time since I came to Meg's place. I hope she remembers me.'

Minutes later a small house with a turf roof came into sight, built into the hillside and half covered in broken trees with moss covered boulders obscuring the doorway. John stopped at the sight of a tall gaunt figure who appeared from behind a large old oak tree. For a moment all was silent, only the unsettling rustle of leaves as the wind made its presence known. Suddenly a stern voice sounded.

'Who are you and what do you want?'

'We were returning home and had an accident. My wife fell off her horse and is injured.' Isobel slumped against him.

'Where is her horse?'

Isobel whispered, 'John, where is my horse, or Margaret's horse. Once they're found the Nixon's will know that two people are unaccounted for. Although Margaret's body will account for one.'

'Yes, we are in a great deal of danger and must hurry.'

He quickly dismounted, pulled Isobel off his horse and, ignoring the old woman's utterances, strode towards the door, kicked it open, cleared the table with one swipe of his arm and laid Isobel down. The floor clattered and clanked as pots found a new place to settle.

The small room was bright enough. The fire was burning well. John brushed his nose and sneezed.

'This place stinks Meg!'

'It's burning peat. If you don't like it, you don't have to stay. What do you want here anyway and who are you? Who's this girl?'

'A warm hideaway is what we need. Won't stay long. Won't trouble you for long. See to my wife.'

There were two comfortable rocking chairs covered in what looked like woollen shawls. A mat in front of the fire was home to two cats curled up asleep, undisturbed by the sudden commotion. The curtains were drawn on the two windows, in the shadows of the fire, the shape of a door with what looked like some sort of badly torn hanging in front of it, perhaps hiding something. Large bunches of drying herbs hung from the ceiling beams. Isobel stirred, groaned, and raised her hand to her head.

'Where am I? What's happening?' Meg took a quick look at Isobel.

The Uncovered Legacy

'There, there now you will be alright. You have a nasty cut on your head and a few cuts on your face.' She went to pour some water out of her kettle into a bowl, dropped various liquids from several little bottles into it, stirred it well, took a small linen cloth, dipped it in the warm mix and returned to bathe Isobel's head.

John rose from the chair to look at her. He gasped,

'There's blood trickling down her face. If she dies, I'll kill that bastard Ridley.' He thumped his hand on the table so hard a pot fell to the floor.

'Out of the way boy, she's not going to die.' She pushed him towards the fire before bending over Isobel. 'There, there now you will be alright, just be patient. You'll have a scar on that pretty little face but not too big.'

Looking down at her, John shouted, 'Isobel! She's bleeding where is the blood coming from?'

'Not from the lass, nothing is broken. Let me look at you.' She led him back to a chair by the fire, but he tried to shrug her off. 'Leave me alone, woman!'

'You won't be saying that if your arm is left untreated.' She pointed to the open wound on his arm.

'Your shirt is torn and, if I don't clean it up, that dirty linen shirt will work its way into the wound, which will become infected, and you will die.'

'Do you always talk to those who are injured like this?'

'No! But you are an unwanted guest. I want you cleaned up and away as soon as possible.'

John sighed. 'I am sorry. It's been a difficult day and, yes, I am grateful for your help.'

She finished cleaning his arm, sat back, and looked from John to Isobel.

'You are a smelly, dirty man. I won't ask why, where you have come from, or what you are doing in my wood, but I want you out.'

'Your wood?'

'Yes, it's mine. I have cast many spells over the years to keep people out. Don't want to be disturbed.'

'It's easy to get lost here, many paths go round and round in circles. They don't go anywhere; brambles and undergrowth blocked our way.'

'But you found me and if you did others will too. I need to make my spells stronger to keep you all out.'

Isobel stirred and tried to sit up. John stepped forward, picked her up and carried her over to one of the rocking chairs, where he sat down and cradled her in his arms. Isobel briefly opened her eyes, smiled, shuffled her body into his chest and fell into a deep sleep.

'Do her the power of good to sleep. She looks done in. Now let's look at your other arm.' John didn't argue but laid his arm across Isobel's legs and allowed Old Meg to dress his other wound.

'Not much damage. Just a bit of torn skin. I'll soon have it mended.' She pulled a small, three-legged stool from under the table and started to tease out the dirt and bits of cloth that had become imbedded in an open sore.

'You have a strong face. Your long hair is worn neatly tied back but its untidy now. Your clothes are of good quality and your boots. You are not a poor man. You have the body and appearance of a Reiver. I suspect you got these injuries from a recent raid.'

He smiled, 'So you've noticed.'

She stared at him for a few moments,

'I know who you are. I remember you as a young boy. You've been here before. Your reputation for pillaging is widely known in these parts. But you are a long way from home now John Tweddle.'

He smiled 'I am a strong and excellent fighter, much admired.' Meg stood back with her hands on her hips and head to one side.

'Are you trying to impress me?'

'He winked at her. 'Do I need to?'

'No. But there are many rumours as to who you've killed, what you've stolen and who you've kidnapped. Didn't you take Margaret Armstrong?'

'She made a good price. Sold her to old man Ogle.'

'That scheming old wretch! Have you no heart?'

'A good bargain. My brother owed him money. Gambling debt. All paid now.'

'And now you have this lovely creature with you. Another kidnap?'

John looked uncomfortable at his rescue attempt being seen as a kidnap and quickly returned the conversation back to himself.

'They take one look at my body, my armour, decorated bridle and saddle, glistening lance, with sacred owl feathers hanging from it, and back away in fear.'

'You have forgotten to mention your magnificent horse,' she said, raising her eyebrows.

'Best there is. Bred him myself from good Irish blood stock, from O'Leary, the horse trader.'

She smiled at him. 'I heard you stole him from Willie Armstrong. I hear a lot living here. Keeper of secrets.'

John paused to readjust himself and Isobel into more comfortable positions. 'I have another five horses. A man of my standing always has more than one horse.'

Old Meg tilted her head to one side and offered a wry smile to herself. 'Were they all Willie Armstrong's as well?

No matter how hard he tried, the old woman wasn't going to fall for his tales. It was as if they both knew he was exaggerating and the best he could do was to shut his eyes and rest.

'Enough now. You rest, lad, and I'll waken you if danger approaches.' She patted his shoulder as she walked away.

As it was getting light John was woken by Old Meg's gnarled hands shaking him.

'Wake up. Wake up both of you. I can hear riders. Men are coming.'

'Nixon's?' he asked.

'Don't know but several riders passed the old thorn down by the river when I was out collecting firewood earlier.'

'Did you see how many?'

'No.'

'Were they coming this way?'

The Uncovered Legacy

John stood up, forgetting Isobel was on his lap. She landed face down on the floor with a thud and a little scream. He took her arm and helped her up. She quickly came round and became aware of the conversation. She brushed herself down and straightened her clothing before going to the window. It was beginning to get light.

'I can see the outline of several horses, trotting in the shadowy distance.' Old Meg took her arm and led her to the old, tatty wall hanging that concealed a secret door.

'Here. Both of you go through here and follow the tunnel.'

'The tunnel, where does it lead?'

'It twists and turns a bit and is cramped in places. Comes out on the other side of the rock face. It's narrow and low so your strong, handsome Reiver had better keep his head down.' She exchanged a wry smile with John who looked anxious to leave. 'Defending two women in a confined space against several Nixon's won't do your reputation any good if they catch you, now will it? Never mind what they would do to Isobel. Now get going...go....go.' She pushed them forward. 'Come, I'll open the door, there is a pole on the other side, lift it across the back. It will hold them for a while.'

'Do the Nixon's know about this secret door and the cave?'

'No, no, no but old man Williams did, and I am never sure who he told before he died.'

'He's dead?'

'Yes, Nixon's drowned him in the Tweed five years ago, or what was left of him.'

'Have you been visited by them before?'

'Only for medicine, healing wounds and such like.'

'Come on, John, we must go.' begged Isobel. 'Here, collect your dagger,' As she turned to old Meg and smiled Isobel put her arms around the old woman and held her as close as she could. 'Thank you for helping us. It's so nice to be held by a woman. My mother Elinor never held me close. She didn't believe in showing affection, although she made an exception for my sister Margaret. Oh, my poor dead sister lying there in that old dirty kitchen with no one to see to her.' She clutched her chest and sobbed.

'Here take this cloth and wipe your eyes. Come on, my dear, you must both go. I can hear men dismounting and moving towards the outside door....be quick, be quick, go, go!'

Once inside, in the total darkness they both scrambled to close the door behind them.

'It's old and rotten. Oh, God, I hope it doesn't crumble.'

'Here, Isobel, help me pull this wooden latch across and lock it in place. Do it quietly.'

'Oh, John, I hope it holds.'

Chapter 8

Nip stirred, disturbing Anne. She rubbed her eyes and stared back into the past. She watched Old Meg collecting the blood-stained cloths and quickly threw them into the simmering cauldron. She rearranged the shawls on the rocking chairs, picked the pots off the floor where they were left from the night before and moved the candle to obscure the light shining on the secret door. She trembled at the sound of heavy footsteps and panting horses. A heavy hand pounded on the door.

'Open this door or I'll knock it down!'

The witch took a deep breath, picked up her gnarled elder stick and slowly opened the door. Richard Nixon stood, red faced, panting and sweating.

'What do you want at this hour?' She croaked.

'Riders! My mother, Katie Nixon, is dead. Found Margaret Elliott in the kitchen and two loose horses. Looking for the Ridleys, murdering bastards!'

'Are you sure it was Margaret Elliott?'

'One of my men recognised what was left of her. A small band of Ridleys were seen driving our cattle west of here. I want them old woman!'

'Well, I have seen nothing, heard nothing. It's quiet here.'

'I don't believe you old woman.' He pushed her aside and strode into her cottage, where he turned the chairs and table over, pulled the rack down above the fire and tore the meagre curtains from the windows before finally satisfying himself there was nobody else there.

In an effort to remind him she could be useful she said, 'I hope your arm has healed well after I stitched it a few weeks ago. It was a very bad wound, so deep you lost a lot of blood. I hope you have looked after it well.' She raised herself to full height, looked him square in the face and stood, arms folded across her chest. 'I have not forgotten the horse your men stole. I needed it to pull my cart, to go to the market and replenish supplies. He was an old animal with poor feet and of little use to you, but you took him anyway. You did not pay me. How can I buy new medicines without money and no cart to carry them home. I am an old woman.' She glanced at his arm. It looked black and swollen. Infection had set in. Death would follow.

'You foul smelling old hag, where are they? You must have seen them.' He took her by the throat and pushed her into the wall.'

'I've seen no…no…' was all she could manage. Old Meg raised her eyebrows and shook her head as she squinted at the inflamed wound on his upper arm. It was raging, the poison oozing out and dripping down his sleeve. Richard Nixon spat in her face, released her, threw the rocking chair into the fire, hitting the cauldron, with the blooded cloths and rabbit stew, so hard it fell off its hook and poured onto the open fire and put it out. Sparks flew across the kitchen floor, landing on the rag mat, and sending both cats flying backwards as the hot ash burned their coats. They landed at his feet where, with a deft swing of his leg, they were soon dispatched through the open cottage door to land in a misshapen heap at the bottom of her log pile. Old Meg put her hand to her mouth to stifle a scream and was lucky to avoid his arm that threw itself her way as he strode out of the door, gathered his horse and men and rode off but not before shouting back, 'You'll pay for this, old woman, if I hear you have been harbouring any of them!'

Old Meg bowed her head and wept. She looked around at her broken furniture. Her two black cats lay outside splattered with blood and disfigured. The candle was out, as was the fire, Wet ash and logs were now strewn across the floor and had soaked the rag mat. She stood, feet wet with the cauldron's contents, shuffled to the door, and muttered to herself, 'There'll be no warmth or rabbit stew for me. It's going to be a long cold night.' She pushed the door closed as best she could and smiled, 'Well Nixon, I am glad I bathed your open wound with a poisonous cloth. I will await word reaching me of your slow death.' She turned, beat the wall with her fists and screamed, 'I will have my revenge, you bastard!'

Chapter 9

John and Isobel inched their way along the slippery, narrow passage.

'I don't know this part of the crag and have no idea where it leads. Didn't know it existed but don't think it can be very long.' He paused for a second to wipe dust and cobwebs from his head.

'Isobel this tunnel is old. I suspect not been used for a long time.' Isobel started wheezing and let out a few short rasping coughs as she stumbled over loose rocks on the floor.

'Be careful.'

'I am being careful. I can't see very much. Shafts of light are peeping through the cracks in the roof openings and it's bouncing off the limestone walls. It's smelly and hard to breathe. My hands are feeling spongy moss and its damp and there are ferns brushing against my legs. We must be getting towards an entrance.'

Minutes later a trickle of water dripped onto her head and Isobel looked up, dazzled by a glint of light.

'Isobel it's nearly dawn. Let's get out of here and put an end to another infuriating mess you have got us both into.' Isobel stopped, pulled his hand back. John screamed and wrenched his hand free of her grip. 'What did you do that for? Stop it, do you hear me? Stop it.'

'Or what? What else can you do to me? I didn't ask to be rescued, leave my dead sister, be thrown onto a horse, dragged through a wood, dropped in a bog and to spend the night in a filthy smelly hovel. And now I am in this disgusting smelly passage. It is not my fault we are here.' Isobel dissolved into tears.

John sighed and reached for her hand, 'Perhaps I should have left you there to be found by the Nixon's.' He squeezed her hand and raised his voice, 'Anyway, I thought you liked adventure. Can't be much further. Come on, Isobel, I need to get back to Wydon and divide up the stolen cattle. I want my share.'

Isobel kicked the stone wall with her foot. 'Ouch…. Is that all you can think about? Is that more important than me?' John ignored her. Soon a light breeze caught Isobel's hair and drips of water turned into a trickle. A wider gap appeared, and more light flooded towards them. The passage narrowed and a gap appeared just wide enough to climb through into a thicket of brambles and thorns. They eagerly scrambled over the undergrowth and were soon standing in the open air where Isobel stood taking several deep breaths. She smiled, 'It's a relief to feel fresh air again.'

She looked down and pointed to the ivy entangling their feet.

'Ivy will help us.'

He looked bemused, 'Help us?'

'Yes, it's showing us we are bound together.'

He laughed, pulled her towards him, threw his arms round her waist and kissed her beautiful face. They stood together in their bedraggled state and for a moment all seemed well. Isobel pulled away and held the ivy in her hands, closed her eyes and began to hum. 'Listen. It's intoxicating. It's talking to us.'

'I can't hear anything.'

'Listen. We need to still our minds. We must resolve any conflict or trouble we have between us.'

'Do we have any?

'My mother is our only problem.'

John looked distracted, suddenly released her and started looking around. 'Isobel, I need to find my horse.'

'What about my horse and Margarets? I'm glad I wasn't riding Molly.'

'Nixon's will have taken them.' After several minutes of looking, Isobel shouted, 'Look, John, he's over there, standing next to that tree.'

'He's grazing. Black horses can be useful on dark nights. He's well disguised and during the night he's wandered away from the cottage and out of sight of the Nixon's.'

John crept towards the horse speaking in soft gentle tones so as not to frighten him. The reins were loose, trailing on the ground and entangled in a broken tree stump, which rendered the animal trapped. He carefully untied the leather straps, stroked its neck, removed the twigs and leaves caught in the various gaps in the saddle and led the horse back to Isobel. 'Mount up, Isobel. I will take you to Tommy Kerr's place.'

'What? Who's he?'

'A farmer. Owes me a favour. He will give us a horse.'

'Yes, John, but is it far?'

'No.'

'Are you taking me home?'

'Yes, I need to see your father.'

'Are you going to explain about Margaret?'

'I am but we must hurry.'

'Why?'

'I need to rejoin my men. They will be nearly back at Wydon by now and the spoils of the raid will be divided and, if I'm not there, I'll not get my share.' He turned away and cursed under his breath.

'That's the second time you've thought about your share of raided goods. I hope I'm just as important to you, but I shall have to be content with your warm body next to mine on your horse.' She giggled. John squeezed her shoulders, stood looking down at her and shook his head.

'Raiding is my life, Isobel, and you know that. You wouldn't have the pretty things you like if we didn't raid, so be quiet. It will be a long hard ride home and I have lost precious time rescuing you.'

Isobel frowned, looked hurt that his focus was on gaining wealth and not on her, but she seemed happy enough to mount up behind him, snuggle into his back and put her arms so tightly round his waist she almost winded him. John kicked his horse hard in the stomach and they set off at a gallop.

Chapter 10

Anne woke with a start. Nip's head rested on her lap, the fire had died down, the shawl lay on the floor where the cats were still curled up asleep on the mat. She shivered, yawned and glanced at the clock which still read ten past two.

'That was a funny dream, Nip, it felt so real. Or was it a dream?' she said, stroking his head.

The dog wagged his tail at the sound of his name and wandered off to rattle his bowl. Anne stirred at the sound of the dish scraping its way across the floor. She felt strangely at ease, sitting in the dark, with only the dying embers of the fire to light the kitchen. As she stretched her arms out her right hand began to itch, as if being scratched. Gazing down she had the faintest image of a bird. Its talons clasped her wrist. She felt no pain, nor could she feel its weight. It wasn't real. As the moon was passing the kitchen window, there was enough light to see it was an eagle. Anne's heart began to flutter as she looked at the resting bird. 'Look, Nip. Look what I can see.'

'Who are you?'

'I am Lolair,' it said in a strong deep voice.

'What do you want?'

'As this magical path opens for you, venture forward into this new world, learn about it and understand what it is asking of you. There is a purpose here. Be courageous and follow it.'

Then with the slightest movement, her arm felt lighter, and it was gone. Anne sat still for a few moments, stunned.

'What was that about Nip? What's just happened? It's been a strange evening and something is gnawing away at the back of my mind.'

Nip, hearing his name again, began to bark, in the hope that, this time, she'd respond to his desire for food. Anne sighed, 'Oh, Nip. Yes, yes, I hear you. I know, I know. But you are not normally fed in the middle of the night, you rascal.' She stood up, ruffled his ears, took stock of her surroundings, and went to the fridge where she produced a plateful of cold, uneaten sausages and dropped them, one by one, into an eagerly waiting open mouth.

'Goodnight, Nip. It's very late. I am going to bed now and will try and get some sleep.' But her thoughts were not on the dog, or the two cats, still asleep on the shawl. Instead, she was thinking about the eagle, Grandmother Crane, Isobel, Margaret, John, Old Meg and Robert Ridley. Yes, it was strange and interesting but, at the same time, there was something familiar about it all and that was the exciting bit.

The Uncovered Legacy

Tomorrow she would go to the library and look up the history of the Border Reivers.

*

Anne woke to the sound of the dawn chorus. Last evening's events were swirling round in her head. She glanced at the bedside clock. It read Tuesday March 14[th,] 06:05. Or did it? Was she still in the 16th century? No, they did not have digital clocks.

Anne sighed, sat up in bed and pulled the covers up around her neck. Her eyes drifted to a picture of the sheep gathering on the bedroom wall and she began to reflect on her childhood, a time of isolation and loneliness, of roaming fields with dogs and ponies and spending hours observing and communicating with animals. It was all so natural and normal.

Perhaps she had always existed in two worlds. However, in recent months, since her return to Wydon, she had been drawn back into the past of long ago more often and for longer.

The cycle of the farming year had given her life a rhythm of time and order. The seasons came and went. Spring was always hard work, full of the sounds of bleating lambs, some lost, some abandoned, some injured or frozen to the ground, needing to be collected into hessian sacks, fastened to the saddle, taken home, and put under the waiting heat lamps in the kitchen lamb boxes. Distraught mothers would follow, calling all the way.

In late March, when lighter days and nights returned, the bluebell wood was a complete joy. Their overpowering scent would drift into Anne's nostrils and dream time never seemed far away.

On cold, frosty mornings the breath of the beef cattle, enclosed in airless byres all winter, left a kaleidoscope of colourful patterns on the windows. A chomping sound from the wet silage pit and the sweet smell of the straw bedding, quickly thrown down to avoid breathing in the ammonia seeping upwards from the pungent manure, heralded the beginning of the day.

Remembering those happy, carefree days brought a smile to her face, although living in damp wellington boots was not pleasant and icy, cold winds biting into her face, unprotected with cream, had taken its toll on her complexion.

May, was the magical time when store cattle would frolic in fresh green pastures. Calves, born indoors, would gallop about the meadows with so much to explore. The smell of the hawthorn flowers and the sharp prick of its thorns on a soft pink nose would make the calves jump, shake their heads and dance away, happy to be unfettered.

Summer was a time of lying under trees and languishing in fragrant hay meadows, daydreaming and sleeping, only to be woken by the wet nuzzling of a pony's mouth on her face. They were safe places to be with the dogs by her side, always alert and only disturbing her with the sound of snapping teeth when an insect came too close.

These were magical times of long hot days and clear skies, perfect for cloud watching and travelling with passing birds on warm thermals. They were days full of treasured memories of journeying to other lands and other places in distant times, when animals would come to her, sit close by, unafraid and when shared communication was easy. Increasingly, Anne had separated from her human family, unable to connect to their lives.

When summer faded and autumn came, the temperature dropped and the workload on the farm increased. Autumn, which brought the fruits of the earth, was an empowering time. Each raspberry was unique, every apple told a story of its visiting nibblers and nesters. Blackberries fought for prime position in the sun, eager to ripen first, drop to the ground in the freshly warmed autumn soil and wait for a helpful foot to take them to earth in anticipation of spring and new life. Jams would be made, and freezers stacked to the brim with pies, crumbles and sauces. Rose hip syrup would be prepared in anticipation of winter's coughs.

Samhain heralded the last harvest. Winter was approaching, a time of quiet on the farm. Livestock were returned to the indoor cattle sheds and the twice daily routine of feeding returned. This was men's work, which allowed Anne to slip away unnoticed to the hillsides and woodlands, to the hidden places away from prying eyes. She would wrap up warm, take sandwiches and a hot drink, saddle Molly, the pony, collect one of the dogs and set off to the woods and freedom. Returning home as dusk gave in to darkness, she would quietly enter the house, collect the cold supper her mother had left out and climb the back stairs to her room, where she would sit on the bed and recall the wonders of the day. Thoughts and pictures would appear in her consciousness, and she would drift into the past. Time would no longer exist, and her life would easily become part of somebody else's.

In recent months memories and images had become more frequent and intense. Why she always went back four hundred years, she did not know. Her rational mind told her these events were not real, which brought up questions about reality. What was it and whose reality she was in. To her right brain all these events were real, the people she observed and the places she was taken to all seemed familiar. The girl, Isobel, haunted her dreams. They looked alike and Anne felt she knew her quite well. In fact, there did not seem to be anything about Isobel that Anne didn't understand. Why was that? And why was she so often at the forefront of her consciousness?

Anne slid down the bed and thought about the times she had slept outside under the stars, having forgotten to go home, so deeply was she connected to the other world. Those were happy carefree days, and they brought a smile to her face. Her thoughts were rudely interrupted by Nip, the Dog, who had run upstairs barking, jumped onto the bed, and begun to lick her face. She laughed and pushed him off.

'Come on Nip, get off the bed, it's time to get dressed, help out with the livestock, have breakfast and then we'll go to the library to do some research.' Nip pricked up his ears, continued barking and rushed downstairs.

Chapter 11

A fter breakfast Anne made her way through the house to the library, a medium-sized room at the end of a long corridor towards the back of the house. It was kept locked and safe from grandchildren who, in the past, had been caught stacking randomly sized books on chairs and climbing up to reach top shelves, only to have them collapse in spectacular fashion. It was a purpose-built, dark room with one small window, designed to prevent bright sunlight fading the book spines and making them illegible. Anne sat down in great grandfather's brown leather armchair and glanced at the papers strewn on the large oak desk. Her latest manuscript was proving a difficult task and most of it lay in disorganised piles on the floor.

She had been wondering what Isobel's life would have been like in the 16th century. Who were her family and where did they live? Gazing round the room, her eyes wandered over the many shelves of books, hundreds of them, all waiting patiently to be opened and read. Somewhere among this rabble of books was an old copy of the History of Northumberland, which had been passed down through the generations and was a treasured family heirloom. All the books were covered in powdered dust and many titles were now obscured. Anne smiled as her eyes settled on the sign she had put up as a child, on the back of the library door, which read:

Dust Experiment in Progress. Do not Disturb the Samples.

At the moment dust was a hindrance. As she started gently to blow off just enough so she could read the spines, her eyes alighted on a dark rectangular shape tottering on the edge of a top shelf. She stared for a moment, then smiled, it was hers, the treasured keepsake box, not seen for many years. She lifted it down and gently rubbed her sleeve across the top of the hand carved rosewood box, with its brass inlaid Awen symbol on the top. She let her fingers trace the flower carvings round the sides of the box before gently prizing open the lid, which revealed an inside lined with red velveteen. Anne sat at the desk and, one by one, removed its contents. First out was the lucky rabbit's foot she always carried in her pocket as a child. It was followed in quick succession by her prefect's badge, her grandmother's ruby encrusted hair clasp, a long, curved, sack darning needle and grandfather's Freemason's fob watch. A small velvet bag contained a broken pearl necklace with string still partially attached. There were her children's baby tags, two gold sovereigns and then, inside the little drawer, she discovered a small piece of grubby, cream paper which revealed two rings tied together with a piece of faded red ribbon, so dry she was fearful it would tear. One of the rings was a posey ring and had the runic symbol of love and the initials I.E., and J.T. She had never seen these rings before. Why were they in her box and who put them there? When? And why had she rediscovered this box today? Anne sat for a while reminiscing then, one by one, quietly replaced her memories and closed the lid. She let out a big sigh and allowed her eyes to drift over the shelves where they soon became fixed on a large green book. The World Atlas. It was much too wide for the shelf it but there sitting next to it, was:

The History of Northumberland 1886 Vol. V
by Professor Daniel Ogle

Anne stood up, replaced the box on its shelf, teased the book from its neighbours, blew the top dust off and carefully carried it to the desk. It was old, torn in places and discoloured, with many loose tissue pages. The red leather binding was frayed, and the front cover was hanging by six threads. Sitting down, she poured a large glass of home-made elderberry wine and opened the book. She found the contents page and ran her eyes down to Chapter 18, which was headed, *"History of the Border Reivers"*. She began to read.

John Balliol ruled Scotland in the name of Edward I. Then, in 1296 he rebelled, made alliances with France and invaded northern England. In retaliation Edward marched North to Berwick on Tweed and slaughtered all 500 inhabitants. It was said that the river Tweed ran red with blood for three days. This was the beginning of the First Scottish War of Independence and the people who lived on each side of the border were caught in the middle.

Anne skipped the next few wordy paragraphs, then continued.

Living on both sides of the divide, Borderers found themselves at the mercy of tides of brutality over which they had no control. Armies large and small marched across their lands, fought on it, burned it, despoiled it and fled. For almost four hundred years until 1603, their homes became battlefields that stretched the length of the North, from the North Sea in the East to the Solway coast in the West.

Over the centuries, Borderers learned well from the early successes of William Wallace and Robert the Bruce, who were skilled at guerrilla warfare and now the Borderers were attacking King Edward's supply lines, by raiding, spying, sabotage and ambushing small groups. Borderers became a flexible fighting force. Fighting on home territory in small mobile groups they could easily destabilise an unwieldy, larger force. This protracted harassment created fear and wore the enemy down. These warfare tactics led to an independent way of living for many of the Border people.

Clans, living on both sides of the border, changed sides and alliances, as suited their family needs at the time. Lawlessness abounded. In the Debatable lands to the west, held by Armstrong's and Grahams, neither Scottish nor English authority was heeded. This was a perfect hideaway for criminals and those who lived outside the law...the outlaws.

The Uncovered Legacy

The difference between war and peace became a matter of intensity. No one ever really won, as conflicts were liable to break out again at any time. In order to survive, many of these Borderers became nomadic, learned to live on the move, to cut crop sustenance to a minimum and to rely on the livestock they could drive in front of them. Homes could be quickly built and often abandoned just as fast, although some of the more powerful families held Bastles, Castles, Pele towers or large stone built, fortified manor houses and had a more settled existence.

Border people learned to travel long distances at speed and to rely on stealing to restock and survive. The men were some of the finest light cavalrymen of their day and in demand from all sides. They wore steel bonnets and rode with the moonlight, armed with long spears.

There could be no future in a settled existence. Crops may be burned before harvesting and homes and property destroyed. Generations of children grew up depending for their existence on raiding. The Borderers became both victims and participants in what developed into a warrior society, having loyalty to neither Scotland nor England. Allegiances were to clan and each other, which caused problems when Borderers were recruited into opposing armies. Conflicts did not break out along the simple lines of England and Scotland. The English feuded with the English. The Scots feuded with the Scots. In addition to cross border conflicts and clan alliances, intermarriage was common, to the frustration of both the Scottish and English governments. Borderers believed that all property was common property, by law of nature and therefore it was liable to be appropriated as seen fit and necessary. Plundering was seen as lawful. ....

The English and Scottish governments tried to enforce control in the 'Marches' with wardens. They divided the Borders into six Marches, three in England and three in Scotland: West, Middle and East.

The English Marches were controlled by southern English landowners and the Scottish March wardens were selected from Scottish Border families. Scottish wardens sided with Scottish claims while the English wardens had no vested interest. Both governments, although deploring the Border economy, exploited it as a source of fighting men. However, they failed to control family alliances.

To keep the peace, the March Wardens maintained garrisons, patrols and watches, to deter raiding and provide justice. They would meet at appointed times, known as "Days of Truce", along the border to settle disputes, which were grand opportunities for socialising, entertaining and lawfully greeting relatives. However, these wardens were largely ineffective and were often raiders themselves, favouring their own families. When nominal peace did break out, Border Law (March law) came into force.

In some Marches, the people who had been raided could re raid and take back their stolen goods, usually cattle, from across the border. But they had to give warning and proceed with "Hound and Horn" to warn the unlawful raiders of their presence. This was known as the 'Hot Trod'.

Valuable Slew dogs and hounds would follow the raiders tracks and the people along the way had to help or be accused of being on the wrong side. The leader of the posse had to carry a lance with a piece of burning turf on its end to guarantee safe passage in enemy territory and had twenty-four hours to retrieve stolen livestock before the raiders were free to keep their loot. A law breaker could cross the border, *seek sanctuary and avoid being taken back, by ringing bells in the first church found on the other side.*

Reivers perfected the 'Protection Racket' and were accomplished at tracking and hiding. They were in tune with their landscape and its hiding places, where upwards of 1,000 head of cattle could be hidden in one of the 100 or more glens where they could wait for the 'Hot Trod' to end. Wardens and Reivers employed a network of spies and many men and women worked for both sides, getting paid twice but their loyalty was always to their own families.

When the Reivers came down from their dales into the Low Countries and carried away horses and livestock, professional thieves were employed by the wardens to retrieve them, although they often worked for both sides and were skilled at generating fear in the population.

As she skimmed over several paragraphs the word "Mail" caught her attention. Fascinated, she read on.

Mail, an old word for tax/rent, was often paid in silver money, which was known as 'White Mail', or paid in cattle or other livestock. Demanding money higher than the rent owed was known as 'Blackmail' or Black Rent. Some reiving families extorted both kinds of rent from farmers, landowners and businesses and it was often known as women's work.

Red handed men where those caught with blood on their hands from just having killed a man or beast. Punishment for being caught 'Red Handed' was often death.

Both governments, although deploring the Border economy used it to their own advantage. The kings of Scotland and England may have ruled their countries, but lance and sword dominated the land in between. The clan chiefs led from their pele towers, bastles, manors and fortified houses. The broken men travelled as mercenaries, the outlaws occupied the mosses and fells, and the peasants possessed the valleys. These were unique people; labourers, gentlemen farmers, peers of the realm, blacksmiths, fighting men, merchants and traders, as well as professional cattle rustlers.

The people of the Borders were self-reliant, had a strong sense of awareness, were resilient in the face of multiple enemies and were shaped by every kind of ordeal imaginable. They lived by continuously feuding among themselves, by robbery, blackmail, stealing, kidnapping, murder, arson, theft and extortion. They needed to be prudent in their alliances if they were to prosper and at the same time be ready to bend to the prevailing wind and make friends and allies wherever they could.

Anne closed the book, gazed out of the window at the rugged landscape beneath the towering clouds and thought it would have changed little since the 16th century; the world Isobel Elliott was born into.

From what she had seen in the kitchen fire, Isobel's family seemed to be powerful, wealthy and feared. John Tweddle had behaved like a leader. He'd been dressed in expensive clothes, perhaps stolen or bartered. Even so, he was not a poor man, nor were his immediate companions. Isobel was also well dressed in a long, good quality, green, wool dress with a fancy decorated jewelled belt, with embroidered edges. She wore good strong leather boots, and her hair was tied back in such a way that someone must have done it for her, perhaps a maid. On the other hand, Robert Ridley looked rough, unkempt, even grubby.

Chapter 12

fter a while Anne opened the book again. She gasped! There on page 493 was a heading in bold type.

The Raid at Wydon

'Wydon…. this Wydon, this house, my home! Nip, there was a raid here! Oh, how exciting!'

It was a small paragraph which told her that, in the 16th century, 500 Border Reivers, led by the Tweddle family, had come down from the Neidpath Castle in the Scottish Borders to five small hamlets: Wydon, Nicol's Barn, Tom's Place, High Dales and Low Croft. Instead of pillaging, burning, stealing and leaving, they had stayed. The land was good, with a large, fortified manor house and several farmhouses built of stone, with good outhouses for livestock. The Reivers never left, and descendants of Angus Tweddle were still living at Wydon.

Anne paused, 'Nip, Nip, I can't believe it!' She bounced up and down, clapping her hands, while trying hard to be calm as she began to count on her fingers how many generations it must have been from John Tweddle to herself, presuming that John Tweddle was her ancestor. Perhaps ten grandfathers, great-greats, great-great-greats…twenty-ish? Some day she would work it out. As she turned to the next page an old, well-fingered, brown envelope fell onto the floor. Bending down to pick it up, she read the handwritten name on the front.

Stories of Angus Twedddle.

Inside were lots of pieces of paper, all written by different hands. Some were illegible but five pieces she could decipher. Two sheets had been fastened together at some time in the past. One was torn and looked like it had been burned, perhaps by pipe ash. A third was blotchy and a fourth had been written by a delicate hand, probably a well-educated woman. The fifth piece of paper had been carefully flattened after having been screwed up in the past. Perhaps someone had found it, disagreed with its contents and tried to destroy it. She surmised that, over the years, as different bits of information had come to light, various members of the family had added to the story. 'Look, Nip, how fascinating!' But the dog only raised his eyebrows. She poured out another glass of elderberry wine, and, feeling a little lightheaded, moved to the sofa and curled up next to Nip, who had managed to get there first. She opened the papers, spread them neatly on her lap and began to read them one after the other.

The Uncovered Legacy

History of Wydon Raid.

Angus Twedle and his two brothers, Willie and Thom, heard a tale, from a travelling peddler, about rich pickings in England, on a large farm with a strong fortified manor house, not far over the border into England, outside a settlement called Haltwezell. Life at Neidpath Castle, near Peebles, was becoming tedious for many of these smaller families; too much fighting among themselves, not enough raiding. Angus wanted to be away from Neidpath, he wanted land, cattle and his own manor. The decades of feuding with the Veaches were getting neither side any richer. Cattle, sheep, horses and, sometimes dogs, were constantly moving from one valley to another. Animals were thin as they didn't stay in one place long enough to put on any weight. Grain stores were fired, and deer were sparse due to over hunting by outlaws. In recent years valuable raiding time had been spent guarding boundaries, reinforcing barricades and escorting their farmers, with whatever remained of their livestock, to Peebles market. The Tweddles and Veaches were evenly matched. Neither side ever truly had the advantage. Even the Crook Inn, a favourite place to ambush, used, often, by the Tweddles to trap enemies on their way past, had lost its effectiveness. After the last skirmish, over a trivial matter concerning one of his dogs' abilities, Angus was bored and was heard to say, 'Nobody worth fighting anymore.'   Jamie 'Long Nose' Tweddle

Vietches Feud.

The chief of the Vietches' had a favourite son, David, who, on his way to Peebles, was ambushed by a band of nine Twedles. A fight had broken out and David was slain. Murdered in a particularly gruesome way, his body had lain in pieces on the ground and the guilty men had fled over the hills to Tarras Moor and safety. When news reached his grandfather, Jack Red hair, a state of inconsolable rage had ensued. They themselves had slain two younger Twedle's in a dispute over a horse only a month before and the Twedle's had sworn revenge. On this day, five of the Vietches' set off to retrieve David's body. The horror of what they saw took them by surprise and it took several hours to collect dismembered body parts. The old man knew the Twedles would be long gone and the trail cold. He also knew that young Tom Twedle, the tutored son of the Laired of Blackwater would be travelling to Edinburgh to the Wardens monthly meeting, the next day. They planned to lie in wait and have their revenge. The following day young Tom Twedle, with his bag of complaints, new alliances, and official documents etc. set out for Edinburgh with two companions.

The track through Coppice Wood narrowed as it approached a large thicket of tightly packed young Scots pine trees. The Vietches' had tied a rope between two trees and left it slack just enough so it merged with the mud. Well-hidden, they waited for their prey to emerge. The five men, two on one side and three on the other were poised and ready for revenge. 'Twedle Bastards' Red Hair had yelled, and the men pulled the rope tight. All three ponies fell, the first caught in the knees. The second fell into the first. The third pony got its front foot tangled in the rope, fell over and crushed his rider. The second rider was trapped under a screaming pony who had had his leg broken and was in considerable pain. Young Tom was no match for five angry Vietches and was soon dispatched to the other world. One horse had its throat cut, the other two were roped together and ridden away, leaving three dead bodies lying in various tangled pieces in the early morning mud. No one was ever caught.

This story has come down to us from a Vietches descendent!

Fergus Kerr Twedel 1806

Memories told to me by Jasper Thomson …taken from his mother's diary that some of you alive after me might find interesting. I am telling this as it was told to me.

Blackwater in Scotland was alive with fighting talk, revenge and destruction of all Veattch's, even though two daughters of the Laird Veattch had married two Tweeddles and one cousin and a sister had been purchased by the Laird of Blackwater himself. Angus's had a pregnant wife, and he wanted his son to be named John, and become a skilled fighter like himself, and a good leader of men. John would be his heir and he wanted more for him, and in particular more land and reliable alliances with other clans but most of all a bigger stronghold from which to govern. If Angus's dreams were to be fulfilled then it was time to look elsewhere, to leave Neidpath Castle and to go south and over the border into England. Angus and his two brothers went to see the Bells, Grahams and Kerr's to patch up their differences long enough to have a large-scale raid into Northumberland and take Wydon. Angus was feared by the Grahams, for his ability to exact revenge on those who betrayed him. The story was told that he once chased a man for three weeks into the Scottish glens to take revenge on the man who stole his horse. Over the decades the story had grown in magnitude and Angus never denied the embellishment.

Johannis William Angus Tweeddle 1701

The Uncovered Legacy

Anne read this extract several times and wondered if the reference to John was to the man she had seen in the fire. Stories, names, dates and spellings, passed down often got muddled. She picked up the next piece of torn paper which appeared to be burnt at one edge. The writing was difficult to read but she managed to make some sense of it as the story followed on from the last.

Some of mother's memories of what her grandfather father told her of the coming to Wydon of our family.

Angus, his two brothers and a few trusted companions, had left Neidpath and travelled south into England looking for Wydon, near a settlement called Haltwezell, to see if the tale of wealth and good land they'd heard about was true. It took many days and nights taking shelter where they could. Important information was gleaned from travellers, farmers, and villages they passed through. Peddlers and journeymen were particularly forthcoming. He discovered the farm belonged to the Ridle's. Angus Tweedle had scores to settle with old man Ridle and the thought of taking Wydon and lands from him was an opportunity not to be missed. Ridle had a reputation as a thief and scoundrel who broke every alliance he had ever made with any family and could not be trusted. It would be easy to rally men to oust him.

Rumours had come to the Tweedle's that suggested Ridle had not held Wydon very long, some said he had won it in a shadowy dispute over cattle where money changed hands. Other tales told of only a few women and children living there, the men having gone and those left would have been easy to dislodge. It sounded as if it had come into Ridle's possession without much resistance. Which seemed odd in these parts, being so close to the border. After many days of scouting Angus had climbed a great hill. Looking down from the top the valley below was flat, with well cultivated meadows, grassland, and lots of cattle pasture. Sheep grazed ahead on the fells. The layout of the houses and building suggested to Angus several small farms, all clustered around the large stone built and well-fortified manor house, built to the east of the smaller buildings. The river Tippalt meandered in the short distance in front of them. To the east the mighty South Tyne flowed and appeared to surround the farm on two sides. The hills to the west were intimidating and offered protection from raiders. The men were pleased with what they saw. The land looked good; livestock healthy and lots of small farms to settle with their own families. But best of all they belonged to the irksome dishonest old man Ridle. They had spent several hours watching the comings and goings on the property, deciding what would be their best approach and how many men would they find. Angus did not think it would be much of a fight. He knew from past encounters that Ridle was a coward. Lived by intimidation and blackmail. A man without honour or loyalty and suspected he would make a hasty retreat at the first sign of danger.

He had been told the farm had only been in his possession for a few months. The previous occupants had tried to regain their territory but had fallen foul of a terrible sickness that had come from the Newcastle docks aboard a merchant ship from the east. It had spread very fast and destroyed many settlements and fighting men, leaving farms empty, livestock unattended and ripe for the taking. Angus had heard of this sickness, but it had thankfully not ventured into Scotland.

Returning home, the three brothers made plans. It was late winter, and spring would soon be upon them. They must hurry. The next few weeks were spent calling men and their families to join them, many of whom had scores to settle with the Ridles. The women began packing household goods, pots, pans, bedding, and clothes. What was left in the grain stores was emptied, livestock rounded up and poultry penned. The Tweedle's knew that once they left on this raid and long march south, they would not be coming back. A new life in a new country awaited them. Angus's wife Astrid had died giving birth to John, born in an old land moving to a new country. They would head for Carlisle followed by a two-day journey east taking the old drove roads, through forests, and woods, over steams, treacherous rivers, bleak moorland, and high fells.

In the last few weeks Angus and his men had ridden many times to Haltwezell searching for less dangerous routes to travel with laden carts, women and children, places to rest up and shelter at night, always following valley bottoms as best they could and avoiding sheep hill passes. He would have to find a gap in Hadrian's wall that was safe enough to travel through.

One fine early morning in February they said their farewells to the remaining Tweedle's at Neidpath. Gathered their livestock, herded them in front, men walked in the middle, outriders and scouts on the edges with women and children in carts behind. These people set off on a perilous journey to a new life in a new country and hoped it would be different. As the days passed men came to join them from outlying villages and farms and the momentum grew. Not all would have stayed, some would need to return home, their cattle would need taking up to the high ground, sheep would be lambing, and crops sewn. Some men would return to Neidpath and their nearby lands, picking up more livestock on their return, as their fear of Angus was too great to endanger taking cattle from Wydon. Although there would be renegades and outlaws who would do as they wished. But rich pickings were to be had on the return journey, if they came back following the western trails. Angus was confident most men would return to Scotland and Wydon would be his, and only his.

Margaret Anne Tweeddel 1784

Anne noticed a small piece of Paper attached to the last page it read…

My Riddlley family ancestors were not as bad as these Tweddl's, don't believe all you read.

Anne Riddlley Tweddl 1802

Anne paused. She thought about their long march and calculated it would have been about eighty miles as the crow flies and taken perhaps about ten to fourteen days, depending on the numbers of livestock they were driving, the weather and laden carts. What an adventure. She felt proud of her ancestor's courage and was pleased that, over the generations, various notes and updates had been added, probably as a result of research, letters and family wills, although a lot of names and places were spelt differently, which was to be expected as stories change with the telling. She wondered how accurate the dates were. But she felt sad so many letters were illegible…a whole history lost!

Nip was looking bored and anxious to be outside. He crept along the floor and quietly edged his paw onto the desk, grabbed several pieces of paper in his teeth and crouched behind the curtain. Anne screamed 'No, No, No, Nip, drop it, NOW!' A scuffle broke out between them as she steadily retrieved each piece of paper and reassembled them into an order. She chastised him as harshly as she could, with lots of, 'You are a bad, bad dog,' wagging her finger and raising her voice. But it failed. Staring into those beautiful brown eyes always weakened her resolve. 'I know, Nip. Please be patient. Just wait a little longer.' She patted him on his head as he slumped away to the hearth rug, where he put his head on his paws and looked decidedly unimpressed, with the look that said, 'wait a little longer!!!' Anne, having reorganised the papers, came across a different hand, skimmed through what she had already read in other pieces and continued to read.

Now in England, Angus Tweedle and his men approached the Wydon settlement, Riidley's dogs seemed unaware of their presence. They were busy scuttling about chasing rats. Most of the ponies were asleep on their feet. The cattle in the low field pastures were quiet enough, lying in small groups, raising their heads now and again as a barn owl quartered over them. The moon was high with only the low mist of dawn to hide the men in the landscape. The farmstead looked vulnerable with herds unguarded and undefended. Angus sent scouts ahead. The others dismounted, tied up their hobblers and crept along the ridge on their bellies. The older women, children, livestock and the old men, past their best fighting days, had been left some distance behind in a steep sided hidden valley, found by the brothers, on their return to Scotland some weeks before. With the narrow entrance gap the livestock could be easily guarded. The heavily laden carts had been left further behind in a secluded wood. The Reivers were well armed with swords, rapiers, daggers, spears, bows and pistols. Some wore thick leather padded jerkins, others an array of breast armour, and all of them wore scarves wrapped tightly round their necks, protection from having their throats cut.

Each man knew his role. Angus and a small group of Reivers moved steadily towards the Manor house. His two brothers Willie, Thom and their men each approached one of the farmhouses. Speed would see a quick and easy victory. Scaling the outside stone steps of the manor house Angus found the deeply carved oak door was not locked, and the latch on the kitchen door moved easily. The servants must have forgotten to lock it before retiring for the night. The room was large and empty. Angus gave the dog lying on the mat a quick cuff along the back of the head to stop it barking and raising the household.

The Reivers had crept up the back stairs, careful to keep their metal weapons from clanking on the stone steps. Faint noises reached their ears as the house was beginning to stir. Turning a corner on the first landing Angus saw Riidley in his night clothes, appear in a doorway. Recognising Angus, he screamed, slammed the *door, ran to the window and with an enormous leap threw himself out onto the bushes beneath. He stood up and ran for his life. This increased his reputation as a coward and plagued him for the rest of his miserable life. By now the house was in uproar but was quickly suppressed by some rough handling. The women were tied up and bundled into a corner of a room to be dealt with later.*

Angus, feeling disgruntled and furious that Riidley had escaped him took his anger out on Riidley's young son Ned, who he found in another upstairs room. He was an insipid boy, a weakling and not worth keeping alive. Angus threw him down the stairs. The boy struggled to his feet, limping badly and dragging his injured leg behind him, fled through a side door that led out into a sheltered orchard and ran as best he could to find safety. Angus searched the house but found no other occupants, surmising they must have heard of their coming and fled. The servants were spared, to be sold later. The Reivers made easy weather of killing the few men that were in the farmsteads. Sometimes their women as well. No property was burnt nor were their children killed but captured and taken back to Scotland for disposal. Killing over and authority gained, the men poured into the house and farmsteads to look for treasure; money, any goods that they could sell or barter.

In a few short minutes it was all over. Angus was surprised, that so valuable a property had been left so badly guarded with only a few men and women about the place. Never had a skirmish been so quick and easy, he was frustrated having lost the potential of a good fight, but relieved it was over, and he could return to the hidden valley and bring his livestock and families through safely. Angus's brothers gathered the men together and supervised the 'spoils of war.' It was still early morning, Angus was anxious that the journey back to Scotland, for those returning, should begin straight away. They left with their stolen goods and slaves, knowing they would be safe, the Hot Trod' would not follow, Riidley had run away and would be unable to raise the warden. For those returning to Scotland there would be a wealth of livestock to plunder on the journey, new homesteads to occupy, slaves to sell and no more Tweedel's to pay allegiance to, once they returned north back to Neidpath.

This story was passed down to me in bits by my grandparents and Great Uncle Angus.

John Thomas Tweedel 1856

The next piece of writing was illegible, covered in smudged ink blots and was of no interest, Anne discarded it. The last letter she found said very little. It was almost somebody's after thought.

The March Warden had not pursued any case of theft, robbery or murder against the Tweddle's. Ridle did not get a mention in any documents that we hold but scribbled notes lead me to believe that some skullduggery had occurred between Angus Tweddle and the Wardens which had enabled them to stay in possession of Wydon.

The Uncovered Legacy

IsaBella Ridle Tweddle 1910.

Anne was fascinated with this history. She presumed Isabella must have married a Ridle. These stories were not always coherent or legible and spelling of the family names had changed over the centuries but nonetheless they were a great story of courage and resilience. She reminded herself that she was part of this family. Although they were thieves, murderers and a rum lot indeed, these Reivers lived in different lawless times, and it was not up to her to judge them. That was how they survived. Part of her was grateful to these ancestors who came from Neidpath in Scotland. Where would she be without her beloved Wydon, which was part of her, part of who she was. It was in her blood.

Chapter 13

Anne sighed, adjusted the cushion behind her back, closed the book, ran both hands through her hair, poured herself another glass of elderberry wine and tried to absorb everything she had just read. Her thoughts turned to Wydon and how it was now; a peaceful, isolated farm with only the slow rumble of traffic on the A69, half a mile away, permeating the stillness and a few ramblers trudging through the middle of the farmyard, on their way to Featherstone Castle. Although, in the recent past, she remembered men with shotguns would arrive, full of their own self-importance, to shoot pheasants at the beginning of the season on the "Glorious" Twelfth of August.

Another memory was of the hunts. The pounding of horse's hooves, tossing up grass sods and leaving a muddy, claggy mess in the meadows which was upsetting, not to mention the churning up of the turnip crops. The hound dogs always seemed to be out of control, barking and barking, dashing through hedge gaps and tearing through the stack yard mopping up any free ranging hens and ducks. A few coppers would be thrown at her father in compensation. Often horses and riders were injured, and some men ended up on the six-foot-long sycamore kitchen table, being patched up. Once a horse with a broken leg was shot. And all for what? There were never any foxes to be torn apart, Anne had seen to that.

She would rise early, collect a sack, impregnated with an odoriferous substance mixed with oil, and lay a false trail for the hounds to follow, having already been out on the previous evening to warn the foxes of the forthcoming hunt and tell them to hide. It seemed to work as no foxes had ever been killed. Eventually the hunt stopped coming; nothing to hunt, nothing to kill.

Anne thought of the last time she had met the old fox. It had been one autumn evening at dusk. She had sat under the old oak in the cool air, lowered her voice and hummed for a while, then gently spoke,

'Hello little foxes, beautiful little creatures, kind and handsome little beings. I am here. It is safe. You are safe. Come to me. I would love to see you. I will wait.' After a while a familiar solitary old dog fox crept out through the patches of scotch thistle. He had approached silently, laid down beside her and put his head on her lap and nuzzled her hand.

'Hello, old friend,' as she had played with his ears, 'Your beautiful coat feels worn and tattered. Too many skirmishes with the running dogs lamping for rabbits.' She had stroked what remained of his beautiful long silky red coat.

'You are such a beautiful creature. You know, foxy, for me you represent innocence, grace and the harmony of the natural world and I never tire of being with you.' He had looked up as if to acknowledge her words and light clouds of dust shimmered across the field as his tail wafted over the grasses, releasing their ripe seed heads.

'I am old now. I'm tired of being hunted and chased.'

'The hunters are coming in the morning. Perhaps it's time you left this farmland and moved your family across the river to the safety of Wydon Nab wood. It's steep and inaccessible to humans.'

'My bones are old and weary, and I fear for the future of the young cubs.'

She had leaned forward and taken him into her arms. 'I love you, my symbol of innocence and beauty in the natural world, that's being destroyed by man's cruelty and greed.'

But her words had been lost on the drifting west wind.

'You have taught me so much about being strong, and I am grateful for your lessons in wisdom. I do love you so. But it's time you left.' She released the fox from her grip. 'You must go tonight. I shall miss you. I've learned so much from you over the years.' She had pushed him onto his feet. He had staggered forward and walked away towards the bramble undergrowth and safety, but he had paused for a brief moment, turned, lifted his head to the stars and howled at the rising moon. Then he was gone.

*

Anne sat for a while in silence and smiled at the outside sound of the "Woolly Maggots" as she called the Scottish black faced sheep near her, chomping away and destroying her beloved landscape.

Her thoughts returned to the past and her childhood. It had been a challenging affair for a strange little girl, a day dreamer, who did not fit in with other children or adults. Her constant arguing and general disobedience had ended by sending her to boarding school.

Seven years of bullying followed. Three episodes of running away, being expelled for bringing the school into disrepute, had changed nothing, even when parental groveling led to her reinstatement. The bullying continued and seeing the inside of police stations became a familiar experience. Eventually, at sixteen, she had attempted suicide and a short experience of freedom had followed. The Catholic convent came next and with the kindness of the nuns, it had become a place of refuge.

At twenty years old she had fallen in love with a hospital engineer, but it was not to be. She had lost him, her job and with it her sense of wellbeing. Two weeks later, on the rebound, she had met and married a communist from a strong working-class family of builders in Manchester. Once more fear had returned as life became a roller-coaster of political meetings, rallies and organising demonstrations, which had led to arrests and living through the unsettling experiences of MI5 monitoring. Escape to Scotland had given some respite. The children were born. Then her husband became terminally ill and, after she had nursed him for seven years, he had died, leaving her widowed at forty-five years old. She had continued with her animal welfare work, become an avid reader and writer of all things in the natural world and through this work she had met people who shared her belief system and discovered she was a druid and had been all her life. A new normality had arrived. It was a way of making sense of her childhood insights, thoughts and dreams. It had given her an understanding and appreciation of her ability to communicate with nature and other worldly beings.

It was through her Druid work that Michael had come into her life, wonderful, handsome, steady, calm and generous Michael, a man who had lifted her spirits and opened her up to love again. They had bought a house together and life had been good. But in recent months his behaviour had changed. He had become secretive, distant and their differences had come to a climax over Jennifer, a woman he refused to talk about. A lack of trust had developed between them. Heartbroken she had returned to Wydon to live with her brother, Jack and father Alan. Here she could be at peace and regain her inner strength, although it was proving to be an impossible task, as Michael was always in her thoughts. She filled her days with writing a column in Cumberland Life and giving the odd lecture on local history and Druidry. She still found time to daydream, to meditate and drift off into this wonderful magical world she knew so well but now the importance of understanding her own distant past was upon her.

Chapter 14

Anne finished her elderberry wine, peeled her cold toes from the dampness of the stone floor and wondered why no one had ever put a rag rug down. Grandmother clock chimed two, it was afternoon already. Nip the dog suddenly rushed to the library window wagging his tail and barking at Grandfather, who was running his fingers up and down the glass, trying to attract Anne's attention. The old man pressed his lips close to the glass and shouted.

'Hello, Anne. I want some help moving some ewes and lambs up from the top field to the pasture. I need Nip the dog.'

Nip, always alert to his name, ran to the door, hit it with full force, bounced back and began pounding on it to be out. Anne loved her grandfather, John Pickering Tweddle (J.P.), a tall, bony man with a large roman nose that dripped constantly onto his chest. He still had a full head of hair, had never smoked, or drunk alcohol and was as fit as a fiddle. He was a real storyteller who seemed to know everything about the family. Anne collected her welly boots, put her coat on and together they walked across the yard towards the field.

'I have been reading the history of Northumberland and the Border Reivers.'

'Yes, interesting stuff.'

'Well, there is a bit in about Wydon and the Tweddles are mentioned. What does Tweddle mean?'

'Well Annie, there are many stories but the one I like best is about the river Tweed.'

'That's a long way from here grandfather.' He paused, his eyes glazed over as he leant on the field gate and started to talk.

'Ah! but in the time of the Reivers, families moved around a lot. Some settled where they raided. Others became outlaws, always on the move, or amalgamated with other families and took more land, Pele Towers, Castles, and Manor Houses.'

'And we were one of those families?'

'Yes. The name Tweddle has many derivatives Tweddle, Twiddle, Twaddle, Tweedy, Twedle, Tweed-Dale and so on it went. Over the generations our ancestors changed the spelling, probably because a lot of them could not read or write.' He smiled and rolled his eyes.

'So, what does it mean?'

'Dale's men from the banks of the river Tweed, men who lived and worked on the Tweed, Tweed-Dales, Tweeds, Tewelde, Twiddles and more.'

'It's a long river?'

'It is but remember Reivers moved around a lot and collected men from wherever they could, often captured as slaves and sold on. Sometimes men were kept, or alliances were forged with new families and many of these people took on the names of their captors. It was quite normal.'

Reaching the Top Field, they quickly moved the small flock. Then, much to Nip's disappointment, they returned to the farmyard and the tool shed for Grandfather's 3 o'clock tea and cake break.

The tool shed was an old building with an arched doorway and a green wooden door, fastened with a rusty bent piece of thin metal fed into the keeper on the other side. Its shape reminded Anne of "Bagend" the home of Bilbo Baggins of hobbit fame, although there was no real comparison. This was a stone building not much bigger than the house bathroom but with no window. It stank of crumbling, rotten wood, mold, disused bric-a-brac and decomposing life, usually in the form of mice or rats that had become trapped in some hideous jar or tin, been unable to escape and starved to death. It was a dark, smelly place, full of old rusty water bowls, a well hacked saw bench and bags of rusty nails and screws filling abandoned paint cans.

Grannie's battered, three cornered dresser leaned on the back wall, full of random bits and pieces, a "Just in case we need it" place. Ancient, but well used, broken hay rakes, spades and shovels, many with holes in from years of use and no maintenance, straddled any available gap. Cobwebs covered almost everything and so dense was the dust they hung like torn curtains draped across pillars of death.

In the middle of the floor stood the iron anvil where John Pickering laid down his bait box and flask of tea. He sat down on his three-legged milking stool, that had been awaiting its fourth leg since he was a boy. After a few minutes searching, Anne found a four-legged chair, brushed the dirt off and sat down. Her eyes alighted on two strange metal objects peeping out of a top draw which was half covered by an old leather dipping coat. She had not seen them before and lifted her hand and pointed.

'What are those?'

He turned, took the coat off its hook, dropped it on the floor, raised his eyebrows and smiled.

'Oh, they're knuckle dusters.'

'Knuckle dusters? Where did they come from?'

He lent forward and picked them up. 'Your dad unearthed them from under the fireplace in Nicol's Barn when we were clearing out the old threshing machine.' He gave one to Anne, who examined the four holes in great detail. 'Here Annie, look. This is how they were put on.' He pushed his four fingers through the holes, clenched his fist, raised his arm, and punched towards her face. Instinctively she leaned backwards to avoid the blow but fell off her chair and landed in a heap of dirty saw dust. Anne lay in an awkward heap on the floor and scowled at him.

'Why did you do that? I could have been seriously hurt!'

'Oh dear. Sorry. I didn't mean to frighten you.' He smiled and held out his hand to help her back onto the chair. 'Now, Annie, these are for hurting people. These pieces of metal were forged to fit round the knuckles and increase the pain inflicted by a punch and were often custom made. They could easily break the jaw.'

'How did they get here, to Wydon?'

'Oh. No one knows. But probably left here after one of the skirmishes that occurred over the centuries.'

The Uncovered Legacy

'Yes! I have been reading about Angus Tweddle and his brothers raid here and the ousting of the Ridleys. I found lots of bits of paper in the library, full of stories. I think it was snippets of people's memories. What stories were passed down to you from your parents or grandparents?'

He smiled, poured another cup of tea from his battered brown flask, and offered Anne a piece of homemade flapjack.

'Thanks,' she said taking a piece while still removing dust from her face.

'You've always been keen to learn more about this family and its history, haven't you?'

'I love it when you tell me things. Wydon is a fascinating place.'

He grinned. 'Well let's see what my memory banks can find.'

'There used to be five farmsteads here, long ago, or so I'm told. These buildings and fields still have the old names. There's Nicol's Barn, which we were just talking about, Tom's Place, that was where we used to put the farm hands when I was a boy.'

'Before you and my father knocked it down!'

John Pickering looked uncomfortable on his three-legged stool. Anne knew that he knew that she knew Tom's Place was a listed building that they had illegally demolished and replaced with a monstrous, new, modern cattle shed. Progress before heritage.

'I remember a farm hand who lived in Tom's Place. He beat his wife up and she came running to our house. Mam took her in and gave her my bedroom. I was only ten years old and was very cross. Mam later told me the woman had been attacked with an axe. Anyway, it didn't last long. The police came, took him away and she went off in an ambulance. I remember being very frightened.'

'He was a good man though, worked well.'

'Well, yes, but what about his poor wife.' He paused for a moment, looked a bit sheepish, cleared his throat and continued with his tale.

'Times were dangerous in the past. It wasn't safe to grow crops, they could get stolen once harvested. The cattle had to be guarded all the time and, in the winter, they were often living under the houses, people above.'

'That must have been smelly?'

'Indeed. But it kept the families warm. Of course, they didn't wash much and rarely changed their clothes. Didn't have many I suppose. Homes were cold and often damp, hot water would be a precious commodity.' He began to ramble on and on about living conditions four hundred years ago. Anne felt she had to bring him back to the present and the history of the Tweddle name.

'Can I have another a piece of flapjack, or have you anything else in your bait box?'

'Here, Annie, help yourself.' Pushing the tin towards her, he stood up and cleared a pile of old green bottles onto the floor.

'Here, Annie. Look at these.' He leaned over, opened a small drawer, and took out several small triangular metal objects. Some were misshapen and chipped, and all were very rusty. Instinctively she knew they were arrow heads. 'They were found in the same place as the knuckle dusters. Must have been there for centuries. Their wooden shafts rotted off years ago. Here, hold them and see what happens.'

As Anne held the ancient arrowheads in the palm of her hand, she closed her eyes and her thoughts became full of someone else's, somewhere else. Isobel was standing, bow in her right hand, nocking her arrow onto the string. She lifted her bow arm, aimed, released the arrow, which flew over a field and landed safely in a tree. Anne felt as if, just for a fleeting moment, she was inside Isobel. She was Isobel, or was she? It was confusing because every time Isobel nocked her arrow, lifted her bow arm, sighted, and released, it was as if she was doing it. Anne herself, was a field archer. Her Amazonian rosewood recurve bow was made for her at Mellistain, in the Scottish Borders and, under the tutelage of the Redgauntlet club, she had become a proficient archer and won many indoor and outdoor competitions throughout Scotland. In 1982 she had come second in the United Kingdom Field Archery Championships.

It was exciting to be reminded how it felt; the build-up of tension, the noise of snapping twigs as your opponent tried to unsettle you, the smell of the forest, the insect that always managed to land on your face at exactly the wrong moment, the sound of the arrow as it was released through the clicker and the satisfying sight of it landing on the target, exactly where you had wanted it to. Then the sound of a man laughing brought Anne back to observing Isobel.

'You have missed me again Isobel!' It was John Tweddle who appeared from behind a tree.

'I won't miss next time!' She stood, with her hands on her hips, laughing. John ran through the trees, threw his arms round Isobel, pulling her to the ground where they rolled around together laughing and giggling, like two young people in love.

Anne sighed and was happy for them. She began to drift into thoughts of her own archery life and how it had all ended so suddenly with her husband's job loss, illness and death. Their home had gone, and Scotland had become a distant memory as England beckoned. Field Archery belonged to another life in another land. Her beloved bow would sit in its case unseen, unheard and lay abandoned in a forbidden loft. Tears flooded her eyes and, as a deep pool of sadness engulfed her, a trickle turned into a stream and Anne found herself drowning in her own sorrow. It was the gentle touch of her grandfather's hand on her arm that brought her back to the present and the tool shed. He pressed his cotton hankie into her hand.

'You are a strange one, Annie. Don't know where you have been, but I know it was far away.'

Wiping her eyes, she smiled at him. 'Thanks. I have flashbacks to this girl, Isobel, and her life in the 16th century. It often seems to reflect my own and I remember what has happened in my life. It is not always good to remember, is it?'

'I have never understood you, Annie, the way you drift off and disappear into somewhere else, but I know how cruelly life has treated you and I hope one day you will find answers. Perhaps they lie in the past.'

Anne straightened herself up, wiped her eyes, smiled, leaned forward, and touched his knee.

'Enough of this grandfather, I asked you about the Tweddle name which seems a long time ago now. Can we carry on talking about it, please?'

Pouring the remains of the, now lukewarm, tea from his battered flask and offering her yet another piece of home-made flapjack, he smiled, took several long deep breaths and continued.

'Of course, there is a place called Tiden in South Lanarkshire, on the river Tweed. The first Tiden was Roger, son of Findlay of Tiden at the beginning of the 14th century.

Then in 1632, I think it was, or maybe a bit before that, they all died out.' He looked upwards rolling his eyes.

'Tiden? Tiden, sounds familiar,' she said, putting her head in her hands, as if to think.

He paused and looked at her expectantly. 'Anyway, before he died, he transferred his name to his kinsman, Lord Hay of Yester, afterwards 1st. Earl of Tweeddale.'

'So that's another connection.'

He sat happily nodding his head. 'But Annie there is another story.'

'Another one, um, it's an interesting name, isn't it?'

'Well, when I was young, we talked a lot in the evenings, sitting round the kitchen table with my parents and sometimes visiting uncles and tradesmen would tell us stories. We didn't have television or radio then, you know.'

'Like the Bards of older times.'

'Very much so. They kept the valleys alive with gossip and families in touch with their heritage. Various people came and went, talking about land prices and livestock movements. Even healers came. Times have changed. I miss all that now I am old, and they have all gone.'

'I miss family talking too. Dad was always working, came in tired and fell asleep every time he sat down or had go to bed to rest his back. He is quite quiet now. You are all I have, and Jack of course.'

Grandfather cleared his throat and looked uncomfortable. 'Your dad has worked hard all his life. He is worn out.'

'I know…Just wish he had spent more time with me when I was young.'

'There is a story of a lady whose husband was away fighting in the crusades. On his return she presented him with a son and told him she had been visited by the 'Tywi', the spirit of the Tweed. Having seen many strange things in Jerusalem he was inclined to believe her, his son Tywi (Tweed) being sired by the water.'

Anne liked the romance of the legend. But her mind was returning to Tywen, and she wasn't sure why. Tywen, Tywen, Tywen kept going round in her head. Then it came to her, 'Wydon. Wydon. Wydon,' she shouted as she threw her arms into the air.

He smiled, 'You have made the connection then. But there are also stories of us coming from Neidpath, near Peebles. Perhaps the family moved from Tywen. In those times families moved a lot and we have to be cautious about what we read.'

She gave him a beaming smile 'Yes, but it's us, isn't it?'

'We were renowned thieves, blackmailers, cattle rustlers, pillagers and leaders of men. And the women were just as strong and powerful. But they were good leaders, protective of their families and survived well in those uncertain times. They did what they had to do to survive, and we should be grateful for that, otherwise we would not be here today, would we?'

'But in the recent generations that I know about, women in this family have not been strong, have they? They have had their power stolen, "bought" or should I say "sold" by men to other families. Wasn't Granny sold to you by her brothers because you wanted her inheritance and they wanted rid of her?'

'Well, Annie, that's how it was then. Wydon was in debt from past mishandling of money and no doubt bits of gambling. Granny's brother, Walton Liddell was my friend, and she was of marriageable age.'

53

'And wealthy!'

'Yes wealthy.'

'And she had no control as her brothers administered her estate!'

'Well Annie that's how it was then.'

'But it was not right was it. It must have been a terrible shock to her to end up living here, on an old rural farm. Her mother died when she was four, she was privately educated and turned out an accomplished, polished violinist.' Anne's voice began to stutter as her bottom lip quivered. Grandfather's face was looking various shades of red and he leant forward and put his head between his hands, taking on the appearance of someone who had been chastised.

An uncomfortable silence followed for several minutes then he said, 'You know, Anne, at that time, in the 16th century the Tweddles were a powerful, domineering family.' He cleared his throat and brought the conversation back to the Reivers.

'But these men, you know, were very well respected. They became rich, mostly from what they had taken. They lived in some of the grandest houses in the north. The women were known for their bartering skills, bribing travelers, blackmailing strangers and peddlers who came through their lands, or any nearby territory. A lot of them had a good life.'

Anne pressed her lips into a fine line and shook her head unable to take it all in.

'And we are the descendants of these people?'

He laughed. 'There is a lot to be grateful for, Annie. Where do you think you got your strength and single mindedness from? Come on, let's finish our cake. Nip, here. You can have this icing left over from yesterday, it gives me toothache.'

Anne sighed and felt sad she had berated the old man. After all, his marriage had happened some seventy years ago. She smiled at him, picked up his bait box, packed it back in the canvas bag, gave him a quick peck on the cheek and watched as he walked briskly across the yard and down the road to Granny and home. Anne returned her chair, closed the tool shed door, dropped the latch, and made her way back to the house.

Chapter 15

I t had been a long, weary day. Anne walked across the stack yard to the kitchen, picking up a bucket of hen food from the meal house as she passed. Loud snorting noises came from over the garden wall and brought her to an abrupt halt. Something wasn't right. Approaching the garden gate, she saw Tom, the Gloucester Old Spot pig, squealing, thrashing about, trying to free himself from the pond fountain. His head was stuck under the waterspout. Anne ran forward, tripped over a loose flagstone, and fell, hitting her head on Tom momentarily knocking herself out. The last thing she remembered was the sudden impact of her body on his back. This had been enough to shock the pig into having one last jerk to free himself, after which he staggered backwards and immediately stuffed his head into the upturned hen bucket, lying next to her arm. The rank smell of the boar's breath and the grunting pig nuzzling her face, with bits of slimy green pond weed, dangling from his protruding upper lip, trailing through her wet muddy hair, quickly brought her round. She struggled to get up and began frantically slapping him on his snout as hard as she could, screaming,

'Tom get off me, get off, get off, AGH! Get off me, get off me, Tom, Tom, get off!'

But Tom wasn't listening, he lifted one of his trotters and stood on her hair, as he repositioned himself round the hen bucket. The excruciating pain of her trapped hair gave Anne the strength to thump Tom hard on the cheek at the same time as giving him a sharp slap on the belly. He grunted, looked around, as if he had no idea what was going on, stepped sideways, releasing Anne's hair, and trotted off towards the garden gate from where he had come only a few minutes earlier.

Anne, dazed, stood up and tried to regain her balance but, at that moment, Nip the dog, just catching up with events, ran forward, wagging his tail, lifted his front paws, launched himself onto her chest and sent her flying backwards onto the stone sun dial. Anne fell clumsily, arms flailing, onto the lawn where she had a vague sense of sweet-smelling spring grass, before the world started spinning and she was riding on a cloud of bright yellow daffodils.

Anne opened her eyes and looked round. She was at home in the kitchen. The room and the people were familiar, but the furnishings, pots, pans, dishes and chairs were all different. Someone else lived here.

*

Jack had been in the Low Byre when he heard the commotion over the wall. He rushed into the garden where he saw his sister spread-eagled on the ground.

'Anne, what the hell? What's happened? What's happened?' He slithered onto the grass and cradled her limp body in his arms. 'What's happened? What's happened? HELP SOMEBODY HELP!' He began to shake her shoulders. After a few moments, realising she wasn't responding, he put his hands on her chest and started to pump her heart with his dirty clammy hands which quickly slipped off her wet slimy top. Jack's lips were trembling, his voice choked with tears as he lifted his head and screamed.

'HELP! HELP! I NEED SOME HELP HERE!.... HELP!.... HELP!' But no one came.

'NO! NO! ANNE, WAKE UP! WAKE UP!' But Anne did not move. Jack fumbled in his pocket for a phone, his shaking hands making pressing the buttons difficult. After a few tries he managed to make the call to the emergency services.

'Yes, I need an ambulance. My sister has had an accident, I don't know if she is breathing. I can't feel her breath. Please help, you must send an ambulance.' At the sound of a quiet comforting voice, he felt calmer and able to mumble enough information to be helpful. The phone slid onto the ground. He readjusted his hold of Anne and continued to rock her backwards and forwards in his arms, as wet tears rolled down his dirty face to form brown puddles on her wet braided hair.

'Help is on its way, please don't die, please don't die.'

Eventually the reassuring sound of an ambulance arrived. Jack stood up, legs wobbling, and ran towards the two paramedics who came forward carrying large bags.

'HURRY UP! HURRY UP! PLEASE HURRY UP! She's over here in the garden...on the grass. Please hurry. I think she's dead.'

'Hello, what's happened?'

'Don't know. I wasn't here. I wasn't here. PLEASE! PLEASE HELP HER! I don't know what's happened, she isn't breathing, is she?' He waved his arms around in the air before stuffing them into his pockets.

'What's her name?' He knelt beside her.

'Anne. Anne Tweddle. She is my sister.'

'Hello, Anne, can you hear me.' But there was no response. He continued.

'Hello, Anne, I am Austin, I'm a paramedic. You've had a fall and I'm here to help you.' Again, no response.

Jack stood still, running his hands through his hair watching the two men work. 'What are you doing?'

'It's the standard Glasgow test for unconscious patients.'

'Glasgow test, what's that?'

'We are checking her airways, breathing, circulation, disability, and exposure. We are making an assessment and now, please stand back and let us get on.... Thank you.' Jack sank back onto the grass, unable to stand upright any longer.

'Is she breathing? Please tell me she is alive.'

'Yes, she's breathing.'

Anne was fitted with a head block, put onto a back board and lifted into the back of the ambulance, where Jack heard one of the paramedics calling ahead to Accident and Emergency for a Rapid Response team to be waiting on their arrival. He began looking round the garden pond for answers. Having touched her saliva covered, muddy hair, decorated with bits of grass and broken daffodils, the slime covering his shirt and a long, wet mud slide next to her feet, he began to put a picture together of what might have happened. Staggering to his feet, he threw his arms in the air and clasped his head.

'Trotter prints,' he yelled, running after the paramedics. 'Trotter prints. It's that bloody pig, he's always breaking through the gate and getting into the garden. He plays in the running water from the fountain. Anne has rescued him before. She must have slipped. Wait I'll come with you.'

'No, it's better if you follow us in your car.'

'Where are you going? Which hospital?'

'Newcastle Victorial Infirmary. I'll have the sirens on so just follow us through. Best if you come and explain what may have happened.'

'Yes, I will.' Jack ran into the house to change his jacket, collect car keys, and pick up some money as, it had filtered through his mind, he may have to pay for a car parking space. A & E seemed fairly quiet but then it was a weekday and late afternoon. Why that would make a difference, he did not know. But random thoughts were all he could manage. As he rushed forward a nurse caught his arm to stop him following medical staff down a corridor.

'What's happening, what's going on?'

'Please, come over here into the visitors' waiting room and sit down. Are you related to the patient?'

'I'm her brother, Jack.' He said wiping his brow with the back of his hand.

'Your sister has had a Glasgow test and gone for a CT scan to look for the extent of her head injury. Please, don't worry, she's in good hands. Please, be patient and wait here, someone will come and explain what is going on.'

There was a lot of activity and an array of people in white coats, coming and going. Eventually a middle-aged man came towards him, offering his hand. 'Hello, I am Dr Swaine.'

'Hello, I am Jack Tweddle, Anne's brother.'

'Can you describe to me what happened?'

'No idea, I wasn't there, didn't see it.' Jack explained about Tom, the Gloucester Old Spot and what he thought might have happened.

'Did she show any signs or symptoms before her fall?' Jack looked confused and scratched his forehead.

'Symptoms of what......No, I don't think so.'

'Can you give me her medical history?' Jack held his head in his hands and realised how little he knew of Anne's life.

'No, I am sorry I can't.'

'Have there been any recent changes in her health or behaviour, drug use, or any prescribed medicines, over the counter remedies she may be taking? Any information that comes to mind may help us.'

Jack shook his head, his mind racing to find something to say, 'I don't know, I'm sorry, really sorry.'

The questions continued. 'Can you tell me if she had been experiencing any problems with dizziness, numbness, vision, fevers, seizures, worsening headaches, confusion. Does she fall over a lot? Is she a diabetic?'

'No, no, I have no idea,' Jack began to sweat under the pressure and, at one point, wondered if he was about to become a patient as well. He knew so little of Anne's life.

He swore it would change. He would try to understand the mystery that was Anne. Then a short stout nurse bustled towards them.

'Dr Swaine, I am sorry to interrupt but can I have a word with you, please?' Jack's ears picked up snippets their conversation……. a spinal lumbar puncture to check for signs of infection in the nervous system……brain injury…… it was too soon for that sort of test…. Jack's mind was racing, he had not thought of brain injury. He stood up and peered through the ward door to Anne's bed. Dr Swaine reappeared.

'Hello, I'm sorry about earlier, it's been a busy time. Please, follow me back to the waiting room and I will explain everything.'

Thankfully, the visitor's room was empty and both men found chairs and sat facing each other.

'Your sister is in a coma.'

Jack reached down and held onto the arm of the chair to steady himself. 'A coma?'

'Please don't worry. We see a coma as a medical emergency, that's why there is all this rushing about. But we have finished now, and she is resting.'

Jack's brain couldn't quite compute what he was being told. Resting! Resting is when you are watching TV, having a cup of tea, taking a cat nap after lunch, not when you are lying unconscious in a hospital bed. Taking a few deep breaths and beginning to think a bit clearer he asked, 'What is a coma?'

Doctor Swaine pulled up a second chair, hunched his shoulders and leaned forward, forearms on his knees.

'Let me keep this simple.'

Jack needed it to be simple, his head was spinning.

'A coma is brought about by damage to the ascending reticular system, either temporarily or permanently.'

'Permanently what does that mean? Permanently …. PERMANENTLY!'

'Shush, shush, please, keep your voice down. We don't want to disturb the other patients.'

Jack looked puzzled. 'But aren't they all in a coma…asleep?'

Dr Swaine continued, 'A coma is when damage has been done across the cerebral hemisphere.' Jack lifted his hand to stop him going any further.

'Do you know what's going on? When will she waken up?' His head was so full of questions he felt his mouth was babbling by itself. The doctor cleared his throat.

'Patients normally come round in two to four weeks.'

'Weeks?' he gasped. 'WEEKS?'

'Please keep your voice down. If she opens her eyes within the first six hours, she will have a 1:6 chance of a good recovery. Otherwise, it can be 1:10. Those with little or no motor response can have as little as three percent chance of a full recovery.'

Jack didn't want to know all this, but the doctor was in full flow, and he couldn't stop him, even when he tried putting his hand up and waving it about. Dr Swaine paused, took a breath, leaned back in his chair, 'But those who show flexion have a fifteen percent chance. Mr. Tweddle, I am one of those doctors who believes, in situations like this, in giving relatives as much information as possible. In my experience of 25 years working in this department I have found that it is best.' He went on and on…. Jack coughed several times to feign a sore throat in the hope that Dr Swaine would shut up. But, instead, the doctor turned to a passing hospital volunteer.

The Uncovered Legacy

'Excuse me, Mary, could you get Mr. Tweddle a glass of water, please. He appears to have a tickly cough,' and he carried on talking.... She soon returned and, standing behind the doctor, rolled her eyes with a look of, "Yes, we know how annoying he can be".

Jack raised one eyebrow and stood up. 'Thank you, Doctor, but I'm not sure I understand you.'

'Oh, I am sorry. I do get carried away. A coma is a deep state of unconsciousness from which a patient can recover.'

'Is she able to move or respond to anything?'

Dr Swaine nodded. 'She's able to breathe on her own, her organs and blood circulation will continue to function without help.'

'Why does she have all those tubes and things attached to her? What are they?'

'The tube up her nose is a nasal gastric drip into her stomach for nutritional support. There is an intravenous line, inserted through the skin into a vein in her neck to give medicines and fluids, and a urethral catheter.'

'Why does she have those needle things in her arms and what are all these monitors for, above her bed? They are very noisy. Will they not waken her up?'

'There is an arterial line attached to the monitor. It's measuring how much oxygen is in her system.'

'So, she is still alive?' He felt awkward as soon as he opened his mouth and desperately wished he could reel his words back in. 'I am sorry to say such stupid things. It is just such a lot to take in.'

'Please, don't worry. Your sister is on a monitor which is above her bed so we can see what is happening. We can look for signs of improvement.'

'What signs?' he said, trying to refocus on what the doctor was saying.

'Eye opening, verbal response or voluntary movements to a command. The ICU nurses are well trained and will monitor her, twenty-four hours a day, ensuring her condition is stable and body functions are normal, such as breathing and blood pressure, while the underlying causes are treated.'

Jack didn't feel he could absorb any more information and held back from asking about 'underlying' and what 'long term causes' were.

'When will you know?'

'It will take time. First things first. Let's wait until test results are back.'

'Can she eat?'

'No, she is on a nutritional drip.'

'But she is so still, can't move.' Dr Swaine patted his arm and both men stood up.

'Thank you. It's a lot to take in at the moment. It has been a difficult day, quite a shock.'

'Please, don't worry. She is in the best possible hands. We have a nurse at the end of each bed and your sister is monitored twenty-four/seven. Please don't worry. I think it's best if you go home now and come back in a couple of days when you can see her.'

'Thank you.' They shook hands and Dr Swaine left.

Jack drove home resolving to be a better brother.

He returned two days later, having phoned the ward several times the previous day asking for an update. But there had been no change. Visiting time had arrived and he made his way to Anne's bed, where he was suddenly aware of a tall, middle-aged nurse, standing over him.

'Hello, I am Sister Jocelyn. Is there anything you would like to ask me?' she said smiling and putting her hand on his shoulder.

'How is she? Any change since this morning?' he said, feeling like a child asking a parent.

'No. No change. We have taken blood tests.'

'Testing for?'

'Kidney and liver function, thyroid, glucose and electrolyte levels. We're looking at her drug and alcohol levels. Its all-standard routine.'

Jack nodded but was unsure if he had taken it all in. Then he screamed. 'NURSE, why is the bed moving and what's happening to her legs? Are they injured?'

'Please keep your voice down, Mr. Tweddle. Anne is lying on a special air mattress. It's turned every hour at an angle of 30 degrees to stop her getting pressure ulcers. Her calves are wrapped in Flowtrons.'

'Flowtrons?'

'They are a non-invasive mechanical prophylaxis system designed to reduce the incidence of deep vein thrombosis.'

'Oh. I see. It's noisy in here. All those bright lights, they're shining in her face and there are no windows…'

'Would you like to sit by her bed for a short while?'

Sister Jocelyn took his hand and put it into Anne's. 'She may find this contact comforting, Jack; may I call you Jack?'

'Yes, of course, that's fine.'

'ICU can be a noisy place. The air mattress is electronic. Some people can hear a faint humming sound. The monitors give off a ping ping-pong sound if the drip is running low. The air conditioning also has a low hum. But she is in a good place, here, with us.' She patted his arm in a reassuring way.

He shielded his eyes. 'What about these bright lights, Sister?'

'Unfortunately, we can't do much about that. Monitors have an intense glowing blue light so we can see them. We try hard to tilt the other lights away from patients' faces.'

He looked at Anne, lying there so stiff and pale, with her face so badly bruised and hands swollen and covered in cuts. Visiting time was soon over and he sat in the corridor where a stout lady arrived, smiling, with a hot cup of tea.

'Thank you, that's very kind.'

'She'll be alright you know. These things take time.'

He nodded, looked down at his tea and thought how English it was. At any time of crisis in our lives, a cup of tea will fix everything.

PART 2
The Dreaming

Chapter 16

While Anne lay comatose in the hospital bed, her mind was at Wydon. She was back in the past, her mind at Wydon. She had left the kitchen in a dazed state and walked outside into a field.

'Oh, there you are Isobel. Where have you been?'.

'I'm not sure, mother. I had this awful pain in my head as if something had suddenly hit me. There were flashing lights as if lots of candles were around me and there was a strong smell of pigs and some snorting.' Isobel wiped her nose with the hem of her dress. 'My hair hurt, as if someone was tugging, trying to pull it out and I was lying on the ground in a bed of yellow buttercups. They smelled lovely and then, well, that's all I can remember.' Isobel shrugged, stood up, ran her shaking hands over her braided hair and said, 'But my headache's gone now.'

'You've been dreaming again. You must stop this, Isobel. Do you hear me?' Elinor pursed her lips and shook her head. 'Now, gather up your herb bag, book and pen, it's time to go to the Pike Wood marsh, while the sun is shining. I want some vervain today.'

A faint ping, ping, pong, noise caused Isobel to look skywards and an image of a woman, lying on a peculiar bed swam into her mind. She sighed and tried hard to remember her dream. It had been so vivid.

*

Together, mother and daughter walked through the fields and pastures, across the Titherthwaite Burn, following the hidden footpath through the valley bottom and up through Strangleton Gap. Elinor, clutching Katie Nixon's herb book close to her chest, picked up the pace, 'Come on, Isobel, stop dawdling. We must hurry. It's a long way. It will take most of the day to get there and back, we'll be well inside other reivers' lands and vulnerable to attack from those thieving rogues. No time for daydreaming.'

'Have you understood her marks and pictures in the whole book, Mam?' She said catching up.

Elinor smiled and nodded her head.

'No, I haven't but there are rough maps of tracks that I can follow. She was a sly old witch, but I do know what she charged for each treatment.'

'How?'

'She kept records of each person, what ailed them, what she used and how much they paid. There is a list of what she was owed. They can pay me now!' She threw her head back and laughed.

'Can you understand her scribblings?'

Elinor ignored the question. 'Oh, a wise woman was Katie Nixon. I knew her when I was a young woman. Both of us learned from old Meggie Pickering; a wizened woman, strange and fearsome but wise, very wise.'

'What was Meggie Pickering like?' Isobel said, raising her voice into an excited tone.

'She was short and round with a rugged face, huge feet. I never did understand how she ever got shoes to fit her, and her eyes bulged.'

'I've never seen anyone with bulging eyes.'

'It was said that an old wizard cast a spell on her mother, and she mated with a frog.'

Isobel frowned.

'She had a moustache that turned grey as she aged, as did her hair. It was never tied back and dangled in the cooking pot and, some say, it made her potions poisonous. Meggie always wore a cap and long apron with two pockets in it, full of things that moved about.'

'Moved? Moved, what things?' she said, alarmed.

'No one knows, Isobel, but some say she made things.'

'Made things? What do you mean?'

'She interfered with nature. That's why the Witch Hunters came for her.'

'The Witch Hunters? Did they find her?'

'No one would give her up.'

Isobel stopped her eyes widened. 'Did they come for you as well?'

'Yes, but I was away at the coast. An outbreak of pox if I remember correctly. They never found me. At that time there was just Meggie, Katie and me to heal their aches and pains, in the March. That protected all of us. But something happened to Meggie a long time ago and she retreated into the back woods and has lived alone ever since.'

'Is she still alive, Mam?' Elinor stopped; her face glazed over.

'When we were young, she was different, open, friendly, then she changed to be bitter and vengeful and full of accusations and blame for those she supposed had done her a bad turn.'

'Did that include you?'

Elinor looked thoughtful. 'I don't know. Rumour had it your father, Thomas, had made some sort of promise and broken it. I don't know whether she is still alive. We have had no contact for many years. She had no daughter to pass her knowledge on to. Katie and I hoped it would be passed on to us. Me.'

'Was Elphin the Bard not a healer and didn't you know him when you were young? You would all be the same age?'

Elinor paused and smiled, 'Elphin the Bard'. She flushed, cleared her throat, letting out an awkward cough.

'Was Katie jealous of you?'

'Maybe. I think it was Elphin that came between us.'

'Elphin?'

Elinor ignored the question and began to hum a happy tune, lost in her own thoughts.

The two women wandered further through the trees and Isobel's thoughts returned to Katie Nixon.

'I am sad that Katie met such a horrible end at the hands of Robert Ridley. It could have been me and Margaret and...' Isobel shuddered at the thought of it.

Elinor wasn't listening but looked wistfully into the distance. 'When Katie and I were young, we were friends and travelled together visiting small settlements and towns, picking up supplies along the way, from merchants and traders we met. Most villages were filthy places, overrun with rats and waste that was thrown onto the paths, making us dart about to avoid being soaked. After a bit too much ale, Katie would slip and stumble for the rest of the day. Always wobbling along in those badly fitted, fancy boots she insisted on wearing, given to her by a young lover she hoped would one day return.'

Isobel laughed, 'Did he return?'

'No, but that didn't stop her talking about him. He married a lass from over the border and never came back.'

Isobel smiled, she loved listening to her mother's stories, few though they were.

'But sometimes Hexham had interesting traders passing through on their way west. They bought trade goods off the ships from Antwerp that docked at Newcastle.'

'Is that where you bought the rarer herbs and plants?'

'Yes, bartered mainly, but usually we just stole them. Katie was good at distracting the men and I would be quick and get extra bags put into my pockets.' Isobel smiled to herself and thought how good she was at beguiling men and getting them to do her bidding... if only it worked on Robert Ridley, she could get rid of him. She shook her head and returned to the matter of Katie.

'Didn't they notice?' Raising her eyebrows at this confirmation that her mother was a thief.

'Sometimes, but Katie had a way with her. She would screw up her face and stare straight in their eyes, look concerned, then tell the traders they were suffering from some strange illness, terrifying them with what symptoms may develop, then she would proceed to offer a remedy.' Elinor smiled. 'Often, they were so grateful she got the goods for nothing. Katie had a good reputation among the traders, no wonder she was so popular.'

'Were you sought after as well?'

'Yes, Isobel, I was, and am still an important person in these parts. I have taught you well.' Isobel detected a hint of jealousy in her mother's voice. 'But there is always more to learn. Sometimes I think other women are afraid I will cast a spell on them if I don't get my own way,' A long smirk crossed her face.

'Would you? Have you?' But Elinor did not reply, and a long awkward pause passed between mother and daughter.

'Isobel, any extra knowledge I can get from Katie's herb book will make me more valued than I am now. You would do well to listen to me more.' She glanced at her daughter. 'Sometimes, Isobel, I wonder if you think you know more than I do.' Pushing her shoulders back she quickened her step.

Isobel shivered and pulled her shawl around her, wondering exactly what her mother meant and how far she would be prepared to go to get what she wanted. She had seen a side of her mother she did not like. She had always known of her mother's jealousy of her and her own popularity in the settlements and villages. But perhaps it went deeper? She would have to be more careful and on her guard.

Chapter 17

T he light was beginning to fade as mother and daughter set off for home. It had been a long day, and their baskets were heavy, full of vervain flower heads and roots. Collecting plants and grasses from the marsh had been a long, tedious task.

'My feet are tired, Isobel, it will be nice to get home to the warmth of my kitchen hearth. I hope that idle Millie has the supper pot on.' Elinor swung the basket onto her other arm and quickened her pace.

Isobel wished she had brought her horse, Molly. It would have made a comfortable ride home. Thinking of the horse made her smile; the pungent smell of the leather saddle, the way it creaked and created sores on Molly's back until she had put a soft wool blanket under it. Ah! The blanket, the blanket, one of her most treasured possessions and her mind drifted back to where it came from. As a young girl it had been her first of many childhood encounters with John who had only lived a half days ride away.

*

Many years ago, on a lovely, warm summer's day, while she was staying at her aunt's house across the border into England, Isobel had ridden a lot further than intended across the fells. But with the wind in her hair, the horse agile under her light frame they had galloped and galloped with not a care in the world. That was until a rabbit suddenly sprang in front of Molly, who had veered to the left, got her feet entangled in some vegetation and thrown her off. The horse had struggled to its feet, had a good shake and ambled off before she could grab the reins. She had landed in a filthy, stinking, peaty bog and slowly began to sink up to her middle. She had felt afraid and fought the panic rising in her throat. Isobel shuddered at the memory of that awful day.

She was used to her own company and wandering off all day was normal. On that day the family were taking livestock to the market and wouldn't be back until the following evening so hopes of a rescue had faded with each passing hour. She had struggled to free herself, twisting her body around to grab an overhanging piece of heather which sadly ripped from the ground, its muddy roots slapping her hard across the face as it plunged into the bog with her and floated away.

After many hours her eyes had closed and she had fallen forward, exhausted, unable to fight the bog anymore. She had felt scared and wondered if she would ever see home again. Her head had slumped onto a mossy outcrop, but the shock of the cold water had woken her up. Her stomach grumbled, hunger had set in hours before and she had wished she had stayed long enough to eat breakfast. Then she had heard a snorting animal and a shadowy figure had appeared over the tops of the heather. As it got closer it had formed into the shape of someone riding a horse. It was a boy, a few years older than herself and her heart had leapt with the thought of a rescue.

Tall, elegantly dressed, with a young face, he had the body of a strong Reiver. Although she shouted as hard as she could, her voice trailed to a whimper.

'Help! Help! I'm over here, please help me.' Thankfully the boy saw her wave her aching arms.

'Please help me. I'm stuck. My horse lost her footing, and I ended up in here. I'm stuck, can't move and I'm cold and and ….' The desperation in her voice surprised her and she had been embarrassed to realise she was crying. Wet, muddy tears slid down her face and dripped into the darkness below.

'Hello. Yes, I saw a loose horse saddled up, covered in dirt and wondered what it was doing, where was his rider? Who are you and what are you doing on our land?'

He had stood there, hands on hips not in any rush to get her out. She had felt very annoyed with this boy. Did he think she was in this bog on purpose? He had just stood there doing nothing. But she had buried her anger and in a pathetic voice had said,

'I'm Isobel Elliott. I had been riding all day when my horse tripped and and and … I am in this bog and its cold…...' then it she fell quiet for a while. She must have fainted, but his voice brought her round.

'I'm John Tweddle, I will get you out of there.' She remembered thinking she was waist deep and must have stunk. Her face was covered in muddy grass and heather, her arms were red from scratching, her braids filthy and she must have looked like she belonged in the bog, a boggart indeed. She remembered fighting tears as he threw her a large branch. 'Hang on to this and I'll pull you out.'

But, feeling too weak and with no strength left in her arms, she had let go and watched it drift down the main water channel, where it stopped, entangled in weed. She began to scream.

'Don't struggle, Isobel, I'll get you out of there. Please don't struggle. Keep still.' John's voice had faded as she had relaxed and slid further into the mire.

She had a faint image of John running to his horse, untying a rope from his saddle, throwing it about his waist, tying the other end round the horse's neck and shouting at her, over and over again, in a harsh, strong voice. 'Isobel stay awake.' He had begun to hit her with weeds. 'She remembered it hurt and felt cross. Then he shouted louder at her. But it was still all a bit of a blur.

'Isobel, stay awake. Stay awake. What did you think you were doing in this part of the fell, you stupid, stupid girl? It's dangerous. What on earth were you doing? And you're trespassing.'

'Isobel, Isobel, stay awake. Look at me.' Then he had laid on the ground and crept gently towards her, caught an arm and managed to slip his arm round her waist. He had pulled hard. His fingers were sharp, and it had hurt. He had kept thrashing at the heather, but the bog was deep and unforgiving and sucked them both further in. Then he shouted, 'Pull, Jock, pull. Pull! Pull!'

He kept shouting. His language was rough and the horse not listening, still busy grazing and paying no attention. John had searched round the wet mud until his hand discovered a large, jagged stone. He had picked it up and, with a huge effort, heaved himself out as far as he could and thrown the stone at the horse, hitting it squarely on the rump. The animal had jerked forward and tried to trot away but the weight of two humans had been too much, and it soon stopped and returned to grazing. But the effort had provided the force necessary for them both to wrench themselves out of the pit. John had scrambled onto the bank dragging her with him and, after an intense few minutes of relief and exhaustion, they had found themselves lying on the heather, arms entwined, dirty face to dirty face. Holding her tightly and looking straight into her face, he had smiled, stroked her cheek, and stared into her eyes, devouring every inch of her being.

'You're a bewitching little creature, muddy though you are.' Then he pushed her away and sat up. She felt disrespected and angry but wondered if the pounding in her heart was only about the bog adventure and rescue.

'You're dressed well, expensive leather boots.' Then he had turned her hands over and raised his eyebrows.

'Not used to hard work, are you? Hands too soft. I bet you are a spoilt little girl with your fancy clothes and I'm presuming that horse is yours, or did you steal it?' He had put his hand round her arm and hauled her up.

She could tell he was cross. She was exhausted. She would have hit him but instead gave in and rested in his arms. And how dare he call her a girl...when she was a woman!

She sagged with exhaustion, and he put one hand round her waist and the other on her breast. 'I can feel your heart. You are going to be alright. You are alive!' She remembered looking up into his dark brown eyes that seemed to engulf her whole being and she had quivered. But had it been from being so close to John or was it the cold?

He had stared at her so intently, looked uncomfortable and embarrassed ... yet in no rush to let her go. Then he had suddenly slackened his grip and untied the rope that had held them together and saved their lives.

'Come on, Isobel Elliott, try and stand up. Please try.' He had dragged her to where his horse was standing, happily grazing next to hers, collected both sets of reins and removed the rope from around his horse's neck. Then he had bent down and, with one effortless movement, lifted her onto the saddle. He had climbed up behind her, put his right arm firmly round her waist and pulled her head back to rest on his chest, inside his open jacket.

The journey had been agony; bouncing up and down, swaying, the changing pace, the sudden veering to the right or left when a bird or rabbit appeared out of nowhere, the plodging through wet mossy ground, the rough, uneven stones on the riverbed as they followed the shallow streams upriver. She had clung onto John's arms as best she could, her head pressed against his earth scented chest. She would never forget that smell, the first time she truly felt the essence that was John.

Chapter 18

It had been dark when they reached Wydon, with only a single light in a round window at the top of the house to guide travelers' home across the treacherous fells. John had ridden into the yard and, as the kitchen door opened, a lone figure had waved. In a low whisper the woman had called,

'John, John, where have you been? You were expected hours ago.'

He had lifted her tired body down from his horse and carried her into the kitchen, clearing the pots from the table with his arm before laying her down. The woman, who she later knew to be called Cook raised her hand to her mouth and followed him inside.

'Who is this? Look at the state of her! John, it's a girl, isn't it? Look at yourself! What has happened, John? What have you done?'

He had stood up, taken a deep breath, clenched his fist and turned to speak to Cook.

'Nothing to do with me. I found her stuck in a bog up on the Brockelhouse fell. Don't know what the hell she was doing that far out.'

'Is she still alive?' She had bent over, put a hand onto her nose and pinched it hard. Isobel remembered gasping for air and coughing, and with Cook's help managed to sit up.

'Well, girl, you are alive. Let's see now, um… Here, John, help me get her things off. Poor child, she's so cold and soaked through.' She began to remove her soaked outer clothes.

'Take her boots off and put them on the hearth to dry.'

John had seemed too tired and weak himself, after all the exertion to argue with Cook who looked at him and said, 'John, go and fetch Mary. She is in the long house. Wake her.' Cook had smiled at the look of relief on John's face, at escaping the undressing of a girl. Moments later they returned, Mary still in her night clothes.

'Mary come and help me with this child. Fetch some hot water and cloths.'

Mary had stood over her, bent down and peered into her grubby face, then lifted an arm and inspected her clothes, before looking at Cook. 'What's your John brought back this time? Looks a healthy one. Fetch a good price, eh, John?' She let out a very satisfying giggle. Mary had taken hold of some hair, jerked her head back, causing her to wince, turned to John and said, 'Who did you say she was?'

'I didn't. But it's Isobel Elliott.'

Cook paused, looked intently at her, then smiled, nodding her head.

'Must be Elinor Elliott's lass. She's a long way from home. I've heard tales of her mother. She's a healer but not one to cross, so the folks in Hexham say. But I think it was her that cured your uncle Thomas last year from that boil he had on his head. Good healer. We had better do our best for the girl.'

'She's not for sale then?' said Mary, looking so surprised her mouth had fallen open.

'I'll go and see to the horses,' said John, looking grateful for the escape route.

'No, John, go bed yourself down with your brother. It's too dark to go out now. Wait 'til the morning.'

'Yes, I'm tired. It's been a long day, but I'll go and bed down the horses first.'

'Mary, I haven't seen John so flustered before. Normally such a calm, confident young man but, as I look at this girl in front of me, a pretty, slim, nothing of a girl, there is something about her that is, well I don't know what, but it's something …. something about this girl has affected my John.' As Cook and Mary had continued to clean her up, Isobel's eyes fluttered open, trying to take in her surroundings before drifting off into a fitful sleep.

'Let's get t' lass to bed.' The two women had lifted, dragged, and carried Isobel upstairs.

As they had left her, Isobel, had woken. Wondering what was going on, she had followed them to the bedroom door where she could hear John, returning across the cobbled yard.

'Where is she?' he said to Cook who sat humming to herself in the rocking chair by the fire.

'Oh, don't worry, she's in bed now, all cleaned up and warm. I managed to get some hot broth down her. Pretty girl, John. You could do worse.'

He had mumbled something and left, at which Isobel had stumbled back to the bed and immediately fallen into a deep sleep.

*

Isobel remembered waking up in a strange bedroom. The furnishings had been unfamiliar. A faint glimmer of light peeped through elaborately decorated wall hangings which had covered a large window. Colourful rugs lay on the floor, but it was the smell of cooking and fresh bread coming under the door that had brought her fully back to her senses.

She sat up in bed and the memories of the day before had come flooding back. She remembered being in the sturdy arms of John Tweddle and how she had lost control of the fluttering in her heart.

Isobel smiled and let out a giggle of delight, before reminding herself she was younger then. But her heart still fluttered. It always did, thinking of her John.

*

The door had opened, and Cook had come in with a bowl of something hot and a cloth. She remembered bits of their conversation.

'Hello. You awake, Isobel?'

'How did you know who I am?'

'John told me. John Tweddle. He found you in the bog yesterday.'

'My horse. My horse! My beautiful horse!' She remembered the panic.

'She's alright. John is looking after her. She's in the stable, fed, watered, not a scratch on her.'

She had smiled at the woman, who had looked nice and was kind. 'Thank you for looking after me. Who are you?'

'I am Cook. Now, come on, let's get you dressed and away home. I've washed your things and, until they are all dry, you can borrow Mary's clothes.'

'Thank you. Who is Mary?'

'She lives in the Long House at the other end of the farm. It's part of Nichol's Barn. Here, these should fit if we tie them with a belt. Mary got too fat for them, had too many young bairn's. Her brother stole this dress from some rich folk who would not pay safe passage through the valley. It was lucky you didn't run into him. It is dangerous to be this far out, away from home. Whatever possessed you to come this far? You are well into England now.'

She had not wanted to admit the time she had spent daydreaming and paying no attention to where Molly was taking her. She had just been enjoying the galloping and the feeling of the wind in her hair. She had told Cook she had got lost looking for wood sorrel. That wasn't really the truth, it was just the first thing that came into her head, but Cook was no fool.

'Looking for Wood Sorrel? You won't find any of that round here at this time of year. But you must have plenty of that where you come from. Where do you come from?'

She had gone red in the face, caught out in a lie and coughing seemed the only solution.

Cook, a kind woman, had given her a hot drink and some breakfast and had stopped asking questions. She had felt relieved. The older woman had helped her to finish dressing and told her she had a pretty face now she was clean, and they had both laughed.

Cook had then opened the kist at the bottom of the bed and pulled out a soft knitted blanket, wrapped it round Isobel's shoulders and led her downstairs to the kitchen, a room with a wonderful earthy smell. She had told her it was John's and that she had slept in his bed. Although shocked, part of her had felt excited and she had wanted to know more. Cook had said the blanket was from his childhood, and it was kept in his room.

*

It smelled of him and Isobel loved it, shivering at the thought. She kept it under Molly's saddle as a safe place, to stop the leather rubbing. Isobel smiled to herself, quickened her pace with the thought of John, the blanket and Molly.

Then she remembered the return journey.

*

Cook had taken her into the yard and shouted for John. 'Ah, John, there you are. Time to take this girl home.'

The Uncovered Legacy

Then her eyes had alighted on Molly, 'Molly, Molly!' She had run to the horse and thrown her arms round her neck.

John looked cross 'If you really cared for the horse, you wouldn't let her back get so sore. If you don't know how to look after such a good horse, then it's time someone took it off you.'

She remembered being furious and not knowing how to defend herself after such a horrible onslaught. Some mumblings had come out of her mouth about the new saddle and her father telling her it would soften with time. Then John had said that her father was an ass. She had begrudgingly dropped her head, smiled thinking he was probably right.

Cook came out with some bread and cheese wrapped in a cloth,

'Here, both of you, this will keep you going until Isobel reaches her aunt's home.... No, John, wait. You had better take her back to Scotland and her father. They'll have missed the girl. I'll send a message to her aunt's, it's not far from here. Goodbye, Isobel. John will come for his blanket in a day or two.'

They rode back in silence. She remembered gazing at his broad shoulders, long legs, the way he guided the horse and she had felt drawn to him. Her mind had played with the idea of a life together with this man who made her heart beat stronger every time she looked at him. She tried to talk to him.

'John Tweddle. I've heard of the Tweddles. Rogues, I believe. I suppose you are one of them. Who is Cook? Is she your mother? It's a funny name Cook for a mother. She was kind. Tell me about her.' But he had ignored all attempts at conversation and every time he had turned round to look at her, she had melted inside just that little bit more and would have forgiven him anything.

*

He never did come back for his blanket. It was still safe under Molly's saddle. Now she was older she knew why he never came back for it.

*

After many long hours of hard riding, John had turned down the track to Fellsend Farm, dismounted and shouted for James Ogle, who had emerged from a low cattle byre. A heated discussion had followed, which had left James Ogle looking afraid. He had taken a step backwards and nodded his head. John had returned to Isobel, tied Molly up to a rail and gestured for James to go.

'Why are we here? What's happening.... John... Are you leaving me here? John. John? Cook told you to take me home.' Her eyes widened, her mouth falling open.

'Yes, James will take you back to your father, at Middle Moor.' John had mounted his horse, lifted his head and for a brief moment their eyes had met. She had seen the beginnings of a smile on his lips, before he kicked his horse and galloped back the way they had come. She had been reluctant to return home to the wrath of her father, as the last scar had still not healed. She had stamped her feet on the ground, kicked the wooden rail, screamed, then raised her voice,

'James Ogle, I can find my own way, thanks. I know where I am now.'

71

B. A. Silcock

She had untied the reins expecting him to let her go. She could wander back over the hills she loved so much, hoping the smell of woodsmoke from Dancing Gate Forest would drift into her nostrils and tell her the old woodsman was around. She would sit by his warm fire and listen to stories of the forest and, if lucky enough, perhaps one of his animal companions would join them. Anything was better than returning home. But the sound of hooves on cobbles next to her had made her look up to see James Ogle returning with his mare. He had raised his hand,

'No, I will not cross John Tweddle.' His dark scowl had taken her by surprise.

'I will leave you a short distance away, I do not want any entanglement with your father. I hope you have a good story to tell. He had laughed, mounted up and in a low growling voice said, 'Your father is a man to be feared. Took twenty-three of my cattle last back end and I have no intention of crossing him, or he'll be back for the rest.' Grabbing her reins, he had led her away.

*

'Isobel, Isobel! What are you doing, girl, it's getting dark.'

Elinor had retraced her steps a long way to find Isobel dawdling. She stood, hands on hips, in front of her daughter, barring her path. Her frustration, at seeing the girl ambling along, head in the clouds, was so great she lashed out and hit her hard across the face. Isobel stumbled, causing the flowers and basket to part company.

'I am tired of you daydreaming girl. It's got to stop. Do you hear me? Stop it! I can imagine you've been thinking about John Tweddle. Well, you can get him right out of your head because it's not going to happen. Do you hear me? Now pick those plants up and follow me and hurry up! When we get home, I'll mix something up for you to drink. I will get that man out of your head once and for all!'

Isobel struggled to her feet and straightened her dress. Her eyes welled up as she bent down to pick up the flowers, her happy memories destroyed once more. She was beginning to hate her mother even more. John would be hers one day and that was that.

Chapter 19

Sister Jocelyn stood by Anne's bedside, taking readings from the monitors and checking the chart hanging on the bottom of her bed. Smiling kindly, she turned to Jack. 'No, she is still unconscious. Doctor Swaine will be here soon but so far there has been no change. We just must be patient and hope she will regain consciousness.'

Jack did not like the sound of "Hope". It felt like such a negative word. We could all hope, hope to win the lottery, hope it wouldn't rain tomorrow, but hope that Anne would wake up didn't seem the right word.' He leaned forward, head in his hands.

'Nobody saw her fall,' he muttered.

'Yes, it looks a nasty head wound.' Sister Jocelyn checked her watch and moved on to the next patient but not before patting his shoulder, making him feel as if he needed reassurance, which he probably did. Jack sat back and tried to relax.

As he pushed his hands into his pockets his fingers discovered the stiff envelope the postman had asked him to sign for that morning. He read the address:

Anne Tweddle. c/o Wydon Farm. Haltwezell. Northumberland.

He recognised the fancy handwriting and knew who it was from, but he had forgotten to give it to her after breakfast. Since she had returned to the family home, a few months ago, several of these letters had arrived. Anne would look sad, quickly stuff them into her pocket, clear her throat and refuse to tell of their contents.

Jack sighed when he heard the noise of the hospital volunteer's tea trolley coming his way. It broke the boredom as it squeaked along the Lino floor.

'Cup of tea, Dear?' she said, peering at him.

'Yes please.'

'Milk? Sugar?'

'Just milk thanks.'

Handing Jack the cup of tea, the hospital volunteer lady leaned on her trolley.

'Poor thing. Is she your wife?'

'No. My sister'

'Just come in, has she? Not seen her before.'

'A few days ago.'

'Ah. Poor thing, been here a while then.' She shook her head with a tut tut sort of smile as if she knew something he didn't.

Jack gasped, scalding his lips on the hot tea, spluttering copious amounts of milky tea onto his jacket as he struggled to put it down.

'A while! A while! What do you mean, a while?' he said, raising his voice.

'Doesn't look so good, does she? I caught a glimpse of her earlier.'

'What do you mean a while? Have you been here a long time?'

'Nearly forty years, part time of course. Only got two more to go, you know. That's the bed they use for them that's…… not going to make it, you know. Bit of an unlucky bed that one.'

She chuckled, making her ample chest heave up and down as if she had had a lot of practice frightening relatives. Jack looked at this misshapen, intimidating old woman standing before him, sounding as if she was a doctor and knew what she was talking about. His heart was pounding, and he desperately wanted her to go away but feared that, having found a fixed audience, she wasn't going to move easily. She rolled her eyes to the ceiling and continued.

'Used to work on the buses, you know, 'til I got sick with all that smoke. It's banned now, you know, and a good thing too. Never got any compensation though, for damaging me lungs.' She started coughing as if to prove it.

'It must have been a difficult job,' he replied, trying to look interested, not knowing what else to say.

'No, not difficult. Driving the buses was difficult. People coming and going all day long, fighting for space with pushchairs, shopping bags banging against you every time you went round a corner, babies crying, kids writing on the back of the seats, that's when they weren't cutting a hole in them. The emergency bell went off a lot but never caught the little buggers responsible. Stroppy loud teenagers giving us a lot of lip. Bring back corporal punishment I say.'

She went on and on waving her arms about as if still directing passengers. Feeling his life beginning to drain from him, Jack stood up, walked to the tea trolley and put his cup back on the bottom shelf.

'Here I'll do that, Sir.' She bustled past him to take his cup. 'Want another one?'

He would have loved another cup but couldn't take the risk of another ear bashing.

'No thanks. Have you finished for today?'

'No. Got Ward 14 to do yet, poor old dears. Some of them have been on that ward a long time. You know, old Mrs. Wilson….'

'Mavis, Mavis where are you?' said a strong voice from the bottom of the ward.

'Patients are waiting. Visiting time is nearly over and no tea has arrived.'

'On my way, Sister. On my way.'

Off she trundled, much to his relief and he hoped to God she would not be on the tea round tomorrow.

Chapter 20

E linor strode off and was soon out of sight across the pasture field. Isobel's thoughts quickly returned to her mother and the last time she had given her "something to drink". But then, for a brief moment, the scent of woodland flowers, as they wafted across her face, and the light breeze, lifting her hair, let her mind wander and, before long, she was searching the landscape, looking up at the hills for whatever caught her eye.

She knew she was wild and wayward, always wanting her own way. She loved exploring the moors where she could absorb the oneness of being with nature. She enjoyed her own company and avoided household tasks whenever possible, much to the annoyance of her family. She resented rules and being told what she couldn't do, especially when her mother forbade her from going into the wood at certain times of the year, which was always when Elphin the Bard was passing through. That was a curious thing. Why did she do that? It was odd and she swore that one day she would follow her mother into the forest.

Isobel was attentive to her apothecary learning, experienced at collecting herbs, crushing roots and berries, making potions and keeping accurate notes, she carried in her healing bag, which she called Freya, after the Norse Goddess of healing.

Her mother, Elinor, coming from an educated family, had taught her to read and write. This made her popular, especially among the wealthier families. She enjoyed the attention although it had brought lots of suitors to her father's attention and potential alliances with the Elliott's.

Isobel remembered her father's first attempt to sell her. He had promised her in marriage to Alan Kerr, a rich farmer who owned a lot of land towards the East of Hoardcross. A man she had never seen. He sold her for the princely sum of one hundred and ten cattle, and two horses. Elinor had kept Isobel locked in her room until it was time for the ceremony. Kerr had arrived with his men, and, at the appointed hour, she had been dragged downstairs into the courtyard where she had stopped and stood ridged at the sight before her.

'So, this is the maid, a fine-looking lass. We'll have a lot of fun with you my lass, won't we lads.'

She had looked at this slobbering old man with his grotesque crumpled faced, and with his sneering companions leering as he stepped forward and slapped her hard across the bottom, much to the merriment of his men. Horrified, she screamed and screamed. So great was her disgust, streams of incoherent words had poured out of her mouth.

B. A. Silcock

'I will not marry you, no matter what my father pays you, you, you, you disgusting old man! I would rather die! Do you hear me? I would rather die!'

She had torn off her wedding dress, run into the stables, leaving a dishevelled trail of blue and white cloth behind her, launched herself onto the first horse she could find and galloped away.

Isobel threw her arms round her body, hugging herself at the memory of that hateful day. On her return home, days later, she had learned of Alan Kerr's fury. He had felt insulted and tried to take the agreed one hundred and ten cattle, and two horses away in compensation for Isobel's insult. However, her father, enraged at the thought of losing his livestock for no benefit, had lunged at Kerr and soon both families were at each other's throats. In the skirmish that followed, five of Kerr's men lay dead, including Alan Kerr's brother, Cameron. The Kerr's had slunk away, disappearing into the glens to heal their wounds, without their prize and, no doubt, to regroup. Alan Kerr, although a large landowner, had few fighting men or strong alliances with other families. He had probably heard of Elinor's reputation as a witch and her ability to curse those that crossed her family. He must have decided to wait for another opportunity to have his revenge on Elliott's because he never came back.

Isobel stopped walking, stood still, dropped her basket onto the mossy ground, stamped her feet over and over again, cracking all the twigs around her, as she remembered the horrible incident. She hated her father for trying to sell her, marry her off to the highest bidder and she had spent years finding ways of avoiding wedlock. What she wanted was to marry John Tweddle and she was determined to have him.

Her father's second attempt, with the help of her mother, had felt more deceptive. This time it was to James Robson, another man as old as her father. Thomas Elliott and her brother had made a pact with Robson; Isobel in exchange for Edgepath Manor and land. Such was the demand for Isobel that her father set a high price. Although she had fought as hard as she could against this union, she had failed and, as the appointed day approached, she had sent a stable boy with a secret message to John asking for help.

When the day of the handfasting had arrived, preparations being finished and families gathered, she had stayed all day in her room and refused to put on the blue silk wedding dress acquired by her father from a large merchant's house in Carlisle. Her father had nailed down her window and she was trapped in her bedroom. In the early afternoon her panic had been compounded by the sound of footsteps on the wooden back stairs and the sound of her father's voice. She ran to the door and pushed furniture behind it.

'Is that girl ready? Elinor, have you got her to see reason yet?'

Later, the two kitchen girls had related the tale of what happened with her mother and they were very, very apologetic for their part in it. Jane had said, 'Your mother came rushing into the kitchen, grabs hold of me and says, *'I need your help with that girl upstairs.'* And Miss Isobel, she was in such a rage we was terrified she'd set the whip on us again. We was both crying and shakin and we knew how unhappy you was but she was bustling about the kitchen with her bottles and things and was shouting at us all the time. *'That ungrateful girl,'* she says, *'I'll show her. I'll get this done once and for all.'* Then she finished crushing up something in that dark blue pot. You know, the one with the black line through it that she keeps in the old, locked cupboard. And then she says, *'Isobel needs a drink to calm her down and I need you two to help me.'* *'Help you we says?'* And we was shakin so much Mary had to hold onto the table. *'Yes, help me,'* she says. *'That stubborn daughter of mine won't take it willingly so you two will have to hold her down.'* Well, Miss Isobel, we didn't knows whats to do. We knew whatever was in that pot wasn't good and, well, what if she made us drink it as well and we was shakin' and me legs was wobbling. And we tells her, *'No, we can't do that, not to Miss Isobel.'* Mary couldn't speak much for blubbering and was pulling another piece of cloth from her apron pocket to wipe away the tears. Then your mother gets real angry and threatens us with chucking us out. Well, Miss, we would have been homeless, nowhere to go, you know. Well, what was we to do, Miss? I am so sorry for it all. Well, Miss, we had to obey. We is both orphans, no family you know. You remember that don't you, Miss?'

Isobel had understood and hadn't blamed them. She knew how dangerous her mother could be and felt her anger rising again. She stepped sideways, bent down, searching the ground to find more sticks and twigs to bash into powder under her feet.

Jane had continued with her tale. 'Then, Miss, she said that you needed a soothing drink, and we didn't know whats to think. And your father stormed into the kitchen shouting. He pushed Mary into the chairs…yelling, *'Where is that girl? If she is not down here now, and I mean now, I will drag her down here myself! I'll be dammed… that girl will be the death of me and I won't have Robson thinking I have changed my mind!'* Your mother smiled at him and she says, *'This will quieten her down,'* and she waved that bowl of cloudy looking liquid in front of him. *'Go back outside. I'll get her,'* she says. Your father clenched his fists, looked as if he was going to burst. He banged the door so hard the latch slipped. Then she made us follow her up to your room. Oh, Miss, I am so sorry. Then, when we gets there you 'd barricaded the door from the inside, and she starts shouting at you.

Jane had paused, bowed her head, and sobbed, then continued the tale,

'Isobel open this door, your father is waiting downstairs and if you don't come down, he will come up and tear the door off its hinges and drag you out. You are going to this handfasting and the sooner you get used to the idea the better.' She was raging, Miss Isobel, and we was shakin and shakin. And then your mother did the most terrible thing, you know the ... do you remember what she'd said? *'If you don't open this door, right now, he will take Molly away, sell her at Hexham market and I will also destroy your herb bag and all its contents.'* And then you gets so cross. You was raging as well. You says, *'You wouldn't dare do that. Why do you say such hateful things. Why do you hate me so much?'* Then she told you she was afraid of your father, but we didn't believe it. She kept winking at Mary and me and then she says, *'Isobel I am more afraid of your father than upsetting you. Now open this door at once. I have brought you a nice warm mug of milk. It will help you feel better.'* Then you moved the furniture and she smiled. Yes, she smiled. She had won. The girl would be wed. Oh, it was awful, Miss, when we gets into your room and saw the state you was in.'

Isobel became tearful and looked at the shattered twigs under her feet. She softly knelt on the ground, held her head in her hands and wept as she remembered that fateful day.

Then Jane had said more.

B. A. Silcock

'Your mother grabs you, throws you onto the bed and shouts at us to sit on top of you and hold you down. Then she puts my arm across your chest, forces your head back and pours the drugged milky liquid down your throat. Of course, we didn't knows it was drugged until later when we saws you going all floppy and talking silly...then we knew what she'd done. Oh, Miss Isobel, we are so sorry. We had no choice. We were so afraid of her. Within minutes the drug took effect, and you became quiet, sat in a chair and allowed us to brush and braid your hair and put the wedding dress on. You couldn't stand up and walk straight so me and Mary takes an arm and drags you through the bedroom door, down the stairs, across the kitchen floor and outside to where your angry father was pacing up and down the yard. He looked red enough to burst. *'So, the girl is ready at last.'* and when he puts his hand out, you wobbled, lost your balance and fell into him, giggling. He picked you up and lifted you onto Molly. But you falls sideways and he starts shouting and pushing you, telling you to sit up and get balance on the horse. But you kept sliding off and fell back into his arms. He gets very cross and was blue in the face. We thought he would burst again... and he was still shouting at your mother...can't repeat what he said.... Oh! No, can't repeat it. Then he stops swearing and says, *'What have you given her woman? She is drugged! Robson won't take her like this.'* Then your mother stares him straight in the face, not feared at all and says, *'Enough to keep her quiet.'* and she stands there with a smirk on her face, as if she'd won. Because she had got rid of you. Then he shouts again, *'Ride beside her. Keep her on that horse at all costs. Hold her on.'* And he pushed your mother's horse close to Molly, gripped her shoulder, squeezed it tight and forced her to stay in the saddle holding you on. Then Mr. Thomas slapped the flank of his horse and galloped off screaming, *'Come on. Let's go! We will be late! I will not lose this husband, by hell I won't!'*

Thinking back, Isobel remembered the day well; dizziness, blurred vision and a wobbly body, refusing to respond the way it used to. She recalled fighting for control of her mind, giggling and swaying. These things and the glimpses of her blue handfasting dress draped over Molly's back all frightened her, even now. Although she couldn't stop her physical body laughing, her mind had been thinking of nothing but James Robson, the old man waiting for her in the wood. She had never forgiven her mother for this betrayal.

Riding away her father had turned and shouted, 'Stop that girl giggling. She looks stupid, mad even. Robson will not take her like this. You stupid woman! You will pay for this!'

Isobel remembered her mother staring and muttering something about, 'Too much skullcap, you will get what's coming to you girl.'

A short time later, as they entered Redpath Wood, she saw her future husband, Robson, waiting by the lake. Her eyes had settled on the short, round, bald but bearded little man standing in the middle of a group of taller men, all dressed in fancy clothes. Although heavily drugged she had felt physically sick and tried to dismount and run away. But Elinor had pushed her back onto the horse and blocked her escape route with the animal's head. The Elliott's had corralled Isobel into the middle and pushed forward to greet the Robson's.

Then a miracle happened. A voice a wonderful, wonderful voice had called, 'There will be no wedding today.'

The Uncovered Legacy

A horde of heavily armed men suddenly appeared out of the woods and headed for the Robson's. They paused in front of Thomas Elliott and John repeated, 'There will be no wedding today.'

Isobel sighed. She could remember the sense of relief she had felt. He had come.

The Tweddles had launched a murderous attack on the Robson's who, having not come dressed for fighting, were at a disadvantage. John had ridden towards her and as he put his arms out her father had hit him hard across the head. John fell off his horse, rolled down the bank into the water and lay face down very still. Isobel remembered how hard she had screamed 'John! John!.....' She had half slithered, half fallen from Molly and staggered towards his lifeless body in the lake. As she had stumbled in her dazed state James Robson, her proposed new husband, had caught her arm, dragged her back towards him and bellowed,

'You're not getting away from me, Isobel Elliott!'

But still unsteady on her feet, she had slipped. Robson had lost his footing and they both fell, she had tumbling into the water, while Robson had landed on a tree stump, which broke his back, and he lay screaming in agony. As he tried to move one of the loose horses jumped over them, missing Isobel but its back foot landed squarely on Robson's chest and he was dead.

According to her father's uncle, Slack Jack, who later told her what had happened, the skirmish between the Robsons, Elliotts and Tweddles, had been a bloody affair. The Elliott's had showed no respect for the Robson's as they had old scores to settle and many of them had taken pleasure in dispatching Robson's to the other world. Some had been killed, others injured, but the majority fled. The women screamed and those who did not escape were captured by the Tweddles and taken prisoner along with their horses and carts full of valuable handfasting gifts.

Isobel turned her thoughts back to that day and remembered how, in her semi-conscious state, she had rolled into the lake and crawled towards John, whose two brothers were hauling him out and trying to bring him round. She had heard him coughing and seen water coming out of his mouth as they had turned him over. But one of the men standing over John had been Robert Ridley and, even in her drugged state, fear had run through her body. What would he do to his rival? Ridley had seen her looking at him and his grin was so wide she had feared the worst. Then rough hands pulled her up out of the water.

'Get out of the water, Isobel.' Her father had dragged her back to his horse, thrown her onto it, turned to her mother and screamed.

'You'll pay for this Elinor! All your fault! By hell you'll pay for this! Clean this mess up!' Her mother had stood shaking and watched her husband and daughter ride at some speed back home. His tight grip had made it difficult to breathe.

'I could lose the ownership of Middle Moor Tower and its lands. You are truly bewitched Isobel. We will have to reinforce our boundary walls. The Robson's are bound to retaliate.'

She had tried to speak but only a muffled giggle escaped.

'The Robson's have fled. Cowards! Living up to their reputation. James Robson is dead; he was head of the family. There will be quarrels now, for leadership and power. The Maxwells or Croziers will hear of this and come for us. We need a handfasting,

Girl, a strong alliance. Damn you, Girl. Damn you!' Isobel, wet and weak had been in no place to argue with her father. It had taken all her strength to stay on his horse.

When they arrived back at Middle Moor the field gates had been open, the outbuildings empty and the kitchen door hanging off its hinges. All was quiet, no livestock, no sounds at all. Her father had dropped her to the ground and raced into the house and found it empty. Their home had been raided, cleaned out. The cattle had gone. Everything was gone. Fortunately, their valuable horses had all been with them. The grain store was half empty. Even the chickens and two dogs were missing. Raiders would have needed the dogs to move the cattle. Then her father stared. With blazing eyes and in a furious rage he had screamed in her ear.

'Isobel, get into the house, Girl. The Tweddles have been here, those thieving bastards. They weren't invited to this handfasting.' He had stepped back and paused his verbal onslaught for a moment before lifting his hand to hit her. She remembered dropping her head hoping he wouldn't ask her if she had been in contact with John Tweddle.

'You told them! He came for you! You told him, murderous bastard. John Tweddle knew no one would be here. He's split his forces, some here to clean us out and some to the skirmish. You did this!' He shook her so hard she collapsed on the ground.

'They've been scouting, leaving men in wait for us to leave. John Tweddle is a cunning man indeed. But I still have you, Isobel! I will barter you for our stolen cattle. He will pay for this. You will pay for this, damn it, Girl, you will pay!' Thomas Elliott paused, turned his head south and after several moments said, 'Indeed, all is not lost. I still have you. He must want you to come so far.'

But she had not been sure if John had not just seen the opportunity of an easy raid, with no one around to stop him. Or had he loved her and come to her rescue? But she knew the answer and smiled to herself.

She remembered struggling to her feet, grasping her father's arm and trying to talk some sense into him.

'All is not lost father he will make a better husband than James Robson and James Kerr. It would be useful to have a strong family alliance across the border in England.' Her father had paused, as if a solution had been presented to him.

'Perhaps so, a bigger prize, I shall wait and see what he offers for you.'

But she knew John was a formidable man, from a powerful Reiving family, who took what they wanted. There would be no bartering but that thought she had kept to herself.

*

'Isobel, Isobel.' She felt her mother's hands on her shoulders shaking her and slapping her across the face. The sudden pain and the sound of her mother's voice intruded her thoughts and reluctantly she came round, still feeling as if she was in the past, drugged and thinking of John. She looked at her mother with a range of confusion and fury, gathered her belongings and followed her down the track.

'Isobel have you been daydreaming about that murderous man?' She raised the back of her hand towards Isobel, who swerved just in time.

'I love him and am going to have him for my own.' She pushed past her mother and quickened her pace.

'He's a murderer, responsible for Margaret's death. He will never be welcome. I will not have it. I will see to it. You will not have him.' Isobel stopped in her tracks, hands on hips and turned to face her mother.

'My father will let me marry him.'

'I will stop him. I have a way to stop him, Isobel. Do not cross me. You will regret it, Girl.' She pointed her finger at Isobel and jabbed the air.

Isobel lifted her shoulders in a defiant stance and hurried on, afraid of what her mother might do. Did she have some unknown power she had not seen?

Chapter 21

A few weeks later, mother and daughter found themselves walking through Foxwood, an ancient woodland laid predominately to oak, ash and alder with an understory of the smaller elder, hawthorn and blackthorn shadowing the paths. It was a long walk up to the small well, which lay behind a grove of weeping silver birch trees, partially hidden by weeds and wild grasses. A single alder tree stood guard against an outcrop of rock sheltering a deep pool, abandoned many centuries ago.

'Oswald's Well. Here at last.' Isobel sat down staring into the water, smiling, her hands making swirling patterns with a soft leaf, and she began to hum a quiet little tune, connecting to the spirits of the water. Elinor watched her and frowned. She was annoyed or jealous, it was not clear. Then, several minutes later, she spoke.

'Isobel pass me those bottles. This water from Oswald's Well is powerful and our stocks are low.' But Isobel was too lost in her own thoughts to hear her mother, who looked at her daughter with a disapproving look.

'I am growing impatient with your daydreaming. I know you are thinking about John Tweddle and running away with him. Not going to happen Isobel.' She would have him, she would, and the thought of John made her feel warm inside. Isobel sighed and, unable to win her mother round, she knelt on the damp mossy grass and did as she was bid.

'Hold your hands over the water. Bless the spirit of the well. Be grateful. Ask for the water spirit to empower your work to heal.'

'Tell me again about the guardian of this clootie well.'

'It is said that Oswald, King of Northumberland passed through this wood on his way from Iona to the east coast. He had been ill for several days and his companions were afraid he might die. There was an old hermit who lived here, in one of those caves up there.' Elinor pointed to an opening in the rock above their heads. 'He came down, bathed Oswald in this water and he was healed. The old hermit disappeared, never to be seen again.'

'Why? Where did he go?'

'Some say he was sent from the Otherworld to make sure Oswald survived. This water became sacred and religious men, witches, traders, peasants came for healing. Then times changed and now, with the Border Wars, no one comes it's overgrown and lost.'

'Not to us. Only stories and legends keep it alive, and the people believe that they will be cured.'

The Uncovered Legacy

'Yes, Isobel. But we know the power of belief, don't we, and use it to our advantage?' Elinor raised her eyebrow and smiled. 'Now, let us bless the well.'

> *'I bless this well with love and gratitude*
> *and may your waters always be pure and healthy*
> *and heal all those who pass by.*
> *I ask that you guide me in the wellbeing of others.*

'Those of us who have the knowledge, tie cloths onto the overhanging branches and know we will be heard and made well. Here, Isobel, tie your cloth.'

The two women sat back on the bank watching the strips of fabric mov e in the gentle wind. Isobel looked sad and her mother took her hand.

'Let's have a look at Katie's book. There may be some new herbs we can collect while we are here filling our bottles. But it's a dirty book, with scratchy handwriting and discoloured pages, making it hard to read, lots of blotches and water stains. There are odd marks and symbols on some of the pages. We must be careful and wary.'

'Why?'

'Katie Nixon had a bit of a reputation of being difficult. Not everyone she healed recovered and it was never a good idea to upset her.'

'Do you think she has put some protection on her book, cast a spell or some other such nonsense?'

'Perhaps.'

'Did you know her when you were very young?'

'No, I came from Newcastle. Something happened in her past and it was always a mystery where she came from, but we were together for a while.'

'Is that why she hid herself in the old steading in Cragg wood?'

'Probably but no one knows. Some say she enchanted the wood to keep people away, a bit like Old Meg. Come, Isobel, let's look closer at the book. It's split into sections. Let's see if we can find anything we don't already know, before some of her family come looking for it.'

'They don't know we have it. Robert Ridley is the only one who does and it's of no use to him.'

'There is a bit here on stomach ills. Slippery elm tastes disgusting but soothes the stomach. Isobel, we have a box full of elm powder.'

'Ginger moves things along.'

'But too much can make things worse. I get it from the dark peddler in Hexham. Comes off the ships at Newcastle docks. It's expensive but I give him a kiss and I usually get a bit extra.' Elinor rolled her eyes and Isobel wondered exactly how much extra she got. 'Agh! peppermint. Picked and dried in autumn. Your father drinks a lot of tea.'

'Hasn't helped his wind though.' Both women laughed and Isobel put her fingers over her nose in memory of the smell. Elinor continued reading.

'Meadowsweet flower heads steeped in water and drunk. It says five cups a day.'

'That seems a lot, how much do you advise?'

'Depends on who it is for. Best fresh and a springtime remedy. Used to give old man Elliott the runs.' They both started laughing again.

'To sniff those feathery leaves and sweet-smelling creamy flowers always makes my heart happy. I feel joyful and sleep well.' She closed her eyes and lifted her head to feel the sun.

'It reminds me of your sister, Margaret, and the long summer days of collecting meadowsweet from the riverbanks and boggy places. She was more reliable and obedient than you, Isobel.' Elinor stared at her daughter and raised her eyebrows.

'Is that why you favoured her?'

'No matter what I have given you, Isobel, you've always been a challenge.'

Isobel frowned and wondered what her mother meant. She flicked through more pages and stopped at the symbol for unblocking.

'There is something here about unblocking.'

'Does she mean getting stuck down below with pain?'

'What does she use to help?'

'Dandelion Root, yellow dock, agrimony, bistort and apple. We use all those.'

Isobel sat down feeling disappointed.

'There is nothing here that we don't know. Wait. Katie used hyssop, drunk in oil or ale. But too much unblocks a lot of their insides as well. She doesn't say how much she gives.'

'No, clever old woman. Turn the page over.'

'BB. I suppose she means broken bones. Comfrey pastes?'

'Isobel, do you remember old Jack Armstrong's broken leg? It took three men to keep him quiet and two of us to pull his leg back into place.' Isobel grimaced at the memory of it.

'It didn't heal well. I think the splintered bones were too shattered. It was a sad day when he died, such a big strapping man with a rotting leg. And the stench! I had never smelled a leg like that before.'

Elinor began to scratch her arms. 'Here is a picture of nettles and leaves being rolled in cloth and put on a leg.'

'I've tried that, it's painful, but works.'

Elinor looked annoyed. 'Child, I don't know where you get these ideas from.'

'There is a reminder here for 'Knit bones, for sprains and swellings.'

'Basic, Isobel, basic. How does she prepare it?'

'Something about boiling leaves and squeezing the oil out for spots.'

'Don't know what she means about oil.' But Isobel knew and decided to keep it to herself.

'Read on, Isobel, find something we don't know.' Elinor shook her head.

'There is a small drawing here, perhaps about bringing things back?'

'Usually too much ale works wonders. But it's not always enough. Needs ginger and large amounts of it'

'Ginger is expensive for that isn't it? I wouldn't use it. Would you get more of it for another kiss? Isobel began to laugh but one severe look from her mother quickly brought her to heel.

Elinor scowled at her daughter. 'You don't know everything, Isobel.'

She stood up and coughed. 'Lemons are best.'

'What are they?'

'Yellow things, like oranges but smaller.'

'Oranges, what are they?'

'When I was a child, my father brought a box full home from the docks. They are round soft fruits grown somewhere over there.' Elinor pointed to the east coast. 'Read on, Girl, read on.'

'It says water problems down below and Katie has put silver birch sap.'

Elinor looked a little alarmed. Isobel, how many pots have you attached to the birch trees in the wood?'

Isobel didn't want to tell her mother that old Winking Willie had already emptied them for wine making. She hadn't had the heart to stop an old man and his pleasures.

'I think we have enough at the moment,' she said, staring at the book and quickly changing the subject. 'Ah, sage for moving poisons. Good for white teeth too.' She opened her mouth just wide enough for her mother to see her sparkling white teeth.

'Betony, for calming down after a raid, and for those who are left behind, worried.'

'Clary sage...use boiled water.... But if it's made up wrong, they could lose their eyesight.' Isobel looked thoughtful. 'Johannes, I remember him, lost one of his eyes last winter. He came to you for help. His barn was burned down, and some ash floated down from the sky and got stuck in his eyes. Burned the middle bit clean out and you didn't have any clary sage.' She glared at her mother. 'How could you run out of something so important? You were lucky he only lost one eye. Wasn't there something else you could have done?' Isobel felt angry with her mother's lack of preparation and wondered if she knew as much as she said she did. Margaret had been a good record keeper of their mother's work. She would have known. Perhaps that was why she was the favourite. She read on.

'There's a list here. Lavender, rosemary, then ... I can't read the rest.' Isobel scratched at the word but only tore the paper. 'Lavender is expensive. Don't see it growing here or rosemary. I think it's too wet. So where did Katie get it from?'

Elinor seemed distracted and then had an emotional outburst. 'I think your father will want to take revenge on Robert Ridley once he can find the slippery little eel, but he's always on the move. And his family as well for killing Margaret. Katie Nixon's lot will be after us for stealing her book.'

Isobel sighed, 'So, John is not to blame anymore? I'll spread the word everywhere I go that it was Ridley.'

Her mother looked pleased. 'Now everyone will have to come to us for supplies.'

Isobel wasn't happy about that. She was protective of her valuable hard-earned supplies, gathered and picked in all weathers from bogs and mossy banks, by climbing trees, scrambling up banks, digging roots out of the ground and getting thrashed with thorns picking soft fruit. She looked at her mother.

'Katie would still have all her remedies in her house. We could go and raid her supplies?'

'No, too dangerous. But perhaps we could get someone else to get them for us?' A mischievous smile passed between them.

Isobel was close to the back of the book and three headings stood out.

'Honey, Vinegar and Oats.'

'What does she say about honey?'

'Boils, cider vinegar and honey. Drink it. Hot packs. There are lots of odd words here, but I understand what she is saying.'

'Good, good, that's right.' Elinor replied as she shifted from foot to foot. Go on read more.'

'Honey for unblocking.'

Elinor smiled, 'Take a lot of honey to unblock. Katie wouldn't have a lot of honey. We have it all. The bees avoided Katie's home. Too dark in the wood, not enough light and few flowers. She would have to buy it and, being a precious thing, would have struggled. Anyway, we have it all. I have controlled the supply of honey coming into this valley for years,' A satisfied smile crossed Elinor's face as she wafted away a passing fly. 'Anything else?'

'Coughs. Let it trickle down. Mouthwash for sore teeth.'

'That would be painful I wonder why she did that? Better to take the tooth out.' Elinor shook her head in such a way as if she had some experience of this herself. 'The word calm has a line under it. Honey and hot milk. Of course, that would depend on the cow not being dry. We have a good store of candles made from bees' wax. Your father lifted a boxful of them from some big house in Hexham last autumn.'

'Seems a strange thing to steal?'

'He was looking for ink for us but didn't open the box. But we have enough for the next few months.'

Isobel had not thought much about her dwindling ink supplies. She would mix honey with the white of an egg and soot from the kitchen fire, mix it into a smooth liquid, pour it into small bottles and carefully store it in her bedroom drawer. She was famous in the valleys for the quality of her inks, and they fetched a high price in the markets when the rich were shopping. But how she made it was a closely guarded secret.

Her thoughts returned to honey, any spare, was traded, but only a little. As a young girl she had found a small amount of honey in a hole in an Aspen tree. It had become diluted with rainwater, fermented with wild yeasts and she made mead. A stimulating powerful drink, much venerated by the ancient druids. Yeast spores were everywhere, and she started collecting unripe pine cones, bark, certain leaves, spruce tips and, of course, apple blossoms. Each batch she made would be different, because of the season, location, temperature, and type of yeast available. Isobel preferred apple blossom brewing and its mead brought the highest price. The stronger the mead the more silver she could ask for. Elinor's voice interrupted her thoughts.

'Vinegar, I have been making it all my life. I learned how to use vinegar for healing from my father, a clever man. He taught me to soften the grain by steeping it in water, allowing germination to occur, drain it, store in large stone pots, and use it for preserving.'

'Why would he know about vinegar?'

'There was a demand for it on the docks, Isobel. Filthy place with sailors coming and going, bringing all manner of infections with them. I learned to dilute it for washing wounds. Good for reducing the itch from Poison Ivy too. Vinegar and honey together as a drink seemed to cure everything over time, from stiff necks, colds, chest cramps, dizziness and tiredness to swellings of all kinds. I've used it for fungus on the feet, when shoes were thin and let water in. When Old Meg ran out of cloths, she would soak bread in vinegar and wrap it round calluses. When she followed the Reivers, she used vinegar to pour on the backs of men who had been opened by the lash.'

'Oh, that must have hurt.' She scrunched up her face.

'Apples are the best for making vinegar, but I have used brambles. The druids planted sacred apple orchards, but it was a long dangerous journey south to the lakes to collect them. They have magical powers, especially those further south in the lakes. That's why I go every year to Ransdale to bring as many back as I can.'

'You were lucky last year not to get caught up in the Thompson raid and get kidnapped.'

'It was the dark peddler who told me of this hidden valley.' Elinor sighed, 'Isobel, many years ago when Margaret and I travelled south to the apple trees, on the way back I met Elphin the Bard. He was travelling with a merchant and a couple of horse thieves when a wheel came off the cart and he rolled down the fell side into a family of adders.'

'Margaret, Margaret, I didn't know you took her. Why did you not take me too?' But Elinor ignored her question and continued the tale.

'I saw it happen, panicked, ran to his side and quickly made a poultice of cider vinegar, mixed with sage, rosemary, thyme, wormwood and lavender blossom. He was very ill but did recover.'

'I remember, you brought him home and rarely left his bedside. My father was angry he was in the house. Margaret sat by his bed a long time, but I wasn't allowed to see him. Why was that?' Elinor ignored her daughter and took the book from her.

'Ah, look there is a section here on Helping Pain. That's what we want to know more about. Wild cabbage? But it only grows in the summer.'

'I once heard Ma Irvin leave cabbage on Jane Oliver's skin too long on a hot day and it blistered her skin.'

'Jane wanted my recipe for removing freckles and softening her rough skin. I told her it was smashed apples and rosewater.'

'You didn't mention the pig's grease we add?'

'No, I didn't. It's our secret and sells well to the fancy ladies in Hexham.'

'Don't think they would be happy if they knew it was pig grease.' They both laughed.

'Isobel, this next page is headed. Oats. That's all it says.'

'When I use oats for pain its best to get them as hot as possible, put them into a linen bag and straight onto the sore bit.'

'I have used it of course. Isobel, our supply of oats is dwindling and you need them for your skin preparations.'

'Do you remember when Cracked Face Bess broke her ankle and you set it badly?'

'I did not,' Her mother replied.

'Well, she did scream a lot and was in considerable pain.'

'She moved too much. The splint you lent me was the wrong size.' Elinor was looking flustered.

'You should have been more careful.' Isobel waved her hand to ward off a reply.

'You have a lot of creams for skin problems but keep your recipes a secret, even from me. I was hoping Katie would share some. Why do you hide your preparations from me?

Isobel quickly turned the page, not wanting to continue the conversation. Her mother had a loose tongue and, in the past, had passed remedies on without knowledge of the proportions and there had been several serious incidents.

'Have you ever wondered where she got her salt from?'

'The Cheshire salt mines like the rest of us, although some came from the West coast, Solway somewhere, I think.'

'There is no mention here of sugar.'

'Sweet, the trader, who comes up from the south in the spring, always has plenty. Bartered quite a lot of sugar from him over the years, in exchange for healing his crippled foot. It was too infected to heal well but he was happy I made the effort and spent time with him. The sugar came into Liverpool docks. Spies on the quayside would steal small amounts from weak bags, although they weren't weak when landed. They bag it up and sell it on to peddlers and shopkeepers. It fetched a high price.'

'We must check our precious sugar supplies are still dry and well-hidden and make sure we have enough to barter our way out of any trouble.'

'Katie has lots of marks here about Valerian.'

'Root for spasms and muscle cramps and, of course, it's a powerful sedative.'

'Yes, very powerful. 'I remember giving some to Mary Kerr when she was in labour with her third child.'

Elinor had never spoken to her daughter before about Mary Kerr. 'Did it work?'

'It worked. I was young then and didn't understand about dosage.' She shrugged her shoulders, which Isobel thought was an apology.

'You gave her too much?' Sounding alarmed

'No, I didn't but I did leave the bottle on a table near her bed.'

'She helped herself, didn't she?' Isobel caught her breath.

'Yes.'

Isobel wanted to know more. 'Was it diluted and ready to take?'

'No.'

'How much did she drink?'

Elinor looked pale and tried to change the subject. 'Read me the next thing?'

'How much did she drink? Tell me!'

Elinor looked trapped, she put her arms on her hips as if to assert herself. 'All of it.'

Isobel gasped. She had always held her mother in high regard but once again she saw her sloppiness. Moving towards her, she asked, 'What happened to her?'

Her mother sighed and tears came into her eyes. 'It wasn't my fault I didn't tell her to take it.'

'NO! But you left it so close to her that it would have been tempting. She was in labour!'

'I was very young and not much older than you are now.' Tears began to roll down her face. 'She died.'

Isobel, shocked, kept repeating. 'She died! She died! What happened to the baby?'

'That died too.'

Isobel put her arms round her mother to try and ease her tears. 'What happened?'

'Mary began to see strange shapes and hear voices and thought she was being chased and had to get away.'

Isobel put her hands to her mouth. 'Oh no! Poor woman. What happened?'

'She got out of bed, screaming with pain, as the baby was on its way. She stumbled over the chair and ripped her nightgown off.' Elinor was moving her hands around as if she was still there and remembering how it happened step by step. 'We couldn't' stop her.... Her maid was with me.'

'Did she get her clothes off?'

Elinor's hands were furiously waving. Tears streamed down her face. 'The. Then, she, err, got to the window, flung it open, climbed out and jumped. She jumped, Isobel, from the top window to the ground!' For a moment they both paused and looked at each other.

'Did you blame yourself?'

'Yes, of course I did. I have never forgotten.'

'Did anyone else know what happened?'

Elinor wiped her tears and regained control. 'No, the maid wasn't very bright. The cook in the house was away at the market and the men folk were around in the buildings outside. No one suspected.'

Isobel was still shocked by what she had discovered.

'The maid, a stupid girl, said her mistress had been possessed by demons and jumped out of the window before we could stop her.'

'That was true, wasn't it?'

'It was awful. The baby was coming. Mary was holding her stomach to keep it in. She was screaming and throwing furniture at us. I am sure she thought we were demons. There was blood all over the floor. The maid was terrified. She slipped, skidded into the window, and collapsed in some sort of vapour.'

The two women sat for a moment in silence and only the noisy appearance of a blackbird flying over them broke the tension. Elinor continued.

'Then the men came running when they heard the noise. But when they saw the mistress lying naked on the hard stone flags with her baby splattered across her body, they just stood there. Couldn't do anything you see.' Elinor was beginning to compose herself.

'What did you do?'

'I quickly collected my things, made my way down the stairs, and explained what had happened. The maid had returned to her senses by then and confirmed what I said.'

'Did you pick up the empty valerian bottle?'

'No Mary had it in her hand when she fell.' Elinor had missed that bit out of the tale.

'But you did get it?'

'When no one was looking I prised the bottle out of her hand and put it in my apron. No one asked any questions. Why should they? I was a wise woman who delivered babies.'

'Except you didn't! How could you have let that happen?'

Elinor tried again to change the conversation. 'No more talk about it now. It was a long time ago. But I do remember the master of the house came and paid me.'

'Paid you! He paid you! And you took it? 'Isobel's eyes widened. She had been paid for killing a pregnant woman and her unborn baby.

'Of course, I took it.' Elinor stood up, lifted her head, took a few purposeful steps to the glade in front of them and put her arms round an old oak.

Isobel wondered if her mother was sorry and asking for forgiveness. It didn't matter because she saw her mother in a different way now and knew it would change how they worked together. She would be more cautious.

A few moments later Elinor returned to her daughter 'Isobel don't think harshly of me. We have all done things we would do differently. I have used a lot of valerian in the past and especially when the fighting was bad. It's a comforting herb to give a wounded man. Helps him sleep.' A small, embarrassed cough followed, as if Elinor was wondering if she should have spoken at all. 'And to their women folk, of course, to stop them worrying about their men coming back alive.'

Isobel tried very hard to believe her mother was being truthful. Perhaps more wounded men had died from "too much sleep". She would have to observe her mother more closely. Elinor sat quietly for a while flicking through the pages of the badly scrawled book.

'Not much in here is useful, Isobel, but I do want to find out what Katie charged. Perhaps we could earn more? I can't find any record of who she has treated and with what. She didn't have daughters to pass anything on to. I have you, Isobel, but you still have much to learn.'

Isobel raised her eyebrows at this comment but decided not to respond. Her mother may be feared among the country folk but she herself had a greater gift for healing. She had kindness and love for everyone in her care. When she was younger, she had found her mother's treasured recipe book, hidden away behind a loose stone in the barn wall. She knew her mother's secrets and smiled quietly to herself.

Although Isobel had learned from her mother, the old Irish hermit had been more useful. Many years ago, she had followed a group of pilgrims through the woods and up into the caves on the forbidden hillside. She had stayed a safe distance behind and when they left, she had approached him.

'Hello, I am Isobel Elliott.'

'I know who you are,' he had said.

'How? I have never been before?'

'I knew you would come to me; I have been waiting for you.'

That was the beginning of her journey into another magical world of healing. She learned to communicate with plants and became more successful. Isobel felt sad that her skills had created so much jealousy between them and had left her feeling more cautious and distrustful of her mother. She had made a sage wand, and each morning would go around her home and clear any detrimental energies Elinor may have laid down and perhaps, any uncaring, unpleasant, or destructive thoughts as well. Isobel was careful to be secretive about this as her mother could react badly. With that thought she put her hand into her herb bag and felt for her lucky rabbit's foot. Reassured that all would be well, she looked forward to the day when she would be free of the dark shadow that was her mother.

As she reflected on her life as a herbalist, a strong breeze arrived and fluttered the pages of the book. The noise reminded Isobel of where she was. Clasping the book in both hands she looked down to see a note that read Infected Wounds.

'This could be useful,' she said, rebalancing the book on her lap.

'Horehound. Don't think I have ever seen that round here. What part. How did she use it?'

'Doesn't say. I don't think this book has much to tell us. She lists plantain for poultices.'

'Yes, yes I know that.' Isobel sighed hoping for something exciting to appear.

'Katie dipped pine sap into open wounds.'

'That was common knowledge. It keeps insects from laying their eggs in the wound.'

Isobel reflected on the common wounds she dealt with. There were lots of eye injuries, infections, swollen faces, broken bones, knife wounds, foreign objects to be removed, shards of wood embedded in the skin and broken pieces of metal or clothing that had been pushed through with an arrowhead.

Sometimes she had followed her father on his raids, secretly hoping to see John, and in case her skills were needed she would take her herb bag, linen bandages, nettle threads, painkilling potions, flax, pignut, needles made from bone for sewing flesh up; her treasured possessions, hidden from her mother who coveted them. It was dangerous work, following the men, but worth it if it led to a glimpse of John. She usually had to sneak away as her mother forbade these journeys. But her father, Thomas Elliott, valued her skills ever since a rutting stag had ripped into his thigh and she had saved his life. Afterwards he told her she could go wherever she wanted because, as her reputation grew, so would her selling price. Isobel had treated many injuries from dog bites, ponies standing on feet and breaking toes and an injured deer that had charged the hunter. Broken bones were common and on one occasion she had amputated a limb.

Trotter, the old woodman, had made her a set of splints, various sizes and shapes, to help set bones and keep them straight. She'd splints for broken fingers, arms and legs as well as upper and lower parts of the body. They were usually worn for a month then removed in the hope that the limb would heal straight.

Finger injuries were common as were string abrasions on the bow arm. But her favourite job was lancing big spots and boils. She took great pleasure in watching a poisonous mass free itself from the body and escape onto a rag and watching it burn on a fire; always a good end when the patient could see a result. Sadly, some wounds were difficult to heal. They could block and fester and become foul smelling. Then the problem could be how to stop the limb from rotting away.

Isobel had heard a tale of fly's eggs hatching and eating dead flesh. On one long winter's night when Elphin the Bard was visiting, he had told a tale about a dog with a bad injury to its thigh. The owner, unable to heal such a big wound, had gone off to find a large knife to slit the dog's throat. Sensing the end was near, the dog had slunk away, travelled some distance dragging his wounded thigh, become exhausted and laid down for warmth next to a dead cow. The animal had been there for some time and stank of rotting flesh. But the dog, too ill and tired to care, slumped beside it and slept. Flies had laid their eggs inside the cow's dead flesh. They had hatched, migrated and feasted on the dog's rotting flesh. The dog slept for days unbeknown to his helpers and when he awoke his flesh was clean and healed over. He was hungry, fed himself on the dead cow and returned to his owner, who was astonished but pleased.

B. A. Silcock

Isobel had enjoyed the tale but was not sure if she believed it. Had maggots cleaned dead flesh? She wondered if the dog had fallen into a bog and been sucked by leeches as they were good little healers and she had used them herself to drain head lumps.

Isobel wanted to learn more, especially about hearing loss, which was a big problem after a skirmish. The noise of clashing swords, men screaming, horses snorting and pounding the earth in panic, left many men unable to hear for weeks.

Then there were lice that created sores on bodies and little creatures in beds that left the sleeper covered in tiny itchy spots. Her mind wandered to the story of an inn keeper in the next valley who swore by putting a pig in the bed first to give them a good feed, as he called it, then letting the room out. He had gained a reputation for a good night's sleep and charged more for his rooms.

This made her think of meadowsweet and the many hours spent as a young child collecting it to throw onto the beds, to aid a good night's sleep.

She was roused from her meanderings by her mother shouting….

'Poisons, Isobel. Stop daydreaming girl.'

'Let me see.'

'There is a list of people Jane Bruise, Alan Robb, Michael Ridley, Mary Johnson… there are many names. The people on this list and I think between us we knew them all.'

'Do you think these were people she'd poisoned?' Isobel opened her mouth wide.

'Yes probably.'

'It's no wonder she hid this book. If some of these families found out she would be done for. But why keep a list? It makes no sense.'

'What did she use?'

'There is a small drawing here of blackthorn spines. If they were scratched into an open wound the blood would become poisoned and death would be slow and painful.'

'NO! NO! NO! We all know about the dangers of blackthorn spines. I've removed many.'

'But the tips carry danger.'

'Oh, look, Isobel, she's been crushing yew berries and adding them to food. Another painful death, crushed and added to the pot. 10 drops to each person, or drip, drip into the ale. Isobel, I wonder if that's what she did to Jane Bruise?'

'Who was Jane Bruise?'

'She was Katie's love rival for Harry Armstrong. The story goes that, the night before they were wed, Jane went to Katie's for a love potion and never came back.'

'Katie killed her?'

'She was found dead in the woods, lying all curled up in a ball clutching her stomach.'

'So, it could have been an accident?'

'No, it was too close to Katie's cottage, and she was holding a handful of black berries, and they weren't brambles.'

'Deadly nightshade?'

'We all reckoned so. Yes.'

'Did Katie wed Harry Armstrong then?'

'No, he wed Jane's sister Sara.'

'Did you ever notice the black line she had round her house?'

Elinor looked surprised at this idea. 'No what was it?'

'Katie used to make a paste from foxgloves and then she drew a dark line round her house.'

'Why?'

'Protection.'

'From what? From whom? I am starting to feel there was more to this old crone than we thought.'

'She even has a mix here using crushed foxgloves. Then it says, more for a big man and feed slowly. Heart and death will follow soon.'

'Look a drawing of hemlock and under it she has written, *calm, drop into water or ale and they fall asleep.*'

'So that's how she did it.' Isobel caught her breath so hard she coughed.

'Did what?'

'Got rich.'

'Perhaps the old stories about her were true.'

'What stories?'

'The villagers up and down the Debatable Lands always reckoned that when Katie Nixon had passed through healing the sick, lots of things disappeared with her.'

'What things?'

'Money mostly. Young Todd Ogle saw her drip some liquid into his grandfather's ale. He fell asleep and she robbed him. It must have been hemlock.'

'Did he waken up?'

'No. Todd was only a bairn at the time and it wasn't clear what he'd seen. The gossip was he'd died of the drink, but rumours persisted.'

'Why did no one challenge her? Stop her?'

'Isobel, it was all about fear. Remember she was the wise woman of these parts and without her they would have died of injuries.'

Isobel was shocked and raised her eyebrows. 'Because of her they died.'

Elinor was staring at two letters at the bottom of the page. They were difficult to read.

'What letters are they?' she asked, pointing.

'Isobel turned the book the wrong way up. They are difficult to read but I think D N?'

'Deadly nightshade,' said her mother. No wonder she just wrote the letters down. Badly prepared as a killer.'

Taking the book from her daughter, Elinor said, 'She's got pain killer, wound dressing, cutting limbs, calming and then number three?'

Both women looked at each other and frowned.

'Three times the dose would be enough to cause death.' Isobel's hand flew to her mouth.

'Do you remember young James Kerr's broken leg. He went to Katie to set it, she was nearer than us, but he became ill and never recovered. She blamed the rough track the cart had taken moving him around too much.'

'That would not have killed him. The thought of a wise women poisoning people is disturbing.'

'Would she have got the dosage wrong on purpose? She was a very rich woman. People were afraid of her and did not ask too many questions.'

Isobel was glad Katie had not lived close by and that they had worked with different people. 'She was a murderer. She had four husbands. They can't all have died quietly in bed, can they?'

Mother and daughter closed the book and sat together holding hands and a sadness passed between them.

'This is a dangerous book, Isobel, we must hide it or, if found, revenge will be taken by those harmed.'

They left the wood and climbed the rocky crag where Elinor found a deep dry hole for the book's last resting place. 'It will be safe here. This path is rarely used, and we will come back to collect it if ever we need to.' Elinor slumped to the ground and looked at her daughter.

'Isobel, Margaret died for nothing. Katie Nixon's secrets were not worth it. Nothing in there can help us advance our knowledge. The woman was a fraud, a murderer and I lost my beautiful girl.' She glared at Isobel and walked away. Isobel stared hard at her mother's back.

'Are you saying you lost the wrong daughter? I lost my sister, friend, and companion! Although she was not very interested in plants. Margaret spent her time pleasing you, Mother, making sure she was your favourite.' Isobel's sadness quickly turned to rage as she saw her mother turn and give her a dismissive look. She shouted after her, 'You sent us for the book. It was your jealousy of Katie Nixon that she had secrets you could have. You killed Margaret. I hate you. Do you hear me? I HATE YOU! I will never forgive you!' Isobel dissolved into tears as she dropped to the ground clutching her sobbing head with only the wind left to carry her words to an unhearing ear.

Chapter 22

E linor stopped, ran back to Isobel, grabbed her by the hair and slapped her across the face.

'You think you know everything, don't you? But you've no idea how hard my life has been and the things I've had to learn.'

Isobel wiped her eyes and rubbed her rosy cheeks, hoping to clear the pain.

'You have never told me about your past. You keep lots of secrets. I know nothing of your life, where you came from and why you married my father. I have always been curious about your knowledge of plants, wines and spices. You are well educated and have taught me all you know. Well, I hope you have?' She frowned.

'Well, Isobel, it's one of those things I've never talked about.' Elinor sighed and sat down; hands clasped on her lap. 'Here sit next to me on this log.'

'I know nothing about your life.'

'It's not important for you to know.'

'It is to me. I want to understand you better, to be closer to you.' She took her mother's hand. 'Why haven't you told me about your past?'

Elinor sighed 'Alright, it's time you knew more.'

'My father, Fraser Kerr, had an apothecary in Newcastle.'

'What is an apothecary?'

'It's a place where you buy herbs, spices, wines, spirits and all manner of things. People came for medical advice and potions to make them well again. The docks brought in merchant ships from far off lands, mainly the Baltic and the East. The Vikings had established strong trade routes with East Europe and brought in silks, spices, strange fruits, dried herbs and all manner of mysterious and magical things. My father had a thriving business selling goods to passing traders and journeymen. He made regular visits to the South Dock to barter goods from the Antwerp based cargo ships. We were constantly restocking our ever-dwindling shelves.'

'It sounds an exciting place.'

'It was. I became a skilled herbalist, gained great respect from my community and we became rich.'

'Did I once hear you mention a grandfather who was an herb person?' Elinor began to smile as she reflected.

'Grandfather Aidan loved nature and would take me into the woods with him. He taught me how to talk with trees and flowers that adorned the paths. I learnt how to communicate with birds when they were singing and be grateful for each herb and flower. He was a well-respected potion maker and taught me how to gather, mix and transform herbs into healing potions.'

'He sounds a clever man.'

'He was. He taught me to always say thank you for everything I took.'

'I do too. We are so close to nature aren't we. So closely connected, as if we are one?'

Elinor nodded in agreement. 'Yes, it's important to be grateful.'

'What happened to him?'

Elinor's eyes filled with tears and Isobel passed her a cloth to wipe her eyes.

'When I was about nineteen years old, he died. I lost him,' She began to cry. 'He told me he would be with me in my dreams teaching and inspiring me.'

'And did he?'

'No, he never did.'

Isobel suddenly blurted out. 'I wonder if he comes to me. Was he a small man, hunched over as if his back was bent and had a long white beard and a green hat? I get thoughts and ideas in my dreams about potions and new plants to use; things I have never thought of. I feel excited.' Isobel paused. 'But I can see by your face you are not happy with this connection I have with him. If it is him? I don't mean to upset you.'

'Yes, it's him. Be careful, Isobel. Do not steal something so precious from me.'

'I am sorry, but Grandfather Kerr comes to me. After all I am his great granddaughter, his direct descendent, perhaps he thought it was best. But I can see you are not happy with me. Please tell me more?'

'I had learned not to trust other people very much. We seemed to be surrounded by thieves, rogues, outlaws, and Reivers who wanted me. I was good looking then and my father had found me a husband.'

'Fathers are like that.' Isobel nodded her head. 'You will always be beautiful to me.' She touched her mother's arm and gave it a little squeeze.

'There were men stealing from us, from our warehouses. It was becoming unsafe, so I started carrying my money round with me and I stitched the money into the hem of my skirt. I made several secret pockets in my tunic and my healing bag, which was always with me and of course my most important herbs.' Elinor sighed.

'For what was to happen, that would prove to be a blessing. We'd been on the road for several days, heading for Coomcatch. It was on one of my regular routes.'

'What do you mean "we" and regular routes?'

'Every few months I would leave my father's work and travel to the outlying settlements helping where I could along the way. It could be a long and hard journey.'

'How did you travel?'

'Usually with bands of travellers, traders, or farmers, getting lifts on their carts or riding alongside.'

'It doesn't sound very safe?'

'No, it wasn't but over the years I got to know the regular merchants, made friends with a lot of them and for a bit of advice on their aliments, or the gift of a potion or two, I was quite safe.'

'Where is Coomcatch? Is it a village?'

'No, it's a farm, a large one but lots of people came when they knew I was coming.'

'Is that near Carlisle?'

'Yes.'

'A long way from Newcastle.'

'It was but there were few healers in the Borders and some of us travelled across a wide area and could be away from home for several weeks at a time. Father didn't need me. He had a young boy he was training to replace me when I left to marry, and I made more money on my own and could keep it.'

'He took your money from you?'

'He did.'

'Was money important to you?'

'It is always important, especially for women, Isobel. It gives us independence, power and some control over our lives.'

'Please go on with your story?'

'The weather turned against us and the roads were flooded and we had to go a long way round, which was well out of our way and through places I had never been before. As we were nearing Middle Moor Tower, we were set upon by a fierce band of Reivers. We presumed they had come out of the Debatable Lands which was only a few hours ride away.'

Isobel shuddered at the mention of that fearsome place, the hideout of Robert Ridley.

'I was cross for getting so close and putting myself in danger.'

'Who were you with? Your travelling companions?'

Elinor looked flushed, blew her nose and continued, 'When I could, I travelled with a small band of traders and usually Elphin the Bard was with them.'

'Elphin the Bard?' she shouted in surprise 'Our Elphin, the one who still travels to us?'

'Yes, in those days he travelled from settlement to steading, from farms to manors and Pele towers, telling stories and passing on news. His reward was a meal and bed for the night. The evenings were cold and dark on my own and could be frightening. Roads were often poor quality and sometimes no more than a rough track which could be slow and hard for a horse and cart. It was good to have him with me. He behaved like a protector.' Elinor smiled and looked a little more flushed. She stood up and stretched her legs, clasped her hands tightly in front of her and paced around.

'Over the years I had built up a strong bond with some of these wandering bands. I gave them free remedies and they offered companionship and protection in return. I tried to time my journeys to the outlying valleys when they were going too. These traders and travellers made the journey shorter. I was respected as a woman and a healer, and I liked that.'

'It all happened very quickly. They were a small band of Reivers blocking our path. Perhaps ten or twelve. All fierce looking, well-armed. Their appearance left me in no doubt they would take what they wanted. They were tired and dishevelled and looked as if they were returning from a raid. Horses were muddy, sweating, riders no better, and there was a stink of farting cattle in the air. Elphin the Bard recognised the leader. He pulled the cart to a halt, stepped down and walked towards a tall uncouth looking man who was sitting high on a black horse and said, *'Good day Thomas Elliott. It's a fine day. Hope we find you well on this fine day?'*

'Elliott nodded his head in acknowledgement. They'd obviously met before.'

'You're obstructing my path. Get out of the way or, by God, I'll run you through, the lot of you and what is in that wagon?'

B. A. Silcock

'We're on our way to Coomcatch but tracks flooded. Had to come up over Carter fell and through Hangman's wood. Couldn't cross Turrets bridge. I have a tale to tell. It'll be a long one. Take all night. Hope for a feast and a bed for the night when we get there.'

'But this Elliott man wasn't listening. His eyes were firmly set on me, and he rode closer.'

'You're a fine-looking lass…. I'll give you a bed for the night.'

All the men laughed. I raised my head and sat on my horse as if I'd been born in the saddle. He kept staring at me and had a leering grin on his face. It made me shiver. I'd heard tales of wild Reivers in these parts but had not encountered this band before. So, I looked straight at him. '*I am Elinor Kerr, on my way to heal the sick. I carry my herbs and potions with me, nothing of value to you.* He smiled and I didn't like it. It was menacing. 'Oh, Isobel, I was so afraid because I could sense this was a man who would take what he wanted. I raised my voice and asked him, 'what is the meaning of this.' How dare he interfere with our journey? I was really shouting at him.'

'What did he do?'

'He went red in the face, and I thought he wasn't used to being spoken to like that and, I suspected, especially not by a woman.'

'I will do as I please and it pleases me to look at you.'

'Then he laughed. It was a loud, raucous sound and my whole body quivered. He sat tall in his saddle, pulled the horse's reins so tight it made the animal snort and stagger back and forth. He was trying to impress me.'

'Did he?'

'Perhaps a little. There was something about him that was quite unsettling. He was tall, had a rugged sort of appearance and dark brown eyes that bored into me.'

'I can see in your face how difficult this memory is to recall. You look flushed.'

'Isobel, I was frightened.'

'Let us pass. We have to be on our way, and I moved forward. He laughed again.'

'None of you are going anywhere and especially not you…Miss Elinor Kerr.'

Isobel put her hand out towards her mother.

'I panicked, kicked the horse, pulled the reins hard to the left and set off as fast as I could down the track. No idea where I was going. I just had to get away. I was frightened. Just frightened, Isobel.' Isobel winced.

'I had only gone a short distance down the track when he caught me. I screamed at him. *Who are you? What do you want? Let me go!* He took my arm, oh and it did hurt.'

'I am Thomas Elliott and am taking you back with me. A fine-looking woman like you would fetch a good price.' His men came forward and everyone was laughing. So, I hit him hard across the face with my reins.'

Isobel's eyes widened in horror. 'What happened?'

'His horse reared up. My rein caught his eye and very quickly red wheals appeared on his face. He lost his composure, lunged towards me and hit me squarely across the face. I was stunned by the unexpected blow, fell sideways off my horse, hit the ground hard and rolled down a grassy bank. I lay on the ground quite still.'

'You must have been terrified?'

'More angry than afraid. He jumped off his horse and stood over me. The look on his face was one of desire. I scrambled to my feet, pulled bits of grass and weeds from my clothing, and stood tall and defiant glaring at him. He was a big man. But, Isobel, I was so afraid and shaking so much. He stared at my body, bent down, lifted my skirt, looked at my shoes and tussled my hair with his filthy hand.

'You're a finely dressed young woman.'

'He looked up your skirt?'

'Horrible man, Isobel, just a horrible man. Anyway, I repeated, *I am Elinor Kerr. No doubt you have heard of me in these parts. I have been here many times before.* I told him I was a valued healer. *Now get out of my way and let me go!* I screeched at him.'

'Did he?'

'He stood over me, hands on hips, looking me over. I was a captured woman after all. I told him he wouldn't dare sell me and I spit in his face. I continued to defend myself. I raised my voice again and again, telling him I was a valued healer, an important person. One day he might need me. There weren't many of us about. Most are witches with poisonous potions, and he'd better not harm me.' Isobel frowned, looked up and her mouth fell open.

'Thomas Elliott! You are talking about my father, aren't you? So, that's how he met you and he married you?' Elinor's eyes flared

'No, Isobel, I am having none of it. He kidnapped me. Do you hear me, Girl? He kidnapped me. He gripped my arms so hard they were bruised for weeks after and he said,'

'Young and strong ...You're a fiery one...Miss Elinor Kerr. From a well-off town by the way you're dressed. Fancy boots. Fancy horse. Fancy voice. I suppose you can read and write?'

'Then he spun me round to face him, filling his eyes with my slender shape. I was so angry, this brute of a man treating me like his possession. Then he smiled. You know that horrible grin he has when he knows you are backed into a corner and panicking?'

'Well, Miss Elinor Kerr, you might be better than the old crone in Hexham. Would do very nicely as a replacement. Think I'll keep you for a bit. Any good and you'll be worth more.'

Isobel looked at her mother. 'Then what happened?'

'He picked me up, threw me over the front of his horse and tied me on like I was a freshly killed stag.'

'He actually tied you down?'

'Yes, then we re-joined my companions. He turned to Elphin the Bard.'

'Follow on.... all of you. We'll see what you're hiding in that cart later.'

'No, Thomas, no...we're on our way to Coomcatch. We were expected. We'll come to you in a day or too.'

'No, NOW! Do you hear me? NOW! I have a mind for entertainment tonight.' His men took hold of Elphin's cart and horse and led the way. The other travellers were terrified and obeyed.'

'Did his men respect him or were they afraid?'

'Oh yes, I think we were all afraid of him. Elphin the Bard looked at me and realised he had no choice but seemed to accept it and went along without protest.

'Where did you go?'

'Middle Moor Tower. The ride was so uncomfortable, I think I drifted in and out of consciousness. The horse was sweating and panting, the reins kept lashing against my body and I was terrified I would fall off. I was also aware of Thomas Elliott's free hand wandering over my body. I felt sick and so angry.'

'Did he speak to you?'

'No, But I do remember being dragged from the horse and carried into a large kitchen. I know it was a kitchen because I heard him shout to old Milly to get him some food.'

'Milly was there then?'

'No. It was Milly's mother. Young Milly wasn't born then. He'd probably been away for days stealing those cattle I saw them with. I looked round for a door and a way out, but it was locked. I was trapped, Isobel. Trapped. I ran to the window and forced it open. I climbed out, fell to the ground, didn't look where I was going but ran as fast as I could, straight into the big fat arms of Thomas Elliott. He was angry and filthy, and he stank of death. It was horrible. I struggled, pounded his chest as hard as I could but he held me in a strong grip,

'And where do you think you're going, Miss Elinor Kerr?'

'Then he bent me backwards, pulled my head down and gave me a filthy, smelly, ale-soaked kiss.'

'Were you afraid?'

'I was more than afraid, Isobel. He was a brute of a man.'

'Did he let you go?'

'He held me at arm's length and told me he would keep me if I behaved.'

'And if you didn't?'

'He was going to sell me to Ned Armstrong because he owed him money.'

'I was furious and told him so, *'How dare you treat me like this? How dare you?'*

'I am so sorry. I can't imagine how horrible it must have been. And he is my father! But I can understand what you say. He has always frightened me and sometimes I struggle being near him.'

'There were lots of people gathering around. I didn't recognise any of them, the rough looking lot, unkempt and they swore, I remember. Most of the words I hadn't heard of before. The men were drawing lots as to who would have me. The women looked tough and no better than the men. Escape seemed impossible. Thomas Elliott seemed to sense that I was afraid. My clothes were torn and dirty and I was beginning to look like them.'

'Then what happened?'

'Well then, Miss Elinor Kerr, what are you about girl…come on…what are you going to do?'

'I think he was enjoying my fear.'

'Make it quick girl. If you don't, there's plenty men here will make decision for you. And I had a sense the men had begun arguing among themselves.'

'What a brute. I always knew father was a brute. All my life I have been afraid of him.'

The Uncovered Legacy

'I think I stumbled but I remember how relieved I felt when a thin gaunt looking woman stepped forward, took my hand, and pulled me away into the kitchen. She cleaned me up. She had some authority, as the men drifted away.'

'I'm in charge here. Don't you take any notice of my son.'

'Was that my grandmother and what happened to Elphin the Bard?'

'Well, that night, as Thomas Elliott, his men, their families, peddlers, and my fellow travellers settled themselves by the great roaring fire in the feasting hall, Elphin the Bard took up his lute and began to play. After a while he paused, cradled his lute in his arms, looked at his host and said,

'Tonight, I shall tell the tale of Rutter. Tis a tale of intrigue, betrayal and murder,

Old Earl of Angus
would not retire,
'You need me sire.'
King James brushed him aside
and with long, strang breath
and mighty force
he killed the man and
seized his lands and took his horse
and saw an end to the Douglas clan.
But he wanted more,
an end to the troublesome
Lords of the Western Isles
and began a plan to beguile.
The pilot Lyndsey then set sail
to navigate the western coast,
'Make sure I can boast
you've mapped every island,
headland, even up to Shetland.'
But English sailors stole the charts
and, with cold hearts,
sold them to the Frenchie's
who were eager to make a start
and paid the map maker, Rutter,
who had an unfortunate stutter,
to make an accurate plan
and get revenge for the Douglas clan.
The French fleet set sail
in wind, sleet and hail
up the Forth to the Clyde
careful to watch the tide
and stay together, perhaps to hide,
but important not to divide.
The battle soon ended
the land well defended, but

Cardinal Beaton was found
with a rope wound round.
A traitor discovered.

'Elphin then paused, took a swig of ale, threw his head back and bellowed….

King James rejoiced…. Although the map was lost, and Beaton was unmasked, the
kings forged will had been discovered.'

A hushed silence filled the room. Thomas Elliott leant forward and threw another
log on the fire. He turned to me.

'First time you've heard that tale? Treachery is all around us, you'll soon get used
to it.'

'He raised his eyebrows and had a menacing grin on his face, and I remember
shaking and wondering what he meant by that but your grandmother was a nice
woman, kind and gentle. Anyway, the days that followed all passed in a blur. The
women were accepting, talked about their families, what raids were successful and
which clans they were allied with. They told me Thomas was in debt and was hoping
to sell me to clear it.'

'But he didn't?'

'No. But the more I heard the more frightened I got and realised my best option to
stay alive would be to make myself indispensable. After all, there did not seem any
way I could return home.'

'What about your father coming after you?'

'My father had arranged a marriage for me to an old man who owned a fleet of
merchant ships. He'd plans to increase his wealth by joining forces with this ship
owner. Isobel, I am shaking at the thought of it. He was a skinny old man, with bent
legs who waddled from side to side when he walked, more like a duck than a man.'
Isobel smiled,'You had a lucky escape.'

'At Middle Moor the women were kind. The men were another matter. But I had
come to like Thomas Elliott over the few weeks I had been there.'

'After what had happened, you began to like him?'

'During the first few days he was polite, and I liked him a little but only a little.
But I was careful not to let him know.'

'Father is a polite man.' Isobel nodded.

'Gradually I began to gain some trust. I began by making teas and potions for
common ailments, aches and pains mainly and then I gradually built up trust among
the people. I wanted to see Old Ma Ogle who lived in the woods, she was the local
healer, but I knew it would be a long time before I was trusted enough not to run away.'

'Did you ever get to meet her?'

'Yes, I did. She was a real old witch. I was never sure how I felt about her. Anyway,
I settled down and began to enjoy my new life. There was a freedom to it I hadn't
experienced before. My father controlled every part of my life. Here I was protected
by the whole Elliott family so travelling round settlements became safer and I slowly
gained a lot of power over them all.'

'Um! You must have enjoyed that! Were many people afraid of you?'

'Sometimes but, being a possession of the powerful Thomas Elliott meant they
didn't bother me much and your grandmother gave me a small room on the ground

floor to work in. The women stole an array of bottles and jars for putting things in and soon I had a manageable apothecary.'

'Is this the room we use today?'

'Yes, but it's bigger now. Years ago, wounded men were brought in, usually with knife or sword cuts or leg injuries not properly treated in the past, damaged fingers, broken bones. Thomas became concerned that, as my reputation grew, I was in danger of being kidnapped for my skills.'

'But that's what he did! He kidnapped you! And your father abandoned you.'

'No, he lived and worked among merchants. We did not live like the Reivers. It was a different type of life.'

'So, no one came, not even your betrothed ship owner? Did your father not want you back?'

'Don't know. I never saw him again. I imagine he thought I had run away from the marriage he'd arranged, and he would have been ashamed and would not have wanted me back.'

'Did you want to go back?'

'I did at first, but women are chattels, Isobel, something for their fathers to sell or barter. I had a better life here and especially after your father and I married.'

'Why did you marry him?'

'It gave me safety to travel, and I loved the freedom of having my own life. I could be away for weeks at a time, had many adventures and earned a lot of money. The Elliott's were a fearsome family, respected or perhaps feared.'

'So are the Tweddle's. I want to remind you of how strong and powerful they are and of how much I love John. Why do you dislike him so much?'

'Isobel, I do not want to talk about that family or that man. You are not going to marry John Tweddle. We do not need an alliance with the Tweddles.'

Isobel frowned and looked at her mother. 'I wonder if there is more to this story you are telling me. Are you hiding something?'

Chapter 23

S ister Jocelyn smiled at Jack' 'Your sister is responding a little better today.'
'That's good news, Sister?'
'But, as you know, these things can take a long time.'

Jack raised his eyebrows, 'How long is a long-time, weeks, months?'

'Let's wait and see how it goes, shall we? You know, there doesn't seem to be any time in a coma. I wonder if time exists at all for them?' She folded her arms across her chest and tilted her head to one side.

'You know, Sister Jocelyn, I complained about her a lot, always daydreaming, drifting off into her own world.'

'What kind of work did she do?'

'She is an animal communicator; helps people heal their animals, writes books and poems, runs courses teaching others. She is a dowser, works with earth energy lines. I think it's called geomancy. Lost her husband many years ago and changed her life completely. She remarried but something must have happened because, a few months ago, she came back to live with us. No explanation was given. No idea what happened. We talk a lot, but I don't know how well I listen. Most of the time she is wandering the woods and fields and I find it hard connecting with her. I don't understand her.'

Sister Jocelyn laughed. 'Interesting person, your sister.'

'She's led a full life, has children and is a grandmother. I wish I'd been closer to her and shared more of my life. I feel there is so much I've missed.'

'I know what you mean. My father is a pediatric surgeon and I never see him. I want to be part of his life, but he is always busy, busy, busy. Life can be difficult. It's only when we are close to losing someone the past looms in front of us.' A subdued silence passed between them.

'Oh, here is Dr. Swaine.' He approached the bed, smiling at Jack and he picked up Anne's notes and began to read.

'How is she doctor?

'No change. Slight finger movement detected. But your sister is comfortable, vital statistics all normal. I'm afraid it's a waiting game.'

'I need more information and reassurance Anne will recover. You're not going to disconnect her then?'

The doctor frowned. 'By no means. Whatever gave you that idea? It's early days.'

He shook Jack's hand and walked off briskly to speak to another relative. Sister Jocelyn patted Jack's arm in a reassuring way, 'He is not the best person at explaining things. He's just lost a patient and it can make him a bit abrupt. He cares so much about his patients he can react badly when we lose one.'

The Uncovered Legacy

Unable to speak, Jack's mouth dropped open. Sister Jocelyn glanced down and chose to ignore his reaction. She cleared her throat, 'Who knows what sort of adventures your sister may be having. It can be a restful time and give her physical body time to be at peace.' She smiled and nodded her head.

'I suppose so. Knowing Anne, she could be in another world, enjoying herself and not wanting to come back.'

'Let's wait and see, shall we?' She pottered off down the ward after the doctor.

Jack felt relieved she had gone and left him to his own thoughts, but no change meant no change. Would she be like this forever?

The work at home was piling up. He sighed as he unbuttoned the top of his shirt. The shepherding needed doing. A cattle feed delivery was due today and could be dropped off in the stack yard. Years ago, when the farm hand was laid up with leg ulcers, his father, Alan, recovering from a recent eye operation, had been told to rest: no heavy work. But the cattle feed wagon had arrived, and it was raining so his father had lifted the bulky paper feed bags and carried them into the "Meal House", stacking them up against the west wall. The strenuous effort had strained his eye muscles, resulting in a detached retina and the loss of sight in that eye, rendering him unable to do the heavy work on the farm. It had left Jack a man down.

Sister Jocelyn's re-appearance broke into his thoughts as she returned to Anne's bedside to change a drip. 'You are a farmer aren't you Mr. Tweddle?'

'Yes, I am.'

'Is it a busy time for you at the moment?'

'To be honest, sister, I am not doing anything useful here and I think, perhaps, I could go home. The work will be piling up and I can't leave it all to the man.'

Jack looked at Sister Jocelyn for agreement but didn't get it.

'Only you can decide. Would you like me to get one of the volunteers to bring you a cup of tea?'

Was she saying no, don't go, or was she expecting something worse to happen? What could be worse. He didn't want another cup of tea, what he wanted was his sister to wake up so they could all get back to normal and get on with life. And when he got back to the farm that BLOODY pig would soon be bacon!

Chapter 24

After a successful raid into the Scottish Lowlands John and his men were on their way home to England and Wydon. They had lifted 400 cattle, 150 sheep, 25 horses, paused to water the animals, rounded up strays and taken a short rest before crossing the long ford. Once across, he dismounted and wandered along the water's edge. Suddenly he stopped and smiled, his attention drawn to a patch of pink flowering valerian. It brought back memories of the bewitching Isobel. He had pulled her out of a bog not far from here, taken her home to dry out and Cook had given her his childhood blanket to keep her warm on the journey home. She had never brought it back and it was not for him, a warrior, to fetch it, although it would have given him another excuse to see her again.

Months later, he had been returning home from scouting Maxwell's lands when he had seen a horse coming towards him. It was Isobel Elliott. She had looked older but still mesmerising. She had pulled up, slid off the horse, walked haughtily towards him and stood with her hands on her hips, smiling.

'Hello, John Tweddle, my father might sell me to you when I'm older. He's always talking about marrying me off to a rich man.'

He had felt shocked and annoyed at being accosted by this young girl with her self-possessed air. *'What did you say?'*

'I've decided I'm going to marry you, John Tweddle, and I always get what I want.'

'Oh, you do, do you? Well, I have no intention of marrying you or anyone else,' he replied but had felt flustered and unsure of himself. Isobel had always had that effect on him. It was unsettling and he had never got used to it. Something about her always unnerved him but he smiled at the memory.

'I am not going to marry anyone. I have no time for girls in my life,' he had told her, although that was not strictly true. He was seeing Mary Ann and Jennie Armstrong but kept Sundays free for Jennie's cousin Flora…… Had Isobel believed him? He wasn't sure. Did he care? He had not been sure of that either. She had walked forward and given him a pink flower.

'Here. This is valerian, you know, makes you dream.'

'Don't dream.' he had replied tossing his head in the air, not wanting to admit to his nightmares of being hunted by six legged beasts.

'Well, I dream but my father says dreams don't come true.' She had danced back and forth, tossing her long blond hair in a tantalising way.

'What are you dreaming about?' he had asked, although not sure if he wanted to hear the answer but felt relieved when she said,'

'Matt Taylor's horse. I want it.'

The Uncovered Legacy

'Well, just take it. Who is Matt Taylor anyway and where is he?' To him it was obvious, if you wanted something you took it.

'He is one of my father's tenants and has a farm quite close to here. I can't get it on my own.' Then she had dropped her head and given him that fetching smile he had come to know so well over the years, as their friendship had grown.

Isobel, hands clasped behind her back, had grinned at him, *'But you could help me get it?'*

This was a challenge impossible to avoid. They had stood together, both looking defiant, neither wanting to give way to the other.

Then he smiled, sighed and said, *'Alright. But the horse had better be worth it. I might even keep it for myself.'* He had grinned at her astonished face.

They had ridden their horses across the river, through the Spring Wood, over the meadow until they had come to the edge of Matt Taylor's place, where the desired animal had stood in a corner of the yard. Isobel had dropped her reins, tied her own horse up in a thicket and run towards the buildings. He rode alongside.

'John lift me up. Be quick.'

He had dismounted and, with one clean sweep, lifted her onto its back and, before he could stop her, she had bent down and kissed him on the mouth, a kiss so sudden and unexpected it had left him dazed.

He had swiped his hand across his mouth to clear the taste of the girl away but it hadn't worked. John smiled to himself as he savoured the feel of her arms around his body, the smell of her skin and the passion of her lips on his.

He had walked forward and opened the gate. As she rode through, he had whacked the pony's backside and watched as she trotted off, happily bouncing up and down, before falling off as she tried to jump the boundary fence. He had stood laughing, the sound of which had alerted Matt Taylor, who came from an outbuilding shouting, *'Hey where has my horse gone. I'll have you for this, thieving kids.'*

John had felt indignant at being called a kid and had run as fast as he could but had been caught as he mounted his own horse. Taylor had slapped him about the head and pushed him down into blackthorn bushes. He had landed badly, hitting his head on a stone, tearing an ear, but managed to crawl away and hide. He remembered his anger at having to hide. He hid from no one. He looked up to see Isobel remount and trot away, leaving him to feel the wrath of Taylor.

John shook his head and rubbed his torn ear in memory of that adventurous day. He smiled to himself and wondered what would have happened to Isobel if Taylor had caught her. Weeks later Johnny Johnson had told him Isobel's father, Thomas Elliott, had bartered two cattle in exchange for the horse she had stolen. A high price indeed.

As he patted his horse, he spoke out loud, 'She's fascinating, fascinating indeed. Unafraid of life.' He bent down and brushed his hand across the pink Valerian flower heads, absorbing their scent and enjoying thoughts of Isobel, his little vixen. The cattle were thirsty and in no hurry to move on. The Croziers, Irving's and Bells were a long way behind and had not yet given chase to their stolen cattle, taken from a remote valley. Looking around him, he saw the strays were in no hurry to be rounded up. He sat down and idly began to play with a twig when his eyes fell upon an arched piece of wood on the far bank. It reminded him of a bow and that tantalising creature once more came into his head. There she stood, slight little thing, holding a bow much too long for her body length, hair loose and waiting to be caught in the bow string if she released the arrow badly.

'I can see you there, John Tweddle. Come down from that bank and show me how to shoot this rabbit. He's a long way off,' she had shouted. Clambering down the slope he slipped, tumbled a few times and landed at her feet, much to her amusement. Laughing, she helped him up. They stood close together, eyes rekindling feelings of past escapades. Only the distant sound of a dog barking broke the tension.

'Someone is coming. Quick in there,' she had said. They had crawled through the undergrowth and crouched down behind a large rock. Two men approached, one a young Robert Ridley, who Isobel hated and was afraid of, the other a man unknown to either of them. Snippets of conversation drifted their way.

'Well, he's forty cattle, shorthorns, I think. Will bring a good price. Let's drive them over the border. Thomas Elliott won't miss 'em 'til later.'

Isobel had gasped so loudly at the sound of her family being the target of thieves, the two men had stopped talking and come towards their hiding place. Fearing for their lives they had jumped up, scrambled to their feet, caught the horses' reins, and fled through the wood to Isobel's home which was close by. Here they had been met by an angry Thomas Elliott, who rushed towards them and lifted his fists in a threatening way.

'What's he doing here? Where is your bow? Took a long time to make that…lost it no doubt, you ungrateful girl.'

Isobel had told her father the tale, but he already knew and had sent several men to capture the thieves. *'You get on your horse, John Tweddle, and get out of here. Don't want your kin round here. Robert Ridley and friend will be done for. I'll see to that.'*

As John had turned to ride away, he had glanced at Isobel who was smiling back at him. She loved adventures. She was exciting to be with, even though he often felt a clumsy youth in her presence. His heart would pound, hands become sweaty, and he seemed to lose all common sense when talking to this captivating creature, who so deeply affected him. One day she would be his and, of that, he was sure. He later heard that by the time Thomas Elliott's men caught up with the thieves one was dead, but Ridley had escaped.

*

John raised his head from his meanderings to the sound of horses and riders approaching and his father's angry voice.

'John! John! What the hell are you doing? Lose your way lad? We've been looking for you. Time to move on…get the livestock moving. Come on, John, get moving! Stop wasting time.'

'No, I'm not lost, I've travelled this route many times before ….' He stood up, keeping his head down, gathering his horse's reins and hoping his father would not ask why his cheeks were flushed.

Angus's horse anxiously paced up and down, sliding on the stoney river bed. 'Willy Ogle says the Irvings and Bells are close behind us. He saw them on the old marsh drove road.…I will not risk losing the herd, chasing after you. Get going. Now! Do you hear me?' His father turned, kicked his horse hard and trotted off.

Chapter 25

Thomas Elliott, his men, Ned Ogle, his sons, Long Faced Kerr, the Johnsons and the Littles, set off from Middle Moor on a raid. They would collect other Reivers on the way. Isobel had heard her father talk of a Mary Kerr, a mysterious old relative, who was to be visited on their way south and she decided to follow and find Mary. It was a long journey, but she felt safe shadowing the band of Reivers.

The men covered their tracks well and as dusk fell the evening's mist blurred the path ahead and she lost sight of them. Isobel shivered with the cold, blew warm air onto her stiff fingers, dismounted, and looked for shelter. An outcrop of rocks came into view and a large overhanging branch hid a small cave entrance.

'We are lost Molly. Hello. Is anybody there? Hello. Hello.' But no one replied. Isobel unsaddled the horse and, clinging tightly to Molly's reins, hoping she would not wander off in the night, wrapped herself up in the horse's blanket and settled down under an overhang. She slept fitfully, to the sounds of tawny owls hooting, small mammals snuffling through the undergrowth and vixens screaming. She was woken by intense sunlight and the intoxicating smell of decaying undergrowth as it wafted past her nose to merge on her face with the drizzled sap from the last of the evening's honeybees' feeding frenzy, on sticky sycamore leaves.

Isobel stood up, stretched her arms to the welcoming daylight and breathed in the clear crisp morning air. The moon was still high and cast just enough light to bounce off the bark of the silver birch and light up an unbroken track that headed north. It was time to forget the foolish venture and return home. After many hours of riding, through scattered woodland and following animal tracks over harvested meadows and flat valley bottoms, the landscape started to become familiar. As she approached the Pelt River, a small, narrow stretch of water where, in the past, she had collected the thickly knotted swathes of watercress, a faint smell of smoke filled her nostrils. She lifted her head to look over the tree line into the far distance and saw faint plumes of grey vapour swirling high in the air, rising to form a dense haze of clouds that covered the woodland beyond her home.

*

Anne shivered in her hospital bed. Unsettling feelings began to make her feel anxious. Sister Jocelyn stood watching her move and twitch as she took Anne's racing pulse. She altered her chart, checked the drips did not need changing, bent down, stroked Anne's forehead, readjusted the bed sheet and walked onto the next patient.

*

Isobel pulled the reins so abruptly Molly spluttered, whined, circled, then tossed her head up and down. Isobel's body trembled, her stomach turned, and, for a few short seconds, disbelief overwhelmed her as she stared ahead. Her home was under attack. The servants would be at market, the men away. No one would be about.

'We must get home. Go. Go. Go!' Clutching Molly's mane and kicking her hard in the belly, she steered the horse across the fields towards the buildings. Fearful thoughts raced through her head, for the safety of her young brother, Fraser. Had he been taken? The cattle in the low fields would have gone first, along with the two black horses and their valuable tackle but other livestock were more securely hidden from prying eyes. What about winter's grain store? Perhaps not. She was grateful her father had dug a secret cellar under an abandoned outbuilding. It would be safe underground from the fire and being discovered by Reivers. Isobel thought of her few precious possessions and hoped they were safe in her old wooden box. It held three magical stones for when she needed comfort, hoping that if she held them long enough her beloved grandmother would come to her aid. There was her mother's crystal embellished cloak clasp, a red wool purse, a piece of soap, a rare thing but a real treasure, a rich lady's pair of shoes, too small, but things of beauty to dream about and, of course, the rose petals that John had given her.

Fears grew stronger as she reached the outer settlement. Molly skidded to a halt. Isobel threw herself off and ran into the first-floor kitchen. Most of the pots and pans had been broken, some of them had even been thrown outside. The servants' beds were upside down and bedding lay strewn across the floors. No doubt they had been looking for money. But Isobel was wise and had hidden her precious box in the rafters, pushed under the beam and covered by old rags. It had not been found and her sense of rage lessened. She heard a noise, turned and there he stood, a short dark figure silhouetted in the smokey doorway, the sneaky little worm, Robert Ridley, who had been spying on her for years. That physically deformed boy, who walked with a limp, no doubt an injury from a previous fight, with unruly hair covering his face, leaving no space for the warming sun to find, what was he doing here? His eyes reminded her of a Scottish Loch, dark and sunken.

'Robert Ridley!' she gasped. 'What are you doing here? Did you do this, ransack our home?' Thoughts and questions came in a rush as she kicked a broken chair out of the way and bent down to pick up a chair leg and wave it in his face.

'Where is my brother? Where is Fraser? He should be here?' Robert smirked as he strode towards her. Isobel stood firm and raised her voice.

'Why aren't you with the others? I thought I caught sight of you yesterday, trailing them, no doubt looking for an opportunity to steal something when you got the chance.'

'I turned back especially for you,' he said grinning at her.

'You will pay for whatever you have done. They will find you.'

'Will I? I have a bigger prize.' He raised an eyebrow and smirked.

Isobel shrieked, 'You have nothing, you miserable wretch!'

'I have you, Isobel Elliott.' He came closer. She backed away from him and tried as hard as she could to feel strong and stop her quivering body abandoning her. With hands on hips, partly to stop herself falling over with terror and partly for reassurance she was in control, she glared at him.

The Uncovered Legacy

'Where is Fraser?'

Folding his arms across his chest he grinned, 'He's where I left him.'

'Left him! Left him! Where?' she threw her arms in the air. 'Fraser is only a child. What have you done with him?' she screamed. Isobel was distraught and ran from one burning outbuilding to another, frantically shouting, 'Fraser! Fraser! Where are you? Fraser! Fraser!'

But all was quiet, the tension only broken by the sound of a scorching door creaking as it fell off its hinges. She feared Ridley, knew he was no good and wherever he went bloodshed followed. She turned back to the main door, went inside and faced him.

'What do you want Ridley?'

'You know what I want. What I have wanted all my life, ever since I saw you naked, washing in Needle Beck when we were young.'

She flushed, more with anger than embarrassment. 'NO! NO! NO! Go away! Leave me alone, you disgusting wretch!'

He stood, tapping his foot on the floor, 'Well, Isobel Elliott, I want you and this time I'm going to have you. No John Tweddle to come to your rescue. I stopped following your father's men hours ago and turned back for you. They didn't even know I was following them.'

Isobel's lips quivered, her voice trembled and she started to feel his power over her. 'Where is Fraser? Where is my young brother?'

'He's in the byre where he belongs, in the muck and shit. He won't trouble me anymore. Put up a good struggle though,' he replied cocking his head to one side and rearranging his ripped jerkin. It was at that moment that Isobel noticed his blood-stained hands and Fraser's leather pouch hanging from Robert's belt. Isobel's hands tore at her face. Stamping her feet, she shrieked, 'You Bastard! You Bastard!'

'I've watched you for years, Miss high and mighty. Well not so much now. I have you now, all to myself.' His face beamed.

'Ridley you are a poisonous rat of a boy.'

He looked affronted at the word boy. 'BOY is it! I'll show you what kind of BOY I am. Come here, you witch.'

Tears streamed down her face, mingling with her hair, blackened by the flying ash from an outbuilding on fire. Isobel turned to run.

'Today's my day!' he bellowed as he lunged forward, grabbed her arm, to spin. her round to face him. Off balance they fell heavily onto the ground. 'I've got you now, no escape this time, Isobel!' Isobel was fighting as hard as she could. She bit, kicked and scratched but felt faint from the dank smell of his ale-stained beard.

'Get off me you pig! You're disgusting! You stink! I hate you!'

The ground was cold, the uneven hard flagstones bit into her back. Isobel turned her head to one side and caught sight of some broken crockery a few feet away. She took a deep breath and, arm outstretched, edged forward, clasped a broken pan handle and in one single motion lifted the weapon and hit Ridley squarely on the head. He released his grip enough for her to slide her hand down the side of her boot, pull out a knife and stab him in the shoulder. Ridley, dazed but aware of the knife, grabbled for it. In the struggle that followed the knife slipped and ripped into his face, creating a gash from eye to chin. He screamed and clutched his face, momentarily releasing Isobel, who scrambled to her feet and ran and ran and ran.

Ridley struggled to his feet and staggered across the yard to where he'd left his horse. He leaned on the saddle, let out a guttural roar, looked into the sky and exploded with rage.

'I hate you all! Father, you bastard for beating me all my life, snapping my sword arm and breaking my fingers! And you mother, except you weren't my mother, were you! You bastard, throwing hot stew into my face…yes, you missed my eye, but the skin peeled off and the scar…look at my scar…look at my scar!' He pointed to his face still oozing blood from his new wound. 'But most of all I hate you women for what you have done to me! I HATE YOU ALL! DO YOU HEAR ME? DO YOU?' He paused, took a deep breath and mounted his horse. 'You witch! You witch, Isobel Elliott! I won't forget this! By God, I won't forget this! You will be sorry! You'll all be sorry!' But her horse was gone and Isobel with it.

Chapter 26

A nne felt her body shudder. She was running, running, then galloping, galloping on a horse. She felt afraid, yet she could feel a warm sensation in her hand. Someone was holding her hand, squeezing it and the sounds of faint mutterings were drifting towards her. A blurry yet familiar voice drifted into her ears, 'Sister Jocelyn.... my sister today.... can I see .... doctor.... please....

Then someone released her hand, and she had a vague awareness that it felt different, no longer warm but cooler and the distant voice had faded.

But then she was somewhere she recognised. She was back home or perhaps it had been. It looked different now. The people wore strange clothes. Looking round the field layouts she knew it to be Wydon and she found herself standing in the stackyard, watching.

*

'Cup of tea Jack?'

'No thank you.'

'Oh well, Dear, I will look in again tomorrow. I expect you will still be here.' The volunteer waddled off, back the way she had come, cup in hand.

'You've been here a long time today.' Said Sister Jocelyn as she stood by Anne's bed taking her temperature...again. Jack raised his eyebrows and looked up.

'Is there any change? '

'No, I am afraid not, Jack.'

'Is that a bad sign?'

'No, not really. Would you like me to fetch the doctor to speak to you? He's just come on duty.'

'Yes, please. Thanks.' Jack sank back into his chair, relieved that no change could be a good thing. He had watched his sister for many hours over many days and thought he could see changes. Sometimes she appeared to smile. Her fingers or legs would move, or her eyes would flicker as if they were trying to open. Moments ago, her mouth had opened as if she wanted to scream or was it a gasp. Thankfully it had not been her last breath. A few moments later he saw the doctor making his way up the ward, pausing to speak to patients' families, no doubt reassuring them that all would be well.

'Hello, I am Dr. Swaine. We met before.'

'How is she, Doctor? Really, what hope is there?'

'It's a waiting game, I'm afraid, but so far so good.'

'I think I see part of her face moving as if she is coming around?'

'Quite possibly but every patient is different.'

'I think I know where my sister is.'

'You do? And where would that be?'

'She has spent her life daydreaming, drifting off into other places, visiting events that happened centuries ago. And she talks to animals. In fact, it was probably talking to the Gloucester Old Spot pig that brought her here.'

Dr. Swaine looked bemused, put his hand on Jack's shoulder and gave it a little squeeze.

'Interesting. Patients can have strange experiences when in an unconscious state.'

'It's normal then?' he said, pleading for agreement.

'It can be but, rest assured, she is comfortable, and I have every belief she will make a full recovery.'

Jack looked reassured and turned to the doctor, 'I think she is waiting for something to happen and when it has, then she'll come back.'

'You could be right. Who knows what goes on in an unconscious mind.'

'Well, Doctor, all her life she has felt that there was something waiting for her; an event, a time, or a place where everything would come together. I am wondering if this is what is happening.'

Dr Swaine smiled at Jack and strode off down the ward to the next patient. Jack sighed. He needed a break.

Chapter 27

A nne's mind was drifting into and out of what seemed to be random events. Her heart would beat faster, her breath would quicken and her hands fidget. She could see and hear what was happening all around her. It was as if she was there with these people, not just observing their lives. No, it was more than that, a lot more. She knew what they were thinking and feeling, and she was at Wydon...a place she knew so well.

*

Edgar came rushing into the stack yard. He ran into the stable, the bye and the calf house yelling, 'They've gone! They've gone!'

Hearing the commotion and the fear in his son's voice, his father, Angus, lifted his head, peered through the crack in the smithy door, where he was sharpening knives, strode out across the yard and stood with hands on hips shouting back. 'What's gone?'

'The cattle, from the West Hill. All of them.' Edgar took a step back to avoid his father's fist.

Angus's face went purple with rage. 'All of them?'

'Yes, all of them.'

'Where were you?' Angus lifted his hand and slapped the lad so hard he tumbled to the ground. Edgar raised his hand, 'I'm sorry, it's not my fault.'

'All of them, all 120?' shouted his father in total disbelief, turning towards his son, who was struggling to stand up with the aid of one hand, the other holding his aching head.

'You were watching them. It was your job and where's the dog?'

He bowed his head and muttered, 'They took him.'

'They took the slue dog. You let them take the dog? They will pay for this and pay heavily.' Angus, enraged, paced up and down, then paused to stare at his young son.

'The sheep?'

Edgar bowed his head, 'In the Hollow. That's when it happened.'

'You're a halfwit boy! A halfwit!'

'I drove the sheep to the Hollow. They must have been watching, waiting until I left. It was getting dark and I was tired and......' his voice trailed to a silence.

'Tired, were you? You'll be more than tired when I've finished with you.' He lifted his fist again, but Edgar ducked the blow.

'I shut the gate and sat down under the ash tree; you know, the one with the loose branch hanging down over the gate.'

'Ash tree, ash tree, what are you babbling about boy?' He threw his arms up in disbelief.

Edgar opened his mouth to reply but his speech stuttered, 'W w… ell I ww…. was h hungry and t t took my bb..bread out.'

'Hungry, you stupid boy!'

'I must have fallen asleep.'

'Asleep…Asleep boy! It's morning now. Have you slept all night?'

'That's not all of it.' He stepped back.

His father shook him so hard his loose tooth dislodged and fell into a pocket.

'What! There is more…. MORE?'

'They raided the grain store in the old steading, you know, the one on the hillside. I passed it on my way home.'

Angus's face was swollen with rage. 'I know where the old store is boy. I built it.'

Edgar stood his ground and turned to his father, 'You said it would be safer out there than down here in the farm buildings. It's not all my fault.' He stood defiantly, waving his arms about, trying to move the blame onto anyone who would take it. Angus lifted his right hand and punched his son so hard in the face he flew several feet in the air and if it had not been for the barn door, perhaps he would not have stopped. Angus spun round to face John who appeared through the fellside gate.

'Where have you been? All hell has broken out here.' Angus explained what had taken place.

'It doesn't make sense. Why would they attack us?'

'Gone, everything's gone, John; the cattle, some of the winter's grain.'

'All the cattle?'

'No, just the herd in the West Hill field.'

'So, all is not lost, we still hold the main herd.'

'Bastards, Ridleys, Nixon's, Grahams, Maxwells. I am undecided who to blame but, by God, they will pay for this.' Angus turned his fury on his eldest son, 'Where have you been, John? You should have been here.'

'Following the deer, took us over the hill onto Fossgill Flats…Davy Nixon's place. Thought I would collect some sheep he owed me while I was there!'

'Where are they now?' A hint of justice lifted in his voice.

'In the High Dales. Who were these? Reivers? Do you know?'

'No. Most likely a rag bag of men. Not many by the number of hoof prints Edgar saw. Must have come down the river side, crossed at the ford and made their way up through the far field. Your halfwit brother fell asleep and didn't wake up until they were all gone. Someone knew you and the others would be going over the hill to Davy's place and be well out of the way.'

'There's a spy among us. I'll find him. Do you think the Ridleys were involved?'

'No idea. They change sides with every fight. Old man Ridley could have sent young Robert, his weakling of a son?'

John, hand on his sword, stared at his father, 'Ever since I was a lad, I hated the Ridleys. Saw young Tunny Maxwell beat Robert up once…pity he didn't finish him off. Robert and I are the same age and Isobel has many tales to tell of his spying and creeping around. By God, I'll kill the little wretch!'

Angus moved and stood over his younger son. 'When I have finished with you…' Edgar looked afraid and knew he would be done for if he was hit again, such was the old man's strength. John stepped forward between them pushing his father back and Angus raised his head and bellowed.

'HOT TROD! HOT TROD! HOT TROD!'

Everyone understood that meant pursuit, fighting, revenge and recovery of stolen goods.

Angus started shouting instructions, 'You over there, get over the hill, fetch Johnson and his two sons and Willie Ervin's men.' Pointing at a random man standing by the byre door, 'Saddle the horses. Bent Nose Bob, go to the house, get the women to pack food. We need to be off.' Angus rushed round the yard and buildings throwing orders, sending men in all directions to round up their allies, collect weapons and supplies.

Eventually Angus quietened, walked to John, and put his hand on his son's shoulder. 'We meet at Mosstorn tonight. Be fully armed. We'll get the bastards before they cross into Scotland. Moving 120 cattle and a cart of grain will be slow. We have time to collect our men.'

'I don't know who they were, but we'll get the bastards father. We will get them! I wonder who has stolen the livestock. The cattle taken are a mixed lot, some Herefords, previously lifted from a Carlisle cattle dealer. There are more than seventy Shorthorns, black and white Galloways, and my favourites, the Kylies, the hardiest and best able to cope on the rough outer fells. Poor grazing seems to suit them, and they do well on our high ground…' John paused mid-sentence and looked thoughtful, 'You took a herd of cattle a while back from Scar Faced Nixon.'

Angus shook his head, 'Can't be certain he knew that, John.'

'They could have come back for them?'

'No, Scar Face would have wanted revenge. Burned our place down. He would want me to know it was him.' He paused, took a deep breath and looked at his son, 'I've been thinking, John, family is important. You're the eldest and will carry the family name on; a name to be feared and respected in these valleys.' His father had a look of pride on his face, then it softened, and he smiled, 'I have seen you look at Isobel Elliott, watched the pair of you over the years playing, fighting, sparring with each other. She's a good match for you, John. Will make a fine wife. Be well pleased if you married the lass.'

John looked down and idly kicked stones into an open doorway, uncomfortable at his father's intrusion into his personal life but inwardly smiling, pleased to have his approval. He knew Isobel would be an asset to the Tweddle family.

'An alliance between the Tweddles and Elliotts would be a strong one. Our lands would be closer, give us a safer passage into Scotland, making us all richer. John, she's a beautiful lass, reminds me of your mother, Anya. Lost her life birthing you. Now here is another strong, powerful woman. Take her John, take the lass.'

This was the first time his father had spoken of these things. He gazed at Angus, a big, tall man weathered from years of riding, raiding, fighting and living outside. His long red hair hung down his back and his braided beard was a magnificent sight. The thumb was missing on his right hand and although he had tried many times to use the sword in his other hand, the skill eluded him, yet he somehow managed to hide his lack of confidence as a fighting warrior. John had observed his father's reticence with a sword but dared not speak of it, fearful of consequences among the men who held him in a position of authority and who showed him great loyalty, although often tinged with fear. But Angus was also a cunning man who knew how to maintain status among his followers and inspire a fighting spirit, something John put down to his Anglo-Saxon ancestry. He was a complicated, clever man, able to build on the work of others to promote his own abilities but hidden deep inside there was a gentleness and a certain amount of humility that did not surface in the company of others. John remembered Cook telling him that his father had once brought Anya a silver bangle, a length of purple silk, two tortoiseshell hair combs and some very fine underclothing from a raid on a merchant's house in Hexham. He had a softer side and had loved John's mother very much. Then suddenly, his thoughts were interrupted by his father's preoccupation with the Hot Trod.

'And that halfwit brother of yours slept all the way through it!' His father began to pace up and down the yard. 'Near as damn it about 120 cattle gone but a few strays will have got away. Two horses left with your brother also gone and I haven't counted the small stuff and there's the grain of course. Quite a haul, John, but we will get the bastards! We will get them! Their horse and cart, or carts, will have to take the bottom road through Lathrup valley. We'll catch them before they cross the border.'

'How many men will come?

Angus's face was red, tears flowing freely down his face so great was his rage. 'All of them, John, all of them! And they will come, by God, they will come! Get your men together, John, swords knives, bows. We meet at Mosstorn tonight.'

Angus waved his men to mount up. They left the yard in such a rush that two buckets of water were turned over, the dairy cow was knocked into the barn door, the calf house gate was ripped off its hinges and various brushes, brooms and farm tackle were strewn across the ground. It had not stopped raining for many weeks and the ground was slippery and thick with mud. It seemed to John it was a poor time to raid as so many cattle would leave heavy tracks and make it easy for them to be followed. Another month and the high pastures would have provided safety. John and his men collected their armour, food from the kitchen, spare clothes, and whatever other provisions they could easily fasten onto their horses and turned through the gate to follow his father and brothers. As John rode down the woodland track his thoughts turned to the raiders and the foolhardiness, they had shown in taking so many cattle from the Tweddles. They would have had either no fear or no sense. But his father was right, someone had been spying on them. His thoughts took him back to Wydon and his visit behind the tool shed to collect the spare dagger he kept hidden under a large stone. He remembered moving the stone and seeing an imprint of a broken shoe next to it. He knew for certain it was Robert Ridley's horse... the spy. He rode a horse with a damaged shoe, the man he despised most in his life and looked forward to killing. It would be justice for Margaret Elliott and the pursuit of Isobel. He would have his revenge for all of it.

The Uncovered Legacy

By mid-morning John had caught up with his father, who had made a brief stop to form a plan and organise who would take the path through the valley bottom. Angus took a stick and drew a map in the mud.

'The thieves will have driven hard to Scotland but stopped to rest the livestock in one of the many hidden glens. Here, here or here is a possibility,' making three large crosses on the ground.

'Now then, Tom Kerr and brother Walter you both know this landscape well. I'm sending you two ahead as trackers. Tom go west to Brusehill and Walter east to Temon moor on the Nooscliff estate. Our cattle are a precious commodity and especially 120. The ransacked grain store was nearly emptied. It will slow them down making their wheel tracks, easier to follow.'

John had spent a successful winter raiding and had acquired four new horses from a dealer in Carlisle, mares he later found had been stolen from Andrew Maxwell the year before. But what of it? Livestock moved so often from one owner to the next it was hard to know who owned what and did it matter? If he wanted something, he took it, as they all did. This was border life, although stealing from the Tweddles was a different matter.

Suddenly, Will Turnbull rode towards them shouting, 'Don't go round that corner, there's twenty men lined up on the skyline.'

Angus shouted, 'We must be getting close. Who are they? Have they seen us? Are they looking our way? Get back. Get back. Go down the slope and quietly. It's the raiders. They mustn't see us. Don't want them to sound an alarm. We'll get the bastards tomorrow.'

John waved his arms in the direction of retreat. Will raised himself in the saddle to try to get a better look, pulled his mare back onto the well-worn track while John and his brother edged forward for a better look.

'Over the past few years, I've had many close encounters with men from the debatable lands. This could be a trap, Will. Their horses don't look lean and under nourished. Ours have thinned out, have a lot of muscle wastage from the lack of good grazing and the meagre amounts of hay and straw that supplemented their diet this past Autumn.'

Jamie shook his head, 'It's been a bad year, John, too much rain, not enough sun to dry the fields and a lot of cattle driven off by the Grahams last back end. Cattle are central to our lives, a sign of our family's prosperity and fertility. Ned Graham insulted us by leaving the old Galloway bull. I know he was lame, no use for breeding, not worth stealing, his fertile days over but it was an insult to leave him. Just like the Tweddles, they thought, no good for breeding. Bastards!'

'I am wise enough to know true wealth is found in the heart and soul of who we are. We're a tightly knit family and have that in abundance. Patience will get all our cattle back and more. The Grahams will pay for what they've taken. I will have my revenge.'

Jamie smiled at John, 'Do you remember a couple of years back when father recovered our five horses?'

'Yes, they had gone up north for a wedding, left the horses unguarded. Yes, I remember. Ned Graham killed my friend Nick Elliott and took his wife. I won't forget.'

It was getting dark. The moon had drifted behind the clouds as they rode through the meadow field and as they approached Mosstorn all seemed quiet. The hill riders had skirted the fell side, seemingly unaware they'd been seen and ridden off towards Whinstone Glen. John had identified a mixture of Bells, Nixon's and Armstrongs and his blood began to boil as the last rider who joined them was Robert Ridley. Treachery was afoot.

Angus and his two brothers, Willie, and Thom, pulled alongside John and the four men rode in silence for several minutes. Then Angus spoke. 'How many men have we got John?'

'Two hundred or more.'

'Good enough. It's getting too dark to see the road, we will rest up at Mosstorn, and wait for the sun to rise.'

Walter rounded the bend behind them and slithered to a halt by Angus's side.

'Have you found the cattle?' all four men shouted together.

He nodded, 'No hurry, I know where they are. Holed up for the night in Brittlestones Gap.'

Angus turned to Walter, 'Have you seen them? Who are they?'

'Looks like outlaws from Scrapshaw Ridge. But I recognise some o' them. Seen 'em down our way.'

John moved to ride beside Walter, 'Was Robert Ridley with them?'

Walter nodded. 'We'll surprise them tomorrow and they will pay. Walter, take some men and keep watch over the hill riders. I don't want anybody raising the alarm. Kill them if you have to.'

Angus steered his horse to ride alongside his son. 'Did you know Mosstorn Manor is the home of Sir Tom Bell, deputy Middle March warden?'

'Is he expecting us?'

'He'll have heard but he wouldn't dare turn the Tweddles away with so many men, John. Do you know what befell my cousin Eddgar, when he stayed here?'

'No.'

'Eddgar was a young man in his early thirties. A few years ago, he'd been appointed deputy Middle March Warden as befitted the status of the Tweddle family.'

'I didn't know we had ever been wardens?'

'Yes, we have. But Tom Bell was determined to have this position himself. He was envious and desperately wanted Mosstorn, which went with the job.'

'What happened?

'Bell had a plot to rid himself of Eddgar. He'd made a pact with the Croziers, who owed him for past misdeeds.'

'Do we know what misdeeds?'

'No. But on this particular day Eddgar was on his way to take up his new residence when a rider approached.'

'Good day, Sir,' he had said.

'Good day.'

'Tom Bell requests you break your journey and rest up for the night with him at Gilsdale Hall.'

'How do we know this father?'

'Travellers were camped nearby, going to Gilsdale and witnessed what happened.'

Angus continued with his tale. 'Edgar had replied, *'That's kind of Tom Bell. I was feeling in need of a good night's rest and some food.'*

'*Who are you?'* he'd asked.

'*I'm Dunc, work in the stables for Bell, look after his horses and stuff.'*

'Was that true father?'

'We don't know. But it was a trap. The travellers knew that.'

'The tale goes on, John. When they arrived at Gilsdale, Eddgar asked where everyone was. Dunc told him most of them had gone to a wedding down the valley, leaving only two men about the place.'

'So the hall was empty that night, just Bell and Eddgar and a few servants in the house?'

'Yes indeed. It had sounded odd to Eddgar but he took the young lad, Dunc, at his word and followed him. It's always safer sleeping indoors than spending the night in the open and being attacked by robbers.'

'What did the travelers do?'

'They followed as well and were invited in for a night's shelter.'

'Tom Bell had greeted him well enough, taken Eddgar in to supper, a small affair, venison and good ale, which lifted his spirits from a long, cold ride.'

'The others where were they?'

'Well, the travellers noticed that the loaf of bread on the table was upside down, a bad omen if ever there was one. Always had a keen eye did Old Fancy Douglas. After a good supper Eddgar bid his host goodnight and went to bed. But in the middle of the night, he didn't hear Bell creep into his room and dampen the primings in his firearm and jam his sword into its sheath with the help of a broken egg. One of the young servants had been out for the night, came back under the light of the moon, heard a door open and followed the noise. She saw what Bell did. Shocked by what she had seen she had run back outside and straight into Old Fancy.'

John couldn't hide his anger and pulled his horse to a sudden halt causing the animal to whine in pain. 'Bastard Bell.'

'The next morning Eddgar rose, bid his host farewell, and prepared to leave. Bell and two of his men, who had not been there the night before, insisted on escorting him some of the way, making up a tale about the Croziers having visited the week before and the road not being safe.'

'The travellers?'

'They packed their animals; said they were in a hurry but hung back and followed a short distance behind the party of four. By mid-day they reached Batingthorp.'

'I know it. A little glen on Cumton Fell.'

'The riders stopped in a glade and seemed to be waiting for something. Then one of Bell's men shouted, *'HORSES ON THE HORIZON.'* Old Fancy, saw Bell smile at one of his men, pull his horse to a halt and hold back. There was lots of yelling, *'Who are they?'* Someone shouted the name, *'Croziers.'* Then Bell rode forward followed by his men, swords out in full war cry but, as the Croziers, riding in a bunch in full fighting mode, got very close, Bell and his men peeled off sideways abandoning Eddgar to the swords, knives and guns of the Crozier murderers.'

Even in the darkening light John could see his father's fury.

'They fell upon him at once. Eddgar tried to pull his sword from its sheath only to discover it was stuck. His gun backfired causing a wound on his chest. By this time he was on the ground being hacked limb from limb, fighting for his life. When the ambush was over, the Croziers with not an injury between them fled in the direction of Liddesdale and safety but not before acknowledging Tom Bell and there was an exchange of money.'

'Murdering bastards! I have heard tales of an Eddgar Tweddle and betrayal.'

'Old Fancy told us Eddgar's remains were taken home on a sheet. The treachery of the Croziers hasn't been forgotten, John. Tom Bell has yet to pay for his part in this. I suspect he knows that I know what happened.'

Chapter 28

Mosstorn was a large manor house with adequate stabling, clean water and fodder for many horses, a well-fortified building with one large gateway, through which everything came; men, women, carts, horses, peddlers, journeymen and all manner of things that were attributed to the workings of such a fine house. There were two courtyards, the outer one used for livestock pens, workmen and visiting friends or foes, the inner one used by the immediate family and their servants.

'What is this man like, Father?'

'Sir Tom Bell is an odd little man. I don't know how he hangs on to his wealth and this manor in these treacherous times. The man is evil, John, nicknamed D.C. Bell... Double Crosser Bell.'

'Why?'

'He has the knack of always being on the right side at the right time.'

'Have you had dealings with him before?'

Angus didn't answer but continued talking about Bell. 'This way of living has made him rich but vulnerable to attack. Some say he buried his money in caves on the fells in case he ever needed to flee in a hurry. Others were more persuaded to search for his wealth in the oak chest at the bottom of his bed.'

'That would be too easy to find.'

'A few years ago, I heard a tale from Bessie, one of his house maids, about a carpenter who came to the house to hollow out the bed posts and old man Bell filled them with gold.'

'She knew this to be true?'

'Bessie had been looking through a hole in the door and saw him gouging the wood out. The carpenter was in the bedroom for three whole days and, when he'd finished his work, he'd flung himself out of the window to his death. He was found with his coat and cap on, and his carpenter's toolbox had flown out of the window after him. It had landed squarely on his chest and finished off whatever job the cobbles had failed to do.' Angus dismounted, lent on his saddle, and continued, 'Bessie thought it odd because that morning the carpenter told her he was nearly finished and asked her to pack some food for his afternoon journey to Woodhall house, several miles away.' Both men sighed.

'Some of us will do for him one day, John.'

A sudden cold wind blew through John's body. 'We must be on our guard tonight. 'As they walked into the house a short, little man came from the oak hall and shuffled towards them.

'Welcome,' said a nervous voice. 'Please come in, good to see you.'

Angus and his men took a quick look round the room, having already inspected the inner courtyard for armed men. The stables had only a couple of horses inside and the few servants seemed calm enough. John looked at his father who was watching the wily old fox, their host.

'Come sit. Plenty of food. Margaret bring wine for our guests. Have you come far?'

John, thinking of past treacherous deeds, looked to the bread on the table to see if it was right way up.

'A distance,' muttered Angus. John thought his father wouldn't want to alert Bell to the reason for their visit.

'It's been a dangerous place these last few weeks. Nixon's and Croziers raiding Tynecome village down the valley and stole their cattle. Cleaned them out.'

At the name Crozier, Angus stiffened. 'Croziers, you say, and Nixon's?'

'Yes, quite a lot of them, well-armed and women with them too.'

'Women travelling with Reivers usually means they've travelled a long way from home and expect injuries which will need to be tended for a safe return,' mused Angus.

'Yesterday two large carts passed along the top of Ash Fell. Seemed an odd place to be. Those tracks are old, unstable, and dangerous. Wheels would be close to the edge of the hill.'

'As warden I expect you will be following these men to see what they are up to.'

But Bell didn't answer. He looked embarrassed, coughed, stood up, abandoned his meal, made his apologies, and left the table.

'Goodnight, Warden Bell,' shouted Angus in a loud voice.

The men sat in silence for several minutes.

'John, did you see the look on his face? The foolish man knew he'd said too much.'

'Yes, I saw it. That's why he scuttled off to bed. Giving strangers this sort of information is dangerous. Who was he covering for?'

John and his father exchanged glances.

Will raised his head to speak.

'The stolen grain will not travel safely along the valley bottom. It's too open, treeless, with no cover. Better to drive the cattle through and take the grain over the older, quieter route along the top of the ridge.'

'They must have split up in the hope of at least getting grain or cattle through.'

'So, Bell knows who they are?' One-eyed Ned raised his fists and shook his head.

'Do we believe him?' asked Willie.

'He's afraid. Too many of us and he won't want to openly betray the Croziers, Nixon's, or whoever they are.'

'Bastards, coming back after what they did to Edgar Tweddle.'

'But he knows, doesn't he?'

'Yes, John, he knows.'

'He must think we don't know?'

'Who is he more afraid of father?'

'Don't know. I have a score to settle with Double Crosser Bell. But that can wait 'til morning.'

The house dogs woke early. Angus dressed quickly and went to find Bell. A short time later he returned smiling and went to seek out Walter and Tom Kerr. Within minutes the horses were saddled, the men armed and eager to be off. Angus walked out of the great hall, nodded his head to old man Bell, mounted up and rode the short distance to where the rest of his men and allies were gathered, waiting.

'Did you get the money?' John asked his father.

'Yes, old gambling debt of my father's, thieving bastard. Double Crosser Bell had a look of fear on his face, John, that's why he paid up. Too many of us. He'd reneged on this debt for years, but I got him, thieving bastard. But that's not the end of it, John…no, by God, it isn't. I've not finished with him yet.' He kicked the horse into a trot. Walter and Tom Kerr were waiting at the entrance to Brittlestones Gap with a large party of Reivers, eager for the fight ahead. Angus and his two brothers, Willie and Thom, greeted their companions then the headsmen sat together and began scratching a quick map in the mud and plans were made.

'With such a large herd of cattle they will move slowly. We have time to catch the thieving bastards,' said Thom.

John scratched his head, picked up a sturdy stick and drew his plan in the soft earth.'

'Look,' he said, 'I know this track over the top of the ridge.'

'Been here before have ya? Up to no good eh!' sneered Walter, grinning from ear to ear. But one glaring look from John and he turned away.

'Once we are in the valley it's a long cattle drive, past Forge Johnson's place, then Tibbies' drinking hole near the Tweed.' The mention of an ale house put a smile on everyone's face.

'There is only one way out of this valley with this amount of cattle.'

'Interesting you know, that,' smirked Walter.

'It's a smallish, narrow passageway with high sided rocks on both sides and well-hidden if you don't know where it is.'

'The day is drying but tracks will still be fresh from yesterday. We'll split our forces. I'll follow the cart tracks through the wood, over the ridge, skirt round in front of them and barricade the far end. You'll follow the cattle track through the valley bottom.'

Angus nodded in agreement, waved to Walter and held his arm aloft beckoning the other headsmen.

John turned and selected the men he trusted. He shouted, 'We must hurry. The carts of grain will be heavy, but it was a clear night, the moon was full and they could've kept moving.' As he bent down to adjust his stirrup, his eyes alighted on the print of a broken horseshoe clearly visible in the dry mud. John's eyes widened and his voice growled, 'Ridley is here. I wonder if he was close enough to hear of our plans. There are short cuts across the top of this valley. Let's take them. We need to get in front. Come on let's go.'

Will turned, 'Ridley may know them too. You're not the only one to raid in this part of the north?'

'He must be the spy. Bastard.' For a moment the two men held a distant gaze. John turned in the saddle and gestured his men to follow.

'I have heard tales of Ridley's fooling around with a maid from one of these villages and it wouldn't be safe for him to enter the valley bottom. He'll be looking for another route, over the ridge? Jamie, hang back and see he doesn't follow. I have unfinished business with that bastard, but it will have to keep for now.'

Chapter 29

F ollowing the muddy tracks of a large herd of cattle, Angus and his allies entered the valley bottom and broke into a steady trot. By mid-morning the trail emerged from Hawksbill Wood and entered the hamlet of St Jack's. It looked deserted, only a few dogs running loose and no livestock in sight.

Stotty Johnson appeared from behind a ramshackle outbuilding,

'Angus, fresh cattle tracks coming from the east side of that cow shed. Bastard thieves cleaned up here too. Taken more cattle by the look of them tracks. If we don't catch 'em soon, they'll be away into the glens of Scotland.'

Angus dismounted and sent the men ahead while he entered the deserted buildings to see if there was anything left worth pinching but pickings were poor. He stormed out of the church, kicked the door, mounted his horse and rode away to see Jock Eliott emerge from behind a crumbling stable with a basket hilted sword.

'Nothing left, taken the lot. Thieving bastards,' he said grinning, swishing his new possession in the air. Angus smiled. 'The plunder will slow them down. We'll push on. John will catch them at the far end and box them in.'

The valley bottom was fairly flat, and Angus's army made good progress. By early afternoon an out rider brought back news he had caught sight of the raiders.

'They're ahead. Keep together and get your weapons ready,' Angus shouted as he pushed his horse into a trot. In his youth he had travelled through this valley many times, raiding into England. The last time was taking cattle from the Trough Head Settlement, and he knew this was the shortest route back over the border. 'The thieves will be pushing the cattle hard, fearful of a blocked escape. We must hurry.'

As they rounded the east side of Low Cragg Fell, the stolen cattle came into sight in the far distance.

Angus paused, then smiled. 'Look, cattle numbers have swollen. There are about fifty riders. There'll be more with horse and cart on the top road.'

Walter came rushing forward, 'We'll go ahead and ambush them. I'll take forty men.'

Angus put his hand on Walter's arm, 'No, wait until they near the end. John must get there first. He must blockade the way out.' Walter frowned but Angus was a cautious man. 'I want all the cattle back, and especially those that aren't ours.'

*

B. A. Silcock

Meanwhile, John and his men rode hard along the top ridge, weaving in and out of narrow thickets, navigating treacherous streams and rock pools, with mile after mile of barren rocks and only a few trees to offer any cover.

The grain cart would be below them on a wider track. John caught sight of his horse's breath in the cold air. It reminded him of how high up they were. Every step was riven with danger. The only casualty was John Irving's son, Michael, whose horse had stumbled over a heather root and thrown him off, only to land under another horse, whose back foot kicked him so hard he died instantly. No one stopped. Time was important. Michael would be collected, or what was left of him, on the return journey. Michael's brother Harry had been lost the year before, crossing the river Eden with stolen plunder. His saddle strap had become loose, then slipped. Man, and horse had fallen into the freezing, swirling water and gone over the weir where their bodies were smashed on the rocks below. Two friends, two valuable Reivers gone.

John had a pang of anger that the dead man was Michael, a valuable lad with a knife. Looking down the hillside he caught an occasional glimpse of the thieves' horse and cart, full of stolen Tweddle grain. He called his brother, Thomas, to ride beside him.

'Go along the lower path, pick up the cartwheel tracks. There is a wide section round yonder bend where it winds down to the valley bottom. They'll have to take it. Ride on. Be careful not to be seen. Just get behind them and follow. The rest of us will ride ahead, get in front and surprise the bastards.'

'John, that cart will be making a lot of noise, they won't hear us coming,' Thomas' face broadened into a wide grin. He turned his horse, gave it a quick kick in the belly and set off, with several others, down the trail.

An hour or so later the high valley track descended along a path that wound its way down the fell to the valley floor. The men dismounted to rest the exhausted horses and walked them through Nobbleton Wood to reach a clearing on the west side. Their prize lay through a clearing in the trees.

'John, there's more cattle than ours down there. The bastards have collected more since yesterday.' Alan Ogle's eyes were as keen as ever and he began to count … 'two hundred, I reckon, fifteen horses and I can see the cart with the grain still on it. We must wait for Angus.'

But John was impatient after such a long hard ride. He stood still, looked around and took a deep breath. 'Stealing is stealing. There are more cattle down there than ours. Rich pickings to be had.' He remounted his horse, let out the loudest war cry his men had ever heard and charged through the trees, heading for the men behind the animals.

The cattle, alarmed by the commotion, began to run on towards the valley exit. Alan Ogle screamed to his companions, 'Forward lads! Get in front of them! Head them off! Turn them, turn them! Get to the cut! Block it off!'

Chaos followed. John's men and horses rushed forward to head the livestock off before they reached the way out. After a lot of yelling, whacking of swords on leather saddles, hitting the cattle on their backsides and swearing, the herd leaders slithered to a halt in front of the small band of horses and riders. The cattle at the front snorted and bellowed then turned and, in one mass of pounding colour, stampeded back in the direction from which they had come, straight through the fighting men.

The Uncovered Legacy

John's men held most of the high ground and seeing the herd coming towards them, he shouted, 'Get back! Get back up the hillside!' The Croziers, Nixons and some Armstrongs were in disarray. Unable to retreat quickly, they found themselves in the path of the rampaging animals. Many men were trampled underfoot, their horses rearing up and fleeing with the retreating cattle.

John, seeing the unfolding chaos, shouted at Jamie Ogle, 'Take ten men! Follow the animals! Get in amongst them, slow them down and head the cattle off to the river. They are running straight towards Angus. His men will be able to stop them on the flatter flood plain.

The Reivers were in disarray and the fighting between some of the men became a battle ground for settling personal grievances. Some of the younger men rode off and escaped. Many were killed and even more injured. It was a bloody battle, but the Tweddles and their allies had the upper hand and, after a short time, drove the offending Reivers away to lick their wounds.

It had been a rout of fifty men. The ground was covered in bodies, abandoned armaments, saddle bags, armour, helmets and swords. Loose horses were rounded up and roped together. Dead men were picked over for their wealth and weapons, which were repacked into saddle bags.

Injured men were seen to as best they could. Some were beyond help and quickly dispatched to the other world. Others were patched up and mounted on a horse. A few were left to die. John looked round for any sign of Robert Ridley. He had seen him fighting alongside Davy Crozier, who was now lying in a bloody pile at his feet. But Ridley, a master of escape, was nowhere to be seen and John again swore that one day he would kill him.

Angus arrived, red-faced and bulging with anger. He rode swiftly towards his son, 'You should have waited. Told you to wait. We missed a good fight. I told you to wait.'

'No time. They were near the cut. We had to strike. Hard and fast.' The two men clasped hands and smiled at each other.

'Are you injured John?' But before John could reply his father's thoughts returned to the livestock. 'How many cattle have we taken?'

'Tom and Fergus are counting the herd now, a lot more than we had.'

'Done us a favour eh, Lad.' He pulled on his beard chuckling to himself, 'How many did you kill?'

'Don't know, lost count.' John grinned, 'The cattle trampled a lot of men when they turned and stampeded back towards you.'

'A wonderful sight it was, coming towards us. Quietened them down quick and settled now on the riverbank.' Angus remembered his son.

'Where is the dog?'

'No, not really, a few scars and stiff leg. I saw someone riding a chestnut stallion on the other side of the cut. I am going after it.'

'Were they part of the raid?'

'No, I don't think so....... I'll send men to round up the strays. And see if they can find the dog but I think he has probably run off.'

'How many strays John?'

'Twenty, or more, I think.'

Angus looked into the distance, 'Is there enough of them bastards to come back after us?'

'No. The few left ran like whining children, scattered in all directions. Take them a long time to round their men up again. Most of the young lads fled when the cattle turned back.'

'What of the grain cart father?'

'Your brother Thomas and Old Mac Ogle have it in hand. Changed horses and already set off back to Wydon. Angus lifted his hand to acknowledge John, who turned and rode out through the cut after the chestnut. Horses were his passion and that one, in particular caught his attention. He had seen the animal last autumn at a market sale in Carlisle, bought by Ben Crozier, the chief of their clan. Now it could be his, if he could catch it. But the Chestnut stallion was nowhere to be seen and, feeling weary, he decided to turn for home and come back another day to find the horse.

Chapter 30

As he was getting closer to Wydon John took a short cut through Chatterspitt Forest and, as he emerged from its southern border into a clearing, the strange site of a black horse, with a long-plaited mane, its tail reaching the ground and a coat glistening in the late morning sun, took his attention. Obviously, it was a very valuable horse. It would nicely replace the chestnut stallion that had eluded him. He sat for several minutes watching the rider turn the horse in one direction, then another, walk backwards then rear up on its hind legs. The rider was a thin lad, well dressed, in what looked like high quality leather boots, sturdy plated jacket and wearing an unfamiliar helmet. Yet there was something familiar about the rider. The way he moved. This black horse was far superior to his own. Indeed, a magnificent creature and he would have it. John calmly rode towards the youth.

The rider spun round glaring and in a muffled voice said, 'Who are you and what do you mean sneaking upon me like that?'

'I'm on my way home.'

'There is no track through this part of the forest. No one comes here. You are a long way from wherever it is you are going.'

'Taking a short cut. I'm John Tweddle, on my way back to Wydon Manor, England.'

Isobel had a wry smile to herself. John had not recognised her. She had purposely dressed as a boy in case she was discovered by outlaws. Her new black stallion had been a gift from her father, Thomas, who had acquired it from an Irish horse dealer. O'Leary had brought several dozen ponies and horses over for the common ridings but lost this one gambling with her father, who she knew hoped someone would take it from her, then he could, with justification, go on the Hot Trod to get it back and perhaps acquire other livestock as well. Her father was a calculating man who only thought of himself. Michael O'Leary had not come across Thomas Elliott before and knew nothing of his reputation as a cheat and a swindler. He had lost two mares to her father and this stallion, that had been on its way to a racehorse trainer on the east coast. Some money had already changed hands for the horse and O'Leary had since disappeared. Isobel, being an excellent horse woman, had begged her father for him. She had spent weeks training him, hoping to prove she was worthy of the horse. Thomas said it would be part of her dowry and, if that was to John Tweddle, she would be quite pleased.

Isobel looked at John and her heart melted. He looked tired and beaten. But what was he doing here so far from Wydon and by himself? Perhaps others were behind him. She was aware of him watching her. How handsome he was in his armour, although his boots were muddy, clothes torn, and his horse's legs were covered in dirt and moss. She thought he must have been in a fight and felt concerned that he was alright, but she was annoyed she was being spied on and decided to have some fun. For once she would have the advantage. This time he would not be rescuing her from the devious robber, Ridley. This time he was the spy.

To disguise her voice further she pulled her scarf up over her mouth, 'Are you on your own?'

'Yes, my men took the long way round?'

'I don't believe you. I suspect you're spying on me. You want my horse and intend to flee through the forest with him.'

John came closer and she became afraid he would recognise her, although part of her wanted him to. She quickly pulled her horse back out of his reach, 'Where have you really come from?'

'You ask a lot of questions for one so young,' John pushed his horse next to hers. He bent down, grabbed her reins and pulled her towards him. Then he leaned across, pulled her scarf down and kissed her fiercely on the lips. He met no resistance.

Isobel pulled herself upright and her helmet fell off, releasing her long blond hair. As she put her hand up to sweep it back, John gasped, with both shock and delight at the same time. His eyes opened wide. Shocked and astonished, he blurted, 'Isobel, it's you. I knew you were a girl. What are you doing here?'

'I could ask you the same question, John Tweddle. You are a spy.'

'No, I'm not.'

Isobel, shaking, took a deep breath. She had been discovered and went on the attack.

'What are you doing here?' she said, tightening her grip on the reins.

'I've already told you that.'

'John, you didn't know who I was when you accosted me.'

He smiled, 'I thought you were a handsome lass in disguise. So, Isobel, let's talk about the horse. Where did you get it from?'

'Don't change the subject,' she was beginning to feel angry, suddenly realising what had happened. 'You bent over and kissed me, not knowing who I was.'

'Handsome lass.' His smile widened.

'I trusted you, John Tweddle! You have betrayed me.'

'I have not. I want you and when I HAVE YOU, I'll have the horse as well.' He began to laugh.

'So that's your game, isn't it? You're like all men, only wanting me for what I have. Well, I've changed my mind, I won't marry you! I don't love you AND you will never get my horse!' She threw her riding whip at him, narrowly missing his left eye.

John dismounted and came towards her smiling, laughing. She quickly pulled the stallion away from him and, with one swift kick, she was off. It happened so fast John was taken by surprise.

'I will have you both, you little witch, Isobel, I will have you both!' he shouted after her, but his words were lost on the wind.

Isobel was racing through the fields. She had given the stallion its head and was struggling to hold him at full gallop. Perhaps he was too strong for her after all. She felt bewildered. Her hair was blowing across her face while floods of tears blurred her vision. What was he really doing on the moor? Did he steal every horse he wanted? Would he have molested any lass or even killed for the horse? All she knew for sure was that she loved him.

*

John watched her go, his heart pounding as if he had been in danger. Isobel was strong minded and willful. He could not help himself loving her, she bewitched him. But Isobel had seen a side of him that he would have preferred she hadn't seen. Would he have killed the lad or lass for the horse? Probably. He was angry that he had been found out. Perhaps he had lost her love, and she wouldn't wed him as they had talked about so often. He resigned himself to the thought that the next time they met he would talk her round. He turned his horse and headed for home, his head full of the encounter with the captivating Isobel and wondering when he was going to take her.

It had been a few hours since he had left his father and men to search for the chestnut horse. He was weary and deflated on both counts, the horse and Isobel. He spurred his own tired horse forward and made his way towards Gilsland Gap. Once the returning men and cattle had crossed the Irthing river they would be safely held, up at Thirlwell Castle, for the night. But try as he might, he could not get the thought of Isobel out of his head. It was time the girl was wed.

Chapter 31

Anne felt calm. She had a sense of being outside, walking along a woodland path. The air was fresh from the passing of a rain shower, birds were chattering, and dragonflies were bussing lazily over the bullrushes. A large pond was nearby, and her nostrils were filled with the sweet scent of meadowsweet. On the path in front of her the slight shape of Isobel was slowly coming her way, smiling. Anne felt herself once again being pulled towards the young girl and, as they got closer, the two women merged to become one and a distant disconnected memory came into her thoughts.

*

Isobel, returning from the fishponds at Holmclose Abbey with three trout and a basket full of freshwater cress, had the uneasy feeling of being followed. She quickened her pace, took a sharp left turn past the gnarled oak and darted into a gap between two large moss-covered rocks. Heart pounding, she waited, unsure of when to come out. Above her a twig snapped as the shrill of two blackbirds took to the air and flew from the tree into the bramble bushes across the track. Bleaks Thorpe wood lit up with alarm calls and the air filled with the birds' music. Isobel crouched forward and peered through the leaves. There he was, walking towards her. She shivered, heart throbbing, hands trembling so hard her basket brushed against an overhanging branch and snagged on an outstretched twig. It was him. He had been following her. For the first time in weeks, she wished John was here to save her and kill Robert Ridley once and for all. She wanted him to rid her of this obsessional man, who pursued her so hard. As he came closer the smell of stale ale and his sweaty aroma wafted into her nostrils and her stomach quivered.

'Ah! There you are,' Isobel stood up, head held high, emerged from her hiding place, stooping to pick up some random greenery and continued along the path, trying hard not to break into a run.

'I knew you would be here,' he sneered in his low gravelly voice.

She stopped, tightened her grip on the basket and turned to face him, 'What do you want?'

'I have this little knife. I know it's yours. Found it at the fishponds.' He waved it in front of her, his smirk so wide she wanted to kick him.

Isobel gasped, 'You have been spying on me all day! Give it back you wretch.' She lunged forward to grab the knife.

'Ha! Not so fast little missy Isobel.' He stepped back and held the knife above his head.

Clasping the shawl tightly round her shoulders, arms folded across her chest, feet firmly placed on each side of the path and fighting hard to control her shaking body, she looked him square in the face and yelled, 'You thief, you grotesque, evil, little man, stop spying on me! I hate you! Do you hear me? I hate you!'

Ridley cocked his head on one side and smiled, 'Well, you shouldn't wander so far into the wood, should you?'

'Why can't you leave me alone? Just GO AWAY! And give me that knife back. And do it now!' She pushed her hand forward to get it.

'You know why. I want you and, by God, I shall have you.' He made a grab for her but, at the same moment, heart pounding in her ears with a mixture of fear and anger, she stepped to the side, bent down, quickly picked up two sticks and threw one at him.

'Give it back or you will be sorry!'

Ridley stumbled, regained his footing and laughed, a horrible sound that reverberated through her whole body and made her want to retch. 'Sorry, will I? Don't think so! You're a weed of a girl, standing in that wet dress. It clings so tightly to your body, can't imagine how you can breathe in it, nor trip over, it's so long, just showing your neat little ankles off when you tried to jump over that stream back there, but fell in didn't you. That pretty little shawl doesn't cover much, now does it, you're no match for me, Isobel Elliott.'

The nauseating smell of stinking sweat and dried ale became too much, and she raised the second stick and hit him on the side of his face. Dazed, he stepped back and his hands flew to his head. Isobel grabbed her knife from his belt and ran and ran and ran.

Moments later she paused for breath, hoping she was far enough away to be safe but the loud sound of rustling leaves, on a track to her left, alerted her to his presence. She needed a place to hide. Looking round, an outcrop of rock seemed a good place and she squeezed under its ivy canopy. But the air was quickly filled with sounds of Ridley crashing through the undergrowth and his demented screaming came closer.

'Isobel, I will find you, you entrancing little witch. I know you're playing games.' His voice was so close she could almost touch his words. Her hands were dripping with sweat, legs shaking so much she was struggling to stand. She pushed her basket against a low-lying branch and clung on as hard as she could to stop herself from collapsing. Perhaps this was the end. This time he would get her and take her to hell. There would be no coming back. She crouched under the ivy and prayed to every god she could think of to give her strength and keep her hidden.

Several minutes passed, with only the sound of her own breathing pulsating in her ears to keep her company and then he was upon her, standing, arms outstretched.

'Oh, there you are, Isobel, hiding again?'

Isobel gracefully stepped forward from her hiding place and with the strongest of voices shrieked, 'I am not hiding! Now that I have my knife back, I can collect galls from this oak tree, I have need of more ink!'

He peered into her basket, 'Don't look like you have collected much.'

'I don't need many.' She laid the wasp galls on top of the fish.

Ridley stood breathless but smiling, blocking the path with his arms across his chest. 'On our way home, are we? Think you have taken the wrong path, Missy.'

Isobel said nothing but wondered how he knew that. No one was wiser than her about the paths in this wood. She knew where the animals sheltered and foraged for food, where they laid up for the day and hid from danger. She knew every dell, stream and track. She glared at him, stamping her foot. 'What are you doing here?' knowing full well she already knew.

Isobel straightened her back, stood tall and, taking a breath so deep she feared her lungs might burst, 'Get out of my way!' She squeezed past and pushed her basket of fish into his chest, in the hope it would momentarily disarm him and allow her to escape. But could she run fast enough? It was a long way to safety. He was right, she had wandered too far from home. She was cross with John for taking up so much of her thinking time. He was always in her thoughts. How she missed him and needed him AND right now. The only way to be safe from Ridley would be to run away and marry John.

She decided she would not be able to outrun Ridley, whose limp did not seem to slow him down, nor his baggy cumbersome clothing, that should trip him up with every step he took. Why couldn't he fall head long into the Wood Boggits, who would kill him in an excruciating way and just before death suck out his blood.

Collecting all her courage she stopped, turned to face him, 'Why are you here. What do you want from me?'

'You know I want you. You are mine, Missy. One way or another, I will have you! Stop this silliness. I've had enough of you pretending you don't want me. Get over here.' He made to grab her arm. Isobel took several steps backwards and stamped her foot on the ground over and over again.

'You can't have me. I am going to marry John Tweddle.'

Ridley looked shocked, bent forward and stared straight into her eyes, 'Oh, you are, are you? Well, Missy Isobel, I think not. He's not here now, is he?'

'You wouldn't dare touch me!' Isobel screeched at the top of her voice until her throat felt raw.

'Wouldn't I?' Ridley went to snatch the basket of fish, but it tipped and the fish slid out. Refusing to make a clean exit, they slithered towards him and became trapped in his jerkin. He screamed, threw his arms in the air and jumped back. Isobel stepped forward, slapped him hard across the face, put her hands on his chest and shoved him backwards as hard as she could. Shocked and moaning with pain, he lost his balance, fell and became entangled in a thick pile of brambles.

Seeing her chance, Isobel ran. Stumbling across dead trees, she ran round a long bend where she paused before clambering over piles of woodland debris and dodging low hanging branches. She turned a sharp corner, squeezed between two staggered oak trees and found herself in a quiet glade looking at a small rickety bridge that crossed the meandering Lowick stream.

Isobel gazed at the scene in front of her. Water buttercups bobbed up and down among the smooth rocks and hover flies darted about, fighting with bees for the nectar of the early flowering wild pink geraniums and yellow crested iris, while avoiding the snacking mouths of the many small fish below. A pair of dippers sped upstream.

Looking skywards she caught sight of witch's brooms hanging from the silver birches, their intense weight causing branches to dance in the warm breeze.

She tilted her head and frowned at the trembling aspen leaves. Were they offering a warning? Glancing at the bridge, which was partly obscured by reed mace and tall phragmites, whose roots she ground and boiled to make flour, she saw a small gateway.

Isobel raced forward, grabbed the damp fence post and jumped onto the bridge. She skidded on the mossy wooden planks, hit a weak top rail which gave way under her weight and together they fell into the stream below. She landed on her side with her face resting on a flat, protruding stone and her legs straddling a mossy outcrop. The warm nurturing flow of the water reassured her that she was alive, and she softly sank into Lowick's supportive kindness.

Everything became peaceful and empty. A bright light glided towards her and through the sound of the gurgling water a soothing voice called.'

'Hello.'

'Hello, who are you?'

'I am a Naiad.'

'A Naiad?'

'Yes, a freshwater spirit.' A small bubble of water bathed Isobel's face, 'I have a message for you.'

'A message?'

'I am here to help you. Beware of your killer.' The surface of the water grumbled as if alarmed.

'My killer, my killer?'

'I am sorry, but he will come for you. He will not give up.'

Isobel became aware of the hammering in her head.

'It is your destiny, there is nothing you can do.'

'Who is coming for me? Who?' Inwardly she began to scream, not wanting to believe it yet part of her knew it was true.

'You already know him.'

'Robert Ridley, that filthy, grotesque, little worm, Robert Ridley. Why have you come to tell me if there is nothing I can do?' The water bubbled and snorted into her face.

'I come to tell you to take a risk, enjoy what you have now, he will come.'

'You are frightening me.' She shivered as another cold blast drenched her face.

'Do not be afraid, it is your destiny.' The voice faded, the water settled, and she began to feel cold; the warm sun hid behind the dappled clouds and the day darkened.

Then a distant voice called, 'Isobel, Isobel wake up. Wake up.' The strong arms of a man, who had a familiar scent on his clothes, lifted her wet, little body out of the stream and laid her gently on the grassy bank. The man cradled her in his arms, held her tightly against his chest and rubbed her cold legs. She slowly opened her eyes and looked into the face of John Tweddle.

'Isobel are you alright? What are you doing here? You're all wet and filthy. I couldn't find you. Where were you?'

'I don't know! something strange happened.'

'Something strange?'

'Yes, I was running through the wood, then the trees parted, and I found myself near Lowick stream and… Oh! John, it was so beautiful. Then a voice spoke to me.'

John frowned and pulled her closer to him, 'A voice. What do you mean? You have hit your head and it's bleeding. We need to wipe it. Be still.' John wiped her head with the bottom of her soaked tunic.

'I fell, I ran onto the bridge and the rail gave way and I fell. Oh, John, I fell, hit my head and …' Isobel cried with a mixture of relief and happiness. 'But what are you doing here?'

'I was coming to take you back to Wydon. No more hiding and secret meetings. I love you and am taking you to Wydon Manor. We're going to be wed.' He squeezed her so hard she gasped, then smiled, curled an arm round his neck, lifted her mouth to meet his and kissed him fiercely on the lips.

'Oh, John, I am so glad to see you!' As her wet arms clung to his body, she sensed all would be well. Suddenly, regaining her senses, Isobel sat bolt upright, brushed the straggly hair from her face, 'John, how did you find me?'

'Old man Johnson saw you leave this morning. He'd asked you to bring back some fish for his supper from the monks' ponds at the abbey, so I knew where you'd gone. He was concerned you hadn't returned so I came to look for you.' John paused to scan the surrounding woodland.

'Isobel where are the fish? Your basket? This isn't the path you would return home on. I have been looking everywhere for you. I know these paths, Isobel, as well as you do. What are you doing here and where are the fish?'

Isobel pushed John away, scrambled to her feet clasped her head and screamed, 'MY BASKET!' The memory of what had happened began to flood back. 'He was here, that loathsome creature, Robert Ridley! He was here, John, he was here! Spying on me.'

'He was here?' John stood up emptied the water out of his leather boots, adjusted his clothing and, taking a firm hold of her arm, 'He was here, Isobel?'

'Yes, following me.'

John spat on the ground and cursed. 'Where is that evil little bastard now?'

'I don't know! I fled! I slapped his face and pushed him away and ran but when I got to the stream I slipped on some mossy wood and then you found me. I don't know how long I have been here.'

John kicked at the pile of debris in front of him, cracked his fingers and let out a long guttural roar. 'This time I am going to kill him,' and he set off at a great pace down the track.

'Wait! I'm coming with you, John. You don't know where he is. I left him by the rock outcrop, the one that is opposite the coppiced hazel. Wait, John. Wait, please wait.'

'I know the one,' he bellowed back.

Isobel broke into a run to catch him up, pausing every few yards to put her hands over her ears as John yelled. 'Robert Ridley where are you, you miserable bastard?' Isobel's heart was beating fast inside her chest. She had never seen him so angry.

'RIDLEY! I am going to kill you when I find you! You miserable, evil boy! Do you hear me? BOY! Yes, I said BOY because that's what you are! … NOT A MAN!

I am going to thrash you to within an inch of your life and cut every limb from your worthless body! RIDLEY WHERE ARE YOU!'

*

Robert, hearing the shouting and recognising the voice of John Tweddle, stopped, turned and fled back the way he had come. His original plan had been to take a short cut past the crumbling barns and catch Isobel as she approached the edge of the wood. But he had been slowed down by a large swathe of thorns and ivy strewn across his path and had lost sight of her. Running for his life, his head consumed with thoughts of escape he did not see until too late, John Tweddle and Isobel Elliott standing on a nearby path several yards in front of him, John Tweddle and Isobel Elliott. He slithered to a halt. Not being a brave man and knowing of John's reputation for fighting and dismembering bodies, he feared his time was up. He knew he was a coward. Chasing Isobel, a weak, pathetic woman was one thing but fighting John Tweddle was quite another. With his heart racing and head throbbing his best option was to run. He remembered where he had left his horse and made straight for it.

'John, look over there.' Isobel pointed to a figure running through the trees ahead of them. 'He's a good way ahead, John.'

'I can see you! Evil little bastard! I am coming! DO YOU HEAR ME RIDLEY? I am coming for you!' Minutes later John had closed the gap and, within seconds, fell upon Ridley. He grabbed his coat and grappled him to the ground. Both men rolled around in the undergrowth, kicking and punching each other. John managed to pin one of Ridley's arms to the ground, bent over and bit off his left ear. Ridley screamed with pain, tried with his free hand to clasp his bloodied ear and at the same time free his trapped short leg from under John's body. John continued to pound Ridley's face. Ridley, panicking that he was done for, slipped his right hand down his leg into his boot and retrieved a knife. He clasped it firmly in his hand and, with a huge intake of breath, stabbed John in his thigh. John screamed in pain, released his hold and, clutching his bleeding thigh, rolled off Ridley just far enough to release the leg. Ridley took his chance, crawled to his feet, tried to wipe the blood from his eyes, hobbled to his horse, untied the bridle and, without waiting to put his foot in the stirrup, lunged at the saddle and immediately fell back onto the ground. The horse, startled, trotted off.

'Come here you stupid animal, get back here!' He stumbled to his feet and, staggering forward, went in search of his horse who had not gone far and was soon caught. Blood was pouring from his nose and lost ear and both eyes were struggling to see clearly. He put his foot in the stirrup, hauled himself onto the saddle, kicked the horse's flank and set off at top speed in fear for his life.

A few miles further on he waded into the middle of Williamsock river and checked he was not being followed. He dismounted and bathed his exposed fleshy ear, while screaming at the landscape over and over again.

'SHE WILL PAY FOR THIS! SHE WILL! THAT EVIL WITCH WILL PAY FOR THIS! DO YOU HEAR ME, ISOBEL ELLIOTT?'

But Ridley knew John was a fearsome opponent and Isobel's father, Thomas Elliott, had an old score to settle and could use this latest incident with Isobel to come for him. Ridley knew that the Tweddle's and Elliott's, both saw him as an outlaw and more so after he had heard of their plans for a raid on Hexham Abbey and warned a warden of the forthcoming raid. Eleven men had died in the skirmish. Silver and religious relics had been stolen, two horses killed, and the families had been pursued for several months to satisfy justice. The relics were never found but the weight of coins in his pocket made up for any guilt. It was always an easy way to make money.

He was an outcast and knew it. Isobel had got the better of him again but being thwarted only made him stronger and more determined to take his revenge. He pulled a cloth from under his saddle, took a chunk of stale bread out of his pocket, soaked it in the water, wrung it out and clamped it as hard as he could on his gushing ear. Putting one hand on the horse's mane, he pulled himself onto its back, waded out of the water, got back onto the track and set off in the hope of finding a healer to help him. He headed west to the Debatable Lands where he had a juicy piece of information to sell to anyone willing to pay and, pay they would the mood he was in. Tales had reached him of some of the Queen's gold treasury moving in small carts on its way south from Edinburgh but taking the back roads to avoid robbers on the main highways between the two countries. His cousin Alan Ridley was privy to the Scottish Middle March Warden and had overheard the plans for moving the wealth. Valuable information indeed.

Chapter 32

John lay on the ground clutching his thigh. Blood was slowly trickling down his leg to settle in a warm puddle inside his boot. He opened his mouth and screamed, 'I'll get you for this Ridley! ... DO YOU HEAR ME? I AM COMING FOR YOU! THIS IS NOT OVER!'

'John, please be quiet. Lie still. Let me have a closer look. John, please! Please be still. Let me do my work.' Isobel took the knife from her wet pocket, cut away his clothing and gently examined the wounds.

'It's alright, John, the gash isn't deep. I can stitch it but, please, be still. The other wounds are small and will heal easily.' Isobel took her healing bag from her shoulder and began rummaging. It was made from linen and had survived the water quite well and most of the contents were still dry. It was lined with green felted wool to stop bottles from clattering into each other and breaking if she fell. The healing herbs were all wrapped in neat little bunches, plaited with a nettle cord. There was a small bowl, measuring spoon and a short thick stick used for crushing and mixing. Her small precious recipe book nestled comfortably in a large front pocket, kept separate in case anything broke and spilled. A small purse sat behind the book with a few coins inside. Torn bundles of linen, carefully wrapped, padded the bottles even more. It was for this she searched; bandages, cleansing liquid but most of all her needle case and accompanying thread.

Lie still, John, don't move.' Isobel took out her bottle of liquid comfrey and cleansed the raw opening. 'The wound is a long gash but it's not deep. I'll be able to stitch it but, please, be still. I can see it's painful. I'll be as quick as I can.' She looked round for a short green stick and put it in between his teeth lest his yelling would alert Ridley that all was not well, and he may return.

'Here, John, bite down on this. It will help with the pain.' John rolled his eyes and shuddered, in pain or embarrassment, she wasn't sure which. The wound was quickly stitched, needle cleaned and bag carefully repacked. She tidied his clothing, bent down and put her arms under his shoulders, 'Can you stand John?' He winced and grabbed the tree trunk.

'I think so.'

'The light is fading. We need to get away. Ridley may be back soon and this time he could have others with him.'

John's rage returned, 'I'll kill him! I'll kill him! Next time! Next time! DO YOU HEAR ME, RIDLEY? I AM COMING FOR YOU!' He slumped against the tree. Isobel looked round for a long wooden staff.

'Here, John, lean on this.' She pushed the waist length stick into his right hand. Together they began the long, arduous walk back through the wood to collect John's horse and continue to Isobel's home. By now it was getting quite dark. The full moon peered through the clouds, guiding them along the woodland paths. At last, the outline of the stables and outbuildings of Isobel's home came into view.

'Look, John, I can see a light.'

'Who's there?' Came the sound of her mother's voice as she emerged from the shadows with a lantern.

'It's me, Isobel, and I have John with me. He's injured. I need some help.'

Elinor raised her voice, 'Don't bring him in here! Leave him to die. I have told you before to have nothing to do with him. He's a murderer!'

Isobel's eyes filled with tears, 'No, Mam. What are you saying? He's injured! I have stitched his wound, but it needs looking at and he rescued me from......... MAM! Listen to me! MAM!'

'Leave him or I will set the dogs on him! Tearing him apart is too good for him! Killing my Margaret!'

Isobel sighed and screamed back at her mother, 'HE DID NOT KILL MARGARET!'

'Come here Girl, it's time you were indoors!' Elinor stormed back into the house.

But Isobel had no intention of leaving John. Together they hobbled through the open stable door. She wedged him between the wall and the door, climbed the ladder to the loft and threw down armfuls of hay to make him a bed.

'Here, John, let me help you lie down. Stay here and I will fetch you some food.'

John winced as he kicked the door with his good foot. 'Damn the woman! Your mother is becoming more of a problem each time I see her. It's time you left here, Isobel. Go and pack your things. We are leaving here tonight. How dare she refuse me hospitality? It is not the Border way.' and he kicked the wall repeatedly, which only aggravated the pain in his thigh.

'My mother doesn't like you, John. She never has and would never let me marry you.'

'Well, I will have to kidnap you then, won't I? That's why I came ...remember?' A weak but wicked smile crossed his face as he pulled her down to lie beside him.

Isobel smiled, lifted her hand and stroked his cheek, 'Oh John, I do love you so. You are so dirty John Tweddle!'

'Well, I am not the only one, but you are wet as well as dirty.' They both laughed.

'John, be serious. Do you really think I could leave here and come away with you to Wydon?'

'Why not? There is no life here for you. Your mother tries to control you. Ridley is often sneaking about. You are not safe here anymore. And I want you. 'He cupped her face in his hands and kissed her.

'What about my father?'

John sighed 'He will be glad of the union; more land, a strong alliance with the powerful Tweddle family.'

'My mother blames you for Margaret's death.'

'I know but I arrived after she was dead.'

'Yes, but if you had arrived sooner, she would still be alive.'

'Maybe, maybe not. But I saved you though, my beautiful Isobel, didn't I?' His fingers played with a strand of her hair as she nuzzled her head into his shoulder. It felt safe and warm. This was where she wanted to be, with John. After a few moments she sat up with a start.

'John, I will come with you! I am afraid of Robert Ridley. That sneaky, little, disfigured creep is everywhere I go. Why no one has killed him I don't understand.'

'I will kill him! Have no doubt about that. He is an outlaw right enough. Plies his trade of stalking, spying and selling information, gnarled wretch of a man. Men like him have their uses in times of war and that is how he survives.'

'Well, we do live in turbulent times. I will go and pack my things and be back as soon as I can.'

John put his hand on her arm, 'Isobel, will your mother let you go?'

'She can't stop me. I love you and want to be with you. I am coming with you to England. Here, John, try to stand and find some strength to saddle Molly and a couple of ponies to carry my things and some food.'

'And the black stallion? What of him? You know I want him!' Isobel smiled and John's eyes followed the line of her finger to where the horse stood, tied to a rail.

'I will have to leave him, for now anyway. He's sensitive and shies when extra things are thrown on his back. He won't carry anything and will make a lot of noise. The stable boys will be alerted.

'One day, Isobel, that horse will be mine.'

'Yes, John, of course, he will be yours.' She frowned, then grinned.

'How long will you be?' It had been a long difficult day and John's eyes were struggling to stay open and he was beginning to yawn.'

'Quick as I can. You will wait, won't you?' Isobel helped him to his feet.

'You know I will.' He took her in his arms and kissed her with so much longing that her knees weakened. Eventually she pulled herself away from him, and floated to the stable door, where she paused for a moment to breathe in the cool evening air, before quickly returning to her senses and quietly making her way across the cobbled yard to the kitchen door. Her head was full of thoughts of what to pack, how much she could carry, and should she leave a note for her father.

John's leg was painful but bearable to stand on. He shuffled round the stable and after several minutes the horses were saddled and bridled. He paused for a moment to rest and, as he leaned against the stable gate and put his hand out to steady himself, he slid down the nearby wall, landing in a soft pile of welcoming hay and, within minutes, was asleep.

Isobel lifted the sneck and opened the kitchen door. All was quiet. The servants had gone to bed. The dogs were curled up asleep in front of the fire. They lifted their heads, recognised Isobel, gave a slow flicker of tails in welcome, before returning to their slumbers. She crept along the back hall and slowly up the stone stairs, being careful her feet made no noise on the middle three steps, which were badly worn, and loose stones often came out and rattled down to the bottom. Reaching her room, she carefully lifted the latch, opened the door and stepped inside, silently closing it behind her.

It was dark except for the moon, which gently created a long shaft of light through the window, just enough to help her find what she needed to pack.

Isobel wondered if she might miss her life at Middle Moor. Life in England would be different. Would the Tweddles accept her? Her magical places to collect herbs and plants would be lost; the caves with secret hiding places, the woods and all the tracks she had known since childhood, the people, the monastery fishponds, her mother.

She paused at the thought of her mother. It was time to spread her wings and fly. To leave her mother's world and find out about John's at Wydon. Her heart pounded at the thought of him. She must hurry, he would be waiting, and they needed to be well on their way before dawn and discovery. From under the bed, she pulled out a brown bag, a present from her father after one of his raids up country many years ago. It must have belonged to a rich woman as the leather was good quality and the stitching was in two colours. A pretty, embroidered clasp fastened the handle. She changed out of her wet things and packed a few clothes, herbal book, paper, writing materials, spare boots, hair ornaments and some treasured soap she had kept for a special occasion. Her precious little box of memories was pushed into a side pocket. Other small bits were added. Glancing round the room she was satisfied she had everything important. She would collect her healing bag, and treasured box from the kitchen rafters when she left along with some potions and food from the kitchen.

Something drew her attention to the window. A Tawny Owl had landed on the sill, its chestnut brown feathers dancing in the moonlight. It opened a wing and turned its head as if pointing but, as she walked forward to touch the magic of the owl, it flew away.

Isobel's eyes filled with tears as she looked out for the last time at the distant hills in front of her. They reflected how she felt, trapped in a wilderness of loneliness that rolled far beyond the skyline. But on the far side lay the English Border lands and Wydon. John had told her so much about England she was eager to get there and start a new life in a new country. She smiled, lifted her hands to her lips and blew a gentle kiss out into the landscape.

'Goodbye hills that I love so much.' Isobel sighed, turned, and saw a dark figure standing silhouetted in the doorway.

'Where do you think you are going, Isobel Elliott?'

It was Elinor, her mother, who stood in the doorway, arms sternly folded across her chest. Isobel, startled, jumped backwards hitting the wall.

'I can hear the opening and closing of drawers, the rustling of belongings and a bag being dragged from under the bed across the floor. What are you doing, girl?'

Isobel took a quick intake of breath, puffed her chest out as best she could, opened her mouth and tried to sound forceful, 'I am going to Wydon, to England with John.' But she could feel her legs wobbling and suddenly she felt afraid because the anger in her mother's voice told her escaping was not going to be easy.

'No, you are not! You are staying here!' Her voice dropped to a low growl.

'I love him. I want a different life. I want to see England. I AM GOING!'

Elinor paused, put her hands on her hips, 'Plenty time for that when you are old enough to join raiding parties.'

'I am old enough.' Isobel thumped the bed as she continued her furious packing.

'You are not going anywhere with John Tweddle. I will see to that. Do you hear me, Isobel? YOU ARE NOT GOING WITH HIM!' Even in the half-light Isobel could see her mother's red face, as if it would burst at any moment.

'I am. I love him!' She stamped her foot on the floor, fastened her bag, picked it up and stood facing her mother.

'No Isobel. Your father has other plans for you.'

Isobel looked defiantly at her mother, 'Well, they're not my plans! He's already tried to marry me off twice and that didn't work. I was old enough then to marry, wasn't I? So why not now?'

Elinor flattened her lips, cracked her knuckles. 'John Tweddle is from a bad family of thieves, murderers, burners of property…'

'Stop it, stop it!' interrupted Isobel. She dropped her bag and glared at her mother. Sweat pouring through her clammy fingers and head hammering, she began to shout. 'SO ARE WE! We are no different from them or any of the other Border families! That's how we ALL live, or have you forgotten that?'

Her mother softened her voice. 'Isobel, do you remember the stories your grandfather told you about the Tweddles and how they got to Wydon?'

Isobel's breath became unsteady, and words tumbled out of her mouth, 'Yes, I do! I do! I remember everything. But, but how did we get to Middle Moor? The same way. We are all the same. This is how we survive!' She stood facing her mother, heart pounding and eyes flashing in defiance.

Elinor lifted her head, flared her nostrils and glared at her daughter. 'No, Isobel! You are not going! I will lock you up first!'

'He is waiting for me. Please let me go. I love him. Please, please don't lock me up.'

Elinor shook her head, 'Foolish girl. You have no idea about love, not true love.'

'Why do you hate him so much? It's about Margaret, isn't it? He couldn't have saved her, Mam. He arrived too late. Please, please understand that I beg you. It wasn't John's fault.'

Elinor put her hands on her hips, 'He managed to save you though, didn't he?'

Isobel winced, 'What are you saying? What are you trying to tell me? Do I not matter? I am alive. Does that mean nothing to you? I am here!' She dropped her bag on the floor, grabbed her mother's hand and put it on her beating heart. 'Here, feel my pounding heart. I AM HERE! I AM ALIVE! My sister was already dead when John arrived. I tried to get back to her, but I couldn't!' Isobel dissolved into floods of tears. Elinor, unmoved by this display of emotion, removed her hand.

'Margaret is dead and with her my hopes and dreams. I have been left with you, the pretty day dreamer who has brought nothing but trouble. Men are always chasing after you, demanding you in exchange for your father's misdeeds.'

Isobel gasped, 'Do you not love me at all? I know you are jealous of my abilities to heal, which are greater than yours. Is that why you hate me so much?'

Elinor stamped her feet on the floor rattling the floorboards, 'How dare you talk to me like that! You think because you are young and beautiful and have the power to enrapture men simply by looking at them, that I am like your father and brothers and will give in to your whims and fancies. Well, my girl, let me tell you, this time you will do as you are told!'

Isobel cleared her throat and raised her voice, 'You can't make me! I am going away with John! We are going to be wed!' She tossed her head in the air and turned back to the bed to pick up her bags.

'I'll tell you another thing, young lady, that black stallion you were given was mine not yours! It had been promised to me. You stole it from me, and I shall have it back!'

'No, you will not, father gave it to me!' Isobel was struggling to understand this onslaught of rage coming from her mother's lips. 'You are jealous that's what you are. People love me... all except you. Why, Mam, why? What have I ever done to you? Let me go and have my own life... please...please.' She fell on her knees, grabbed her mother's skirt and sobbed and sobbed.

Elinor prised her hands off and hauled Isobel to her feet. 'You get too much of your own way. Well, this time you are going to do as you're told and do what I tell you! You are not going with him!'

'Isobel began to scream, 'I am! I am! I love him! I am not going to lose him! It would be unbearable.' Fists flying, she hurled herself at her mother.

Elinor grabbed Isobel's hands and pushed her away, before carefully stepping back through the bedroom door, slamming it hard shut, dropping the latch and turning the key.

Isobel ran to the door, frantically rattling the latch up and down and kicking the wooden frame. Nothing moved and, after several exhausting minutes, she stopped and slithered to the floor, where she lay crumpled in a heap of weeping frustration. Her fists pounded the floor. There was nothing else she could do. She suspected the house was empty apart from herself, the servants and her mother, who would have given them instructions not to let her out no matter how much she screamed. The dogs had stopped barking, and she could not hear any voices.

After a while Isobel sat up, slumped against the door frame and dried her tears. No one was coming to help her. She struggled to her feet and rattled and rattled the latch until her fingers began to bleed. 'LET ME OUT! LET ME OUT!' Isobel kicked the loose wooden rail on the bottom of the door, hoping against hope it would clatter off and let her crawl under and get out onto the landing. It was a desperate idea. She knew it would be too narrow to crawl through but that did not stop her kicking it. Her rage knew no boundaries as she flung herself on the bed and started to tear the bedding up in a frenzied attack which was occasionally interrupted by running across the room from window to wall, hoping against all hope that some magical door would open and set her free. Eventually physical exhaustion took over and she fell on the bed and was quickly asleep. It had been a very long, frightening day.

The dawn light peeped through the window. Isobel woke up, shivering. It was cold. She could hear the sounds of the house at the start of the day. Her eyes were stuck together with the tears of the night before. The blood on her fingers had dried but they did their best to tease the tangled hair from her face and clear her vision. She lay on the bed and gazed at the ripped bedclothes strewn across the floor.

As memories of the previous night circled her thoughts, she was wondering what to do. She had to get out. She remembered the owl on the windowsill. Why had it been there? Perhaps it was a sign, showing her a way out? The window was big enough to get through. The only problem was the height from the ground. As a child she had spent many happy hours climbing trees but the branch outside the window in her childhood had withered and died. Isobel sighed with the hopelessness of it all. Her chest tightened. She was trapped. There really was no way out except through the door. But the owl had come to her for a reason, if only she knew what it was.

She returned to the window and gazed onto the landscape beyond, waiting for a sign. The sound of rumbling cartwheels on the cobbles drew her attention to the lane. She saw her mother leave the house carrying large, heavy bags. Elinor stood waiting for the horse and cart to stop. A man stepped down. Isobel thought she recognised him as Elphin, the Bard. Elinor smiled at him. He put his arm around her, bent down, gave her a kiss on the lips, picked up her and her bags and off they drove.

Isobel, seizing her chance to escape, rushed to the door and shook it hard but it was still locked. Then a tuneless singing voice alerted her to look outside. Running back to the window, she saw Millie, the house maid, walking across the moat bridge. 'Millie! Millie!' she shouted, trying hard not to sound hysterical. The plain, dull-faced girl looked up.

'Hello, Miss Isobel.'

'Millie, Millie, I need some help.'

'Help?' she said, not being the brightest of girls.

'Yes, Millie, help.' Isobel paused. Millie would be cautious of making Elinor angry and would not want another thrashing. Isobel lowered her voice and tried as best she could to sound kind.

'Millie, I think my door is stuck. Can you come and help me?'

'Stuck, Miss? What do you mean stuck?'

'I think the latch is stuck. It's stiff and I can't open the door. Please come and help. I have important calls to make today.' Dim-witted Millie stood, staring up at the window, looking confused and Isobel's fears increased that she would not come.

'Millie, would you please put that bucket down, stop what you are doing and get up here now. Please, Millie.'

Several minutes passed and nothing happened so Isobel raised her voice, 'Millie, get up here at once. Do you hear me? NOW! AT ONCE or I'll thrash you so you can't stand anymore, and you'll get no food for a week.'

No rabbit stew for a week seemed to move Millie into action. Dropping her bucket, she waddled her plump little body back across the bridge, into the kitchen, along the back hall and up the stairs to Isobel's room.

Isobel, heart throbbing and fearful Millie would see the door was locked with a key and ask why, 'Millie are you there?'

'Yes, Miss Isobel, I'm here.'

'Good. Now lift the latch and push.'

'It won't move, Miss.'

'Ah Millie the key must be stuck. Can you see it? It's under the latch. It's black, a black key, Millie,' Isobel took a deep breath.

'The key Miss?'

'Yes, Millie, the key. Can you turn the key and lift the latch at the same time?'

'What time?'

Isobel's panic was growing. First with the thought she would never get out of this room and then, that this stupid girl could not turn the key, 'Millie, you turn the key, and I will move the latch from this side. Have you understood what I want you to do?'

'Yes. Alright, Miss, I understand.'

'Alright, Millie, I am going to count to three and we will do this together. Ready…ONE, TWO, THREE,' and with one united movement, CLICK, the door opened, and Isobel stumbled out.

'Oh! Thank you, Millie, thank you! I am so glad you were here to help.' She flung her arms round the confused girl. Millie hugged Isobel, looking like she had no idea what had just happened. 'Now, Millie, tell me where has my mother gone.'

'Gone with Elphin the Bard.'

'Yes, but where has she gone?"

'To Carlisle and the Solway. Folks there have some new disease and people can't breathe.'

'Can't breathe?'

'Black spots and evil things coming out of their mouths.' She contorted her face so much it made her cough. Isobel realised she should not have asked for more information.

'When will she be coming back?'

'Don't know. But she made me pack her night things and that special bag she takes when she goes off with that man.' Millie lowered her head and flushed.

'So, she is not back tonight?' Isobel nodded her head and smiled.

'No.'

'Thank you, Millie. Thank you. You may go now.'

After another quick, grateful hug, she went back into the room and picked up her leather bag. She ran downstairs, paused for a few seconds to collect her healing bag, box of treasures, refill little bottles and untie some plants that had been left to dry over the fire. Then she ran out of the house, across the yard to the stables where she had left John hours before, hoping against hope he was still there.

Did he love her enough to wait and know that something or somebody must have stopped her return? With one hand clutching her chest, she gently pushed open the stable door, then let out a sigh of relief as she saw John lying on the bed of hay, with his clothes disheveled and one leg trapped under the other. She paused, gazed lovingly at this man she was about to run away with, then wondered why he wasn't moving.

'JOHN. JOHN.' She dropped the bags, rushed over to him, put an ear to his nose and felt relieved, he was breathing. 'John wake up. It's going to be light soon, the sun is rising. We must flee. Millie may tell. John wake up. Wake up.' She began shaking him. He awoke with a start, staggered to his feet, swayed, lost his balance and fell into the stable door.

'John, John are you alright. You've slept all night. It's morning and we must go.'

'I fell asleep waiting for you. I am stiff. My leg aches, Isobel.'

'Here let me look. Your wound probably needs cleaning.' She opened her bag and inspected her stitching.

'It's alright, John. Healed well overnight. The sleep has done it good but, come, we must go.' As she helped him to his feet he yawned, stretched his arms up and caught her round the waist and planted a huge kiss on her lips. She stifled a giggle and pushed him away.

'John, no. No time for that now. We must hurry.' She took his arm and led him outside where he took a long breath of fresh air and quickly regained his composure. Picking up her bags they crept to where only a few hours earlier he had left the saddled horses. The animals were untied and walked as quietly as possible out of the stable, across the cobbled yard, through the outer courtyard and onto the grassy lane. Isobel, relieved and glad the dogs had made no fuss arousing the servants, mounted quietly and together they walked further down the track until she felt safe. John gave her horse a hard slap on the rump, which startled the animal into a canter and soon they were fleeing for their lives, from the wrath of Elinor Elliott and the probable anger of her father, Thomas.

By midday, John stopped at a shieling on the far side of Knackerby's wood. 'We need to stop to rest the horses.'

Isobel turned in the saddle to look back along the track, 'I don't think we are being followed. Where are we?' She slid off her horse and landed with a slow thud on the soft earth. 'I am so stiff after all these hours in the saddle. I think we should rest here John; I'll change the dressing on your leg.'

John stepped forward, put his arm round her waist to steady her. 'Come, Isobel, let's get you inside. You feel cold and the weather is turning foul. There is usually some dry wood in here. We can light a fire; get you warmed up and find something to eat.' Isobel gave him a halfhearted smile; John was in charge, and she had no idea where she was.

'First, I need to look at your leg. Sit down, lean against that wall.' She took out her healing bag and cleaned up his wound.

'It's clean and seems to be healing well. Oh, John I am exhausted.' She slumped onto the floor beside him, put her head on his shoulder and they were soon both asleep. Sometime later Isobel woke with a start.

'Have you got any food with you?' she asked.

'Isobel, I don't like being questioned. Where is the food you went into the kitchen for?'

She spun round, eyes flaring, 'What did you say? It isn't my fault we have no food. I was locked in I…I…I.'

John stood up, held his aching leg and went outside to search through his saddle bag. Returning with a lumpy cloth, 'Here it's cheese and bread I packed a few days ago when I set off to find you. There's not much of it.' She took it eagerly, opened the cloth and it was soon gone.

'Thank you, John. It was good. I feel so much better.' She threw her arms tightly round him, humming a happy little tune of contentment.

'I do love you, John, and I am glad I have left.' Standing in the doorway she lifted her arms skywards and shouted, 'ENGLAND I AM COMING!'

She reached up to kiss him, but he held her at arm's length. 'We must go. It is not safe here.' He pushed her away, looking as if he was not able to trust himself being so close to her, 'Leave the fire, the wood is too damp to light. Mount up, Isobel, we will go.'

As she closed the door her eyes caught sight of arrowheads etched into the lintel and she knew it to be where reivers rested.

Their journey continued through smaller settlements and outlying farms. Isobel was very tired after yesterday's events and the frightening night's encounters with her mother. She slouched in the saddle half asleep and slipped forward causing the horse to shy. She slid to the ground, rolled down a grassy bank into the steep sided Brothers Tarn and began to sink.

'John, John I am sinking!' she screamed. He turned to look over his shoulder, jumped off his horse, skidded down the bank and tried to grab her arm to stop it flailing about as her body desperately tried to stay upright.

'Stop struggling, Isobel, or you will sink further. Wait, try and be still. I will fetch something to pull you out.'

'John, I'm sinking, I'm sinking. My feet are stuck in heavy mud and it's slippery. It's pulling me down. John, help! Help!' She reached forward to catch a small overhanging branch and managed to pull herself closer to the bank side before it broke free from its roots and floated serenely away. John wrenched several large, rooted heather plants from the ground, rushed back and held them over the tarn bank side. Panic had set in, and Isobel started screaming even more.

'John, John, get me out of here! I'm so cold! Cold and I'm sinking, John …....'

'Here take hold of this heather. Put both hands on it and I'll pull you out. Isobel, wake up, you are starting to fall asleep. Fight it, Isobel. Fight it. Listen to my voice. Look at me. Get hold of these roots. ISOBEL! Listen to me! I will get you out, but you must grab hold of these roots.'

Several minutes of thrashing about passed without any change. John shouted, 'Isobel, grab hold, I am not going to lose you now.' He leaned over the steep edge, grabbed a cold hand and pulled a wet, smelly Isobel to safety. He pulled his cloak around her and sat, cradling her in his arms, gently rubbing her back.

John sighed, 'I'm grateful you're alive.' Her eyes opened and a glimmer of a smile passed her lips. She laughed, lifted her arms and placed them around his neck and, as they clung to each other, she knew this was the beginning of adventure and life with John. There would be no turning back. John smiled,

'Isobel, this is the second or third time I have rescued you from water. I shall have to watch you very carefully on the moors. For God's sake make it the last time.'

Isobel smiled but her attention was drawn to the lords and ladies flower half hidden behind a mossy rock. She smiled as she looked at the large glossy leaves as they were emerging from their sheath-like leaf, blotched and black. 'Look John, look at the inside of this plant it carries the potential union of male and female flowers and represents a meeting of minds, harmony and union with the person you love. 'Isobel sighed and looked at him, 'John my mother is a dangerous person.'

'I always liked your mother. She is a good healer. Not as good as you, of course.' He squeezed her body closer to him.

'She has a dark side and sometimes I am afraid of her. I know I am a powerful healer, but I do not know much about cursing and that frightens me.'

'Cursing?'

'Yes. I heard her talk about cursing to Bran the Hermit. You know, the old Welsh hermit who lived in Windsill Valley. I sometimes wonder if he is still there. Anyway, we used to visit him when I was young. He lived in a cave hollowed out by lead miners of long ago. It was hidden by ivy and overhanging plants, very hard to find. There was a small hole directly above which acted like a chimney. Smoke came out into the trees, but the tall oaks absorbed the smoke into the low-lying mist that frequently hung over the treetops. It was an invisible place to those passing below.

Mam had bottles, jars and supplies hidden there and she processed herbs, made poultices and kept expensive supplies on the cold stone shelves. Sometimes Elphin the Bard was there.

'What happened to the hermit?'

'He was tied up by two young men, robbed of his meagre possessions and left to die.'

'What did that have to do with your mother?'

'She knew who they were and weeks later we came upon them. They asked her for some medicine... bad stomachs, I think. I was picking flowers and hidden behind some trees and watched.'

'And cursing? Where does that fit in?'

'Well, I was very young at the time, but I saw her open a secret pocket in her bag and take strange things out and mix them up in a pot over the fire. Then she put a cloth over the flames and said some strange words I had never heard before. She was shaking and swaying with her eyes closed. I was frightened. She then gave it to one of them with a tincture wrapped inside the cloth. They paid her and left.'

'Then what happened?'

'A few days later both the robbers' gnarled bodies were found on the open road. They died in some sort of agony. John, I know she had cursed them. She has secrets.'

'What secrets?'

'It's something to do with Elphin, the Bard.'

'The bard?'

'Yes. He used to call a lot when my father was away, and that cave seemed important to her.'

'She can't hurt you now, Isobel.' John held her tightly against his body, turned to face the wind, tears slowly falling, and he whispered, 'I swear, in the name of my ancestors, I shall always keep you safe.'

Chapter 33

S omething inside Anne shuddered. Her heart was pounding, and, for a moment, her breathing felt laboured, as if she was drowning. She remembered two young people with pack horses, mounting up and riding hand in hand down a lane, unable to take their eyes off each other. Now there was the sound of wheels coming towards her, getting louder and louder, distant voices mumbling, and the image of the two young people began to fade.

*

'Hello Jack. Visiting time is never long enough, is it? Earlier today your sister was smiling and one of her hands moved, as if she was happy about some thoughts she was experiencing.'

'She smiled? Are you sure?' Jack gasped.

'Yes, I am.'

'Is that a good sign?'

'Could be. It means her thought processes are working. Always a good sign. She is in good hands. We are looking after her well, but we just must be patient. She will waken when she's ready.' The nurse smiled again and gave his shoulder a little squeeze as she moved off down the ward. Jack looked at the pale face of his motionless sister and wondered what was going on in her head. Perhaps she was where she had always wanted to be.

His thoughts were suddenly interrupted by a scruffy, middle-aged woman who had been sitting by the bedside of a man in a nearby bed. The woman had been peering through a gap in his curtains trying to catch his conversation with the nurse. She stood up and waddled towards him. Jack lifted his newspaper, trying to hide behind it, hoping she would keep moving but she did not.

'Hello. Is that your wife?'

'No. My sister.'

'She looks very pale, but I've seen worse. My Bill was that colour in the beginning.' She folded her flabby arms across her chest.

'The beginning?'

'Yes, he had a fall, months ago. They don't come round you know.' The woman leered at Anne and was about to bend down over her when Jack stood up to put his body between them. Anxious to get the woman to leave, he said, 'Her name is Anne. She had a fall too. Knocked herself out. We're waiting for her to come round.'

The Uncovered Legacy

The woman turned and put her arm around his shoulder giving him a hug. The stench of body odour mixed with tobacco smoke made him nauseous and he extricated himself as soon as he could.

'You alright love?' she said, smiling.

'Yes, thank you. I am fine.' He stepped forward trying to use his body to push her away.

'Today they are going to switch my Bill off.'

'Oh! I am sorry.'

'Well, it's time isn't it.'

'Is it?' Jack raised his eyebrows and took a quick intake of breath.

'We've all had enough now, visiting every day, buses not on time. Sitting here for hours on end. It's boring and I've got me kids to think about.'

'It must have been difficult for you going on for so long?'

'He was a wrong un. No good as a man, or a father. A man of drink he was. Never brought any money home. Always kept me short. And me with five kids.'

'How awful for you,' he said, wishing she would shut up and go away.

'Never cared for him really. Be glad to be rid. But then there will be all that paperwork.'

'What paperwork?'

'You know, death certificates, funerals, and all that. And it will cost a packet. And who's going to pay for it? Well, not me!'

Jack's legs began to wobble, and he sat down. 'Oh, yes I see.'

'And my dogs have had a rough time. No walks in the mornings. Having to do their business in the garden. A right mess it is.'

Jack took deep breaths and sighed several times, hoping she would take the hint and leave him in peace. 'Perhaps it would be best if you went home and saw to the dogs?'

'Can't go yet. Not long now.'

'Not long?'

'Until they switch him off, you know, unplug the bugger.'

'Do you know when? Do you have to be there?'

'They said when t'ward rounds have finished and visitors is gone. They like to do these things when nobody is around. Anyway, I want to make sure the bugger's gone. Gone for good.'

'Have they given you a time?' Beads of sweat were running down his face. What might happen to Anne once he left for the night?

'Their time. I'm at their beck and call, just hanging around waiting.' she said, folding her arms to rest on her protruding stomach.

'Do you want to be here when it happens. Have you said goodbye to Bill?'

'Said goodbye years ago when he left me for Peggy Wilson, cheating bastard. She dies and t' hospital called me. Next of kin and all that.'

'So, he is not your husband?'

'He's a miserable liar. Would not divorce me until mother died and left me her house. Wanted me money you see.' The woman was becoming agitated and kept looking at her watch.

'Can't wait all day. I'll miss me bus. I'd best be off.'

'Okay, goodbye then.' Jack's shoulders relaxed. He looked at Anne and sighed, then his heart thumped as the voice came back.

'Hope you don't have to wait long for your switch off.' Jack turned a strange shade of grey.

'They all get it in the end, you know. Bye bye, luv, nice talking to you.'

With that she waddled her fat, smelly, little body down the corridor and out into the hospital grounds. Jack was relieved she had gone. The thought of Anne not coming round from the coma had not crossed his mind. But she was still breathing, vital signs were normal and, although he had not seen it, one of the nurses said she had smiled. What was going on? But knowing Anne as he did, or did he? She would not easily leave her children, grandchildren, or her animal communicators.

Chapter 34

L ater that day, Anne watched Thomas Elliott's homecoming.

*

The horses were unsaddled and stabled. Stolen goods and captured livestock from the raid in Thorp Glen were shared out among the men, who then set off for their homes. Millie was walking across the yard when Thomas called her name.

'Millie, Millie! Where are you girl? Millie, go and get Isobel. I must speak to her.... found her another husband. Will Armstrong wants her. He has offered 40 cattle and two farms. I'll be rid of that girl once and for all and this time she will do as she's told, by God she will.' He slapped his thigh and rubbed his hands together.

Millie appeared from the cow shed, dropped her head and muttered, 'She's gone.'

Thomas glared at Millie who stood shaking so much she dropped her pail of milk. 'Who's gone?' he bellowed, racing towards her.

'Miss Isobel. Run off with John Tweddle,' she mumbled.

'What? Speak up girl! What did you say? She's run off with John Tweddle?'

Millie nodded, 'Yes. And when her mother comes home there will be trouble.' She began to ramble.

'Be quiet girl. When did this happen?' he shouted, as he ran across the yard, threw the kitchen door open and ran up the back stairs to Isobel's room, with Millie hard on his heels.

'It wasn't my fault. I didn't know she was locked in.'

Thomas took hold of Millie's shoulders and shook her, 'Locked in, Girl! What are you talking about? Why was she locked in?'

'Don't know. Don't know,' said Milly flattening herself against the wall, trying to look invisible.

Thomas returned to the kitchen where old Ma Blenkinsop was cooking rabbit stew. 'What's going on here Ma?'

Ma Blenkinsop, without lifting her head from the stew pot, replied, 'Isobel and her mother had a fight and she got locked in her room.'

'A fight? A fight? What are you talking about, Woman? What was the fight about? Why is everyone talking in riddles?'

Ma Blenkinsop stopped stirring and looked at Thomas, 'John Tweddle. Isobel's run off with him.' She turned back to her cooking.

'What! That girl's money! Money, do you hear? I have already promised her to Will Armstrong. Damn the girl and damn John Tweddle!' He swiped his arm over the

155

table and cleared it of pots, scattering them over the kitchen floor. The remains of breakfast's porridge clung to the wall, slowly dropping to form thick puddles on the stone flags.

Thomas turned to find Millie, who had followed him downstairs and was trying to hide behind the door.

'Do you know what you have done, you stupid, stupid girl? The money I have lost. Isobel would have fetched a high price, paid off debts!' He began to shake her shoulders with such force her head bounced off the wall.

'Stop shaking the child. She only has half a brain. She'll be no use to me in the kitchen if it's gone all together.'

'You stupid, stupid idiot!' he yelled.

'Here.' Ma pulled him away from the quaking girl, who had dissolved into floods of tears. She pushed Thomas into a chair, pushed a large mug of ale into his hand and stood facing him with her arms folded across her chest.

'She won't come back, you know. She loves him.'

'Love. Don't talk rot, Woman!'

After several mugs of ale, the situation did not seem too bad.

Thomas looked at Ma and sighed, 'Perhaps my senses are dulled. I am exhausted after several days on the road and the thought of gathering up the men again and setting off after my wayward daughter, doesn't seem the best thing to do.'

He became silent for a few moments, scratched his chin and looked thoughtful. 'The Tweddles are a powerful family. My sister, Meg, ran off and wed Bill Tweedy. Uncle Duff had entanglements with Flo Tweddle. Now Isobel is to wed another. This new alliance could bring wealth, new land and strengthen family, making raiding into England easier.'

Ma stood nodding her head, 'Well you don't care much for the girl. She's a commodity, something to be sold. You've tried, twice before, to marry her off to rich men and both times it's failed. Now she's gone off on her own free will.'

'Um! Money. A daughter married into powerful Tweddles will increase my status among other border families. Our kin sometimes ride with John Tweddle, so I don't see any trouble coming from them. No, it's best to leave well alone. After all my long-term plan for Isobel's future has happened without me having to do anything. But still I have lost the gift of cattle and two farms. One day I will make her pay for that and the Tweddles. There will be other ways to get paid for the wretched girl. But you're right. I care little for the girl's happiness, but family wealth is another matter. I will do nothing. Ma, nothing at the moment, fetch more ale.'

Chapter 35

Anne's awareness shifted to the next day and the return of Elinor.

*

Millie was sitting at the kitchen table in tears.

'Hello Millie. What are you doing, sitting down, you lazy creature. Get up, get on with your work. Have you done the milking this morning?'

'She's gone.' Millie mumbled.

'Who's gone?'

'Isobel. She tricked me. It wasn't my fault. I didn't do anything wrong. Please don't beat me. It wasn't my fault.'

Elinor dragged Millie to her feet and slapped her hard across the face. 'What are you talking about girl? Who's gone and why is that milk pail empty? You're lazy. Stupid girl.'

Millie stepped back just in time to avoid another slap. She knew well enough the temper of her mistress and wasn't as daft as she led them to believe. Over the years she had learned to play a halfwit. It had kept her safe and especially from the boys.

'GONE! Run off with that John Tweddle has she!' Elinor's rage began to grow. The veins in her neck stood proud, her hands were waving about, beads of sweat running down her cheeks and her eyes were bulging like a mating frog. Such was her shock that for several seconds no words came out of her mouth.

'Isobel thinks she can defy me, does she, get her own way over this man, thinks she will be happy, does she? I will not have it. Do you hear me, Girl? I will not have it! She has defied me for the last time!' Elinor picked up a stool and threw it at Millie, who managed to cower just low enough for it to fly over her head and collide with the door.

'Get up! Stoke the fire, Girl! Get it hot, very hot! I will show them not to defy me! I'll show them! This is the last time! No more will I put up with her selfish ways!'

Millie crawled along the floor to the log pile and began feeding the fire. 'What are you going to do? Please don't be angry with me, don't hurt me,' the girl pleaded.

Elinor stood glaring at Millie and gave her a quick kick. 'Get that fire hot, you stupid girl! What's the matter with you? Move, Girl. Move! Get on with it!' She was screaming, yelling and shouting, throwing pots and dishes at the walls until nearly everything was broken. It looked as if the kitchen had been raided. She glared at Millie.

'So, she's gone far out of my reach, or so she thinks, but my reach goes a long, long way! Now I will give her what she deserves. Isobel thinks she is a better healer, loved and adored by the men and the women trust her. No matter how far I send her out into new settlements, she always returns well and happy and with a renewed sense of who she is. I'll not have it! Do you hear me, Girl? I'll not have it!' Elinor's anger continued to grow. She looked round, screamed, picked up the last unbroken pot and threw it at the door. 'Run off with John Tweddle, has she? He killed my daughter, Margaret! Thomas Elliott's a thief, a liar and a brute and his daughter, Isobel, has betrayed me!'

Elinor paused, glanced at the drying herbs and grasses hanging from the ceiling and smiled to herself, 'I know of the old ways and now is the time to use them.'

She walked to the fire and swung the hot cauldron back onto the stove, over the roaring flames. Into it she put large amounts of dried herbs. Some had come from foreign lands and had destructive powers. She added blackthorn, water hemlock, monkshood, deadly night shade and mullein. She had used mullein as graveyard dust, in the days when she dabbled in darker magic and understood its potency.

Elinor, the hedge witch, went out into the cobbled yard, stood with arms skywards, and called to the four elements.

She stood in the north and shouted, 'I CALL TO THE POWERS OF THE NORTH TO BRING ME THE STRENGTH OF THE EARTH DRAGON!'

She then moved to the East, 'I CALL TO THE POWERS FROM THE EAST FOR THEIR INSPIRATION AND THE FLIGHT OF THE MIGHTY EAGLE!'

Then she moved to the South, 'I CALL TO FATHER SUN IN THE SOUTH FOR THE POWER OF FIRE!'

Finally, she moved to face the West and spoke, 'I CALL TO THE STORMS FROM THE WEST AND ASK FOR THEIR FORCE AND ENERGY!'

Returning to the kitchen fire, she took three deep breaths and began to speak, 'I know the power of words can create a different reality. In the past, I have stirred potions and blessed the men folk who went raiding, wishing them a safe return. It hasn't always worked perfectly because sometimes they returned injured but alive. But this time it is different. Margaret has gone. I hate my husband Thomas Elliott with every bone of my body. Isobel has run away with John Tweddle, a man I despise for not protecting Margaret and for allowing her to die. He thinks because his family is big and powerful and quite some distance away into England that they are safe, and I have heard from travelling merchants that Wydon is an impenetrable manor house.' Elinor screwed up her face and winced. 'But you Isobel…Isobel…I shall have my revenge on you. DO YOU HEAR ME ISOBEL…DO YOU? I curse you Isobel Elliott to a short life. May you lose everything you love. I curse all the women in your family down the generations. May they all have loveless marriages, lose any inherited wealth and be sold…become slaves to men. And to you John Tweddle.' She closed her eyes, stared at a still cowering Millie and yelled, 'I will have my revenge for taking away my daughter!'

Elinor took hold of the large wooden spurtle, 'I stir this pot widdershins, which is backwards and guaranteed to bring bad luck and, as my left hand stirs the pot, it increases the power to destroy!' As she began screaming into the cauldron, an evil looking liquid spat back at her, catching her in the left eye. She screamed, then Elinor smiled. It was as if the pot was acknowledging her thoughts. Her rage was greater than the pain and she stirred with more fury than ever.

Then she began her rant.

'I curse all the hairs on every part of John Tweddle's body from the top of his head to the bottom of his feet. May raging storms rattle his bones and lightning seek him out, strike and deform his wretched body. I curse his home, his health, his wealth and all he possesses in this world and any other world. May he eat only diseased food and may poison seep into his being, that even witches struggle to heal. I curse the Tweed, Tipalt, Tyne and all rivers, becks and streams that he drinks from and bathes in. May he fall and drown when crossing any stretch of water. May he get lost on the moors and bogs trap and endanger him and heather roots trip and entwine his feet. Let Boggits feed on his flesh. May the dry earth crack and open wide and swallow him whole. May branches in woods break, come down quickly and sweep him from his horse. May the great north wind lash him to pieces, rip his skin to shreds and tear his face. May all families reject him and neighbours plot against him. May he not know love or kindness but lead a miserable unhappy existence and be worn down by responsibility!' Elinor paused and took another deep breath. 'I curse future generations down the male line of this Tweddle family. May they have hard, difficult lives, uncomfortable illnesses and painful deaths!' She continued to stir the cauldron anti clockwise, for visitation of maximum harm.

The pot began to boil as Elinor's voice rose in a terrifying crescendo, but the curse seemed to be too powerful, even for a skilled wise woman. The boiling concoction in the cauldron began to bubble upwards and, as it reached the top of the pot, it erupted with a bang and the scalding liquid poured out onto Elinor's chest, slithered onto her abdomen and travelled down her legs, before settling in puddles of gunge at her feet. The spurtle flew into the air, Elinor screamed, and her hands grasped her chest as she choked and struggled to breathe. Millie ran towards her but was beaten back by the heat and the spitting steam arising from the fire. It was as if the cauldron's contents were fighting the flames which refused to be extinguished. Elinor tried to speak but no words came from her burnt, disfigured lips and she fell silently to the floor in a distorted mass, a victim of her own hatred.

Millie screamed, 'What have you done? You put agrimony in, and I heard you once say that if you added that plant then any curse sent would come back in some form to the sender. What have you done? Oh! What am I going to do? What will happen to me now?'

Chapter 36

It was getting dark when the barking dogs announced John's and Isobel's arrival. He dismounted and tied up his horse as a half-dressed boy, wearing only a night shirt ran out of the shadows towards him.

'Didn't expect you back tonight. Your father hasn't returned.'

'Any word from him?'

'No, but one of the farm lads thought he saw cattle moving down the drove road over Waterbog Moor. The river is in flood and too deep to cross safely with so many livestock. They've been holed up on the other side for the last couple of days.'

'Thanks. See to the horses. I will rouse Cook and get her to make us some hot food. It's been a long time since we ate.'

'Yes Sir.'

Isobel had jumped down and looked around her new surroundings,

'The manor house looks large and fearsome in the dark. Something about it feels familiar. Have I been here before?'

'Yes, you have, when you were younger. It was after the first time I rescued you from a bog, I brought you back here. You were visiting with some relatives on this side of the border. You stayed overnight and took my blanket away with you. Come, let's go in and get dry, Cook will soon get us warmed up.' He took her arm and led her through the gateway.

'I remember the blanket. I still have it on Mollie's back.' She gave his arm a little squeeze and smiled. An iron bracketed oak door came into view and a large brusque woman in her night clothes stood with arms folded across her chest.

'Hello, you're back then? A peddler passed by here yesterday and said you'd left the men and gone off somewhere. Seems your father is holed up on the other side of the border, waiting for the weather to change. The commotion woke me up. And who is this you have brought with you?'

'Oh, Cook, this is Isobel… Isobel this is Cook,' he said, bending over to give Cook a quick kiss on the cheek.

Isobel clenched her fist and frowned at John greeting the Cook in such a way and felt resentful. Why did he treat her so respectfully? … she was the cook after all… a servant.

'Hello.' Isobel replied, staring at Cook.

'On your own, just the two of you?' She held the door open as if expecting more people. Isobel wasn't sure about Cook, a big bossy woman, someone who knew she was in charge.

'Been riding a long time by the look of you both. Well, come in and be quick. It's cold standing with the door open. Get in and I'll get you some hot food.' She ushered them in to get warmed by the fire.

Isobel saw Cook raise an eyebrow as she looked her over; the filthy tunic, the torn shawl, the wet matted hair the muddy boots and she took an instant dislike to this servant. After all this was her house now, John's mother being dead, she would soon be in charge.

'John sit down and take those dirty boots off. You know better than bringing mud into my kitchen.' Cook was definitely in charge. He sat by the fire, took his boots off and quietly ate the bowl of hot lamb stew that she'd pressed into his hands.

John grinned, 'Cook is used to strange comings and goings in the middle of the night and always has the stewpot on the fire for our men when they come back from reiving.'

'So, you are Isobel?'

'Yes, I am,' she said, wondering how she knew that.

'John has talked a lot about you. Don't know what took him so long to get you back down here. I remember you from years ago. A scrap of a little thing you were then, coming across the moor on your own, getting stuck and arriving here all wet and bedraggled. You never returned John's blanket,' she said, wagging her finger, 'Precious blanket, been in the family a long time.' Cook, hands in pockets, turned back to the fire.

Isobel felt like a cow being herded, rounded up and kidnapped. She slammed her fist on the table and stood up, 'I am here of my own free will. John has not bought me. Yes, I am Thomas Elliott's daughter. I imagine you have heard of him?'

'Who hasn't?'

Isobel was not getting anywhere with this annoying woman. She sat down at the table and ate some stew and thought it might be better to be nice, 'This is excellent food. It has a special unfamiliar flavour. You must let me know what it is.'

'My secrets, stays my secrets.' she said, folding her arms across her heavy chest.

Isobel looked at John who shook his head, as if to be quiet, which only infuriated her more. She was not going to be spoken to like that, and by a cook. Millie would not have dared to speak to her mother like that. This woman needed to show some respect.

'When I am the lady of this house, I expect you will tell me everything, secrets or not.'

'You're not the lady yet, Miss Isobel Elliott.'

Isobel couldn't contain herself any longer, stood up and threw her empty bowl across the floor. She heard it break into many pieces against the oak door.

John stood up and caught her firmly by the arm, but she pulled away from him and put her hands on her hips and turned to face Cook.

'You will show me respect.'

Silence followed as Cook stood transfixed, unable to move. She looked up and her face went pale, as she quietly opened her mouth, 'No one has ever spoken to me like that before.'

'You seem to forget who you are in this house. Been in charge for too long, I think. I will do something about that.' Isobel turned and saw a look of shock and horror on John's face.

161

'Come, Isobel. It's late. There are things you don't know. We are both tired. Let's to bed.'

He turned to Cook, 'Is there a room for Isobel?'

It seemed to break the tension between them. Cook nodded her head and turned away, leaving Isobel with a wry smile on her face. She had won the first battle.

Moments later a boy entered the kitchen and John went outside with him, followed by two dogs, tails wagging, happy to see him return.

Isobel looked at Cook and sighed, a long-drawn-out sigh. This woman had obviously been here a long time. Probably since John was born, his mother having died in childbirth. She was a big woman with a kind face and gentle smile despite her sharp words. Her long grey hair, neatly braided and tied with a piece of worn ribbon looked heavy, as it swung down her back to reach her knees. Looking round the large kitchen with its stone flagged floor, long sycamore table and oak chairs, Isobel began to have some sympathy for her hard life and did not want to get on the wrong side of her, this woman who behaved as if she'd always been in charge and perhaps, she had. Pangs of pity wrestled in Isobel's throat. She walked over to Cook, took the pot rag out of her hands and lifted the kettle onto the hot coals.

The older woman looked at Isobel and tears welled up in her eyes, 'I am sorry. I am not used to company and other women being in my kitchen.'

'I'm sorry too.' She put her arms round the older woman and hugged her. 'I am very tired, and it's been a long journey, full of dangers and accidents. I have left my family and come to a strange place. I think I would like to go to bed now. Please show me where I am to sleep.'

Cook took her arm and led her through the passage, up the back stairs, along the corridor and into a room. 'I'll pull the curtains. The bed is clean, but I expect you will not be awake for long. You look the same as the last time we met; cold, weary but a bit older of course.' She smiled. Cook continued to prattle on but Isobel was too tired to listen to anything and was grateful the older woman helped her off with her boots and tunic, lifted her legs onto the bed and pulled the blanket over her. She vaguely remembered a wet cloth wiping her face before drifting into a deep sleep.

*

Isobel slept late. The light, shining through a gap in the curtains, alerted her to a new day. She sat up in bed with a start, the events of the night before rushing through her head. The room was large. The two big windows faced east, drapes hanging to the floor. Two chairs sat, one on each side of a lit fire. Someone must have come in while she was asleep and warmed the room. It must have been the crackling of the logs that awakened her. A large wooden chest sat at the bottom of the bed, probably full of linen, blankets and nightwear. A short wardrobe, on the wall near the door, stood next to a set of tall drawers. A few pictures of fells and animals hung on the walls. She supposed someone in the family was an artist. Above the bed was a tapestry wall hanging. She had seen one before in a rich merchant's house in Carlisle. It had been brought back, from the low countries, by some marauding villains, intent on making a profit. This one, above the bed, must be of a similar origin. Isobel stood on the bed to examine it in more detail. There was much to be admired; the needlework was fine and delicate, the colours bright. It was a hunting scene; horses, dogs and people, dressed in strange looking clothes she had never seen before.

Suddenly, the door flew open and Cook entered in such a flurry that Isobel lost her balance and landed on the bed. The two women looked at each other and laughed.

'It's good to see you up and about. Did you sleep well?'

'Yes, I did, thanks.'

'It's afternoon now. You must've been exhausted.'

Cook put a tray down on the bed in front of her; eggs, bread, some hot liquid in a ceramic mug and a bowl of something that looked like porridge.

'Here, Isobel, get some hot food inside you.'

'Thank you. I am hungry. Where is John?'

'Up and away. He came downstairs and found spurs on his breakfast plate. He smiled at me, knew what it meant. No meat. So, he has gone hunting.'

Isobel realised Cook had authority over the men in this house and she remembered the words that passed between them the night before and felt sad. Cook obviously cared a lot about this family and Isobel wondered if she was more than a servant.

'How long will they be gone?'

'A few days. It depends where they've gone. Last time outlaws sneaked in while the place was quiet and stole two horses. Angus said they'd been watching and waiting for our men to leave.'

Angus. She had forgotten he had a father who was master at Wydon. As an alarmed look crossed Isobel's face, Cook was quick to reassure her that all would be well.

'Don't worry, he will like you. He's spoken many times about, Isobel Elliott, how you would enhance the family's wealth and John should marry you.'

Isobel frowned. Had she been baited like an animal in a trap, kidnapped? Was John no better than Robert Ridley? She was beginning to feel caught. Thoughts were crashing through her head of what to do. She could not go back. How would she get there, although she would find a way?

Would her father come for her? After all, he had tried, twice before, to marry her off to rich and powerful men and it had not worked. The Tweddles had large estates and many farms. Perhaps he would be glad, because she'd gone willingly, and he was rid of her. Thomas Elliott would be well pleased with this new alliance and would not be coming after her.

She thought of her mother. Would she round up the Kerr family and take her back? But did she want to go back? Her mother had locked her up, refused to tend John's wounds and she hated him.

Isobel fell back onto the soft pillows and thought about what she had done. She stayed in her room for the remainder of the day resting and sleeping.

The next morning, she came down to breakfast to find a young girl in the kitchen.

'Hello, who are you? Where is Cook?'

'Me Mam's not well, Miss. Cook's gone to see to her. I'm Kitty, her daughter.'

'I'm Isobel. What are you doing? Have you cooked before?'

'No.'

'Do you know anything about cooking, Kitty?'

'No, Miss, sorry. I'm always in the fields with me sister. Mam says kitchen's hers and I gets in way. Says I am not bright enough to follow what she tells me.'

'Here, let me show you how to make porridge.' Isobel walked across the floor, took a large glass jar of oats from the dresser, and poured some into a dry cooking pot.

'All you do is put water in and set them on the fire. Sometimes we add herbs and things to change the taste.'

The girl smiled, 'Thank you, Miss.'

Isobel continued with her instructions, handing the girl a large spoon, 'Keep stirring to stop it sticking. The Anglo Saxons made porridge from rye, barley and oats and called it Brew. It's important to keep grains dry.'

'Grains miss?'

'Oats in particular. If the weather gets too hot, the grains can ferment. So, a warm moist spell can create havoc with stored cereals.'

'What about using flour? Me Mam has flour sometimes. Gets it from peddler.'

'Wheat must be ground, and you need an oven. Not every kitchen has one. Look there's one there.' She pointed to a small black door. 'We must always be careful not to waste any. Don't leave a trail of bits on the ground for raiders to follow and steal from our secret stores.'

'Secret stores?' Kitty went pale.

'They have lost a lot of grain in the past. Raiders cause havoc. Disrupt the agricultural rotation system. You will know all about that working on the land.'

'The land becomes bare, nothing grows. A time ago, don't remember when, me father had no food to feed us and the little ones he joined a raiding party to get some with old man Ridley and his son Robert. But they gets caught and sent to garrison at Carlisle.' She began to cry. Isobel went towards her and put comforting arms around her scrawny body.

'He was hung, Miss, but Ridleys escaped.'

Isobel's heart began to quicken at the sound of Robert Ridley's name, but she was not surprised, he was a master at escaping. Isobel sighed. Was she never going to be free of this man?

'Come now, let's wipe these tears away and keep the porridge stirring. We'll have a fine breakfast. Afterwards I will find Cook's book and you can follow what it says.'

'I can't read Miss,' she said sheepishly, dropping her head.

Isobel smiled and gave her another hug. 'Never mind, we'll manage.'

*

The next few weeks passed quickly as Isobel spent her days riding through the Tweddle lands, visiting farms, villages, hamlets and remote settlements, meeting the Tweddle tenants. She asked about their health, offered tinctures and healing herbs, successfully birthed two healthy babies, and tried to gain the trust of these people, with their strange northern English accents.

One day, as she returned home from one of her foraging trips, her horse wandered up an overgrown, winding dirt track that led to the top of the fell, where a ruined stone building came into view. A broken sign read Thropplestead Farm and she knew this to be the boundary with the Kerr's land. Isobel looked at the long since abandoned farmstead. The roof, having been ripped off by the wind, lay strewn across the carpets of purple heather. Cawing crows were squabbling over a dead rabbit's carcass and a sudden blast of wind rushed through the crumbling stone walls disturbing the fledgling blackbirds. Doors had long since rotted away and the only signs of human habitation were the ash scars on the blackened chimney breast and the remnants of a broken cooking pot. Only the misshapen elderly sycamore betrayed the extent of what had once been a home.

'Whose home was it?' she shouted. The overpowering dank smell of fermenting peat made Isobel shiver and she covered her face and turned to embrace the forbidding northern moorlands and the flat rolling hills that lay to the east. The silence was only broken by the crackling sound of the South Tyne River as it wound its way down the craggy fellside and deep ravines to the valley bottom from its source on Tynedale fell, a landscape so different from the land she had left and the tightly woven glens of Southern Scotland. Isobel wiped her eyes and tried hard to control the flood of tears. There was a sense of sadness and loss of what she had left behind, not just the land but the people too. She felt caught between tragedy and triumph in this desolate vast wasteland that had no end.

Isobel sighed and reminded herself she had run away from her jealous mother, who had imprisoned her, a father who had tried twice to sell her into unwanted marriages, and Robert Ridley and a lifetime of his unwanted attentions. It was only John, her rescuer, Reiver, and lover, who cared, the man she had loved from the first time he rescued her from a peat bog. The thought of John made her smile. Her spirits lifted as she turned the horse down the track and took the lower fell paths back to him and the preparations for their forthcoming handfasting.

Chapter 37

The day of John and Isobel's handfasting was fast approaching. Cook stood at the kitchen door, smiling; arms folded across her chest, 'It'll be a grand affair, Angus's eldest son wed. People will come from great distances to celebrate with us but there's so much to do, Isobel. You'll need a new dress.'

'My mother was keeping her green hand-fasted dress for my sister, Margaret.'

'Not you Isobel? But you are the eldest.'

'No, not for me. I was not the favourite, although it lived in a bottom drawer in my room.' Isobel frowned, 'I sometimes wonder if my mother misses me.' Isobel sighed, looked at Cook and smiled at the warm friendly face of the woman, who treated her like a daughter, and Isobel loved her for it.

'Follow me upstairs. I am sure we can find something for you to wear.'

In the first few weeks Cook had fussed about showing her all the secrets of the house, the hiding places, and the special hidden door in a wardrobe, in case she ever needed to escape. It had no handle and was not easy to open and she would never have found it on her own. It led into a small space, just big enough for two people, that had been used many times over the years, as a refuge from Wardens and sometimes priests, who could arrive unannounced with bands of religious fanatics to convert the household to Christianity. Isobel knew of the witch hunters and, as a healer, she could be one who was named, and this tiny room might one day save her life.

Cook opened the bedroom door and knelt by the chest at the bottom of the bed.

'I have kept John's mother's clothes for all these years. Let's have a look, shall we?'

'What was she like?'

Cook sighed and looked sad. She sat on the bed and lifted a cloth to wipe her watery eyes. 'A beauty. That's where John gets his good looks from. Not his father with all that red hair and long beard so it's hard to see his face sometimes.' Cook put her hand to her mouth, as if she had spoken out of turn. 'John's mother, Anya, was fiery, fierce, clever, well-educated and something of a Reiver herself. On many occasions she rode with the men and was equal to many of them. She was a strong woman; a mother John would have been proud to ride alongside.'

'Anya, a strange name?'

'Angus changed it to Annie, so Annie it was.'

'Did she mind?'

'She did but the gift of two black Irish ponies soon changed her mind. He also gave her a basket hilted sword as well.'

'Quite a gift.'

The Uncovered Legacy

'Yes, a real Reiver she was. Loved it, born in the saddle.'

'She died giving birth to John?'

'He came backwards, couldn't get him out. Warm and comfortable he was. Didn't want to leave her. He's always liked being warm and at home. Couldn't get him out of the kitchen when he was little. Loved the fire. Something about it fascinated him.'

'I once lost a mother, birthing. It was horrible, I didn't get there in time. It was snowing and I got lost in the dark.' Isobel bowed her head and took a deep breath. She had known Ma Johnson well and had helped her other two little ones into the world.

'Did you lose the baby as well?'

'Yes, lost them both and left two little girls motherless.'

Cook put her cloth away in her pocket, cleared her throat and ruffled Isobel's hair. 'Now then, Isobel, let's look inside, shall we'. Cook opened the lid and began to unpack clothes that had lain there twenty years or more.

'I don't think I should wear them. What about Angus? They did belong to his wife.'

'Never you mind about that. I will see to him.'

The dresses, much to Isobel's relief, did not fit her. They were old, worn and unlike anything she had seen before. Annie had been taller and a different shape. Isobel took each garment, folded it neatly and replaced it in the box. She smiled at Cook and said, 'I will go to Hexham tomorrow. I am sure there will be something there to fit me.'

Cook raised both eyebrows and held up a green tunic with flowers embroidered on the edges. 'I can change this one.'

'Thanks, but I would like something of my own, for such a special day.'

'I understand. My father used to bring me old clothes. They rarely fit. He blackmailed people for goods of all kinds. He stole clothes for my mother, to make her like him better. Do you miss your mother, Isobel?'

'I don't think so. It's good to be free to be myself. I miss our walks, collecting herbs and listening to her stories but, after Margaret died, we grew apart.'

'What about your father?'

'No. He didn't like me much. Tried to marry me off twice but failed.' She shivered.

Cook tilted her head to one side. 'He must be happy now because he hasn't come to get you, has he?'

'No. He wouldn't risk a fight with the Tweddles. My father's a coward and a bully.'

'Did you know that Angus has sent for him?'

Isobel went pale, 'Why?'

'A handfasting is a joining of families, yours to ours.' Cook folded her arms and smiled.

Isobel felt bewildered, 'Ours? Are you related to the Tweddles?'

'I am Annie's sister.'

Isobel grinned and her eyes sparkled. She had thought of her only as the cook. 'You never married?' she asked.

'I had my sister's four boys to bring up.' She nodded her head. 'It's been wonderful. My family, my lovely family. They will always be mine. I love them all.' Isobel was sad about the life Cook must have had and now understood why she ruled the house so strictly and why Angus and his sons accepted it.

'Why did Angus not remarry?'

Cook looked flushed and quickly changed the subject. 'Now then, enough of this talk. Let's get back to your handfasting.'

Now, for the first time, Isobel thought about the creaking floorboards in the night, the sound of bedroom doors opening and closing, and ideas began to form in her head. She had only been in Cook's room a couple of times, but it was sparse with no personal possessions in it, no clothes, a room for visitors, not a bedroom for a woman who had lived in the house her whole adult life. Then she thought of Angus and how he looked at Cook and the way she dropped her eyes and giggled. Why had she not made any connection before? It all made sense. Angus had no need for a wife. He had Cook. Isobel felt happy for her. A woman who had carried a great burden all her life. Then she thought of Jamie, Jack, and Will, John's brothers. She had also come across a distant brother called Edgar, but no one spoke of him. How could John have three younger brothers if his mother died birthing him? Ah, because they belonged to Cook. All three boys were Cook's sons. Her face spread into a wide grin. Isobel was brought out of her daydream by Cook's return to planning.

'Then there are the flowers, of course. The girls in the village will do that. Ribbons to be fetched.'

'Who will come?' Isobel said, continuing to fold clothes and re fill the box.

'Everyone from round here, Your father, of course, and his family.'

'I don't know if my mother will come after I ran away. I expect she was glad to be rid of me.' Isobel looked at Cook and saw tears rolling down her face and she jumped up and took hold of her hands. 'What's happened? Why are you sad?'

'I thought they would have told you.'

'Told me what?'

'About your mother'

'My mother? What about her? Tell me what's happened.' She released Cook's hands and stepped back.

'She is gone, Isobel.'

'Gone? What do you mean gone? Gone where?'

'Passed away. She is in the Summerland's.'

Isobel sank slowly onto the bed, put her hands on her face and wept, 'When did it happen? Are you sure she is gone? My mother? Are you sure?'

'The day after you left.'

'What happened?'

Cook sat on the bed beside her, 'When she came home and found out you'd run off with John, she flew into a terrible rage. She went to the cooking pot and filled it with handfuls of dangerous herbs, plants, a rat's head and other things and she cursed all the men in the Tweddle family to horrible illnesses and painful deaths down the generations and she laid a curse on the women as well.'

Isobel gasped. Her mouth dried up and it took her several seconds to speak.'

'No! She couldn't! … She wouldn't! How could she? She must have really hated me to do such a thing. I know Margaret was her favourite and she blamed John for not saving her. I know nothing about cursing. It's a dark art. I know she dabbled in it when she was younger, but I don't know how to lift curses. Oh! What am I going to do? Oh no, no, no!'

'Let's hope she didn't know what she was doing, and it won't happen. We will find someone who knows and ask for help.' She pressed a small linen cloth into Isobel's hand to wipe away her tears.

'Your mother's rage was so great that, when she was stirring the cauldron with all these despicable things in and chanting incantations, the pot started to grow. Then it boiled over and hot, scalding liquid poured down her body. I think she died quite quickly.'

Isobel paused her crying, lifted her head looking puzzled, 'How do you know all this?'

'Millie told me.'

'MILLIE! MILLIE! how did Mi Mi Mil...Millie tell you? I am confused. How could she have told you?'

'Well, Dear, she saw it happen.'

'She was there? 'Isobel's mouth fell open. 'How do you know that?'

'She told me.'

'Told you? What do you mean she told you?'

'Yes, told me.'

'When?'

'A few days after you arrived with John.'

'I don't understand. Are you saying Millie is here at Wydon?' Isobel threw her arms up, ran to the open window and took several deep breaths.

'No, not at Wydon dear.'

'Where then?'

'Millie is staying in Park village across the fields.'

'Why is she not here?'

'Angus thought it better not to have her in the house.'

'Why? What's going on? I want to know what's going on.' Isobel began to pace the room, back and forth to the window, holding firmly onto the sill, unable to believe all she was hearing.

Cook shook her head, 'I told him you should be told.'

'Why didn't he want me to know?'

Cook raised her eyebrows, sighed, stood up and closed the window. She put her arms round the girl, 'He was afraid she would persuade you to return. The tale of your mother's death might have been too much for you and he wants you to stay. He is very fond of you. He wants you to be wed to John... it is important to him.'

Isobel glared at the older woman, 'How dare he presume to know how I would feel! What's right for me!' She stomped across the floor picking up random objects and throwing them across the room.

'Would you have gone back?'

'I don't know. My mother did a terrible thing to this family. If I have sons, they will be cursed. Daughters destined to have unhappy lives.' She flew onto the bed, pounding the pillows with both hands and weeping with rage.

Cook sat next to her and stroked her tear-soaked hair. After a while, she stopped crying and sat up. Cook wiped her wet face and they sat together in silence holding hands.

'I know that my mother never loved me, not really loved me and was always jealous but this! I wouldn't have even dared think she could do such a thing, something so evil.'

'Come on, it's still early. I will take you to Millie. We can talk about your handfasting dress tomorrow.'

Chapter 38
Millie's Story

Isobel and Cook left Wydon Manor, walked down the track through fields, over the Tipalt bridge, up a narrow twisty path, as yet undiscovered by Isobel, onto a woodland track that led up a steep hill and through a pine wood before emerging onto a moor. In a short distance lay a settlement of five houses.

'What's this place called?'

'Parkfoot.'

'Is this where Millie is? How did she get here?'

'After your mother had, er…. moved on, so to speak… Elphin, the Bard, happened to be passing and, when he discovered what had happened, he collapsed on the ground and was inconsolable. Millie had to give him a potion to calm him down. Your father had left, almost immediately after seeing her dead, and gone hunting. Elphin, the Bard, was left in charge of burying your mother. Millie washed and dressed her as best she could.' Cook paused and gave an embarrassed cough.

'Go on, please, tell me everything. I want to know. Please go on.'

'Elphin, the Bard, gathered friends and tenants together and they dug a hole in the orchard and laid her to rest.' He was very upset. No one could make any sense of what he was saying or why he'd taken your mother's death so hard. Millie was frightened and asked if he would take her away to find you. She'd quickly packed her meagre possessions and they both left for Carlisle. When they got as far as Gilsland, some travellers took her with them the rest of the way.'

'How did she know where to go?'

'She kept babbling about Wydon and one of the peddler's was a local man and understood some of what he was saying.'

'Poor Millie, awful things could have happened to her. She was brave and had a lot of courage, coming so far with no idea what would happen when she arrived, or even if she would get here. She must have been frightened, but courageous to make such a long journey.'

'Well, Isobel, in all her babbling she'd mentioned the Tweddles, and that name had been enough to protect her. News of John Tweddle going into Scotland to fetch his bride had travelled far and wide and no one would have wanted any trouble. Millie walked up to Wydon, and you were out when she arrived. Angus and I listened to her story about your mother's death, curses and things. He wanted to protect you and he was not sure if your father would be coming after you, or even Millie. After all, he had just lost his wife, his daughter and then their servant and all because of John so Angus brought her here.'

'A convenient plan, I think!'

'Look, Isobel, we are nearly there. Open this gate and follow the track.'

As they approached the largest house in the settlement, a stout, grey haired old woman came out of the steading.

'Hello, Audrey, and who is this you have with you?'

Audrey? Audrey? She was called Audrey. Isobel hadn't thought Cook had any other name, although she did remember Angus calling her Aud.

'This is Isobel Elliott, our John's lass.'

'So, this is her, bonny lass, bonny lass.' She began to stroke Isobel's hair, took her hand and gestured to follow her inside.

'I suppose you've come for the young lass?'

Isobel could see a door slowly opening and there, in the darkness, was the silhouette of Millie, who stood for a moment frozen to the spot. Isobel smiled, 'Is that really you, Millie?'

'Yes, Miss, it's me.' Both girls ran to greet each other.

'I am so glad I have found you. Are you angry with me? Please don't be angry with me. I had to leave. I didn't know what your father was going to do, he was so angry. He said he had lost everything, and it was all my fault.'

'No. I am pleased to see you,' Isobel hugged Millie, who began to cry.

'I couldn't stay any longer, not after you'd gone. Everyone left and I was frightened and didn't know what to do.' Cook led them into the house and sat Millie down, where they took turns to dab her wet tears with small linen cloths.

'Please don't be cross with me. Don't send me back. I won't go, I won't.'

Isobel held out her hand to the girl and squeezed her's in a reassuring way. 'I won't send you back. You can stay with me. I want you to come to Wydon to live. We will have a new home together.' That seemed altogether too much for Millie and her tears changed into uncontrollable sobbing.

'Stop that. Stop crying. I am not sending you back, but I want to know how you got here?'

'I was with Elphin, the Bard, and we met old man Trotter. You know, the one who works with wood, made your splints for broken bones.'

'Yes, I remember.'

'He was coming south with Elphin, and he looked after me.'

Isobel thought she was either very brave or very stupid. Old Trotter had a reputation for having his way with young girls.

'I stayed a long way back, especially when Elphin, the Bard, wasn't around. I didn't trust Totter. He tried to er....' Her voice trailed off. Millie stopped crying, dried her eyes and, as she looked up, a faint movement occurred at the side of her mouth. It was a smile trying to emerge. Isobel put her arms round the girl's shoulders and gave her a reassuring hug.

'I must have collapsed somewhere, I was so tired and cold and had no food for two days, Miss Isobel, then these men found me and brought me here. I remember babbling something to them about Wydon.'

The old woman went into another room and returned with a large bag, which Isobel recognised as Millie's. It was her clothes and few possessions, and she laid the bag on Millie's lap. 'Right then, Millie, it's best you be off now they've come for you.'

Millie stood up, thanked the woman. Took Isobel's arm on one side and Audrey's on the other and together the three of them walked down the track, back towards Wydon.

After a short distance Isobel stopped, looked at Millie and said, 'What about my father? How did he respond to my running away with John Tweddle?'

'He was pleased, very pleased. Not at first, of course. He was very angry but then he thought of how rich he would be, you know, you joining the Tweddles.'

Isobel winced, John rich? Well, they do own a lot of land, but it is constantly changing hands. But perhaps she did not know everything about the Tweddle's possessions. Maybe her father knew more.

'He said that, if he didn't come after you, all would be well, and he'd get you married without having to pay for anything.'

'That sounds like my father. His first thoughts were always about money, land and allying himself with powerful families. But he will want something in return.'

'I couldn't stay there by myself, not with your father. I didn't want to end up like Mary Thomson and Jane Ridley over the fell top.'

Isobel spun round and glared, 'Millie what are you saying?'

But the girl bent her head and went silent.

'Millie, do they have his children? Is that what you are saying?'

'Yes, both of them. Jane had a boy called Thomas and Mary has two of 'em.'

'What? What? Two? Two children? What are they?'

'Little John and Mathew.'

'Millie how do you know all this?'

'Oh, Miss Isobel, everyone knows. Jane used to come to the kitchen for your old cast offs for her twins when they were little. And to see your father of ....'

'Did my mother know?'

'She knew about some of them but was glad because he left her alone, if err.... you know what I mean?'

Isobel frowned and stood with hands on hips, 'Are there any more children belonging to my father?'

'Oh, yes. Your father has children all over the fells. There was Meg Ogle. She had a son and Kate Ridley had a daughter, but she died young and there was a pretty young thing from Hexham. Can't remember her name but she had a little boy, sweet little thing but...'

'Millie STOP! Just STOP! I don't want to hear any more.' She flopped onto the ground and sat, with her head in her hands, unable to take it all in. 'Not only is my mother dead, killed by her own rage, leaving a legacy that will affect our descendants forever, but my father had children all over the Borders. How did I not know? Not even a whisper over all these years.'

Chapter 39

A few days before the handfasting Thomas Elliott arrived at Wydon with his extended family, some Kerrs and Ogles among them. This could lead to a useful and profitable gathering. Thomas sat at the kitchen table having breakfast when Isobel arrived. She had risen early, ridden over to old Janet Tether at Tibble village to collect linen for her handfasting and returned in good spirits with arms full of gifts.

She crossed the yard and, as she opened the kitchen door, stopped suddenly at the sight of her father, sitting between John and Angus.

'Hello Isobel,' he said in a lower tone of voice than she was used to.

'Hello. I didn't know you had arrived.' She clutched her basket tightly to her chest.

'Yes, late last night.'

'Did you have a good journey?'

'Yes, probably better than the one you had.' He lifted his head and stiffened his body.

Isobel flushed, glared at her father, banged her fist on the table and struggled to control her voice. 'I HAD NO CHOICE!' she screamed back at him.

'Perhaps not but you could have waited until I returned.'

'No, I couldn't! John was injured and needed help. Mam threatened to kill him, she hated him so much. I was afraid for his life.'

Thomas looked down at the table, 'But she didn't, Isobel, did she?'

'She meant what she said! She has cursed him and all his male descendants. Did you know that? Did you know what she has done?'

Thomas Elliott looked up. His embarrassed face turned to one of anger, 'You drove her to it, Isobel. You were always disobedient.' His voice was shaking as he thumped the table so hard the bowls jumped, and wooden spoons splattered porridge over the floor.

'I did not! It was not my fault Margaret died. Mam sent us into danger, following the Reivers, to steal Katie Nixon's book.' She threw the basket at the table so hard the linens fell among dirty bowls.

John cleared his throat, stood up and laid a steadying hand on Thomas's shoulder, 'Yes, Thomas. Sadly, I arrived too late to help Margaret. Robert Ridley had already killed her. It was lucky I arrived when I did, before he realised his mistake and went back for Isobel.'

Isobel covered her face, desperately trying to control her weeping, 'Yes, father he'd killed the wrong sister! Mam changed towards me after that. Her jealousy got worse, and she became more cruel and made my life miserable. Did you not notice? Did you? Did you?'

The kitchen fell into a long period of silence. Thomas Elliott sat for a long while and said nothing. Then he stood up walked over to his daughter and held out his arms, 'I'm sorry, Isobel, I didn't know. Your mother told a different tale.'

'I knew she would. I have never understood why she disliked me so much.' Without thinking she threw her arms round his neck and sobbed. For what, she was unsure, after a lifetime of not being loved by her mother or understood by her father.

Thomas seemed taken aback by such a sudden display of emotion. He sighed, relieved. 'One day, Isobel, you will know why.' He released her grip and they both sat at the kitchen table.

Cook smiled, cleared the linens off the table, poured fresh hot porridge into four clean bowls and placed them in front of |Isobel, John, Angus, and Thomas. In a firm voice, standing with hands on hips, she said, 'Well, I am glad that's settled. We need to pull together and look after each other's interests.' She patted Isobel on the shoulder and with a wide smile across her face wandered over to the fire humming a merry tune.

Moments later Angus cleared his throat, pushed his chair away and stood up. 'Ah, Thomas, come to the stables, I have three new horses you might like to see. Got them from a dealer in Gretna last week. One is a big bay. Think she might be in foal.' The conversation tailed off as they left the room. John gave Isobel a long, lingering look, gently brushed against her hand as he left the table to follow the two older men out of the door.

Cook came over to where Isobel sat and took her hand. 'That went well. How are you feeling now you have spoken to your father?'

'Glad, perhaps part of him did love me after all but, you know, he said something odd about my mother. He said that one day I would find out why she disliked me so much. I wonder what he meant by that?'

'Men are strange. Perhaps he didn't treat your mother well. After all, he kidnapped her and had children with other women, all over the Borders by the sound of it.'

Isobel's mouth dropped open. 'Who told you all that?'

'Millie. She told Angus and I when she first arrived.'

Isobel's eyes widened, 'Millie? Millie told you. So, you knew before I did?' There are so many secrets... so much I don't know. But I will find out.'

'I am sure you will but, not now, we have a handfasting to organise. Let's go upstairs and have another look in the chest.'

Isobel bowed her head, nodded, and followed Cook up the back stairs, 'I am glad my father is here, and things seem settled between us. Now I only have mother's Kerr relatives to worry about. Will they come and what will happen? But I am happy at Millie's return.'

'Isobel, do you like the green silk gown I got from the trader in Hexham yesterday? It's a lovely shade for a handfasting. Or would you like something different? Let's have another peep in the chest and see what else we can discover.'

'Yes, I do like it. It's a lovely colour. Goes with my hair.' Isobel lifted the gown to her face and both women giggled.

'Come and sit next to me. Lots of old treasures are in this chest. Let's have another look.' She patted the bed for Isobel to sit down and began talking about her sister, Annie.

'You are very similar to his mother: long fair hair, blue eyes, slim, tall and elegant.' Cook gazed out of the open window onto the distant hills, sighed, then returned to emptying the bedding chest.

'Oh look, I remember this bracelet. I gave it to her when we were children and she kept it all those years. We made it from seashells that our father brought back from one of his trips.' Her eyes filled with tears.

Isobel saw a pair of woolen gloves, worn and faded with age, a small box with a dried petal inside, a pair of tattered shoes, hair fastenings, a chain with a blue stone hanging from it and a ring, a plain band, perhaps her wedding ring.

Cook took out a silver clasp with the initial A on it, held it to her lips and kissed it.

'Was that a precious clasp?'

'Belonged to our mother, Agnes. I haven't seen it in many seasons. I'd forgotten it was in this chest.' She quickly put it into her apron pocket.

Cook pulled out a carefully folded linen cloth and neatly placed inside was a small, dark book. 'This is where we wrote our hopes and dreams for the future.' As she turned the pages, beautiful drawings appeared from aged papers, colours only slightly faded.

'See, Isobel, this is my sister's writing.'

'She was very neat and careful. I imagine she was a gifted and lively person by the way her letters dance on the page.' Isobel caressed the words with her fingers.

The older woman smiled, and a single tear rolled down her cheek and landed on the word "love". 'You know Isobel, I cannot remember the sound of her voice.' Cook trembled. Isobel held her hand and they sat together for a while in silence.

'It has been a long time since she went to the Otherworld. I love John dearly as if he was my own.'

'Yes, I do too.'

'I am not surprised he wanted you.'

'What do you mean?'

'You are so like her.'

Isobel looked surprised, 'His mother? But he never knew her.'

'Interesting, isn't it, that, somewhere in the depths of his being, he knew.'

'Knew what? Was he searching for a mother?' Isobel's heart began to beat faster. She wanted to be his wife, not his mother. Cook, seeing Isobel's alarmed face, patted her arm.

'No, no Isobel, I know John loves you. But part of him is his mother. Perhaps it's his mother's way of finding happiness for him. Something she lost.'

Isobel wasn't sure where the conversation was going, as Cook continued to reminisce and ramble on about their childhood. She wiped her eyes and returned to rummaging through the chest.

'Please don't be upset, Isobel. I am sure John loves you for who you are.'

'I'm not sure,' she said, shaking her head, having difficulty hiding how she felt.

'It's just the ramblings of an old woman reminiscing… Please don't begrudge me that.

Chapter 40
The Handfasting

Mayday arrived, the time for Isobel's and John's handfasting. Families had come from distant settlements, glens, valleys and villages to celebrate with them. The women had spent many days baking and preparing food and extra ale had been brewed. The men had returned from hunting with a few rabbits, pheasants and pigeons. It would have been a poor affair if Edgar had not brought down an injured stag two days earlier.

Costumes had been made, antler headdresses brought out, dusted and redecorated, hats with fresh flowers and ivy garlands made and hung in the shade. Ribbons and silks had been collected and fastened onto the old hawthorn faerie tree in the pasture, making it ready to dance round, there being no maypole again this year.

Elphin, the Bard, usually came to Beltaine ceremonies but this year he was late. After a long search, Angus had found him in Corbridge and brought him back to handfast his son to Isobel Elliott. The young and the old had been sent into a nearby field to build a labyrinth, a physical, symbolic representation of a spiritual journey, for those who wished to walk a meditative path to the middle and seek answers.

On Beltaine eve, the night of men's mischief, John and his friends had waited until the sun had long since set before gathering round the houses of their brides and, knowing they would be asleep, quietly tying garlands of greenery, birch, ivy, nettles, thistles, weeds, briar or holly to the doors of the girls' houses. Each garland carried a secret only known to the couple. Then the men had stood as one, blown their horns in unison and watched as candles were lit in windows and weary faces looked out to the sight of their menfolk, jeering and laughing.

Isobel awoke at dawn, very excited. The sun had peeped through a gap in the curtains and shone onto her pillow. She blinked, lay still for a few moments, yawned, had a long stretch, then leapt out of bed, dressed quickly, ran downstairs bouncing into the kitchen so fast she tripped over the broom. Struggling to her feet, she looked at the women in the room.

'Morning Cook, Millie, Martha, Jane, where are the Kerr girls, Mary and Margaret? Are they not up yet? They are being hand-fasted today as well.'

'Isobel it's early. Most sensible girls are still abed. You be careful. Have you hurt your leg on that broom? You'll have a bruise. Just as well your dress will cover it,' and, hands on hips, she shook her head.

'Oh, Cook, it could have been worse. It might have scratched my beautiful little face.' She tilted her head sideways and ran into Cook's open arms, smiling, 'Oh, it's Beltaine, my handfasting day. It's going to be a perfect day.' She kept giggling and dancing round and round the kitchen table pulling out chairs, chased by the barking dogs.

'Isobel, get you head out of the clouds there is much to do.'

'Yes, Cook. Oh yes. So much to do.' She skipped out of the kitchen and all the way across the yard to the stable.

'Millie, you had better go after her. I hope she's not off to find John. If she does, it'll bring bad luck on a day like this. The sun will go in. No good will come of it. She needs something to do. Here, give her these baskets to fill by the stream. Tell her I want them full of watercress. Oh, Millie, if you see Martha's mother send her in. The children need to be sent out to make a green man.'

Millie frowned, nodded, raised her eyebrows, shrugged her shoulders as if unsure if picking watercress was the answer.

Isobel opened the pasture gate and danced among the wildflowers. She looked up at the sun and smiled, knelt in the tall grass and washed her face in the early morning dew. 'Please make me more beautiful and remove those brown freckles from my nose,' she asked, as she giggled and rolled down the grassy bank, with her heart full of joy.

Millie and Cook spent the day trying to keep Isobel busy, welcoming guests, helping to unload stable carts, carrying goods back and forth from the kitchen and erecting temporary shelters for the children. As the day wore on, the anticipation grew, as more and more people arrived.

By midafternoon the pasture was full of excitement and Isobel made her way into the house to get ready. Martha Robson, her cousin Jane Armstrong and Mary and Margaret Kerr joined Isobel in the house, where the five girls, Cook and their mothers, all laughing and giggling, got themselves ready for their handfastings.

Isobel had not seen John or any of the other men to be tied all day and suspected they were off somewhere doing some male druid preparations.

Chapter 41

It was early afternoon, and the sun was still high in the sky, warming the land, when, from deep within the nearby woods, came the distant sound of the druid's ceremonial horn. Everyone paused. It was time to begin the handfasting ceremony. The horn was followed by a slow, quiet, rhythmical sound of drums which kept a steady beat as guests walked into the pasture, adults and children all forming a large circle round the flowers in the middle, women standing in the east, men in the west. The noise became louder as the drumming intensified and the assembled gathering cheered and chanted in praise of the trees and the land.

Cook made the final touches to Isobel's braided hair, laid the flower crown on her head, tied knotted bells round one ankle, smoothed her tight-fitting green silk dress and then, with a small tear, turned to Isobel, 'I am giving you John's mother's broach, worn on her dress when she married John's father and I think it's only right you have it now. Bend down dear so I can put it on.'

Isobel gasped and gently traced its shape with her fingers, 'It's beautiful. Emeralds set in silver Celtic knots. Oh, Cook, thank you so much, it's beautiful. Will Angus mind? Is it alright with him?'

'Now don't you worry your pretty little head about that. He will do what I tell him. Annie would want John's wife to have it. I know she would.' Once more tears welled up in Cook's eyes. Isobel opened her arms and hugged her. 'I am so grateful to you. You've been more of a mother to me than my own.'

Cook took a cloth out of her pocket, wiped her face, straightened her dress, and opened the kitchen door, 'Now, come on, let's have no more of this. It's your handfasting day and everyone will be outside waiting for us. Let's go and join the others.' She bent forward and gave Isobel a quick kiss on the cheek.

Isobel took a deep breath, smiled, hitched her dress up in both hands and skipped down the field, through the gate into the pasture. She made her way to the Eastern gate, the place of the rising sun. The women stood together in the circle holding hands and, as she approached, hands parted, space was made, hands were rejoined, and the circle was again closed.

John entered the circle at the Western gate, the place of the setting sun. The men's hands parted, space was made, hands were rejoined, and the circle closed once more, men standing together in the West and women in the East. Isobel raised her head, looked across the circle to where John stood, tall and proud, in his brown leather trousers and red embroidered shirt, with dappled leather jerkin over the top. He wore an elaborately decorated headdress with a stag's antlers as its centre piece.

He caught her gaze, and a quiet, gentle smile could be seen spreading across his face. Isobel closed her eyes and flushed. She tapped her feet up and down, turned sideways to look at Jennie, who was standing beside her, and squeezed the girl's hand so hard she winced with the pain.

'I'm sorry, Jennie, it's all so exciting. John is just so handsome. He's there, over there, waiting for me.' Then both girls were startled into silence as the great horn was blown once more.

All eyes turned to follow the sound and there, standing in the North, was Elphin, the Bard. He laid down the great horn, took several deep breaths and, in a deep, loud voice, began to speak.

'John, you are Cernuous the Hunter, come to take your bride, the May Queen. This night will be spent in the wildwood, to ensure the fertility of the land, to make love under the trees, to sing and dance and awaken to bathe in the early morning dew. Through your union at Beltaine, together you will share your knowledge of the power of the great circle of life and death through the seasons.'

'Who comes to this circle walking the path of the sun?'

John walked sun wise to the middle of the circle. 'I do.'

'Who comes to this circle walking the path of the moon?'

Isobel walked to stand opposite John. 'I do.'

Elphin, the Bard, stamped the ground three times with his Oak staff and looked directly into Isobel's eyes. 'Isobel, what do you say to this man?'

It took a few moments for Isobel to reply. A troublesome flower had fallen from her May crown and was dangling over her brow and her rehearsed words had flown away. She took a deep breath, raised her head, and turned her gaze to the face of her lover.

'I love you, John, and I will always believe in you. I have total trust. I have no regrets about running away with you. I want to spend my whole life with you and bear many sons. I want us to sing and dance together in the summer meadows. I want to harvest our fields together and walk beside you on the cold wintery nights. Sometimes you will be ill or injured and I will always do my best to heal you. I look forward to spending the rest of my life with you. Our old age will be full of wisdom. I will love you forever and am so blessed to have you in my life.'

The women stood smiling, hands on faces wiping tears from their eyes.

Elphin, the Bard, stamped the ground three times with his Oak staff, 'John, what do you say to this woman?'

John smiled, took a long deep breath, pushed back his shoulders, and looked directly into her green eyes, 'I love you too, Isobel. I will keep you safe and hunt well for the pot. I am proud of you, for who you are and what you have done. Isobel, you are valued by all of us. I want to waken with you in my arms each morning, where I will give you my strength and protection and I want, each night, to comfort you from the troubles of the day.'

Elphin spoke once more, 'John, what is it you bring the May Queen?'

John put his hand in his jerkin pocket and gave Isobel a silver amulet, embossed with a grey wolf, 'Isobel, this wolf will bring you inner strength and give you courage to take risks to become a great healer. He will guide your inner power.' He lifted her hand, gently placed the amulet on her wrist, raised her hand to his lips, kissed the wolf and said, 'Wear it always.'

Elphin spoke again, 'Isobel, what is it you bring to Cernuous the Hunter.'

Isobel carefully put her hand down the front of her dress and brought out a golden pin, so bright it dazzled. The dragon was curled twice round itself, its head tucked beneath folded wings. The emerald jewelled eyes sparkled, and she looked directly into John's piercing brown ones, 'John, I give you the special gift of the Earth Dragon. He is a fierce guardian who will protect you and your reiving ways. Keep him by your heart and each time you touch him, he will sing, and you will know I am calling you safely home.'

Elphin, the Bard, let out a long sigh followed by a wide smile, 'It is now time to bind you together.'

He joined their hands, right to right and left to left, and bound their hands together with the braid of spun wool, leaves, twigs and mosses that Isobel had collected from the Wydon fells and carefully woven into an intricate pattern, an expression of her love and commitment.

'Isobel and John, I unite you together. I invoke the protection of the five elements: Air, Fire, Water, Earth and Spirit. Bless you both as you weave your lives together.'

Tears flowed down Isobel's face as Elphin, the Bard, gestured they should sit down on the warm meadow grass. 'I shall give you the loving cup to seal the bond between you.'

He poured mead into a silver goblet which he gave to John who held it to Isobel's mouth for her to drink. Then he put the goblet into her hands to hold to John's mouth for him to drink.

Then Elphin held the goblet to the sky. 'This mead, the nectar of the druids that you have now shared will bring balance when you are apart and bring you together in future lives.'

Elphin, the Bard, took the cup and gave it to Angus. He stamped his Oak staff on the ground three times, 'You will take the first drink of the circle, share the hopes and dreams of these two young people and wish them well.' The goblet was passed round each person in the circle and had to be refilled many times, the men taking their vow very seriously.

Elphin, the Bard, looked to the sky, lifted his arms to the heavens and spoke,

> 'Above you are the stars.
> Below you are the rocks.
> Your love will be strong like the rocks
> And as constant as the stars.
> May you both be guided by the greater power that
> Connects us all together.'

He then untied their hands, turned to those in the circle and with the biggest smile on his face that Isobel had ever seen, shouted, 'What gifts have you brought, for John and Isobel, be it ale, verse or song?'

The young couple stood together, hand in hand, and welcomed a long procession of people bearing gifts. Mary Johnson gave Isobel a woollen tunic from her family, a rich prize indeed. The Elliott men gave John a basket hilted sword. His father, Angus, had purchased a dagger with an inlaid crystal handle. Cook was in tears of joy with Isobel's response to her gift of a linen underdress with the initials I.T. embroidered on it. Other gifts included a woollen blanket, leather strips for tying boots and a wide, soft, embossed belt for John. There were lots of flowers and herb plants. Old Meg sent a basket of bottles and containers to help stock Isobel's new apothecary.

Suddenly, from among the crowd, Thomas Elliott walked forward, leading Isobel's black stallion, 'Daughter, you left your horse when you fled. I return him to you and may his strength keep you safe. I am pleased with your match. The alliance will be a good one for all of us.'

'Thank you, father. I am pleased to have him back... and ... I am pleased you are here.'

Thomas Elliott put the reins into her hands, gave them a little squeeze, nodded his head and walked back to his men. The stallion lifted his head and snuffled her chest. Isobel dropped the reins and smiled, threw her arms round the animal's neck and wept with joy. It was the only thing she had regretted leaving, her beautiful Irish stallion.

Other gifts included a brown leather book for journaling, a hair clip in the shape of a letter T, several bars of soap, all different shapes and sizes, a drawing of Wydon from Mrs. Mary Ogle, a few bags of oats, two cockerels, a woven wall hanging and undergarments for Isobel. Meggie Johnson gave her a tortoiseshell hair comb she had bought from a trader in Antwerp and long woollen socks for John.

Cook had made John a new jacket with a brightly coloured, embroidered badge sewn inside his tunic so, when he was injured or lost, all who found him would know of his clan. John was given two new shirts and many ornaments for his horse's bridle. The Robson family presented Isobel with new bed linen embroidered with the initials I.J.T. A pair of much sought-after silk stockings appeared, along with a bottle of rose perfume. A pair of rabbit fur mittens came with a smudge wing from a fallen raven, inlaid with quartz. There were lots of pots and pans for the kitchen. Totter, the old woodsman, who used to make Isobel's splints had sent a rocking chair, which she immediately sat in and rocked to and fro as her lap quickly filled with more gifts.

Thomas Elliott came to John carrying a large rolled up bundle. He showed no signs of animosity, frustration, or anger towards the kidnapper of his daughter. 'Here, John, I give you this long leather coat. Should fit you well enough. Keep you dry in the winter.' He pushed it into John's hands, turned to walk away, cleared his throat, 'Mind you look after that lass of mine.' He lowered his head and returned to his drinking companions.

From the outskirts of the circle the old women wove their way towards the bride. Nellie Oldbottom was first. She approached Isobel grinning and giggling and laid a knitted blanket on her lap, 'For the little ones, Dear.' She tapped Isobel's hand, bowed in acknowledgement, turned, and shuffled away, leaving Isobel flushed, hoping no one noticed.

Grandmother Ogle, was the first to bring writings, 'I bless you, my Dears, that the sun will always shine on you both like a great fire and bring you lots of little ones.'

Jenny Tomson was next, 'May the rain fall on your fields and wash away troubles. May it cleanse the earth and make it fertile.' She trickled a handful of seeds in a circle around Isobel.

Ma Oliver said, 'I give you the blessings of Mother Earth under your feet and wish you a long life together.' She gave Isobel a kiss on the cheek as she picked a daisy from her crown to sniff. She smiled and said 'Perhaps a memory dear? Just a little memory for an old woman.'

Old Mother Elliott staggered forward, grasped Isobel's arm and said, 'Always be kind, my Dear, always be kind.' Then she winked and patted Isobel's arm as she hugged her, an acknowledgement of something unspoken between them.

John Scott approached, 'I hope, Isobel, that you will keep the candle lit in the north window to guide us wanderers in from the storms.'

Isobel smiled. 'Yes of course. Wouldn't want you thieves to get lost in the dark.' She raised her eyebrows and smiled at the old rogue. When the gift giving was over Elphin the Bard stamped his staff three times on the anchor stone, 'Hail! hail and welcome to all. Gather round, it's time to jump the broom.' Excitement rose among the crowd. The broom had been made by John, from a hazel shaft with a birch brush fastened at the bottom and tied with braid woven by Isobel. The word, MORNING, in the Ogham alphabet was engraved onto its shaft. The word meant, new beginning, hope, fresh start, freedom from darkness... light.

'Who will hold the broom?'

'I will, I will!' Millie ran forward, closely followed by John's younger brother, Jack, who gave Millie a deeply desirous smile as he picked up the other end and they faced each other, holding the broom.

Elphin, the Bard, called, 'Who will sweep away their past?'

Angus approached, standing tall and proud. He above anyone else, was aware of the struggles Isobel and John had been through. This, for him, was an important moment. 'Come, Children....,' he said, then paused as Elphin the Bard shouted to the crowd.

'This broom represents the boundary between your lives as Isobel and John and the life that you wish to move towards together. In jumping this broom, you are leaving your old lives and old ways behind and starting afresh.'

Elphin, the Bard, stamped his staff three times and, on the third strike, Jack and Millie lifted the broom high as Isobel and John, holding hands and smiling at each other, jumped the broom, to great cheers from everyone. Angus stepped forward, took the broom from Millie and Jack, and began to sweep. He bellowed, 'I sweep your past behind you! It is all done and gone.' He swept so heavily that the fresh grass was torn from its summer roots.

Isobel and John returned to the circle to watch their friends enter and be hand-fasted. Their turn had come.

Chapter 42

At the end of the afternoon and before the maypole dancing began, the Beltaine fire was lit. Elphin, the Bard, walked over to Isobel, whispered in her ear, took her arm and together they wove their way through the merry crowds and into the old barn. He cleared the wooden bench, leaned down and retrieved something from underneath.

'Sit down, Isobel, I have some things to give you.' He passed her a small parcel carefully wrapped in red cloth. 'Here, my Dear, I have this precious gift for you.'

She unwrapped the cloth and gently caressed a book. Raising her head, she smiled.

'Yes, my Dear, it's old Katie Nixon's herb book.'

'Where did you get it? Where? Where? I never thought I would see it again.'

'Where do you think?'

Thoughts of home came rushing into her head; Margaret's death, John's rescue, walking through the woods with her mother, going through the book page by page, understanding, learning and then the horror of knowing that Katie had been a murderer.

'From my mother. You took it from my mother?'

'She had no need of it. Not anymore. Not now. She would want you to have it.'

'But I remember we hid it when we were together. So how did she have it?'

'I don't know, Isobel, perhaps she went back for it at a later date?'

Isobel sat transfixed, clutching the book to her chest.

'I have another gift for you. Come, I will show you.'

'Where are we going?'

Elphin ignored the question, took her hand and together they went through the farm steading to where his horse and cart were stabled.

'It wasn't the only thing I took from your mother's house.' He pulled out a large brown, leather shoulder bag that was wedged under his peddler's goods.

Isobel gasped and her eyes widened in surprise. The bag was full of things she recognised; bottles and jars full of dried herbs, tinctures, sachets of sweet powders, potions of various sizes and quantities, cloths, strips of linen, a batch of needles and various other bits used by herbalists.

'Elphin, these are my mother's supplies. Oh, Elphin! Running away with John meant most of my herbs were left behind and I fear it will take me many years to find where some of them grow here. I am very pleased, very happy. Thank you very much.' Isobel paused and threw her arms round the old man. Then she rummaged through the bag and frowned, 'But there are more here than she kept in the house.'

'Well, my Dear, they didn't all come from the house.'

'You bought some from the market. Oh, Elphin, how kind.'

Elphin shuffled awkwardly. 'No.'

Isobel's eyes expanded so much they were in danger of popping out. 'No? Elphin, have you been to the cave where we kept our stores? But it was a secret place. No one knew it was there.'

He bowed his head and looked embarrassed. 'I did, I have always known.'

'How did you know? I don't understand.'

He cleared his throat several times, then lifted his head, 'When your mother was young, she would travel with me on my journeys round the big houses. I was an important bard then.'

Isobel put her hand on his arm, 'Oh, Elphin, you are still important. Your wealth of knowledge is so valuable to us all.'

He patted her hand and cleared his throat again. 'Thank you, little one. I was there when your father kidnapped her. Over the years, we became close friends. I used to visit her, bring herbs, things she needed and, while she made her preparations, I would tell her stories of my travels.'

'In the cave?'

'Yes, in the cave, up on the hillside.'

'How did you know where it was? You were always travelling.'

'One day, many years ago, I followed her back from Hexham market.'

'You and my mother were friends? I am trying to understand. She was a cold unfeeling cruel woman, and you are so gentle and quiet.' Elphin blushed and Isobel thought something was amiss. His eyes filled with tears that slowly trickled down his face. A long pause followed. 'Elphin, she meant a lot to you, didn't she?'

'Yes, she did.'

'Oh, Elphin I had no idea that you two were close.' Then Isobel began to remember that, whenever Elphin was passing by on one of his trips, her mother always disappeared, and she was under strict instruction to stay at home and usually given a list of unimportant things to do. She looked at this sad, old man and her heart melted.

She sighed, took his arm and gently said, 'You and my mother were lovers?'

He turned and looked into her eyes and slowly nodded his head.

'Had you always been lovers?'

'Yes, from the first time we met. We were very happy. I loved your mother, Isobel, and she loved me.'

'Did my father know?'

'I suspect so. But he didn't care. He had enough women to satisfy him.'

Isobel was trying hard to understand...... her mother and Elphin the Bard? She had only recently learned about her father and his other women and children, scattered all over the borders.

'Did you have children together?' She sank back, unsure of why she had asked.

Elphin began to pat her hand again. 'My Dear, it does not matter now.'

'I expected you to say NO.' There was a long pause as Isobel gasped and sat with her mouth open.

'You did! You had children together! Well, where are they?

His eyes welled up with tears and she gently pushed a linen cloth into his hands, as he began to sob. He was so upset that Isobel wondered if his heart would break with … with what?

'We had two. A daughter, Margaret……' His voice trailed off.

Isobel thought she was going to faint and put her arms out to steady herself against the cart, 'Margaret. Margaret! My sister? My sister Margaret?'

'Yes, your sister Margaret. We loved that child and Elinor brought her to me whenever she could.'

Isobel's legs wobbled and she felt herself slide and land with a thump on the ground. Suddenly lots of things began to make sense, like why Margaret had always been the favourite. Because she had been fathered by the man her mother loved.

'Fraser, was he yours as well?'

'Yes, he was mine. Both are gone now. I will never see my children again.' He wiped his eyes and took a deep breath.

Isobel didn't know if she dared ask about herself but desperately wanted to know the truth and began to secretly pray that he would say yes. 'And me?' she said in a sheepish voice.

'No, Isobel, not you. But I wish I had been your father. You are so lovely, clever and everything I could have wanted in a daughter.'

Isobel fought back her tears, stood up and made herself busy, brushing imaginary grass from her dress.

'Margaret was a silly girl, hard to understand and your mother spoilt her too much.'

'My mother hated my father. Is that why she was cruel to me? Because I was his daughter?'

'I expect so.' Elphin put his hand under a grubby, dark sheet, opened a box and took out a book. Isobel recognised it.

'I brought you her herb book as well. I know she would have wanted you to have it. After Margaret died, she wanted to spend more time with you, walking, talking, herb gathering and doing things together.'

'So, I replaced my sister, did I? Well, it was all too late, wasn't it?' Isobel clenched her fists and thumped his chest fighting the desire to strangle the messenger. Part of her wished he had not told her.

'Perhaps so,' he said, gently taking hold of her hands. 'Yes, perhaps so. Isobel, you must forgive your mother. In her own way she did love you. Remember the life she had, brought up to be an independent herbalist in a wealthy household, kidnapped by your father and forced to lead a rough, tough life that she hated, well at the beginning anyway. But she was a lovely kind woman and I think you are very like her. If only you had known her as I did.' Elphin, the Bard, dropped his head and sighed, put his hands on her shoulders and gave them a squeeze.

'And now you have both books, and it is your wedding day so let us return to the festivities.' He wiped his eyes, gave her the cloth to wipe hers and, together, they walked back to the pasture to join in the Maypole dancing, to eat and drink ale.

It truly had been a momentous day.

Elphin the Bard put his hand on her arm and said, 'It is all as it should be, Isobel.'

'I know. Thank you for telling me. Elphin, so much of my relationship with her makes sense now. It's such a lot to think about and today is my handfasting,' she sighed.

Elphin turned to look at her, 'Isobel, I am the keeper of secrets. I know things no one else knows or cares about.'

The Uncovered Legacy

She smiled, 'No one else could have told me what you have. I know that.'

'Come on. Let us join the festivities. I think tonight I shall get very drunk.' He took her arm and he laughed and laughed. As they reached the gate, Johnny Johnson emerged, grinning, carrying a flagon of ale and shouting a raucous greeting to Elphin, who quickened his pace to join him.

Isobel smiled and watched Elphin… for an old man he moved remarkably quickly. She paused, smiled to herself in gratitude for his honesty. It had been a strange encounter.

Chapter 43

I sobel looked around at the throngs of people merrymaking and waved as Mary and Jane ran towards her. 'There you are, Isobel. Come. It's time to take our baskets of rosemary round.'

The three girls held hands, whirling round and round giggling, as they skipped to a small, hastily erected shelter and picked up their baskets of rosemary.

'Let's find the other brides, Mary. Come, Jane.'

The blue and purple flowerheads released their intoxicating oils, making the girls a little lightheaded as they ran, in a daze, among the crowds, looking for the other brides. Each was given a sprig of rosemary, always accompanied by lots of laughter to a repetitive verse,

> 'Remember not to wear new clothes tonight,
> lest they be torn in the woodlands flight.'

Clootie strips of cloth were tied to the hawthorn tree as gifts to the Fae who lived within. Men and women were holding hands and dancing round the hawthorn, singing to the spirit of the trees, their interweaving energies asking for the fertility of the summer lands.

The girls smiled at each other as they wandered off, arm in arm, to the far corner of the field, where a solitary, mature sycamore tree stood, with its leaves open just enough to allow the green flowers space to dangle in the light breeze.

A loose sheet of old linen hung between two branches and under it sat an old hag. A faded woollen shawl was wrapped round her thin, little body, her hands lay on her lap, where she held a large crystal ball. She was calling to all who passed, 'Come, my pretty ones, and I will tell of your future.'

Jane took Isobel's hand and pulled her towards the old woman, 'Let's have our fortunes told. Come on it'll be fun.'

'I'm not sure.' She pulled away.

'I'll go first.' Jane sat down and gave the old woman her hands. Isobel stepped back, unwilling to intrude. It wasn't long before Jane came out dancing in circles.

'You seem very happy did you have good news?'

'Yes, lots of children. Isobel, you know how much I love children.' She took Mary's hand and spun her round and round as they skipped off to the other tents, leaving Isobel alone.

Moments later a quiet, gentle voice floated towards her, 'Are you afraid of me, Isobel?'

The Uncovered Legacy

She spun round to look at the old hag, 'How do you know my name?'

The old one nodded and held out her hand, 'I know who you are. I have always known about you and your destiny.'

Isobel put her hands on her hips, lowered her head and stared, 'How could you?' This was all a bit frightening and annoying. After all, she did not know this old woman. 'What is it you think you know?'

'Come, Child. Sit with me. Give me your hands and we will look into the ball together.'

Isobel had heard of these old hags before, travelling through the Borders, telling tales. On one visit, Millie had given a precious loaf of bread to an old hag and come home in tears, although unwilling to tell. But this old woman had a compelling way about her, and Isobel moved forward, sat down and placed her hands round the ball. For a while nothing happened. Then her hands warmed and flashing lights appeared.

Startled, she tried to pull away. 'What do they mean? What are they?'

But the old hag held them firm. 'They tell of your future.'

'My future? What do you know of my future?'

The hag looked deep into her eyes and stared for several seconds.

'You will have children.'

Isobel smiled and nodded while the old one went on about good crops, harsh seasons, children running around Beltaine fires, lots of travelling and new things to find in distant places. Suddenly she stopped and became silent.

Isobel's heart began to beat faster. 'What is it? What do you see? Why have you stopped?'

'Oh, just an old woman having a rest.' She began to fidget.

'No, it was more than that! You saw something! Tell me! Tell me, what was it?'

'It's getting late and I'm weary. There now. Be off with you.' She pushed Isobel's hands off the crystal ball and began to wrap it up in a brightly coloured cloth.

'Tell me! Tell me what you saw, please! Please!'

'It's of no matter. It's getting dark. The light is fading. It's hard to see.'

But Isobel suspected this was a lie and put her hands back onto the ball, 'Please tell me!'

'Some things are best left unsaid.'

'You're frightening me now. What things? Please, tell me!'

'You will have two sons, healthy ones.'

'And daughters? Will I have daughters? I want a daughter to pass on my skills.' She smiled, her heart skipping a beat.

'There will be no time for more children.'

'No time? What do you mean, no time?'

The hag shook her head and held firm to Isobel's hands. She looked deep into her eyes, 'There is darkness coming to you, little one.' A single tear rolled slowly down the old woman's wrinkled face and landed, trembling, on the crystal ball.

'Darkness? What kind of darkness? What form does it take? What do you mean?'

'A man, an ugly man, a deformed being. Be careful, my Dear, be careful.'

Isobel withdrew her hands, held her head and stood up shrieking at the sound of the words 'DEFORMED BEING.' 'It's Robert Ridley! I know it is! No, no, you must be wrong! Please be wrong. Are you sure? Look again!'

'No names. I cannot see names.' The old hag kept shaking her head.

'I know it's him!' Isobel clasped her dress and tried hard to fight back the tears.

The hag smiled but would only say, 'He will come. He will come.'

'When? When will I know he is coming?'

'Enjoy what you have now, Isobel. Be happy, my Dear. Be happy.' She quickly gathered her belongings and disappeared into the wood.

'Enjoy your life' felt, to Isobel, like it wasn't going to be very long. Panic gripped her mind. It became a bloody kaleidoscope of Ridley. Yet the thought of two sons lifted her spirits and the sight of Jane running excitedly towards her momentarily took her thoughts away.

'Isobel, come over here. Come and look at this.' They ran barefoot, hand in hand, hair flowing in the evening breeze, to join the other women and children, who were singing and dancing. As she danced the conversation with the old hag faded and became a forgotten memory. Some of the old men sat together with their animal hide shamanic drums and kept a good rhythm for the girls, who danced until they collapsed, laughing into an exhausted heap on the meadow grasses.

Chapter 44

The sound of the ceremonial horn caused everyone to turn and run to the far end of the pasture, where men and their horses were jostling for position on the starting line. The highlight of the day, the Reiver Race, was about to begin. Isobel struggled to see John in the throng of riders, but he was there, on his bay mare, pushing her father, Thomas, out of his way.

The horn sounded a second time, and they were off, galloping across the field, onto Middle Fell, through the Tootup Wood, where they momentarily went out of sight, back up through Crow Hill dip, over the near side of the fell and back into view to lots of cheering and shouting. Each rider had a price on his head. Successful gambling on this race meant a man could win enough money to keep his family through the dry summer months. After several anxious minutes the riders came back into sight and crossed the finishing line, a flax rope tied between two oak trees.

Isobel heard herself shouting, 'Come on, John! Come on, John!'

Several horses crossed the line together, which resulted in a lot of shouting and arguing. Reivers jumped off their horses and very quickly fighting broke out.

Loose horses, sweating and foaming at the mouth after a hard ride, stumbled and trotted away in various directions, much to the joy of young children, who ran after them. It was a great game to catch a horse, mount it and have your own race. Anxious mothers screamed as they ran after their children in the hope of catching them, but the children were too quick and were soon riding round the course at full speed. Often horse and rider returned separately.

John decided he was the winner of the race, took his prize money and followed by many others, strode to the slu dogs. He approached the pen, where the dogs were all tied up, barking loudly, looked them over and pointed to a young black and white collie, 'I'll have that one.'

'He's not for sale,' said a large, rough looking man.

'Everything's for sale and that's the one I want. I always get what I want.' He stepped forward, wide eyed and shouted. 'Do you know who I am?'

'Don't care who you are. He's not for sale.'

John did not listen. He strode into the dog pen, untied the dog and walked off. 'I take what I want.'

It was met with a loud, 'Hey! Come back here! That's my dog, you thief! I will have you for this!' He ran after John, grabbed his shoulder and spun him round so fast John lost his balance, helped to the ground by a heavy fist in his face, momentarily knocking him out. As he came round, dazed, he lay still, hot, sweaty, dirty and in no mood to be thwarted. John's father and brothers arrived on the scene along with several other drunken men. Angus lifted his son by the scruff of his neck, checked he was alive and dropped him back onto the ground. Then, looking at the sturdy man, he bellowed, 'Enough! Enough, it's Beltaine. My son wants that dog. He's for sale is he not?'

'No.'

'Why is he here then?'

'He's mine. Bought him from Matt Crozier this morning.'

'Where?'

'Down Hexham way….in the shire….' and he began to mutter some incoherent nonsense.

'Liar. I know Matt Crozier. He never owned a dog in his life, and I saw him not two days ago laid up with a broken leg in the Debatable Lands.'

At this accusation the man picked up the dog and put a knife to its throat, 'I'm having him or nobody's having him. Do you hear me? Do you? I'll kill it!'

The sight of the knife quickly brought all the drunkards out of their stupor. John struggled to his feet and stood behind man and dog.

Angus's face set in a furious rage. 'You wouldn't harm the dog. It's young and valuable. Who are you anyway? You are not from these parts.'

The dog was whining and struggling to be free, which only tightened the man's grip. The other dogs, still tied up waiting to be sold, were straining on their ropes and barking, increasing the tension. Then one of the younger men turned to Angus and screamed, 'I know who he is! Spent three months in Carlisle jail with him two years back!'

'Who is he?'

'Halflug Ridley.'

'What?' exclaimed Angus. 'Ridley! Ridley!'

'Brother to Robert Ridley,' said Tom Armstrong. Everyone stared…stunned.

John, overhearing the conversation, stood to his full height, nodded to his father, pulled a dagger out of his left boot and stabbed Halflug Ridley in the back. 'You bastard.'

Ridley screamed and dropped his knife. His arms flew wide as he staggered forwards and slumped on the ground. The dog fell heavily, whimpered, and limped away, holding its right leg in the air.

The noise brought more people to the scene to see what the mayhem was about. 'What is it? What's happened?' they shouted in a disorganised union.

Isobel was one of the first there and pushed herself to the front. After seeing the fight at the end of the horse race and John stride towards the dogs, she feared the worst. 'John? John? Where is John?'

Angus took her arm and pushed her away. Before the crowd, lay a sturdy man, face down, framed by a ring of daisies, one knife lying on the ground, the other in his back.

'Is he dead?' someone asked.

'He's dead.'

'John! John!' she screamed. Then she saw him move forward, pull the knife out of the man's back, wipe it on his shirt and replace it in his boot.

John turned, either unable or unwilling to make eye contact with her, picked up the lame dog, tucked it under his arm and walked back to the farm steading.

Isobel ran after him, shouting, 'John! John, are you alright?'

The dog yelped as he readjusted it under his arm. 'Get your herb bag we will need it.' Reaching the kitchen, John kicked the door open.

'Wait John. Let me put a cloth on the table first.'

'He's a young un and from good breeding stock by the look of him.' He gently laid the injured animal on the kitchen table.

Isobel carefully examined the whimpering dog. 'Hold him down John. Put your arm across his back. I'll get something to calm him and dress the wound.'

'Is the leg broken?'

'Yes, I think so. Try to keep him still while I fetch a splint for the leg. Isobel rushed off into the back kitchen, to return moments later with an armful of bottles and bandages.

'I'll have to reset the leg and it will hurt. Today of all days. John it's my handfasting day.' But the noise of the injured animal soon brought her attention back to the present problem.

'Oh, you poor thing. Please be still while I mend your leg,' As she worked, she made lots of calming, nurturing noises to still the frightened patient. She cleaned and reset the leg, gave him a strong sleeping draught and he quickly fell asleep.

'Where shall I put him? He'll roll off the table when he comes round?'

'Over there, on that blanket by the fire. It will be a few hours before he wakes up. He'll be safe and warm there.'

John carefully carried the floppy body to an abandoned blanket, lying on the floor next to the fire, laid him down and covered him with it.

John looked shaken and, with a soft smile, she touched his arm and watched as he caressed the dog's ears, 'You'll recover, my lad. You're in good hands now.' He stood up, gave Isobel a lingering kiss and disappeared outside.

Isobel sat with the dog, put a small cushion under his head, readjusted the blanket and thought how gentle and caring John had been with the wounded animal.

As she leaned forward to put another log on the fire to keep the room warm her thoughts were interrupted by Millie, who came rushing into the kitchen.

Chapter 45

M illie shouted. 'He's still there!'

'Who, Millie? Who?'

'The fat man John stabbed!' She bounced up and down, hands in the air. 'Has no one moved him?'

'No! Come on, come and see!' Isobel followed Millie outside, to the far end of the pasture where the dog pens were. Isobel bent down over the body and stroked his head. 'Oh, Millie, he looks pale, uncared for. Why has no one come to claim him? Here, help me turn him over.' Millie frowned but knelt down and together they turned him onto his back.

'Look. There is blood seeping out from his wound, his clothes are discoloured, he's lying in a pool of red. It's quite beautiful in a gruesome way. It's the glistening of the moon as it shines through the dappled shade of the evening light. Poor man.'

'Don't touch him, Isobel! Don't touch him.'

'He's gone, Millie. Let's close his eyes so he can travel back to the Summerlands in peace.'

'In peace, Miss? After what he did?'

'He's gone, Millie, and, whatever he did in this life, it's over.'

Millie screwed up her face. She wasn't convinced, 'After what he did!'

'I'm sure it was no worse than the other men.'

'Not cold murder! No, that's wrong! Not cold murder!'

Isobel looked up at Millie, who was shaking her head.

'Murder, Millie? Murder? Who had he murdered?'

'Mary Lee Nixon,' she said, lifting her chin up. She knew something Miss Isobel didn't.

'I don't think I know her. But her name? Who was she Millie?'

'His wife and he murdered her.'

Isobel stood up, clasped her hands to her face and stared at the lifeless body, 'Who was he?'

Millie dropped her head and muttered, 'Well…. err … Halflug Ridley?'

Isobel gasped, 'What did you say? Speak up, Girl!'

'Halflug Ridley? '

'Ridley, you say. Was he a brother of Robert? NO! I don't believe it! Can't be! No! How do you know, Millie?' Isobel's legs felt weak and she slowly sat down on the grass.

'Yes, it's him and he killed his wife. The old woman sitting over there, talking to Jean Johnson, told me.' She pointed to a group of old women watching children play.

'She was friends with his wife. They all lived in Bewcastle. He got drunk and they had a fight.' Millie paused. 'Well, no one knows, really.' She opened her hands as if unsure of the truth. 'But she was dead the next morning, covered in blood and found tied to a chair. And her new baby was dead. And the dog.'

Isobel wasn't sure what to think. At least one of that hateful family was dead. It just left Robert and his father. There was also Tom and Dandle Ridley who had different mothers and had been brought up at Wydon. They were good raiders, loyal to the Tweddles and treated their women and children well. John and Dandle had grown up together and shared a close friendship. She loved listening to him tell tales of their failed hunting trips as boys. Not all Ridleys were the same.

'Millie where did you say he came from?'

'Bewcastle village. It's somewhere near them Debatable Lands where the rest of them thieves and rogues live, outside the laws of decent folk.' She wagged her finger at Isobel, who had a wry smile on her face, at the thought of decent folk.

'Who do you think will come for the body?' Isobel's heart began to thump at the sudden thought his brother Robert might come and the conversation with the old witch came flooding back into her head.

Millie bent down and poked the man's ribs, as if to check he was really gone. 'His father might come. He has a grievance against John.'

'John? Why, Millie? How do you know all these things?'

'It's the women, Miss. They tells all sorts of tales. They says family feud goes back so many generations nobody knows anymore. But it was something to do with stealing a wife.'

Millie looked away. Something had caught her eye. She trembled and put her hand on Isobel's arm. 'Come with me I want you to meet someone.' Millie, blushing, took Isobel's hand and pulled her away to where a group of young men were standing together teasing some young girls. They were waiting for the wrestling to begin between last year's champion Matty Ogle and Ian Kerr. As they approached, a boy, not yet old enough to be called a man, glanced over in their direction and came towards them.

'Hello, Millie. Decided to come to the wood with me?' He caught her round the waist and laughed.

She flushed, her face matching the colour of her dress, and giggled, 'I haven't decided.'

'You must be Isobel.' He stood squarely in front of her. An arrogant presence, she thought, and had the sudden urge to push him back. Only the adoring look on Millie's face made her pause.

'I am Isobel Tweddle.' She smiled to herself. Yes, she was a Tweddle now.

'Saw you fasted. Grand affair. That Elphin is an old rogue,' he said, puffing himself up to tower over both girls.

Isobel, hands on hips, looked him straight in the eyes. 'Rogue or not, he is my friend, a valued member of this community and I'll thank you to show him some respect!'

The boy lifted his hand and clenched his throat, as if to strangle himself. He staggered backwards pretending to groan. Isobel quivered and wondered who this cheeky, overconfident boy was.

'Elphin the Bard is not to be harmed!' Her voice was so forceful, the boy stepped back, released his hands and looked like he knew he had gone too far. 'I am mistress here. Who are you?' But before he could reply Millie interrupted. 'This is Michael Tweddle.'

Isobel raised her brow. 'Are you related to John?'

'Different family. We are from Wrae, far end of Neidpath Castle, near Peebles.'

She knew of Neidpath Castle, the original home of the Tweddles and she remembered the tales of Angus and his brothers leaving their ancestral home, the long trek south to England and their new home at Wydon. 'I hope you are returning tomorrow?'

Michael curled his lip at the edges creating the appearance of knowing he wasn't welcome. He turned to Millie, his smile reappeared, 'You've decided, you're coming with me.' He took her hand and together they ran off in the direction of the woods.

Millie turned back only once, to wave, before sliding her arm through his and giving it a little squeeze. He bent down and planted a kiss on her forehead. Isobel watched; pleased Millie had found her lover.

Chapter 46

Walking back to the hawthorn tree, now bedecked with colourful ribbons and cloths, Isobel paused and suddenly realised it wasn't a maypole. She frowned. 'No maypole.' she said out loud several times and, seeing Cook in the crowd, she had to find out why.

'Where is the Beltaine maypole?'

'We don't have one.'

'What do you mean, we don't have one? Every hamlet, village and settlement have one. Why don't we?'

Cook looked a little drunk and Isobel wasn't sure she knew what was going on.

'Gone. Gone. Gone. Only the tree now.' She pointed to the hawthorn.

Isobel, confused, stopped Cook from dancing and put her hands on her shoulders, 'Stop! Listen! I want to know why?'

'Well, my Dear, now, let me see…May.May. Maypole…oops it's gone again…' She couldn't stop giggling and Isobel could get no sense out of her.

John's brother Jack came up behind her, 'Now we are related, Isobel…Dear Sister,…let's dance.' He put his arms round her waist and whisked them both away to dance and sing to the fiddler's tune.

After an exhausting half hour, she pulled him to a halt, 'Please can we stop. Put me down. I only came to ask a question. Do you know why we have no maypole? Please tell me. You must know.'

'Ay, I know, Lass.' He took hold of her hand and continued to twirl her round.

'Tell me.'

'What's it worth. Give us a kiss and I'll tell you.' He picked her up in his arms.

Isobel slapped his chest hard, 'Jack, be serious. Please put me down.'

'Oh, it's a dark tale. You won't want to hear it.'

'But I do. Please tell me. I am beginning to think it is something sinister'.

'Well, when he was young, Robert Ridley….'

Isobel froze at the sound of his name. Why did it keep appearing in her life and today, of all days?

Then, as he looked over her shoulder, he became distracted by the sight of a pretty, servant girl so he released Isobel and walked towards her.

As he did that, an old woman, Isobel recognised from Fat Sow Hall, came over. 'Hello, Isobel. I will tell you. Come let's find somewhere quiet.' Together they moved away from the festivities and sat down under a large flowering sycamore tree. 'I saw the look of fear on your face when Jack mentioned Ridley. I know all about his stalking.'

'How do you know?'

'Cook told me.'

Isobel took the woman's hand, 'I am frightened of him. He's tried to take me so many times.'

'My name is Rosy Kerr. Cook and I have been friends all our lives so, yes, I know he is a bad man, hated by everyone but there are reasons for his behaviour.'

'I thought, when I was here at Wydon, I would be free of him.'

Rosy nodded her head and sighed. 'Sadly, I don't think that will happen until he's dead.'

Isobel shuddered and nervously looked round. 'Is he here?'

'No, he's not here. He wouldn't dare with so many Tweddles, their tenants and villagers about.'

'What do you mean?'

'You are not the only woman he chases. It's all the daughters of those involved.'

For a moment Isobel was unsure how she felt. Was she shocked or pleased she was not the only one? What was going on? Rosy took a deep breath, held Isobel's hands, and began her tale.

'Many years ago, when they were young, Robert and his friends got drunk on too much ale and fell asleep between the Beltaine fires.'

'How many of them?'

'No one knows exactly, but a few. It was a warm night that year and most of us had gone off into the woods to spend the night….' She paused, looked flushed and let out a small giggle. 'The story goes that some of the boys woke in the night and decided to have some fun.'

'How do you know this?'

'One of Ridley's friends, Michael Johnson, wasn't as drunk as Robert and crawled away and watched. Months later, when he was in another drunken stupor, his mother found out but there could have been more to it. I don't think we will ever really know who the other boys were.'

'What happened?'

'James Nixon was lying under the Maypole asleep. He wasn't a boy who was able to hold his ale.' Rosy paused, her voice began to shake, she took a deep breath, then continued. 'Robert set fire to the maypole. Some braids were dangling in the cool night breeze. The flames quickly took hold.' Isobel's hands flew to her face. Her mouth opened in a gasp of horror.

'Ridley and his friends were so drunk they staggered around laughing in a stupor and slept it off.'

'What happened to James Nixon?'

'According to Michael Johnson, he was burned alive. He woke up screaming but was too drunk to move. It must have been a horrible death.'

'And this Johnson did nothing to help?'

'No nothing.'

'Why?'

'Possibly unable to. Perhaps it was too late, flames too fierce.' Rosy began to sob uncontrollably.

'Did you know the dead boy?'

Rosy nodded and wiped her tears, 'He was my sister's son.'

Isobel put her arms round the older woman and together they sat for a while in silence. Isobel stared into the flowering long grasses, waving in a light breeze, struggling to get a sense of the maypole fire. After a while Rosy wiped her eyes, took a deep breath, and sighed.

'I didn't know any of this and I'm wondering why my mother didn't tell me. Was she here?' She wondered if her mother had had a secret hope that Robert would rid her of her existence.

'Yes, she was here Isobel. It was a big gathering that year and many families came from over the border. There was a large market as well. But, you know, Isobel, there has always been a maypole at Wydon. Villagers took it in turn to cut down a tree each year. People felt a new pole would bring hope and fertility to the land for the coming season. It became a tradition. Now we use a hawthorn tree in the pasture. No one wants a maypole anymore.'

'Who found the boy and how did the others know what they'd done?'

'The smell of burning flesh and the sight of smoke brought us running from the woods. Everyone was screaming and trying to fight the flames. His mother was badly burned trying to save him. Ridley was still drunk when they found him. The others had run off. He was covered in white ash and his hands were still holding the rope that was singed but not burned through.'

'The rope?'

'James had been tied to the maypole. Not all the braids were gone. Some must have burned through and blown off. They were lying about on the grass, evidence of what had happened. The boys ran off, leaving Ridley, who was dazed and staggered to his feet.'

'He should've been killed for what he'd done.'

Rosy sighed, wiped her eyes again and then a stern expression covered her face. 'We tried. The women were screaming and shouting. We wouldn't let our menfolk anywhere near him. I think, in truth, they were afraid of our anger. My sister ran forward and picked up sticks. The rest of us followed, gathered anything we could find and began to beat him until his face and body was bloodied and unrecognisable.'

'That must have been when he got the scar above his eye and why he limps so badly.'

'He never fully recovered. Grew into an ugly, deformed young man. We made sure no woman would ever look at him and he would never be able to father children.'

Isobel thought it was a shame they hadn't killed him.

Rosy picked up a long stick and frantically snapped it into many pieces and was soon surrounded by a pile of sawdust. She collapsed sobbing onto the warm grass. 'We thought he was dead, and we left him for the crows.'

'Who took him away?'

'We think his father, Buckle Knee Ridley. We came back the next day to burn his body, but he had disappeared.'

'That's an odd name? Where had they goner?'

'Yes, an odd name isn't it. He fell out of a tree when he was young and landed badly. But we think, they would have gone into the lawless, Debatable Lands.'

Isobel bent down and helped Rosy to her feet. 'Come on let's return to the festivities. I am so sorry for what happened.'

'That's not all.'

'There's more?'

'After that his reputation was in tatters. He was a murderer and to murder one of your own in such a cowardly fashion meant he was shunned by everyone. Destined to be alone.'

'Was Robert Ridley related to James Nixon?'

'Their mothers were sisters. Different fathers but family just the same.'

'I wondered why he was always alone skulking around on the outside of raids.'

'He was shamed by women and seeks revenge on their daughters. But, you know, Isobel, he had a terrible life with his mother. She was an angry woman and did terrible things to him. Her favourite trick was to lock him up in the grain store for days on end, without food or water, and it was very hot in there. She would curse the day he was born. His father beat him when he was young, probably still does. He became a frequent visitor to our home to be patched up. He was just an abused young boy, growing up with fear and hatred.'

Isobel began to make sense of his behaviour. 'So that's why he stalks us. But why was he never caught and hanged?'

'He has his uses as a spy, a go between. But everyone knows he's not to be trusted. His father has a similar reputation. Isobel, the Debatable Lands are a fearsome place. Wardens never go there. Not much to steal by all accounts. Home of the outlaws.'

The two women smiled, something important had passed between them. They held hands and walked back to join the others.

As they approached the gathering Rosy paused, 'Look, Isobel, how beautiful our hawthorn tree is. Do you see the red, white, and black ribbons tied together? They're lost among the other brightly coloured ribbons. But they represent blood, earth, and seed. The maypole is how we make our connection to earth, sea and sky.'

Isobel smiled, 'I think it's a good idea to have a new tradition, a new pole, a symbol of the incarnation of the nature spirit and the importance of the women choosing the tree. The magical hawthorn. It's perfect, isn't it? It encourages us to discover the challenges within ourselves and move forward with courage. If we focus, it will help us explore new places to test our strength and gain new insights into the meaning of our lives. It energises our being.'

Isobel stood for a long time absorbing its significance and tried to make sense of what Elphin had told her.

Then Jane broke into her thoughts, 'Isobel, come over here. Let's join the dancing. Oh, look, there's Calum with his brother, the blond Scott Come on. Let's go.'

Chapter 47

Towards the end of the evening the sky began to darken. The evening's festivities quietened. Some people were already asleep, others were packing their wares, and some parents were bedding children down somewhere safe for the night. The rest loaded their carts and drove away, no doubt hoping to travel home while the moon showered the tracks with light.

'Isobel, where have you been?' It was John. He took her hand, pulled her towards him and held her so tightly she was afraid she might break. But the sensation of his lips on hers and the pounding of his heart against her chest meant nothing else mattered. The conversations with Elphin, the Bard, the fortune teller, the injured dog and Rosy, all drifted away, taken by the wind and blown to a distant land.

After what seemed to Isobel an all too short embrace, John let her go, laughed, and swept her into his arms. Then he spun them both round and round until they collapsed on the ground laughing. All too quickly he became serious,

'Come, Isobel, it's time to jump the Beltaine fire. We will join with the land, and we will also be fertile. I want many sons.'

Isobel flushed at the thought and joy of begetting John's children. Hand in hand they jumped the Beltaine fire to the raucous sound of a crowd cheering them on. The other hand-fasted couples followed, Then the cattle and animals were driven through the smoke to protect them from disease and to empower the fertility of the land. It was a noisy affair with much shouting and animals being afraid, causing havoc as they desperately tried to avoid the flames. Children were running and screaming, trying to escape the frightened animals. But it was a joyous affair with people laughing and singing. The old people sat and watched with pleasure and amusement, drinking their ale and talking about the past. They had seen it all before.

John turned to Isobel, 'Take a burning log. Put it on one side. It belongs to our hearth now. The spirits of Beltaine will stay in our house and light our fire tomorrow.'

Isobel picked a thin, half burned log, blessed it with love and good fortune, ran back to the kitchen, where she checked on the injured dog, who was, thankfully, still asleep and put the sacred log safely on the stone floor to await the lighting tomorrow. Then she picked up a woollen blanket, she had earlier hidden behind the door, fled the kitchen and ran with joy in her heart towards John. He caught her hand in his and together they ran towards the wood, casting off their clothes as they went.

The night was warm and full of promise for their life together.

PART 3
The Awakening

Chapter 48

S ister Jocelyn put her hand on Jack's shoulder and gave it a comforting squeeze. 'Hello,' she said in a soft gentle voice.

'Why don't you hold her hand? Talk to her?'

'Will she hear me?'

'We think so, from what patients have told us when they've come round.'

'Talk about everyday things. Perhaps read the newspaper?'

As he shuffled his chair forward, a rustle in his pocket reminded him of another one of those 'posh' handwritten letters. It had arrived that morning, for Anne. He could read it to her but then, it was hers, not his. He knew who it was from, but Anne had not shared any of the other letters' contents. Why had she left Michael remained a mystery but would reading his letter to her help or hinder her recovery? He didn't know what to do. He felt uncomfortable holding her hand, after all he was a grown man, and they hadn't held hands since childhood.

His thoughts were interrupted by Sister Jocelyn who was looking at Anne's chart, adjusting the drip and changing her outflow bag, 'She is doing better this morning.'

'What do you mean, better?' He straightened himself in the chair, his hopes raised.

'The doctor would like a word with you,' she said smiling in her reassuring way.

'Would you like to go and get a cup of tea? I'll call you when the doctor comes. Try not to worry. It's better for your sister if you're rested.'

Jack inwardly frowned and wondered if the staff were telling him everything. Or were they hiding something? As he walked down the corridor the pervading smell of bacon loosened his nostrils and reminded him, he was hungry. He followed the sign that read, Cafeteria. Perhaps a cup of tea and a bite to eat would make him feel better.

'Hello,' said a stout middle-aged woman, who plonked herself down next to him holding a tray of five cups of tea.

'Hello.'

'Seen you before. Been here a while, haven't you?'

'How do you know that?'

'Been watching. We're both here at visiting times.'

'Are you visiting someone on the same ward? I haven't seen you before.' Ignoring his question, she chatted about the ward staff. She did not trust them. She took the five cups from their saucers, carefully lined them up in order of how much milk they contained, then took a sip from each in turn. As the last cup was emptied, she stood up, walked to the counter, and returned with a bowl of sugar cubes. She continued to chatter. Each cube was laid out in a flower pattern around every cup. Jack began to sweat. He desperately wanted her to shut up and leave him alone with his thoughts and half-eaten bacon sandwich. He pushed his chair back and stood up,

'Please excuse me I am going back to the ward now.'

The woman frowned, put one hand on his arm and renewed her efforts reorganising the sugar cubes, while continuing her confusing babble about hateful staff and various unnecessary medications. Jack suspected she was not being told everything. Perhaps beyond her understanding? Was she visiting someone in the same ward as Anne? He hoped not. God, he hoped not. Or was she a patient? Possibly she had been in a coma, just woken up, got out of bed confused and wandered off and drifted into the cafeteria? The woman began sneezing. Clouds of snotty pustules were sticking to her face, some landing on her sugar cubes, which she didn't seem to notice, others on her clothing. She lifted her hand, wiped the snot onto her sleeve, seemingly oblivious to the fact she was sneezing at all. Jack offered her a napkin to clean her face.

'Thank you,' she said and put it straight into her pocket.

He became alarmed that Anne might come round and be like this awful woman. He quickly pulled his arm away and fled back to the ward where he found Doctor Swaine, leaning over Anne's bed talking to Sister Jocelyn.

'Good afternoon Mr. Tweddle.'

'Hello doctor. Any change?'

'Yes, I am pleased to say, I think we are seeing signs of recovery.'

Jack's heart began to pound. Hope was stirring in his mind.

'Patients usually come around gradually. She may be a bit confused and agitated for a while.' Doctor Swaine continued, 'Some people completely recover; others may have some disabilities caused by the damage to the brain. She may need physiotherapy, occupational therapy, and psychological support to regain a full life.'

Jack's thoughts returned to the woman in the cafeteria. He smiled to himself at the thought of Anne undergoing psychological assessment. She had always been a challenge and now she may have heightened awareness. God help any psychiatrist.

'Of course, it depends on the severity of the brain injury. So many unknowns.' Jack felt the doctor was too full of doom and gloom but listened as he continued to ramble...

'Speed of coming out depends on the severity of the injury. It may take weeks, months to be fully aware of who she is and where, even to be fully conscious of her surroundings. It's impossible to accurately predict if she will make a full recovery or have any long-term problems. Sometimes they stay in a vegetative state.' Sister Jocelyn rolled her eyes, put her hand on Dr. Swaine's arm and tried to lead him away, obviously concerned about the way the conversation was going.

Jack stared. 'Look, her eyes keep opening, fingers moving. They're all good signs, aren't they? Is she dreaming?'

'Unlikely,' he said in a very dismissive way. 'Although some patients tell us they have been dreaming yet still have an awareness of what's happening around them. They can have nightmares that go on and on.'

Sister Jocelyn cleared her throat, 'Doctor, I think Mrs. Thompson is waiting over there to speak to you. She's been here for quite a while.' She tugged his sleeve and dragged him away, as if he was a naughty child.

Jack felt relieved he had gone and wondered if he was related to the woman in the café. His hopes were rising that Anne would wake. Was she journeying back in time? Could there be an upside? He hoped she'd been travelling back to the time of the Reivers and found some resolution for herself. He wanted her to come back happy and to have some relief from the constant uncertainty of her life since childhood. He prayed she would wake up, healed and perhaps this trauma had a purpose? He returned to his chair, held her hand and smiled. He reflected on how much he loved her, his gifted sister.

Chapter 49

Anne stirred in the bed, her eyes flickered and her fingers twitched. She was remembering Tom, the Gloucester Old Spot pig, had been making squealing noises, which were coming from the garden. Something was wrong. She had rushed round the corner of the house to find his head stuck in the water fountain. As she ran towards him, she had tripped and hit her head on his broad back. Then everything had become blurred. She remembered pain shooting through her brow, her legs crumpling under her and slowly slumping onto the flower bed. There was the smell of lavender and the tickling feel of flower stems as she lay on the grass in a semi-conscious state, with the noise of Tom's snorting reverberating through her head. Then a herd of horses was galloping and gathering speed but, as suddenly as the memory came, it faded.

*

Then Anne was back with the Border Reivers. It was Samhain and she was at Wydon. The last harvest of the year was upon them. A large gathering of many people was milling around a huge bonfire, some of them singing and dancing. It was a happy occasion.

She stayed with the scene for several minutes smiling to herself and becoming immersed in the joy and happiness of the celebrations. Old man Kerr and his clan stood outside the kitchen door. There was a smell of fresh bread and ale. The women seemed busy, rushing about fetching and carrying pots, pans, dishes and bowls. Snippets of broken conversations drifted Anne's way.

'Get out of this kitchen Will.' ....

'When is that lazy boy coming with more wood for the fire?' ....

'Mary, take this tray of cake outside. Give it to Ma Nelson and don't let old man Johnson see it.' ....

'Where are Isobel and her children? The bread's ready.'

Anne could see the familiar face of John, who was with Isobel's father, Thomas Elliott. They looked to be in a deep discussion about something important. Cook was standing near the fire and shouting various instructions to Millie, who was struggling to manoeuvre a large pot onto the flames.

'Hurry up, Girl, and be careful it doesn't spill and put the fire out.'

Cook coughed. 'Millie stop that fire smoking.'

'Cook, where shall I put these skinned rabbits?'

'Give them to Meg, tell her to cut them up. Oh, and don't forget to put your Samhain frock on for later.' She winked at the girl.

The sound of laughing drew Anne's attention to the outside barn where Will came rushing out, closely followed by Matt Thomson, who tripped over one of the dogs, fell headlong, stood up, wiped the mud off his face and, much to everyone's amusement, gave the dog a quick kick up the backside.

This happy scene was interrupted by the sound of a woman screaming and Anne could hear the pounding of horse's hooves on stone. She looked away from the throngs of revellers and saw Isobel, fleeing across the yard screaming and screaming as if the devil himself was behind her. A rough looking horseman was trotting behind her. He grabbed Isobel by the hair and dragged her along the yard, arms flailing, feet slithering, her body bouncing along the uneven flags, whilst hooves clattered on the mossy cobbles.

'Let me go!' she shrieked over and over again but her words soon became an incoherent muffle of sounds. Isobel's bright red and orange Samhain clothes dulled as they were pulled through the dirt.

Anne could see bodies lying around the yard. An old man lay on his back, a pitchfork in his chest. A couple of younger men, with various injuries, were straddled over a water trough in the far yard. Vague shapes hung over the barn door. They could have been animal or human, she was unsure. Several people were walking wounded. The air was filled with ear splitting rhythmical wailing sounds. Anne, ears pounding, breath shortening, tried to clutch her chest, her attention suddenly taken by the tormented pain of Isobel. Then the rider paused, hauled the struggling woman onto the front of his horse, turned, kicked the horse's belly, and set off at speed for the stack yard gate.

Suddenly he reined in the horse, 'Now I've got you, you witch. Now you will be mine. I told you I could wait. I would have you in the end.' He spun the horse round a couple of times yelling in his triumph. Isobel's head flopped against the horse's flank. She looked to have slipped into an unconscious state and would be unable to hear his taunting voice. Noise and chaos followed as many men rushed to catch the horse and rider, with his hostage, before they reached the open gateway.

'Get that bastard! Stop him! Get round that hemmel! No, the barn! The other way Tom! Tom go the other way!' yelled David Ogle.

'Michael, block that gate! Run, Lad! Run! Hurry!' Thomas Elliott turned, took a sharp left and ran between the low byre and the stables in the hope of cutting off the rider's exit and reaching his daughter. On rounding the corner, he skidded to a halt, his quarry not five yards in front of him.

'It's Ridley! It's Ridley! Let her go, you bastard! I'll kill you for this!' he shrieked. The startled horse sheered to the left, giving just time for Thomas to pull a knife from the outside of his boot and threw it full pelt at Robert Ridley.

'I'll kill you for this, you bastard!' The knife hit its target and became embedded deep in the middle of Ridley's back. A scream of excruciating pain followed, as Ridley jerked the reins upwards, causing his horse to rear up and lose its footing.

Both horse and rider fell heavily into the Sheep Hill field wall. Ridley was thrown over the animal's neck and landed with such force that his head became wedged in the moss-covered wall top. As the horse tried to find its feet, its rear end smashed Robert's body against the stonework, crushing it into a tangled jumble of shattered bones and flesh.

The beautiful, flaxen haired Isobel, fell under the horse's feet, her body pounded by its hooves as it panicked. In seconds her body lay on the ground, a mangled mass of blood and hair, a wife, a mother, a daughter no more. Her body lay there on the cold stone cobbles, abandoned and alone.

Anne screamed, clutched her chest and sat up in bed with a jolt. She looked at Isobel, lying on the cobbles, who opened her eyes and smiled. Anne nodded to her on the ground and, momentarily, gently floated back into the soft comfort of her hospital pillows, before returning to the scene at Wydon. The horse, once back on his feet, shook the torn bridle off its head and ambled slowly down the track into the meadow field.

'Robert! Robert!' screamed his father, David Ridley, who emerged from the back of a stable and ran towards what remained of his son.

'Robert, you were my last hope. All my other sons are gone. You were my last hope.' He collapsed over the lifeless body of his son, head in hands, weeping like an inconsolable child but only for a moment as his rage seemed to heighten and he slowly rose to his feet.

'You will pay for this Thomas Elliot! That daughter of yours has always bewitched my boy! Now he is dead I have lost everything! Do you hear me, Elliott? They are gone! All my sons! I will have my revenge!' David Ridley turned, with vengeance in his head and grief in his heart and ran towards Thomas Elliott. Before anyone could stop him, he ran Thomas Elliott through with his broadsword.

'That will teach you, Elliott! You're a murderous thug! That's an end to you now and that witch of a daughter of yours! She bewitched him! All Robert's life she's brought trouble to the Ridleys!'

Thomas, blood seeping out at a steady pace, clutching his chest, slumped forwards onto the ground. His eyes were still open and there, in his line of sight, was his daughter, now only a brown-haired deformed figure, lying in the filth of the yard. John, his two sons, his father, Angus, and many other men raced forward as the murderous scene unfolded before them.

'Father, what the hell is David Ridley doing here at our Samhain gathering?'

'He's up to no good, John. Evil bastard and that son of his, been spying on us again!' For a moment Angus paused, then yelled, 'Isobel! Isobel!' John looked up, followed his father's pointed finger, and screamed, 'Isobel! Isobel!'... He raced towards his wife, fell beside her and gathered her broken body in his arms.

'Isobel! No! NO! It's not you! By all the gods, it's not you! no! no! no!' John's whole body shook with a mixture of rage and grief. He looked skywards and yelled, 'WHY! WHY! WHY!' as he rocked backwards and forwards cradling the mangled remains of his wife's body. He gently picked strands of hair away from her face, bent down and kissed her forehead and then lowered her body gently to the ground. John stood up, white with rage, and ran to join the many screaming men who were tearing through the farm buildings, chasing the elusive murderer.

Then David Ogle, stepped from behind the byre door and came face to face with David Ridley, 'There you are you shrivelling, murderous excuse for a man!'

'He got her though, didn't he! Little miss precious! Had her in the end!' He threw his head back and laughed. Then his face paled, and David Ridley took flight. He doubled back, raced round a corner and hurtled straight into John Tweddle, and found himself standing over the body of the dead Thomas Elliott. David Ridley staggered backwards, wide eyed, spittle foaming at the corners of his mouth.

'You Tweddle bastards, think you can have everything, don't you? Well not now. Lost your precious wife eh, John Tweddle?' As he went to pull the broad sword from his belt, he paused, then shrieked and fell forward.

'You murdering bastard!' John Tweddle had withdrawn a dirk and stabbed Ridley's heart. It was a clean kill and Ridley, a heavy man, dropped to the ground to land on top of Thomas Elliott's body. There they lay together, two Reivers, two fathers, two heads of two border families, two sudden unexpected deaths, while a few feet away lay the hopes and dreams of their futures, Isobel Tweddle and Robert Ridley.

Chapter 50

Anne sat straight up in bed, silent tears streaming down her face. Her vision was foggy. The room was bright, white, noisy, and full of strangely dressed people she didn't recognise. She turned her head and tried to move her heavy limbs, then sighed and sank into the pillows, her head full of confusing thoughts. Where was she? Where had she been and what had happened? Isobel felt so familiar; her thoughts, ideas, feelings, high spiritedness, lack of willingness to follow rules? Why did she feel so close to this woman with her two sons?

Her thoughts were interrupted by a quiet voice drifting into her head. Almost inaudible at first, then a muddled set of gentle sounds, peaceful and calming, which filled her whole being with an extraordinary sense of wonder. Absorbing these feelings of oneness, she drifted further into the softness of the bed.

She had an image of Isobel being with her. This tall, elegant, beautiful, flaxen haired woman was smiling. Blurring images of various people and places came into her mind. Anne recognised Wydon and felt she was at home again with Cook, John, and Millie.

Then the quiet voice became clearer and said, '*Hello, Anne, welcome back. I have been waiting a long time for you.*'

Anne found herself replying, 'Me? Why?'

'*There are things you must do for both of us?*'

'Us?'

'*Yes. All will become clear but first you must lift the curse my mother, Elinor, laid on the Tweddle men and women.*'

Anne had a clear memory of Elinor laying a curse, 'I will. But I don't know how.'

'*You will find a way.*'

'Will I?'

'*I will help. I will always be with you.*'

'Will you?'

'*Yes, I have always been with you. We have always been together. I have been waiting over four hundred years for this moment.*'

'What?'

'*You must set us both free.*'

'But how? Why? I am feeling confused.'

'*Rest now, Anne. You have been away a long time. When you are fully recovered, I will come to you again, when the time is right for both of us. Be patient we will be together again.*'

Then the voice disappeared, and all became quiet. Anne smiled and felt at peace. She'd understood what Isobel had asked of her. The adventures were over for the moment. It was time to return to her other world.

*

Anne was suddenly brought out of her dream state by the pain in her hand. Someone was squeezing it. The sound of chairs scraping across a floor and people chattering made her frown. Bright lights, in her eyes, made her squint and shake her head.

Then a dull voice that was vaguely familiar was speaking, 'Anne. Anne, wake up. It's me, Jack, your brother.'

Anne tried hard to focus on his voice.

'Nurse. Nurse! Anne's coming round. She sat up, tried to speak and was making mumbling sounds but I couldn't understand what they were. Look, she's smiling, there are tears running down her face, her body is moving. I can see it. Look. Look!' He stood up and began shaking Anne's hand.

Sister Jocelyn smiled and came over to the bedside, 'It happens sometimes and can be a good sign.'

'Good sign that she is coming around?' He wiped his forehead.

Sister patted his arm in a reassuring way, 'It's always a good sign.' She smiled, 'Now, please, sit down, Jack. There is so much we don't know about people in comas.'

'Why don't you know? You are experts, aren't you? Deal with this sort of thing all the time? I think I need to speak to someone who knows more than you do. Someone in authority.' He rubbed his scalp with his hands in sheer frustration that no one was giving him a straight answer.

'Please, Mr. Tweddle, be quiet. You are disturbing others. Every recovery is different. We must just wait.'

'Yes. But they were good signs, weren't they?'

'I am sure they were.'

'You know, Sister, I didn't know how much I loved her. Never paid her much attention before now.' He sat, head in hands, and began to sob. His hopes, once raised, were now dashed.

Sister Jocelyn looked round the ward and noticed how Jack's outpourings had disturbed other visitors. 'You must wait. Some patients never have any facial changes and come round. I am sure she will return to you.'

He wiped his eyes, feeling somewhat embarrassed at his outburst, 'I'm sorry but I have made a pact with myself that, when I get her back, I'm going to be different, to get to know her, to really know her.'

'That sounds a wonderful idea and a real blessing for you both.' Sister Jocelyn moved away leaving Jack to his own thoughts.

Jack wasn't sure about the last comment because Anne was still unconscious. After a few moments the atmosphere around Anne changed. The room was filled with silence as deep as the sky itself. He watched, with hope in his heart and excitement in his mind. Anne's fingers on both hands had begun to move. Several minutes later, her body began to shuffle down the bed, as if taking an enormous stretch after a long heavy sleep. Her eyes flickered, her tongue protruded from her mouth and gently caressed her dry lips, which appeared to try to form sounds, but none came out. Jack sat beside her, holding her warm hand, squeezing it, desperately willing her to wake up, to see him, to remember. Anne's eyes fluttered, as if opening for the first time to a world of light and strangeness. Moments later they opened fully. She turned her head, looked him full in the face, squeezed his hand and smiled. But, as suddenly as she had awoken, she closed her eyes, smiled and returned to the comfort of her pillows.

Jack, shocked, lent over the bed and, without thinking, began to shake her, 'Anne. Anne. Wake up Wake up.'

Sister Jocelyn came running up. 'No. No, Jack. It's alright. Don't shake her. It's all good. She is coming back to us, just taking it nice and slow. We must be patient. After all, she has only been here a few days. I will go and see if I can find Dr. Swaine.'

Over the next few hours, Anne came round from her long sleep and was able to sit up and have brief but muddled conversations with the staff.

'Hello Anne. My name is Sister Jocelyn. You are in hospital. You had an accident and hit your head. I am Sister Jocelyn. Do you understand me?'

A hesitating nod followed.

'Your name is Anne, Anne Tweddle. Your brother, Jack Tweddle, is here. You are in hospital. You have had an accident, hit your head. You are well now. Do you understand me?'

Anne's eyes flickered. She rubbed her face, yawned then smiled, 'Who are you?'

'Hello, Anne. My name is Sister Jocelyn,' squeezing her hand and smiling. 'We are all very pleased you have returned to us. Your brother Jack is here. It's visiting time and you are awake. You are in Newcastle Victoria Infirmary.'

'Newcastle? Where's that?'

'Yes, Newcastle. It's the nearest hospital to your home.'

'My home?'

'Yes. You live at Wydon Farm with your brother, Jack.'

Jack was beaming, took her hand from Sister Jocelyn and sat down. 'Hello, Anne. It's me, Jack.' He let out an uncontrollable gasp of joy. 'It's so good to have you back, I've missed you so much.'

Anne took both his hands in hers and held them tightly as she nodded her head.

Jack, overjoyed his sister had returned, was careful what he said, not wanting to bombard her with questions. Instead, he kept the conversations short and talked about mundane everyday things. 'It's a nice day outside. Mrs. Clutterbuck has been laying lots of eggs but is as clumsy as ever. Still managed to knock the hen corn bucket over, this morning.'

Anne raised her eyebrows.

'Old Mrs. Pike has been coming round at night with her casseroles, not quite as much beef in as I would have liked but very kind of her, very kind indeed.'

'Isn't she a vegetarian?'

'Yes. Well, that might have something to do with it.' They both laughed. 'I'm so glad you are feeling better, Anne. It's great to have you back with us.'

'I remember what happened. How is Tom the pig?'

Jack panicked and took a sharp intake of breath. He didn't want to tell her that Tom had become the chief ingredient of his breakfast. He quickly changed the conversation in the hope she would not ask about the pig again. 'Things are running smoothly at home. Nip, the dog, is missing you. He doesn't think I give him enough to eat.'

'What day is it?'

'Saturday and it's about ten o'clock.'

'So, how long have I been in here?'

'A few days.'

'I remember what happened. Some of it is still a bit hazy. My head's a bit fuzzy. But I am okay. I think I would like to lie down for a few minutes. I suddenly feel quite tired.'

Jack eased her back onto the pillows. After a short nap Anne woke feeling refreshed, had some lunch and by midafternoon wanted to leave.

'Can I go home now, Sister?'

'No not quite yet, Anne. We must keep an eye on you for just a little bit longer. We want to make sure you're fully recovered so you are being moved to a Neuro Rehab ward for a day or so. Let's see how you go. All being well, you could go home on Monday.'

Chapter 51

The next few weeks passed by at a gentle pace. Brother and sister sat together in the long evenings, talking about what had happened. Anne's memory, now fully restored, enabled her to recount conversations with their grandfather and the whole of her journeys into the sixteenth century; the raid on Wydon, the Tweddle's, Isobel and John, their lives and, of course, Robert Ridley's, as well as the stories around the various characters and incidents that had occurred along the way.

'I am glad you are back, Anne.' Jack said, after supper, one night.

'Me too.' Anne paused as she sat watching the flames dance and crackle around a damp log in the kitchen fire. 'You know, Jack, it was so real.'

'What was?'

'Living in the 16th century. One minute I was in our garden with Tom the pig, and the next I was with Isobel. But I wasn't with her because I was her. I could think like she did, feel her emotions and have all her memories. They came in sudden bursts and often went backwards and forwards. Then sometimes I wasn't Isobel but observing others and always knowing what they were thinking. So strange, it was as if I was in their heads. Then I could hear vague voices from somewhere else, people touching my body, moving my limbs and always a low humming sound.'

'That must have been in those moments when you were coming round from your coma. The humming would have been the machines that were monitoring you.'

'Um, yes, perhaps.'

'You know, Anne, I thought I'd lost you.' He suddenly went a peculiar shade of red.

'It's not something we have ever talked about, is it, our feelings?'

'No.'

'We have a lot to catch up on, don't we?'

'Yes, we do.'

'Jack, there is something I haven't told you.'

'Is it about the letters that have been coming for you ever since you returned to live with us?'

Anne flushed, 'Yes, it is.'

He learned forward and held her hand. 'You don't have to tell me if you don't want to.'

'I don't know whether there is anything to tell, really. I think it's over.'

'Over? Is this about Michael? Is he dead?'

'No, he isn't. At least, I hope not.' Her hand flew to her chest. 'He was everything I ever wanted; kind, generous, financially independent, intelligent, considerate, loving, too good to be true, really.'

'Yes, I get the picture.' Jack rolled his eyes hoping she wouldn't notice.

'Then about a year ago he changed.'

'Changed? What do you mean changed?'

'Yes, a few months back he became distant, worried all the time and he started staying out late, coming home at strange hours, always without explanation. We argued about it and he kept asking me to trust him.'

'I can see why you would find that of concern.'

'He kept reassuring me that all was well, and he wasn't up to no good.'

'Odd though.'

'He became secretive. One night, when he was having a bath, his phone rang, and I picked it up but it rang off as soon as I said '*hello*.' Then I found a woman's name in his phone. She was called Jennifer and he'd various appointments made with her in his diary.'

'Wow, that doesn't sound good! Do you think it was something to do with his past? Is that why you left?'

'Yes. It had gone on for too long, I just couldn't make any sense of it, and I was starting to live on my nerves. I even went to the doctor.'

'Did it help?'

'No, he offered me counselling and that would have meant months on a waiting list.' Anne's eyes filled with tears, 'You know, Jack, I really loved him, and I still love him but now I feel that my whole world has crashed down on me.'

'Why does he write to you? His penmanship is quite something. Wish I could write like that.'

'Everything about him is perfect!' She dissolved into more tears. 'He tells me he still loves me, and I have to be patient and he will soon be able to tell me the truth.'

'Do you believe him?'

'I want to! But there is just this woman nagging at the back of my mind. Who is she?'

'It sounds, to me, like Michael really loves you and there is no way he is going to give up on you.' Jack handed Anne another hankie. 'You haven't had much luck with men, have you? Your first husband, Jeff, died. Michael seems to be doing strange things. Then there was that stalker. Whatever happened to him?'

'Michael sorted him out.'

'Really? How did he do that? Beat him up?'

'I don't know. The man used to follow me home each night from the railway station. He'd hide in doorways when I turned round. He knew where I lived and would stand outside our house. Sometimes he jumped out and said all sorts of obscene things…you know… what he wanted…' Anne lowered her head and cleared her throat. 'It was frightening. I didn't know what to do. I didn't tell Michael for a long time.'

'How long?'

'A couple of years.'

'What! A couple of years? What were you thinking, woman?'

'I was frightened. He was clever and, whenever Michael was around, he would disappear, and I was afraid he wouldn't believe me.'

'So, what happened?'

'One night he grabbed me, and I was dragged into a garden. A passing motorist stopped and helped. Don't remember much about it but there was a bit of a scuffle, and I ended up in A&E and the whole sorry saga came out. Michael was furious and went to look for him.'

'He found him?'

'When I next saw Michael, he said the police had sorted it out. But I never heard anything after that and wondered if there had been a court case or something. But then, I would have been involved, wouldn't I? It was all a bit odd, and Michael was a bit sheepish and wouldn't discuss it but kept reassuring me he was gone.'

'Um! odd indeed. I wonder if Michael had done something illegal. But it all ended a few years ago and you haven't seen him since?'

'No.'

'Well, it's over now. Gosh, we have churned some stuff over, this evening, haven't we?'

'Yes. I am glad you know. I always wanted to tell you, but it never seemed the right moment.' Anne held his hand and they both smiled.

'Come on. Enough for tonight, I'll let the dog out. You go on up to bed.'

Chapter 52

Months passed, walking the dog, reading, doing bits of writing, talking to her brother and regaining her strength. Life was different now. She was no longer plagued by dreams. Her meditations had taken on a calmer, deeper form and she no longer travelled back to the 16th century. Anne felt well, really well.

One winter's evening, as she was closing the sitting room curtains, the sound of distant bells coming across the valley from Haltwezell Parish Church alerted her to the darkening sky. Anne smiled, went upstairs to take the Harris Tweed overcoat out of last year's hibernation box and laid her sheepskin boots to warm by the kitchen fire. She found her grandmother's woolly gloves, collected her seasonal scarf, rescued it from the back of the wardrobe, and returned to the kitchen. Opening the back door, torch in hand, she was met by a cold north wind that blew ice covered leaves into the kitchen.

'Nip, come on. Let's go for a walk. It's a beautiful clear night.' After a lot of persuasion, Nip begrudgingly left his cosy bed, stretched his legs and ambled to the door, where he yawned, took one look outside, decided it wasn't for him and returned to his bed.

'Come on, Nip.' She bent down and fastened a lead to his collar. Then she stepped outside, adjusted her scarf and, with muffled footsteps, as they crunched through the freshly fallen snow, she walked several yards down the lane. There she paused and turned to smile at Nip the dog, who was trailing behind, keeping his head down, unhappy to be out in the cold and longing for the warmth of the kitchen fire.

The snow reminded Anne of the previous winter when Michael had made her a sledge. They had veered from the run and collided with a wall, broken the sledge and rolled about in the slush laughing like two carefree children. She pulled her collar tighter, smiling to herself, lost in thoughts of happy times.

Suddenly Nip the dog began to bark. Lifting her eyes to the sky, Anne saw a distant blue light coming towards them. 'Nip what is it?' The dog stood fast, hackles up and refused to move forward. Green, opaque lights flashed across the night sky... a changing shape billowed across the landscape and a beautiful calming presence held her transfixed. Nip the dog continued to growl. Anne bent down and unleashed him. 'Go home Nip, go home.' He turned back to the house and very quickly was lost in the darkening light.

As the shape came closer it changed into something familiar. It was a bear, the great bear of the starry heavens. She had spent many years following Ursa Major across the night sky and stood in awe as it gracefully approached her. The shape floated closer and soon a large brown bear landed gracefully at her feet, so close she could feel its breath on her face.

'Hello, you magical creature, I don't know what to say to you.'

The bear looked bemused, lifted his paw and rested it on her shoulder. It didn't feel heavy but delicate and made her tingle all over.

'Have you come to tell me something?'

The bear nodded.

'I am not sure that I will be able to understand you. I have never communicated with a bear before.' She looked up into the night sky and saw he was missing. The seven stars were in front of her. He made a strange sound but in her head she understood.

You will need strength. More than you have. I have come to give you, my strength.'

'Why? Why do I need to be strong?'

'It is not easy to move the soul.'

'The soul? I have done it before, many times,' she replied lifting her eyebrows.

The bear's brown eyes looked deeply into hers.

'This time it is about you and your soul.'

'My soul?' Anne frowned.

'Isobel's soul is here on this earth plane, as is yours.'

'Yes, I know.'

'Be careful. Take my strength to guide you.'

Anne's heart began to beat faster, 'Thank you but why? Am I in danger?'

'You could be.'

Anne frowned. 'Why?'

'Releasing trapped souls is a difficult process.'

'I know. I have sometimes found it difficult but always managed it.'

'This time it will be different.'

'Different? How?'

'Because you and Isobel are the same person.'

Anne had come to that conclusion herself but to hear it being said by a mystical being was an earth-shattering moment and profoundly moving. After a few moments of stillness, she asked, 'How is it more difficult?'

'Be careful that you do not lose your soul.'

'Oh! can I lose my soul before I am physically dead?'

'It is possible. But of course, I am always here for you.'

Anne knew bear energy was important. They held a deep connection with the ancestors, their purpose, to protect humans from danger and it was vital to listen to the power of the bear who would guide her.

'You must listen to your intuition and trust yourself. I will be with you on the journey ahead. You are a spiritual warrior, like Arthur.'

Anne smiled. She had worked with Arthurian energy before. He had taught her how to integrate her primal power and intuition. Now he had returned in the form of a bear to guide her, to unite with star and animal power.

'There are others.'

Anne's eyes widened, 'Others? What others?'

But no words came, and the bear closed his eyes, took a deep breath and, with his paw still on her shoulder, sent his strength to her. Almost immediately she could feel her energy rising. Her body felt bigger, wider, taller, and strong, very strong. After a few moments he lifted his paw, nodded, acknowledged she had understood and turned his head to the sky. It was time to return to the starry heavens. He stepped back and, as the image began to fade, green, pink, blue, orange, purple and yellow lights slowly appeared and swirled round in the dark sky. For a few seconds this aurora wafted around her, dancing and bathing her in a colourful cascade of awe and wonder. The great bear silently drifted skywards to take his place in the night sky once again. Anne looked up and there he was once more, the seven stars pointing to Polaris, the North Star.

She stood for a long time absorbing the magic of the meeting. It was only much later she became aware of how cold it was and, pulling her coat tightly round her, she returned to the farmhouse full of joy. Everything in her head was becoming clearer. Soon she would be able to free Isobel's soul, although when to do it was unclear and she hoped for a sign to guide her.

Chapter 53

As the weeks went by Anne's strength grew day by day. One afternoon, while walking with Nip the dog, she noticed the tool shed door stood open. Her grandfather was having his 3 o'clock tea.

'Hello. Is it that time of day already?'

'Hello Annie. I was just packing up but there is enough tea left in the flask if you want a cup, gingerbread too?'

'Thank you but no. I have just seen a jackdaw hanging by its leg on the fence. It took me back to the tale you told me years ago of Uncle Edward and how he lost his leg.'

'Agh, awful death! A lot of the Tweddles have had horrible deaths. Many met a gruesome end. My father used to talk about ghosts, spriggans, hobgoblins and other strange things that came in the night.'

'I would have liked to listen to his stories. I know about some of them, of course.'

'Do you want me to show you where they are recorded?'

'Recorded! Oh, yes, I would. I didn't know there were any recorded.'

'Come on then. I've finished for the day so let's go to the family bible in the library. That's where we need to look. Some records are only on scraps of paper but readable none the less.'

'Have you recorded any?'

'Only in my head. Best place for them. Stories passed down from relatives and travellers, passing through, told tales of long ago but I don't know if I ever wrote them down...not in the book, since my father died.'

'Myths or truths grandfather?'

'I don't think there is a difference. All myths are based on truths. There's always been a dark cloud hanging over the Tweddle men. Some tales go back to the times of the Reivers. It's as if we are cursed, Annie.'

Anne shuddered. She remembered Elinor and what she did. Perhaps it was true and time to find the truth.

Grandfather finished his tea and gingerbread, fastened his flask, and repacked his bait bag. 'Come, Annie. Let's go and find this bible. Together we will read the stories of these Tweddle men.' He winked, 'But you know, Annie, I don't believe in witches and curses.'

'Do you think they were all accidents?'

He smiled and took her arm. Together they walked to the house, entered through the back door, and walked along the passageway that led to the library, a room situated on the north side of the house, visited only by Anne, who used it as a quiet space to write. The old oak door swung open, the room was pulling her back, as if to tell her something.

J.P. turned towards the small alcove and pulled back a faded green velvet curtain, which Anne hadn't noticed before. It revealed a pile of aged books. Under them, hiding, was a battered brown leather suitcase. Anne wondered why, after all the hours she had sat at the desk, this curtain and its secrets had been invisible.

'Here, Annie, help me. They're a bit heavy for my old bones. Don't want to hurt myself or I'll have your grandmother to answer to.' He laughed with that naughty boy look on his face she knew so well. Removing the books, from the decades of dust covering them, and lifting the suitcase out of the way, the family bible finally emerged. It was a large suede and leather-bound book several inches thick, the size of a small coffee table. The date on the spine was faded, scratched and impossible to read. On the top in perfect gold script was a plaque which read:

The Tweddle Bible

Feeling very excited at the prize she had found and looking eagerly at her grandfather to make things happen she tried to open the book. But the Bible was bound in two places by brass hinges attached to a lock and a mass of clouded dust covered the key holes.

'Have you got the keys?'

'No. Lost them years ago,' he said apologetically.

'Are there any spares?'

'No.'

Anne sighed. 'No one has looked in here for a long time, have they?'

'No. My father took me through some of the papers a few years before he died. But he thought it was best not to dwell on the past.'

'He attached the lock?'

'Um. I think so. To keep me out no doubt.'

'It's important for me to know. Please help me. How can we get in?' She returned to fighting with the lock.

J.P shook his head, 'Annie, you'll have to break it.'

'Break it? With what?' she said, stamping her foot on the floor.

'There's a paper knife over there. Try that.'

'I don't want to damage it, Grandfather.'

'Wouldn't worry about that. Nobody else is ever going to look in it, are they?'

This sounded plausible and she went over to the desk to extract the letter opener from a desk caddy full of old pens, well sharpened pencils, and a surprisingly well used goose quill. The opener broke at the first attempt. The bible was not ready to reveal its secrets. She then found a dinner knife but to no avail. After several minutes of no success Anne gave the knife to her grandfather, 'Keep trying while I go back to the tool shed and get a screwdriver and hammer.'

On her return, J.P. was sitting on the floor looking exhausted, nursing a bleeding finger.

'Oh, that looks sore. Here let me wrap my hankie round it.'

The Uncovered Legacy

'It's nothing,' he looked at what she had in her hands and gasped, 'Annie, you can't use those. They are much too heavy. You'll smash it to pieces.'

'That's the idea, isn't it? After all, we want in, don't we?' She wedged the screwdriver into the lock hasp and hit it over and over again with the hammer. Bang. Bang. Bang. The sound was beginning to hurt her ears and she feared her tinnitus would return. Eventually it relented and the lock flew open. Carefully lifting the front cover and blowing away even more dust, a batch of papers, all different sizes and colours, some wrapped with bits of worn string or thread, lay before her.

'Here, Annie, let me show you the family tree.'

'We have a family tree?'

'It's quite near the front and, if I am careful, I'll find it. These pages are crusty, faded and delicate. Some of them have been well read. Other pages, probably left open on the desk in full sight of the north window, have faded in the light.'

Anne put on her reading glasses, 'I want to read the well-read pages first.'

'Annie look at this.' Before her lay a list of Tweddles, all in date order, her brother being the last entry.

'Why is Jack here and not me? Why am I not recorded?'

'Because you're a girl, Annie, and, as you know in the farming world, not important.'

Anne sighed and shook her head. 'I feel incensed at the injustice of it all. For generations the women in this family have been excluded, bought, sold, and written out of history. It's time this historical, patriarchal error was corrected.' She thumped the table with her fist so hard the book cover jumped.

'Here now, Annie, be careful.'

She sighed again and took a deep breath to steady her frustration. 'Some of these names are hard to read.'

'Yes. Well, different families have written entries over many generations. Most of them couldn't write and had to wait for the travelling bards to record births and deaths and some of these people were only just literate themselves. So, these dates are not as accurate as they could be but it's of no matter. It begins with Erik born in 1502 … no death recorded, then Angus, born 1523, died 1580. He was 57 years old. He was the father of John, born in 1548, died in 1585, only 37 years old. That will be the John Tweddle you're interested in, won't it? Cuthbert, who was born in 1570 died in 1597.'

'Yes, it would seem so, Grandfather. Remember, Isobel and John had two sons.'

'Cuthbert and Edgar. Edgar died when he was 33 years old. Cuthbert had a son Will in 1591, who died in 1640.'

'Grandfather, this is quite complicated to follow.'

'Yes, it's a bit of a muddle, isn't it? Some of them look confusing chronologically but all the same it's a record of our Tweddle ancestors.'

'I suppose we have to accept it for what it is and be grateful that we have it at all.'

'Quite so, Annie. Quite so.'

'Oh look, Will, who was John and Isobel's grandson, had a son Thomas born in 1635 and he died in 1673. He was thirty-eight years old. Some of these men did not live very long, did they?' Anne was starting to realise that perhaps the curse Isobel's mother, Elinor, had put on the Tweddle men had some truth in it.

'Ah. Look, Edgar appears, over there, born in 1570.' She pointed to a very faded entry.

'Under his name is Conall 1603 and under that is Mathew John born 1655 and died 1711.'

'So, he was thirty-six when he died, another young life.'

'But old enough to father the next generation. James was born in 1695 and died when twenty-five years old in 1720.'

'Now we have another John born in 1720. He was born in the same year as his father died?'

'It would seem so. But he lived twice as long as his father as he reached the age of fifty.'

'Plenty of time to father children but there is only one recorded here. George was born in 1750 and died in 1782. Then there is John Ridley Tweddle born 1780. Is that what it says John Ridley?'

'Yes, must have been a lot of marriages with other families and names passed on. He had a good long life and died in 1840 when he was sixty, or so they thought.'

'A long life, I wonder if that was some sort of justice for perhaps what happened to an ancestor Robert Ridley?

'This John Ridley had three sons William 1800. Hew 1802. Jamie 1806. Meg 1808. Oh, look there is a note here that says…. transported to Australia 1807.'

'She must have died as soon as she arrived, or perhaps on-board ship. But that's the first girl we've seen recorded,' Anne sighed as her tears welled up. She really was in a family where females were written out of history.

'Anyway, Hew had a son Jack 1830. There is a Todd 1838 – 1867 son of Jamie 1806. This Todd had a son William Ridley who had four boys, Edgar Ridley 1883 – 1853. James Elliott Kerr 1884. Todd Elliott 1886. John Ridley 1888.'

'We are getting a lot more detailed information now aren't we. That poor woman was pregnant all the time. They are so close together I wonder if some of them died?'

'More than likely, the death rate among children could be high then.'

'Oh, look, Grandfather, there's your name, son of Edgar, John Pickering born 1923, no death date yet fortunately.' She looked into his eyes and smiled, took his arm and gave it a loving squeeze.

'Yes, Annie, now we are into our names and dates. There's my son Alan 1939 and his daughter, that's you, Annie, 1957 and your brother Jack 1959.'

'So, you were only 17 years old when you had my father?' Annes mouth fell open. 'So young?'

Her grandfather ignored her remark.

'Let's see if we make some sense of it all. Tie up information to names on the tree?'

'Good idea.'

'We'll sift through these bits of paper. Some are neatly folded, others just a few words added onto the bottom of something else. There is quite a few too faded to read and they're not in any order.'

'What does the first one say Annie?'

'Lost in a snow drift. Christmas 1840. Sheep beyond Far Field wall covered in snow. Tried a rescue. Got trapped under them. Froze to death. Body found in the spring thaw.'

'It happens. I've lost many a sheep over the years in snow drifts, stupid buggers all huddled on top of each other. Them at the bottom suffocate and them at the top are too exhausted to dig their way out.'

'Wouldn't badgers and foxes have smelt them out for food? Shepherding was poor if they weren't missed until spring?'

'Yes, a lot of unanswered questions.'

'There are many men recorded with the same name.'

'It's back to spelling, I imagine, and who recorded what.'

'Anyway, a James Tweeddle was born in 1806 and died in 1836.' There is a reference to manure and suffocating.'

'Perhaps he lost his balance, fell in the pit and couldn't get out. Middens could be treacherous places, especially when soft.'

'Todd Twedle, 1886, died in 1917. That's probably World War 1? Who was he?'

'My father's brother. Never came home. Died of trench foot, a painful, horrible death. Annie, John James Tweddle, my father's brother, born in 1900 and died in 1942. You know all the farmers were in reserved occupations, staying on the farm to produce food for the nation. He was a Captain in the Home guard. They were known locally as the "Luck Duck and Vanish Brigade".'

'What does that mean, it sounds odd?'

'Local Defence Volunteers. They practiced with wooden rifles and only my father, who was in charge of them, had a real one. It had been decommissioned from the First World War. These were the only weapons that the army could let them have.'

'But what would have happened if the Germans had crossed the channel and come up north.? Were they able to defend us?'

'No, but your father-in-law, Harry Silcock, remember him? He was a leader of a communist cell in Lancashire. They'd arms caches hidden in the Derbyshire dales and had formed units to fight Hitler. They said the Home Guard was ineffective. You know they may well have been right, but it made the men left at home feel they were contributing to the war effort.'

Anne's body stiffened. 'I was unaware of my father- in- law's role in the early part of the second world war. I know he was conscripted and sent to Italy. So, what happened to your uncle John James?'

'One night they were out training and saw a rabbit ahead. Deciding this was easy game and my father having the only working weapon, they persuaded him to shoot the rabbit for the pot. He took aim and fired but the gun malfunctioned and backfired. It exploded in his face, and he bled to death.'

'What a horrible thing to happen. Did you remember him?'

'No. Mother said the farm workload increased dramatically and we had to employ veterans from the Great War to work on the land to get crops in. We had Land Girls, of course, but that's a long set of stories and not for today. Come let us continue.'

'Yes let's. So, you had two uncles who died in the First World War and the Second World War in horrible ways?'

He ignored her last comment and continued to go through the pile of papers in front of them. Then John Pickering paused, his eyes filled with tears as he turned to Annie, 'I don't know whether you know this, but I had four brothers. Two sets of twins, all still born, and their mother died having the second boys.'

Anne sank back in the chair and went pale, 'No, I didn't know that.'

'Well half-brothers. After their mother, Kate, died, my father married my mother Eleanor, and I was born in 1923.' He wiped his eyes, sighed and then his face lit up. 'Oh, look, Annie, John Pickering Tweddle born 1923. That's me and look no death date as I am still here,' he squeezed Anne's hand and smiled.

'My father has a mention underneath as well. Alan John Tweddle was born in 1939. Then there is my brother John Jack born 1959 and me, only the second female to be recorded! It's so sad....annoying.... disrespectful 'Anne sighed, relieved that her grandfather, father and brother were all still here and desperately hoping the power of Elinor's curse had petered out.

'Look, some of these papers have a few odd words on, others have phrases, but they do seem to be a record of what Tweddles died from. It's odd isn't it grandfather?'

'I have memories, Annie, stories, tales. You know, they are not good stories. I think the Tweddles have been quite unlucky, more so than other farming families.'

Ann wondered about her interesting ancestors who had kept these records. Had someone, apart from her, understood what had happened long ago and kept these records. It was an unsettling thought.

'Grandfather let's begin with Uncle Rob, Dad's brother. He's not on the tree and I'm not sure why?'

'An arrogant son, he was, and a bully. Wouldn't listen to anyone. A wild lad, lazy too. He had a horse called Jock and rode him like the wind was behind him. Rough he was and treated that animal badly. He wasn't fit to have a horse.'

'But he did?'

'Yes, he did. Anyway, one day he and his friend, another stupid lad, drove the stock to the out-bye fields. They had a race and Jock, his gelding, jumped a gate. He'd done it many times before but this time he slipped on take-off and threw him off. Rob landed badly. The time the ambulance arrived he was in a pretty bad way, and they couldn't save him.'

Anne gasped, 'Oh! He was your son. How awful for you.'

But grandfather rolled his eyes and shrugged his shoulders. He seemed accepting of what had happened.

'Annie, it was many years ago and I don't think about him anymore.'

'Look there are names here of men who were not mentioned on the family tree.'

'Probably brothers, uncles, cousins. Whoever collected this information must have thought they were worthy of note.'

'And they were all Tweddles?'

'Yes, it seems so. I had a cousin, James Angus Tweddle who emigrated to Australia. He died of "Farmers Lung" not long after he got there.'

'I know about "Farmers Lung". I wrote an article on it for Farmer's Weekly, years ago. Horrible debilitating respiratory disease that affects your breathing. It's when you inhale spores from moldy hay or straw. This dust passes through the immune system in the nose and throat as it travels to the lungs. They get fever, chills, a constant dripping nose, a nasty cough and laboured breathing. They can have muscular pain, lose weight, suffer from night sweats and when it's at its worst they can suffer depression.'

Anne paused and looked at the old man. 'Your nose drips all the time. I hope you just have a cold?' Anne handed her grandfather a hankie and picked up two bits of paper from the floor. 'Who were Mathew and Thomas Twedle?'

'Father and son in the 1610s and 1620s?'

'It mentions America?'

'Ah! I know about this. When James I came onto the English throne in 1603, he wanted to sort out the Border Reivers so in 1605 he forcibly cleared out the Borders of men, women and children. He broke up the Reiver families by sending them on ships to Ireland and America. One of them, can't quite remember the story very clearly after all these years, but he fell sick and died, don't know whether it was Mathew or Thomas. Today we would probably call it dysentery. He was thrown overboard into the Atlantic Ocean.'

'How do we know this?'

'When the survivor arrived in the Americas he wrote back to his family. There's a copy of the ship's manifest somewhere in these archives.'

Anne quietly began to weep. It was hard to listen to family trauma, yet her grandfather seemed philosophical and accepting. But then, he didn't know what she knew.

'There's a note here of a David Tweddle who was on the roof of the Round Hemmel fixing the guttering. He had crackling breath and was coughing so much he lost his balance and fell into the grain store and, with no one around to hear him scream, he suffocated. That's what his family thought. Horrible way to go, Annie, just horrible. He wasn't found for months. It was only when the cattle refused to eat the spoiled grain that he was discovered.'

'There is a John Tweddle mentioned here. Could that be Isobel's husband, 1585?'

'The date's about right.'

'What does it say?'

'Leg wound, black blood and the word pox?'

'Probably an infection from a knife or sword injury. Pox? May have had gangrene set in?'

Anne felt profoundly sorry for this man. Over her life in the 16th century, she had spent many hours with John Tweddle, Isobel's husband, and had grown to love him as much as Isobel did.

'Is there any more grandfather? I think I don't want to hear any.'

'Just bits and pieces really. Do you want me to briefly cover them?'

'Yes, but not too much detail. Were they all related to Tweddle men?'

'Yes, some mentioned in this bible, others not.'

Anne collected all the papers she had in her hands and gave them to her grandfather, 'Just give me the gist of what they say.'

'Let me see.

Alick Twedddle, gored by a bull, left a cripple.

Jasper James tangled in horse straps, lost a leg and died soon after.

Seth John Tweedled fell under a cart, and the wheel crushed his legs.

Little Michael, kicked by a horse. It says loose saddle. That's probably why.

Scar face Tweed stumbles in a cow shed, crushed into a wall.

Tom Twedle beaten in a brawl, died of his injuries.

Long Nose, murdered by his brother Chesty Tweddle.

Cattle stampede at Willison Town raid, trampled Alan, Natty and Ian Twedddle.

Edgar Twedle caught in threshing machine, lost his arm.

His brother got his head stuck, trying to save him, the machine jammed and work for the day stopped.

Clem Willie Tweeled's cart overturned, landed in a ditch and his son was thrown under the wheel.

Young Norman Tweedle's horse bolted, foot caught in stirrup, and he was dragged down a field and into a tree. Bled to death.'

'Stop! Just stop! I've heard enough.' Anne sat with her head in her hands, shaking in disbelief.

'There is one story that might cheer you up, Annie. Shall I tell it?' he grinned.

'Alright but no gruesome ending.'

'Can't promise, can't promise. There was a family called Irvin who stole 40 sheep from the Tweddles. Unfortunately, the sheep in question had sheep scab or some other disease. Anyway, they infected Irvin's own flock. Irvin's were mad and drove the sheep back to the Tweddles and slaughtered many of the men folk in revenge for infecting their sheep.'

'That was so wrong. The Irvin's were the "Baddies" so to speak.'

'Yes, they were but that was how things were then.'

'So, some of those who died were our relatives. But not recorded here?'

'Perhaps not. But I did hear tell of Rob Tweddle kidnapping Irvin's three daughters in revenge. Didn't have to buy them, just took them. Married one of them, I think?'

'As you know there is a long history of buying women in this family.' Anne sighed and as she turned her head sideways, she noticed a piece of pink paper peeping out of the edge of the book, near the back. 'Look here grandfather this is a list of women's names. Someone has collated them, tried to make a record, and somehow managed to get them in the book. They must have hoped somebody in the future would find it. That is me.' I wonder why it is me that has found this list. Anyway, I am going to read it to you.'

'Oh, Annie please don't I am tired.'

'No, it's important you hear this.'

'Most of these names do not have a surname. I can imagine they were not important enough to have a surname.

Meg, taken on a slave ship to Jamica. Morag, daughter of Lord Temmon sold to Michael Armstrong. Mary Ann, killed running away with her lover. Jeney Wilson, mother of 11, taken away.

'I wonder what that means?'

Eleanor, died in childbirth 8ᵗʰ child. Nell, beaten to death. Margaret, died in prison. Elizabeth Twaddle had inherited wealth but died in mysterious circumstances. Ann, sold to Bell family. Polly bartered for a horse. Jenny Tweddle, died in childbirth 6ᵗʰ child. Mary Lee, widow, killed by brother-in-law. Anne Tweddle sold to Michael Kerr for two cows. Hannah, Janet, Emma, three sisters died in house fire. Kate, beaten to death by husband. Isobel, had 3 still born children, hung herself. Isla, exchanged for a debt. Jane fell into boiling water. Alice and sister Anne transported to Americas. Janet, sent to Ireland. Helen given to O'Leary, Irish horse trader. Elizabeth disappeared. Rose, a widow with 5 children lived on the fells. Jane Tweddel, abandoned, stripped of her fortune and sent to Newcastle docks to find a living.'

Anne stopped reading out loud.' I don't want to read anymore, it's heartbreaking. Oh, there is a note over the page, it says.'

I have created this list, which is only a simple trace, there will be many more that I do not know of, but I just wanted to acknowledge and honour their existence

Annie Tweddle 1805....

John Pickering sat back in his chair and yawned. 'Annie, I am very tired now and going off for a nap in front of the kitchen fire. I'll leave you to tidy this mess up. Don't look so sad, my Dear, it's alright. It's just life you know, just life.' He pottered off into the warm kitchen, where he put the kettle on the Aga, sat down in his mother's rocking chair and fell asleep.

Anne sat in the library with tears in her eyes, knowing that these men and women had been cursed. Many of them had had miserable lives and painful deaths. Elinor had done her job well, a gruesome business indeed. So powerful had her cursing been, she had sacrificed her own life. Anne collected the bits of papers, straightened, folded and then, with great care, replaced them in the family bible, perhaps never to be seen again. Tears rolled down her cheeks. One drop landed on the death date of Robson John Tweddle; his name obliterated. He no longer existed. She sank back into her chair and thought about these families, torn apart over the centuries. Had Elinor's curse really been so powerful? Deep down she knew it to be true. It became clear to Anne, one of the tasks that had been awaiting her for over four hundred years was now here.

Chapter 54

It seemed strange to be thinking about the men in the family. Anne had always been more interested in the women, most of whom had been bartered or sold off to other farming families, to keep 'money safe' and out of their hands. It was traditional in farming circles; women were not to be troubled with money. Daughters who inherited a share of farming land had an alleged reputation for selling, leaving the farms smaller and less economic for their brothers to farm. Anne's family had followed the same pattern.

She thought about her grandmother, Mary Lee Liddell, who was the youngest of four children. When both her parents, wealthy agricultural merchants, died, they were schooled by a strict Victorian governess who kept the two girls on a tight leash, educated as 'Proper' young ladies who spoke French and played the violin. At seventeen years old her uncles married her off to their friend John Pickering Tweddle, in payment of their large gambling debt and her inheritance now belonged to her new husband, J. P., who invested most of it in the farm and the remainder in worthless War Bonds.

M'Lee swapped a comfortable life, in a large house with servants, for Wydon farm, a cold, dark, windy house with no help and a life of drudgery and isolation.

Anne's other grandmother, Henrietta, at nineteen years old, was forced to give up her career, to come home to cook, wash and clean for her father and four brothers. She was trapped. Other women in the family had had similar horrible lives. Winnie, a crippled spinster, ran a sweet shop in the back streets of Newcastle. Aunt Susie lost her husband and six sons in the First World War. Nora drowned, saving her daughter, who survived but with brain damage. Aunt Isabella ran away to marry her lover. She was found and killed by her father. And so, the list went on. Perhaps the women were cursed as well.

Anne sat in silence for a long while, saddened by what she had read and remembered. Her tears continued to flow as she reflected on the destructive powers of the unseen world. Anne wondered what to do to lift this curse for her male descendants and her thoughts turned to Elinor. Yes, that was it! Talk to Elinor. After all, she had laid the curse on the Tweddle descendants so she could lift it. She decided to ask Archangel Michael, her guides, Gwyneth the Welsh Witch, St Cuthbert, Gaerr, her guardian angel, Merlin, and her new animal communicators for help.

Anne closed her eyes and cast a small circle around herself, spraying the essential oils of Lemon, Rosemary, Juniper, and Scots Pine to help spirit connect to her third eye and, for good measure, she charged the circle with a Lapis Lazuli crystal and an Amethyst crystal, which, when working together, encourage spiritual awareness. She pulled her chair closer to the desk, lit a large white candle, put four sheets of clean paper in front of her and picked up her fountain pen.

She sat very still, inhaled the pervading vapour and, with the reassurance her spirit guides were with her, allowed her mind to wander into the past. It wasn't long before familiar images drifted before her. 'Elinor, Elinor I call to you to come to me. Come and talk to me.'

After a short while Anne began to feel words forming in her head. It was the beginning of a conversation, and she began to write, 'Elinor, are you there?'

'Yes, I am here.'

'I send you peace and love and hope all is well in your world. I am pleased I can communicate with you.'

'You have always been able to communicate with us, Anne, even from childhood. You know this. I chose the life as Isobel's mother. I wanted to experience love, real love, but it was hard and not what I expected,'

'In what way?'

'The people I loved were hurt by my actions.'

'Can they be undone, Elinor? I am struggling to know how to lift a curse that you laid on the Tweddle men throughout time.'

'It seemed right at the time, to do it. I was angry and torn apart by grief at the loss of my daughter.'

'I can understand that, but you cursed your own family, Isobel's sons, their sons, and so it went on down through time, the women too. Can you release this curse that has had such devastating consequences through the centuries?'

'I can. But these men who died so badly will have on a soul level chosen some of this. As will the women.'

'Yes, I understand, on a soul level, we all choose our own lives, and they don't always work out the way we envisaged. We may have to come back in another form to relive the experience in a different way.'

'All lives are multidimensional and linear, and we connect with each other when and if need be. Anne, we are all masters of our own destiny. It is good that you have found me. The curse can be released.'

'Are you willing to let it go, Elinor?'

'Yes, it has brought you to me.'

'How?'

Through your connection with Isobel. Through re-experiencing her life and understanding it, your journey work animals, communicating with us in the Otherworld. You have a willingness to learn. Anne, do you know you and Isobel are the same soul, born centuries apart? You must be careful because, if you release Isobel's soul you could lose yours as well.'

'It has taken me a long time to understand it all and I am not sure if I really do.'

'There is more to learn. One soul moving between two bodies can be a difficult thing to separate. Isobel has been drifting, searching for you and you have spent many years wandering, not being fully in your body but lost in an unknown void. If Isobel had not been communicating with you, making you search for answers, nothing would have changed and no resolution, no completion would have been possible for either of you. Anne, you are blessed and much loved by your soul group. We await your return.'

Anne's limbs were tingling, her breath shortening, 'I'm not ready to return. I have so much to do here.'

'Releasing the curse is the next step.'

'I thought it might be. Do I have the power to lift it?'

'No, but I do.'

'What do I do?'

'Anne, my work is done, you have come to me, and all is as it should be. We have waited a long time for you to connect to us. Isobel is still waiting.'

'She is waiting?'

'Yes.'

'Why?'

'You are not yet in the right place to help her. Your energy is not strong enough yet.'

'I am still recovering.'

'Yes, be patient. She has waited many centuries for you. Listen to the animal communicators we have sent you, take heed of their words.'

'I am feeling humbled by this talk. How is this going to work? Will something just come into my head to write down?'

'It will.'

'How will I know when to begin?'

'Be patient. Remember everything happens in the right time and space sequence.'

Anne sat in stillness for quite a while. Then, after more anxious moments, the pen in her hand began to move on the page.

'I release my curse on the Tweddle men. Any trapped souls of these cursed men are now free to journey safely back to the otherworld, if they choose to do so, leaving all their earthly trappings behind. May future generations always feel safe, wherever they choose to travel in any world, be healthy and happy. May all food and drink nurture their bodies and nature's powers be kind to them. May their relationships be loving, supportive, fruitful, and blessed and responsibilities be only what is manageable and acceptable. I release all future generations on the male Tweddle line. I lift the curse. Be free, be safe, be happy and fulfilled in all your lives.'

Anne's pen stopped writing and, hand trembling, she took a long deep breath, uncertain of what to do. Elinor's voice returned and her hand moved again.

'I lift the curse I laid on Isobel and all the women who came after her. May they be truly valued for who they are. May they be safe in childbirth, be loved, and keep their own money. I wish them happy, healthy, fulfilled lives.'

Anne shuffled in her chair.

'Anne, thank you. The release of the curse has released me too. The rest will follow.'

'What do you mean the rest will follow?'

'Wait and see. Some of our ancestors are trapped here with me and you have the power to help them return. We shall not communicate again. I am free now.'

Anne's pen came to a sudden halt. It fell from her hand and rolled silently onto the floor; its work done. It was over. She blew out the candle, uncast the circle and looked round the room, dazed and confused. Waves of exhaustion embraced her. The room was stuffy. She pushed the chair back, steadied herself on the table and slowly made her way to the door, where Nip the dog, jumped up, tail wagging, pleased to be with her.

'Come on, Nip, let's go for a walk, a long, long walk. I think we both need lots of fresh air.'

Chapter 55

Early one morning, several weeks later, Anne awoke early, blinded by sunlight as it peeped through the bedroom curtains. She let out a long sigh and smiled. She was home, back at Wydon, fully recovered from her coma and at peace with herself. The memories of her experiences in the library with her grandfather and the lifting of the curse had begun to fade. Life was good and gave rise to a satisfying calmness. She would be patient, wait for Isobel's return, trust herself and her spirit guides and know that everything would occur at the right time.

Through the open window she could smell freshly cut grass and hear a distant cuckoo. The sight of an orange tip butterfly, fluttering among the ox-eye daisies, warmed her heart. She quickly dressed and went downstairs. Today would be a good day.

'Morning Anne.'

'Morning Jack.'

'This letter came yesterday. I forgot to give it to you.' Anne took the letter and, without looking, stuffed it into her pocket. 'Going for a walk?'

'Yes. It's a lovely day. I think the fresh air is just what I need today.'

'I am sure it is. Come and have some breakfast with me. Are you going to read Michael's letter? He's persistent, isn't he?' Jack grinned as he put his hand up and ruffled her hair.

Anne flushed and pushed past him on her way to the kitchen, 'I shall read it later.'

After breakfast Anne collected her jacket from the coat hook in the hall. The pockets were bulging with random pieces of stale, broken dog biscuits, a damp notebook, pen and pencil, bits of string, an old brass ring and small, pretty stones collected from various streams. The large inside pockets were a home for her binoculars, phone, glasses, keys and Nip's lead, in case he was in a car chasing mood. She turned out the bottom pocket and watched as a flurry of grass seeds descended onto the floor.

Then her hand rested on a long, hard, shiny object. It was her knife. She had named it Tyme…. Tyme to cut plants, herbs or twigs. Touching it brought back a memory of Isobel and her little knife and the incident with Robert Ridley trying to steal it. A knife was a valuable possession that neither Anne nor Isobel would have wanted to be without.

Having recovered one of her walking boots from Nip the dog's bed, where he had succeeded in pulling out one of the laces, she put them on, stood in the kitchen doorway, took a deep breath, and gazed across the fields.

'Where shall we go today Nip?' The dog barked.

'I wonder if it matters. Come on, Nip, let's walk the farm boundaries like we used to do. I feel something important is going to happen today.'

The cattle shed stood empty in the cobbled stack yard, the greening pastures having called for the cow's return. Anne lifted her head and filled her nostrils with the deep, satisfying smell of spring. She crossed the yard into the Low Field, which was full of sheep, who had been up with the dawn light and were now, heads down, grazing, and watched small gangs of lambs, racing up and down the hillside.

'Look Nip.' The dog seemed to take the mention of his name as a signal to chase. 'Nip! Nip! No! No! Come back here NOW!'

Walkers had left the Tootup field gate open. 'Funny name for a lopsided hill field.' Anne paused and shut the gate, remembering the whirlwind she had seen here, as a child, parting the corn. Dorothy in the Wizard of OZ came to mind.

A sharp nibble on her fingers broke the reminiscing and together they walked on into Nichol's Fell, where the smell of bluebells drowned her in clouds of scent. 'Another field with a strange name, Nip.' The dog stopped dead in his tracks at the sound of his name, expecting action. 'It's named after one of the five hamlets at Wydon raided by Angus when he came down from the Scotland's Neidpath Castle.'

The dog wasn't impressed and continued shuffling around in the soft rush looking to raise something to chase. The thought amused her as she climbed the gate into the Pike Field, so called from the old days of 'piking' hay. She walked diagonally across the field to the primrose dell, a deep ravine, damp and soggy underfoot, covered in mossy carpets of yellow glory.

A long, low stone wall separated the Pike from the Far Field. 'Nip,' she shouted pointing to her left. 'Look, Nip, TOURISTS!' He followed her pointed finger and set off at top speed to send the five sheep and lambs back to where they had come from "Tourists," escaped livestock from a neighbouring farm, truly believing grass was greener on the other side of the fence. She made a mental note to remind Jack to fix any new gaps in the dyke backs.

Nip turned and set off towards the television repeater mast, a field known locally as the Pinkinscleugh. Anne couldn't see the dog and began to panic. 'Nip. Nip, come here. Where are you? Then she caught sight of a rabbit running for its life. The morning haze was playing with her eyesight, and she thought, for a moment, she saw figures in fancy dress and legs, perhaps those of horses, gliding by. And then they were gone. She paused, became excited and shouted, 'It's the ghosts of Pinkinscleugh. It's the wedding party, I have never seen them before. I always struggled to believe what grandfather told me.' The dog gave up his fruitless pursuit of the rabbit, returned and flopped by her side exhausted, seemingly grateful for the break. Anne tousled his ears. He looked up and wagged his tail.

'I have remembered the story of Pinkinscleugh.' She smiled at a disinterested dog, who, still panting, looked up at her, confused.

'Nip, a wedding party came along this road,' and she pointed to it. 'They were set upon by a jealous suitor who wanted the bride. All the guests were killed. No one knows who they were. It's said they are visible at a certain time of day. Horses and carriages rattling through the air. It's a haunted place and I have never seen or heard of it before. I wonder who they were, perhaps our family?' She pulled a half biscuit out of her pocket and threw it towards the dog.

'Come on. Let's go.'

Anne lifted her head into the breeze and caught a faint scent of corn. She could hear the cracking of stems. It took her back to childhood, playing in the stooks with her brother, Jack. That was a great game, making dens, while trying to avoid the wrath of their father as they inevitably collapsed. But, as nimble kids, they could both outrun him, only to cop it at supper time. Anne smiled.

The gate at the bottom of the hill led into the Hollow Field, a deep grassy ravine where livestock were easily hidden in the days of the Border Reivers. A metal gate was the exit into the Tyneside, a large field split into two sections, the Pea field and the Thurlehaugh, a strange name of unknown history. Anne turned right and walked the edge that bordered the Primrose Wood and the South Tyne. On the wood side of the fence, she saw the remains of the rabbit boxes her father had dug into the hillside many years ago.

'Nip, get your nose out of there. They're all empty now.' He looked up, as if unwilling to believe her. 'They've gone, Nip, all gone. No more dead rabbits.'

A trap door had been laid across the top of the box. Rabbits fell in and could not escape. The boxes would be checked daily, (except when they weren't). The rabbits would be pulled out, their necks wrung and left in a pile as a warning to others. Sometimes boxes were so full the rabbits suffocated or starved to death. Anne could still hear their muffled screaming.

'Get your nose out of that box. You know, one summer my dad caught over a thousand rabbits in these boxes but no more now, Nip, all gone.' She wagged her finger at a disinterested dog. 'But you know, they had no chance. Trapped, flooded out on the riverbank. Cut off for decades from land, they made their way to these Tyneside fields to eat the grass. Over the years they multiplied to dangerous levels. Look up there.' She pointed to the top of the West Hill. 'Jack and I would clap our hands, shout and watch as a brown cloud emerged from the grass and fled under the wires, back to the holed riverbank. Impossible to count.' She smiled to herself and patted the dog.

'They were fun days, Nip. You'd have been in heaven chasing all those rabbits.' Come on, let's get through that bottom fence. Must be a gap somewhere?'

The riverside field fence posts were rickety. The wire was loose and covered in sheep's wool. The top strand, barbed wire, had been forced down by local fishermen, seeking access to the salmon runs in the autumn. Anne bent down, prized apart two strands, and crawled through.

'Nip, come on, jump through here.' But the dog had other ideas and, with one great leap, he cleared the top barbed wire. She threw her arms in the air and screamed, 'Nip, you stupid dog, don't do that! You'll rip your legs on the barbs!' But he was off snuffling, no doubt following a mysterious scent.

The riverbank was noisy and blooming with life. Anne paused to absorb the beauty of it all. The marsh pennyworts were competing well with the water crowfoot, as they were both creeping along, forging pathways between the stones. Clumps of red campion were straddling the grassy banks and watching the yellow monkey flowers nodding their heads at passing insects. The creeping waterwort was struggling to leave sodden edges, perhaps afraid of the carnivorous greater bladderwort, who were dancing mid-stream, hoping to catch unsuspecting lava. The cow parsley was wilting, leaving gaps for solitary ragged robins to take hold. Anne listened to the low-pitched buzz of flies, hovering, and magical columns of midges dancing over the water. Small shoals of early minnows darted under stones as her shadow passed. Trout were occasionally surfacing to catch newly hatched mayflies, causing a "Plop", then several rings of water would ripple out and become absorbed into the shoreline, a joy to watch.

It was a beautiful day and she had had such a pleasant morning, remembering stories and incidents that had occurred in various fields. Anne smiled, bent down, blew colts foot seed heads from their stalks and hummed a joyful tune.

Her attention was drawn to a grey/brown stone, further upstream, lying close to the fence in the Pea field. She stopped humming for several minutes, staring at the stone, then her face beamed, 'Oh, Nip, look. Look. Come over here. Look, it's not a stone, it's a Butter… Butter – Bump, a hedgehog.' Hands trembling, she sat down and picked up the small prickly mass of flattened spines, rolled it round in her hands and delicately stroked its back. She looked at the hole in the ground, bent down and puffed gently in the hog's ear. Slowly he unraveled and they met face to face, his piercing tiny black eyes searching her larger green ones. Anne smiled.

'Hello, you lovely, little creature. I can see your burrow. Why is there a small pile of crab apples outside the narrow entrance?' The ball in her hand shuffled, raised its front feet to rest on her chest and then a deep gentle voice spoke.

'It's a hog's hoard.'

'Is that to keep your tummy full in the winter?' She let out a little giggle.

He glanced sideways, *'Anne, I am here to tell you to uncurl your inner thoughts for the drama that is to come.'*

She frowned. 'Oh, how do you know my name?'

'We all know your name.' The hog looked skywards. *'We have all been assigned the task of helping you?'*

'Helping me?'

'Yes, you have had many visitations from other creatures.'

Anne nodded, 'Yes, I have.'

'Listen to us. You must listen to us. Your time is close, very close.'

She raised an eyebrow 'My time?'

'Please put me down. All will become clear. Remember, your life's purpose is rapidly approaching.'

Anne stroked the hog one last time, laid him on the ground and watched as he scuttled away into the long meadow grass but after a few feet he stopped, turned, stood on his hind legs and gave her a nod of his head.

Anne looked round for the dog, 'Nip, Nip where are you?' She lay back on the warm earth and let her fingers play with the soft grassy blades. He arrived with a twig in his mouth, settled down and put his head on her stomach. Anne sighed and fondled his ears, her eyes playing with the puffy white clouds as they followed the course of the river downstream. 'It's a good day, Nip, interesting too.'

Suddenly the dog stood up, alerted by a passing cricket, and darted after it. Anne turned onto her side and watched as it jumped from stem to stem. Was this an enchanted creature who would bring good fortune? Perhaps an opportunity was coming, and she must be ready to take advantage of it. She tried to capture the little creature in her hand but missed. It jumped away and she wondered if something was flying away from her, leaving, or perhaps not going far, as the cricket flew back and landed on her hand. She smiled, lifted it onto a blue cornflower and gently blew it away.

Moments later a small white feather floated silently down and landed on her face, then a sudden breeze caught her hair and a light rose fragrance drifted across her nose. She sensed someone or something was nearby. She sat up with a start, sneezed and looked round.

'Is that you Isobel?'

Nothing. No sound. After a few moments, Anne got up and returned to the riverbank, her head full of curious thoughts; Was it Isobel? Perhaps a spirit guide, a guardian angel or just her imagination? She wandered on, pausing every few steps to pick up a stone and skim it across the water. She took her shoes off. The sandy shore was warm under her shoeless feet as her toes dallied with the water's edge. The heavy rainfall of the last few weeks was still gushing down the hillsides to fill the rivers with urgency. Her attention was drawn to a large, round, grey rock bobbing up and down in the middle of the river. The sun was reflecting onto a blueish quartz disc, on top of the stone/rock. It glistened, then faded, as the shadow of the clouds passed over. It felt odd. Had the sun selected it for a special purpose?

'Look, see if I can reach that rock. It's a long way off.'

As she bent down to select another flat stone, Nip stood, ears erect and tail on full alert, transfixed to the spot. 'What is it? What have you seen?' She followed the dog's eye line, but nothing appeared. The water continued to rush past, carrying masses of discarded debris. An odd fish surfaced to blow the occasional bubble. A broken branch floated past carrying smaller twigs on its back and the sound of water lashing random stones was all that broke the stillness of the moment.

'I can't see anything,' but the dog, stood rigid, unwilling to move. No matter how much she patted his back and ruffed up his ears, the dog would not move. 'Nip, I can't see anything. What is it?' Anne's eyes skirted the water's surface, looking for what she wasn't sure. Her heart began to flutter. Something was out there. 'I know, I know, something is out there, Nip. I sense it but can't see anything unusual.'

Anne looked up and down the river, saw nothing odd and walked downstream a little further.

'Come on, I will get cross with you if you don't stop this staring. There is nothing there.' But still the dog refused to budge. She continued to skim stones across the water towards the glistening rock, hoping to break the dog's concentration and began to count the bounces before the stone fell to the river bottom. 'One, two, three, four.' Then she paused and looked around and frowned. 'Nip, the rock has gone. It's not there anymore. How could that be. It can't just disappear.'

But the dog had turned his head upstream and looked as if he was going to growl. A rock was moving in the water.

'Is it bobbing up and down, or is it a different rock being chased by the eddies of water trying to dislodge it? What is going on?' Reaching for her faithful binoculars, that she always carried in her coat pocket, especially at this time of year in case she heard the call of a cuckoo in the far distance, she scanned the surface, 'Nothing, Nip, nothing. Oh, that rock has gone too.'

The dog seemed to have no interest in her voice and continued to move his head looking left and right then fixating upstream. There was something in his line of sight.

Suddenly, river life seemed busy. Two oystercatchers were turning pebbles over on the water's edge. On the far bank a lone heron stood in the shade of its umbrella wings, hoping a fish would chance by. A couple of grey wagtails were courting on the moss-covered outer shore. Two common sandpipers, newly arrived from Africa, were calling to each other as they laid claim to territorial boundaries, occasionally alerted to potential danger as the resident dipper flew past, eventually to land on a large rock a few feet from where Anne was standing.

'Look, look. The rock the dipper was standing on has moved. It went under the water and disappeared.' Nip's head followed the bird downstream. 'There must be something out there.'

Anne sat down on the grassy riverbank, hugged her knees close to her chest and watched the life on the river as it passed by. Her mind went back to childhood and life with her brother; the building of dams, fishing for tiddlers in the forbidden oxbow pool, climbing the scar cliff, slipping, then grabbing onto the broom and hanging on for dear life.

'You know, Nip, we used to raid birds' nests on the lower slopes. You would have enjoyed rummaging up there on the steep scar sides, so full of rabbit warrens,' she smiled and ruffled his coat. 'Dad hated pigeons or "Cushettes", as he called them, and corbies, or crows. He would pay us to destroy the small round twiggy nests and break their eggs.' Anne shuddered at the memory. 'Nip that was a terrible thing to do, raid pigeon nests and destroy their eggs.' He put his head to one side, as if trying to understand what she was talking about.

'Dad said they ate the corn, wheat and barley in the fields. When he was young, he saw a whole flock clean a field out in one afternoon. I suppose it's the same as locust flocks in Africa. I hate myself for the destruction I was involved with, but I was too young to understand. On the other hand, how do you stop pigeons eating winter's cattle fodder?' She laughed. He seemed uninterested in the conversation.

Anne continued to gaze into the water. Lots of things were bobbing up and down. Perhaps they were stones being moved on the riverbed by fish hunting for food. Then a large round dome shape lifted out of the water a couple of feet away from her. Anne gasped, both with delight and joy.

'Nip, Nip it's a seal and so far up the river from the sea. We have never seen a seal on this part of the Tyne before.'

He had seen it too but became distracted by the sight of a young rabbit, who had just popped out of a hole and was holding his gaze. The head of the seal was bobbing up and down looking straight at her, before submerging and reemerging a few yards further on. Then it came back and lifted out of the water, fixed its gaze on her, dived and swam upstream. It continued to repeat this behaviour for what seemed to Anne a very long time.

'Nip, what's it doing?'

But the dog had lost interest in her conversation and had his nose well and truly down the rabbit hole.

'It's bobbing up and down, I think it is trying to tell me something. Does it want me to follow it?' Anne knew that seals and humans had a very close relationship. 'Nip, I remember stories Grandfather told me as a child, when all the world seemed magical. The story of the Selkies, the seal people who lived in the ocean. Nip, leave that rabbit alone, come here, sit down and be quiet and I shall tell you a story. One day a young man was walking along the cliffs, when he saw a small band of selkie folk emerge from the sea. Once on land they discarded their seal skins in the warm sun and danced naked, played among the rocks, and laughed in the sheer joy of freedom. The young man crept down to a rock pool and stole one of the seal's skins. The Selkies became alarmed. All but one grabbed their skins, fled back into the sea, and swam out into the safety of deep water. At the sound of a girl sobbing, the man looked around and saw the stranded girl, who begged him to give her seal skin back for, without it, she could not return to the sea. The man felt sorry for the girl and beckoned her closer, whereupon he fell instantly in love. He wanted to marry her and haggled until she relented and agreed to live with him on land. In time, she bore him seven children that she loved dearly but in her quiet moments she would gaze mournfully out to sea and call to her Selkie family. One day the man took his boys fishing and the girls walked along the seashore collecting shells. But one little girl had a cut foot and stayed behind. Her mother wanted the seal skin to bind it. Although she had spent many years looking for her skin, she had never found it. But the Selkie's daughter knew where her father had hidden the skin and gave it to her mother, who raced to the beach, put her skin back on and dived into the sea. She swam to a nearby fishing boat, lifted herself out of the water, looked upon her husband and sons, said her farewells and dived back into the sea. The children and their father never saw the beautiful woman again.' The dog momentarily looked up.

'Oh Nip, that was such a sad tale. As a child I used to sit here on this bank and wait for her to come back to visit her children, but she never did, not while I was here, anyway. Granny Tweddle used to tell another tale.' But the dog was not listening. He jumped up and started digging furiously into the soft, sandy bank, hoping to get the rabbit out for lunch. Anne smiled at this happy animal she loved so much.

'The rabbit's gone, Nip. It's gone, not there anymore. Look it's above you on the grass, watching.' Anne laughed at the sight of the hunter and prey, standing transfixed by each other. How quickly the roles had reversed.

Her focus returned to the river. The seal was still there and, as she de-focused her eyes, she saw a faint image, the outline of a familiar form, in the distance where the seal had just been. At that moment a light breeze swept across the water carrying clouds of sycamore flowers, which landed on the surface, carpeting the water in green and yellow waves and the image faded. Anne sighed and returned to her thoughts of Selkie stories.

'Nip, listen and I will tell you another tale. My great grandmother told me that, as a young girl, she'd been walking along the riverbank with her mother, who, herself, was a 'Strange One' and was often seen walking the fields at night, spending hours by the river and was known to disappear for days at a time.' The dog yawned.

'Nip pay attention. Anyway, on this particular night, great grandmother had been walking by the water's edge and had seen naked women dancing on the far bank. One beautiful young woman was standing by the water's edge and singing a soulful song to the water to draw out a Selkie lover from the depths. Oh Nip, those were stories of the ocean, but this is the river, the South Tyne. Why is there a seal here?' As she spoke, the faint image of a Selkie reappeared before her eyes, and began to sing. 'Listen, it's the haunting song of the seal. It's said to upset humans and make them fearful, but I think it sounds beautiful. It's a call to the unconscious. It's something that resonates within the depths of my being. It touches my soul, a primeval sound from the waters of my birth calling to me.' Anne's body quivered and legs tingled as she sprang to her feet, picked up her shoes and smiled at the dog.

'Nip, come on. Let's walk further up the bank.'

Chapter 56

Anne's mind was in a quiet turmoil. Something was wanting her attention. As she walked, the seal followed and when she stopped, it stopped. She even tried walking backwards but that didn't work either. The seal would flip over and change direction, always keeping her in its eye line. She stopped and stared, searching her mind for what it all meant.

Leaning forward and opening her hands she said, 'Hello, you are following me. Are you trying to tell me something?' Nip stood by her side transfixed as the sleek grey seal slid effortlessly towards her and closer to the shoreline. 'You are a handsome creature,' Anne said.

Then she heard a beautiful gentle voice drift along the surface of the water towards her, like a distant cloud in a sunlit sky. The voice brought the faint smell of roses as it wafted through her mind, beautiful, calm and serene. Anne's mind easily flowed into the power of the words.

'I am gone from this physical world and have been waiting many centuries for you to find me. This shoreline is a magical boundary between your world and the other world. I am in the in-between. It is a constantly shifting tide, do not be afraid.'

Anne stood upright and walked slowly backwards, away from the shoreline and up onto the stony beach. She whispered to the dog, 'Nip, come here. Come here.' He didn't need telling twice but shot backwards and hid behind her legs. Then she heard the voice again.

'Do not be afraid, the call from the water is strong.'

Anne was not afraid and smiled with love in her heart as she witnessed the seal slowly emerge from the water and the faint image she had seen, only moments before, returned, clearer this time and taking the form of a beautiful young woman. She stepped gracefully across the shoreline, glided over the stones, as if lifted by angels, and held her arms out in greeting. As this captivating apparition came closer, she took on her human form. Anne walked towards this enchanted being. Both women held out their hands and smiled.

Anne gazed deep into her eyes. 'I know who you are.'

'I am glad. It has taken me a long time to find you,' she said, her face full of love.

As Anne looked into this exquisitely beautiful young woman in front of her, she gently stroked her fingers, a perfect human being.

'I have been waiting over four hundred years for you.'

Anne looked puzzled, 'Why so long?'

The girl smiled, *'It had to be you, but you chose not to come back until this lifetime.'* She looked into Anne's eyes with an intensity that flooded her whole being with unconditional love.

'You are Isobel. I have been witnessing your life ever since I was a young girl. It was only when I experienced your death that I understood its purpose.'

'I have been observing your life too. It was hard when you went inside, into the bed in the long room with lots of noise of others round you. There was no air, and you went into the long dream time and it was easier to connect with you.'

They smiled and squeezing fingers, a knowingness passing between them. For Anne it was tinged with a mixture of excitement and wonder.

'Isobel, your life was a magical tale of love, passion, war, death and loss, while mine was about love, loss, loneliness and isolation.'

'Between us we have lived, really lived a full life.'

They put their arms around each other and stood together for several minutes, finally reunited as one being.

Nip emerged from the trees and ran towards them. He began to bark, turning his head in a confused way, unable to understand what he saw. Both women turned to look at him and smiled. He wagged his tail and stopped barking, laid down, head on paws, unafraid and accepting of who they were.

'My boys, my beautiful sons, Cuthbert and Edgar. I watch Edgar. I will not leave him.'

'And Cuthbert?'

Isobel smiled, *'Cuthbert spent his life in the fields and meadows, the old woods and never left Wydon. He did not follow his father, John's, ways and they became estranged when he was quite young. He married and had a son. Then he fell in love with a mystical being from the forest who whisked him away into the Faerie realm and was never seen again by his family, but Cuthbert is with me. I sense his soul, it's still part of me. We have not let each other go.'*

'What happened to Edgar, what sort of life did he have?'

'He followed my teachings, grew up to be a great healer and fell in love with a bone setter when he was young. Under her guidance he established himself as an important healer in the Scottish court. His wife died giving birth to their fourth son. He was unable to save her. Such was his grief that he took his own life. He came to me, fleetingly at first then more frequently as the centuries passed. He wanders the earth looking for her still.'

Anne gazed at this beautiful creature and tears welled up inside her. She looked deep into her own soul, 'Isobel, raising our children is a wonderful, joyful thing but we must set them free. Isobel, it is time to let them go. It is time you were free too.'

'I am afraid to leave. My death was sudden and unexpected, and I had no time to prepare to leave my body. My love for my children holds me to this place. They are here with me. Caitlin, Edgar's wife, is drifting between worlds searching for him but now she is here with me. Sometimes I get a glimpse of Cuthbert. He is here too. He has escaped the faerie realm. There are others with me, Anne.'

'Others?'

'Yes, souls who are trapped with me. Others come to comfort and guide. They move between realms.'

Anne nodded her head, 'Your sons, Cuthbert, and Edgar, have not moved on to the Summerland's? They are still here with you? It is time you all went and set yourselves free.'

'Yes. You must do this for all of us, Anne. Will you come with us?'

'No, it is not my time. I want to stay here a while longer, but I will help you all to go.'

Anne began to remember the soul release work she had done in the past, valuable experiences for the task ahead. Isobel's soul had been trapped on this earth plane for over four hundred years. She had wandered these lands, drifted through many people's lifetimes, always searching for Anne, the reincarnation of herself, the only person who could set her free. Anne briefly closed her eyes, looked skywards, nodded, and was engulfed with a huge sense of relief. This momentous time in her life had arrived. In the past few weeks, since her awakening, she had understood the meaning of the daydreaming and the animal communicators who had come to guide her. Always she had questioned them, unable to understand their confusing messages, but now she knew. She turned to gaze at Isobel, 'I don't see your children, Cuthbert and Edgar, with you. I only saw them as little ones. You died and they were left.' Anne's chin trembled. She wondered if they had been her children as well.

But Isobel, reading her thoughts, quickly reassured her, *'No, not yours.'*

Anne tilted her head to one side, 'I saw your children hiding in the stable as you lay dying on the ground, your mangled, bloody body trampled by the pounding of hooves.'

'They saw it all. Anne, do you know that Robert is here with me now? Can you see him?'

Anne took a step back, shivered and turned pale. 'I don't understand, Isobel. Robert Ridley your tormentor?'

'We are in the same soul group. We are all in the same soul group.'

'Hello Anne,' and the familiar but untarnished face of a handsome young man, no longer disfigured and scarred, came into focus to stand beside Isobel, his arm round her shoulders. They smiled at each other. Anne took a sudden step backwards. Robert lifted his hand.

'Please do not be afraid. I chose a life of hardship and pain. Through my experiences on earth, I was able to help Isobel fulfil her soul's purpose. My earth life was brutal. I was my father's bastard. His wife hated me and began a lifelong pursuit of cruelty and abuse. In my formative years I was refused food, became under nourished and small. My bones did not form properly were easily broken and did not heal well, I only felt safe on horseback where no one could see my deformed stature.

I disgusted my father who would take the flat of his sword across my back to show his displeasure. My brothers were a mixed bunch of thieves and rogues. I easily slipped into their ways and became a useful pawn in their adventures. Together they gave me the skills I needed to pursue Isobel.'

Isobel smiled. *'I chose to experience what it would feel like to be hunted, to live in constant fear of being killed. He came to teach me to be strong and find my inner warrior. I discovered I had an overwhelming desire to heal others, to be selfless and share my healing gifts. I was living with people who had suffered great loss, a situation not of their making but one of constant upheaval and war on so many fronts. Their injuries were frequent, sometimes life threatening. I was often alone and exposed to many dangers.'*

'Do you think you were given the opportunity to gain knowledge of healing, when you were a child?'

'Yes, I do. I was born into the right family. They could offer me teaching in the healing arts.'

'In what way did Robert Ridley help you?'

'He challenged me, on a deep level, to be kind, to heal and ultimately to learn about unconditional love. I had many opportunities to destroy him, but I didn't.'

'Only injured?'

'Yes, hoping he would not be able to come back, although I wasn't doing it on a conscious level.'

'Your guides were with you?'

'Yes.'

'Well, Isobel, observing your life as I did over a period of years, it did not seem like that. You were terrified of him.'

'In the physical world, in human form, I was.'

'And now?'

'Now I understand he was an angel sent to show me the path of forgiveness and the oneness of all beings.'

'Did he succeed?'

'Yes indeed. I am grateful for the path we both chose.'

'Although not at the time?'

'No.' Isobel laughed, *'We have been together before. Shared many lives together. Always torn apart. Endings not of our choosing. There is another here you know, Anne.'*

'Is there?'

'Yes. He has always been with you but in different forms.'

Anne frowned, 'And this time?'

'He suffered a long slow death and was taken from you.'

Anne thought hard for several minutes. Then her eyes filled with tears when she realised who it was. Isobel smiled and squeezed her hand.

'Jeff came to challenge you. Your twenty-three-year marriage was always about pushing you into situations you were afraid of, forcing change when you didn't want it, making you fearful of the outside world and reinforcing your isolation and sense of not being heard. Then he left you.'

'Yes, he did.'

Jeff stepped forward and beckoned Anne towards him, *'And, in leaving, I set you free and, in that freedom, you have blossomed.'*

'Yes, I have and for that I am grateful. But I did and still do miss you. Our children miss their father. They spent their teenage years watching you die. It was cruel.'

'Yes, I know.' Jeff said *'But it has all come full circle, Anne. Everything is as it should be.'*

'Yes, it may be for you, but they still suffer. At the time all this was hard to understand. Everything is easy in hindsight.'

'I know. I have always been with you, observing you and sending unconditional love to you for the life you have chosen and the hardships it has brought. The love of your soul group will always be there in the ether of the universe.'

Tears ran down Anne's face.

Isobel stepped forward and put her arms round Anne. *'Anne, our soul group were sad when you chose this life.'*

'You know, Isobel, I believe the universe sends us nothing but angels to help us learn who we truly are and to complete our journey to oneness with all. But I am happy now. Over the years I've learned so much. I've recognised patterns of behaviour in my relationships, have learned how to connect them up and gain successful resolutions and, like you, I have learned the power of forgiveness and the value of blessings. Now I am free to be me and do as I wish. The hard work is over.'

'But you are still here in human form.'

'It's a magical place, this beautiful earth and a blessing and privilege to live on it.'

'I understand and feel it too. But I long to return to source.'

'Isobel, I feel I've more to do. Each time I consider leaving, the land calls me back, the old oak tree, my animal guides, and my human family. They want me to stay longer, for a while anyway. But the oneness we've shared, the knowing of who we are is powerful. I feel we are at one with each other because we are one. We are one soul, now reconnected, united in thought. We have found each other at last. We chose lives to develop our understanding of forgiveness, kindness and happiness towards ourselves and all life forms, lessons to be truly grateful for. Anne mirrored Isobel's smile and for several moments they stood in silence, holding hands, treasuring their last moments together.

Chapter 57

I sobel spoke. *'Anne, you must set us all free.'*

'I know. I just wanted to hold on to this time with you a little longer. It has been so long in coming. It will be strange living without you being in my consciousness.'

Isobel lifted her head and smiled.

Anne nodded, closed her eyes and tuned in to the deep silence within, before she could begin the healing process of releasing Isobel's soul to the Otherworld, from which she came.

'This is a powerful time for both of us.'

Anne took several deep breaths and spoke out loud, 'Before I begin, I ask to be shown a beneficial place to stand to do this work?' She paused and waited for a sign. After a few seconds she was pulled to the left and took a few steps forward and stumbled, momentarily losing her balance. Anne smiled at the unseen energies. All was well.

Anne lifted her arms to the eastern sky and began her ritual. 'Isobel, to begin I must ask for our psychic protection. Please stand with me.' She put her hand into Isobel's and together they stood looking skywards.

'As I look into the vastness of what lies above me, I see clouds of dazzling rainbow lights. I pull this splendid wave towards us and ask that they pass through our auric fields and physical bodies. I ask that all energies detrimental to our wellbeing are removed, taken away to the light and disposed of in a safe and appropriate way, leaving us in peace, balance and harmony. And so, it is.' Anne swayed ever so slightly, as if caught by a light breeze.

Then she closed her eyes and slowly circled round, pointing in turn to the four directions: East, South, West and North.

'I call to the Air Dragons in the Eastern skies, whose wings move the clouds and blow the great winds across the world. I ask for your inspiration.

I call to the Fire Dragons who live in the mountains and unsettle the earth. I ask for your energy and passion.

I call to the Water Dragons, the guardians of the oceans. I ask for your wisdom.

I call to the Earth Dragons who roam the tunnels of the earth. I ask for your strength.'

Anne paused. Her face lit up with joy, 'They have heard me…they are here! Great spirits of this place, I greet and honour you. I come in peace and love. I ask for your blessings, guidance, and inspiration for this important work before me.'

She stood still and allowed the dragon energies to fill her being. 'Thank you. I call to my guides, seen and unseen; to Gwyneth, my Welsh witch, to St. Cuthbert, Arthur and Merlin, to all my animal guides, to Grandmother Crane, to Swan, Eagle, Bear, Hare, Hedgehog and Cricket, to the White Wolves and all nature spirits who I have worked with over the years. Please come and help me. I call to the Archangels for guidance and support in this important work.'

Anne opened her eyes and searched the passing clouds, looking for a distortion, an opening, a sign. The day had changed, it was now damp and cool. Darkening puffs of rain threatened to fall to earth. Then, quite suddenly, two argumentative clouds parted and, from behind, he appeared…the Sun, the bringer of life, bright, sparkling and glowing with a force so strong that Anne shielded her eyes lest she lose her sight. This was the moment, a portal to the other world.

'I look to the gap that has appeared between the clouds and I ask that a beam of light be opened to the heavens.' Anne stood very still and watched. After a few moments a wondrous stream of pure energy cascaded down to earth, surrounding them both in a large circle of light.

'Thank you for hearing me. I humbly ask the ancestors to show Isobel the peace and beauty that lies beyond this earth realm, a place of no judgement, only the joy of return to her soul group from which she came. Please bring her ancestors forward to greet her. Show her familiar places, people and, most important of all, the unconditional love that awaits her return.'

Stillness followed, then a blinding light cascaded upon them. It gently flickered as an angelic being glided down, holding out its arms in a welcoming gesture.

Anne turned to gaze once more on the beautiful Isobel, her face wet with tears of happiness. 'Isobel, are you ready to go? Now is the time to return to source. Your journey on this earth plane and your wanderings through unknown dimensions are over. Your soul group awaits.'

She stepped forward, looked deeply into those beautiful green eyes, and smiled. Anne held her gaze and watched Isobel's image begin to fade as she drifted effortlessly upwards, wrapped in the arms of the golden angel, leaving only a faint outline as she moved towards the light. Isobel had a blissful smile on her face, as she turned and blew a single kiss back to Anne. Then, very gradually, she became absorbed, merged to become one with the iridescent brightness of love. Anne's pulse was racing, her cheeks were glowing, as she was overwhelmed with the beauty of what she was witnessing, a rare moment of purity and oneness with all that is.

Then Anne's body began to sway. There was a buildup of energy behind her, a powerful force, a strange sensation of invisible energies rushing past her, almost lifting her. As the minutes passed, she felt an increasing number of 'taps' on her shoulder and could sense the words, 'Thank you,' in her head.

Other trapped souls were moving into the brilliance of the open portal. From her memory banks she recognised some of these people. One was Robert Ridley, who turned to look at her, smiled and nodded his head. She recognised his father, David Ridley, Isobel's two sons, Cuthbert and Edgar, John Tweddle, his father, Angus, Thomas Elliot, Isobel's mother. Jeff was there too. There were others who she did not recognise. There was a rush of earth-bound spirits coming from all four directions. Anne stood waiting, just waiting for it all to finish, for them all to be free to return home, back to the spirit world and their soul groups, back to source from where they had all come.

Anne stood quietly for a long time, until the atmosphere around her became calm and still. It had ended. It was over. Those trapped souls who had wanted or been able to return had now gone. Others, for various reasons, would still be here, waiting, unable or unwilling to leave.

Anne had experienced this before. When a portal is opened and communication made with the other world, trapped souls from many places, over many centuries, rush to go through before it closes. At this moment in her time Anne had counted several hundred passing through, knowing they included men from her family, from past generations, men who had been trapped on this earth plane, unable to leave, perhaps some of them because of Elinor's curse. Anne stood, overwhelmed, tearful, weak and unsteady on her feet but most of all she was feeling exhausted. Her energy was drained, and she was left wondering if part of herself had gone too.

Looking back at the fading beam of light, she once again lifted her arms to the heavens. 'Hello. Can I ask for a sign that everyone who wants to go, who wants to leave this earth plane, has gone?'

Moments later Anne's body stopped swaying. It became still. She felt a gentle angelic kiss on her forehead. She looked skywards once more, 'Thank you, thank you angels for your love and support. I honour you, my ancestors. I am grateful to have been given this opportunity. It has truly been a privilege. I feel humbled in your presence. I will now close this portal to protect not only those who have left and returned to you but also, to protect the earth from any detrimental energies, tricksters or the like that might come down.'

Anne put her hands to the ground and held the bottom of the beam of light which was now beginning to fade. She lifted it up, threw it skywards to the heavens and waved her hands across the top to seal the beam. The portal was now closed. The dark clouds merged once more, and the sun was hidden. Anne felt a faint wet sensation on her face. It was beginning to rain, a slow trickle at first, that grew with urgency and an intensity that fixed her to the ground. The rain was purifying, washing away all that she had brought with her, all that she was and had ever been. She was cleansed of her past, her misdemeanours, her unpleasant thoughts, and wrong actions.

Anne was free and had been blessed. Moments later the visible mass of condensed, watery vapour moved on, white clouds puffed, and the hot sun briefly appeared. It shone just long enough to dry her wet hair, before continuing its journey across the afternoon sky.

The sound of Nip the dog barking drew her attention once more to the shoreline and there in front of him was a grey seal, bobbing up and down in the water. It raised itself high onto its tail and gave Anne a long, lingering look. It dived back into the deep water and swam downstream towards the sea. Anne waved and stood for a while watching until it was out of sight.

She bent down and ruffled the dog's ears, 'Come on, Nip, let's go home too. It has been a good end, the right end, the way things had to be. Isobel has returned home, and I am free too.'

Nip ran by her side and together they walked back along the riverbank through the fields towards their home. Walking into the wind made Anne's eyes water and she put her hand into her pocket to retrieve a hankie but instead found a folded up white envelope. It was a letter that had arrived that morning and she had put it into her pocket with the intention of reading it later but, in all the excitement of the day, it had become forgotten. Taking it out she recognised the handwriting as Michael's.

'Nip, perhaps this time I will read his letter. Maybe I will be able to forgive him but for what? I don't actually know.' But the dog had seen a pair of rabbits and ran off across the field.

Anne found an old tree stump, sat down, and gazed at the handwriting gently caressing it with her fingers. She opened the envelope and, with shaking hands, pulled out two pieces of cream paper

Dearest Anne,

At last, I am able to share with you what has been happening in my life and the circumstances I found myself in that have so badly affected both our lives. I could not defend myself against your accusations but am now in a position to reveal the truth.

Let me begin by explaining that I wasn't entirely truthful when I told you I was a retired police officer. I was more than that. I worked undercover with criminal gangs, involved in people trafficking and money laundering on an international level. In recent months a cold case came to light. I was a witness in the original case. Jennifer, which is not her real name, was a Detective Inspector and contacted me several times about a review of evidence.

But the defence was not allowed to see or hear new evidence and after many months of legal argument the case has collapsed. That is often the way with these high-profile cases as evidence can be too sensitive to the security of the state to be made public.

But it is over now so I am freed from all this turmoil.

I am so glad I found you, the love of my life. Anne, it seemed such a blessing to have you to share my remaining years with.

Please believe me when I say how deeply sorry, I am for all this trouble that I have inadvertently landed us both in. I understand why you left.

But now it is over, and I am free, safe and well, and long to see you for without you my life is worthless. How cruel it would be if I lost you now.

It will take me several days to sort things out down here, but I should be with you by the end of next week.

I long to see you, I love you so much.

All my love Michael xxxx

Anne brought a shaking hand to her forehead, let out a long uncontrollable sob and, after a moment or two, a beaming smile crossed her face. Jennifer was not the 'OTHER WOMAN'. Michael had not betrayed her. Tears rolled down her face, wetting the letter so much that the inky words blurred after the hundredth time of reading them and were no longer legible. She crumpled it up into her sticky hand and kissed it over and over again before returning it to her pocket.

Nip had returned and seemed to sense something was different. Anne began to hum… a tune she did not know but it did not matter. Her pace quickened and a lightness, that she had not experienced since her youth, returned to her feet and she ran home through the wildflower meadows. All was well in her world.

THE END

Glossary

Awen
Inspiration. Flowing spirit.

Barnkin
Medieval defense enclosure found round Pele Towers, bastle houses and small castles.

Bastle
Fortified house. Cheaper alternative to a stone tower.

Blackmail
Illegal rent. Money extracted by threatening coercive behaviour.

Borders
Southern counties of Scotland and northern England.

Clan
Can be used interchangeably with family. Although Clan is bigger than family.

Clootie
Rag tied to a tree giving a blessing.

Clootie Well
A holy well in which a rag, or clootie, is dipped and tied to a tree in the hope that a sickness or ailment will fade as the rag disintegrates.

Deosil
Clockwise, turning from east to west. Considered the prosperous course.

Dirk
A long-bladed thrusting knife.

Drove Road
Track used by shepherds and cattle herders to drive livestock to markets.

Dyke
Hedge, wall, boundary between fields, stream and river.

Handfasting
Symbolic marriage ritual. Dates back thousands of years.

Hobbler
Small sturdy sure-footed ponies, common in the Borders. Now extinct.

Hot Trod
Practice of retrieving stolen livestock.

Kist
Scottish bedding chest with drawers. A place to keep important papers.

Ogham
Ancient British, Irish alphabet.

Shieling
Rough, often temporary shelter in remote places used by people tending cattle and travelers who need a dry place for the night.

Slue Dog
Used for hunting and tracking game and fugitives.

Warden
Official in charge of administering justice.

Widdershins
Anticlockwise. Considered unlucky.

Whitemail
Legal rent.

Acknowledgements

Many thanks are due to those who have helped me in producing this book.

To James Nash, poet, and all-round lovely man for suggesting that my short story could be a novel.

To Maria Frankland for her enthusiasm, encouragement and guidance in the early stages and her constant reminder of 'from whose point of view are you writing.' Such a hard one to master.

To Sarah Nicholson for invaluable information and support about hospital procedures.

To Otley Writers for their support and friendship. Our weekly writing prompts have been challenging but have kept me on track. To James, Jan, Pam, Mark, and Sandy for all your editing and offering so much useful feedback. I love you all.

Above all to the help and encouragement from Sandy Wilson who has tried so hard to keep me on the right path. Sending back my manuscript so many times before eventually publishing my novel for me. A valued friend and I am indebted to you.

Final thanks go to my long-suffering husband, Dave, for his unending patience and tolerance in reading my manuscript over and over, always finding something to edit. He has spent the last few years listening and encouraging me to keep going.

Without you all this novel would not have been possible, and I truly offer you all my undying love and gratitude.

A final note to Mollie, our Border Collie, much as I love you, writing this book has been hard with your constant interruptions. Toys arriving on my knee, barking, whining to play with you, or walkie time, supper, or snack time. Did you really have to alert me to every human who passed the front door and not just the postman. The list goes on. It has all been exhausting and interrupted my flow on so many occasions. Without it perhaps it would not have taken me five years to finish, who knows! But I love you and forgive you. xxx

About the Author

For over four hundred years Barbara Silcock, (nee Tweddle) and her ancestors have come from the wild lawless places of Northumberland. Her writing is inspired by this inherited history of stories, tales and legends passed down through the generations.

Her druid life, observing and listening, has helped her understand better the natural world and, through these connections, magic has appeared from a place of respect and honour.

The seasons turn and she turns with them.

Printed in Great Britain
by Amazon

33645410R00148